The Cross: Culmination of The Nation

The Crowning: Culmination of the Nation

The Crowning, Volume 1

Thomas J. Feely

Published by Feely.Life, 2023.

This is a work of fiction. Similarities to real people, places, or events are entirely coincidental.

THE CROWNING: CULMINATION OF THE NATION

First edition. January 19, 2023.

Copyright © 2023 Thomas J. Feely.

ISBN: 979-8987292907

Written by Thomas J. Feely.

Table of Contents

Prologue | January 30th, 2025: Tampa, Florida 1

Chapter 1. | Nation In Crisis | January 30th, 2025: Tampa, Florida 4

Chapter 2 | A Desperate and Dangerous Time | Tampa, Florida | January 30th, 2025; 8:00 p.m. 15

Chapter 3 | Shadowland | Tampa, Florida | January 31st, 2025 20

Chapter 4 | Until the Storm Has Passed | Tampa, Florida | Saturday, February 1st, 2025 25

Chapter 5 | That Day Has Come | Tampa, Florida | Feb. 2, 2025 33

Chapter 6 | Just Bad Luck | Tampa, Florida | February 3rd, 2025 40

Chapter 7 | Blinded by the Flames | 10 Miles South of Tampa | Feb 10th, 2025: 46

Chapter 8 | She is Going to Die Soon | Tampa, Florida | February 11, 2025 55

Chapter 9 | Take Back our Country | Tampa, Florida | Evening of February 11th, 2025 59

Chapter 10 | A Nuclear Option | Tampa, Florida | February 12, 2025 66

Chapter 11 | What Do They Know? | Tampa, Florida | February 13th, 2025 77

Chapter 12 | Internal Divide | Tampa, Florida | Feb. 14, 2025 85

Chapter 13 | They're All Gone | Tampa, Florida | February 15th, 2025 93

Chapter 14 | You Are Not Replaceable | Riverview Florida | February 16th 106

Chapter 15 | Looks Like We're Under New Management | Tampa, Florida | February 17, 2025 120

Chapter 16 | We Can't Just Give Up on Her | Tampa, Florida | February 17, 2025 144

Chapter 17 | Peaceful Political Discourse | Tampa, Florida | Feb.18th, 2025 148

Chapter 18 | An Extraordinary Danger to the Nation | Orlando, Florida | February 19th, 2025 157

Chapter 19 | Destitute and Homeless | Tampa, Florida | February 19th, 2025 171

Chapter 20 | Political Malpractice and other Illicit Behaviors | Tampa, Florida | February 28th, 2025 175

Chapter 21 | Hovering a Bit Above Empty | Tampa, Florida | Saturday, March 1st, 2025 183

Chapter 22 | Standing There, Helplessly | Detroit, Michigan | Sunday, March 2nd, 2025.. 188

Chapter 23 | Any Sign of Grady | Tampa, Florida | Sunday, March 2nd, 2025 194

Chapter 24 | The President is in His Cross Hairs | Tampa, Florida | Monday, March 3rd, 2025: 199

Chapter 25 | The Vulture Looms | Tampa, Florida | Monday night, March 3, 2025.. 204

Chapter 26 | Donald John Trump vs. The United States of America | Tampa, Florida | Tuesday, March 4, 2025.. 212

Chapter 27 | The Verdict | Wesley Chapel, Florida | March 5th, 2025 227

Chapter 28 | Transfer of Power | Tampa, Florida | March 5th, 2025 . 257

Epilogue | American Carnage 268

April 1, 2025 (30,000 feet above Madagascar) 275

Note: This story continues in the sequel, The Crowning: Exodus from Cerberus due to be published in late 2023. | BIBLIOGRAPHIC REFERENCES.. 277

Dedication

Dedication

This book would not have been possible without the love and support of my wonderful family. You all have my most profound appreciation for your contributions to the success of this endeavor.

First, I thank my wife, Adrienne, for being my strongest supporter, rock, and most demanding critic throughout this journey. Your quiet and steadfast love for our children and grandchildren served as a model for us all. You have infused your warmth and grace into one of the main characters in the story. Completing this book would not have been possible without your unwavering support and encouragement.

To all of my children and grandchildren for being my inspiration for writing this book. Your love for our family and your spirit have inspired me immensely, which is reflected in the book's characters. I am also blessed to have our children and grandchildren as my source of joy and inspiration. You have shown me the true meaning of family and given me the courage to pursue my passion.

To my three brothers, Pat, Richard, and Daniel, as well as my good friend, Geno, for your sage wisdom, insightful advice, and enthusiastic support. I am enormously grateful for your invaluable guidance, feedback, and encouragement. You have helped me shape this book with your wisdom.

I thank Dr. Brian Greeno for his expert advice and content suggestions. Your vision and insight have enhanced the quality and depth of this book. Thanks, Dr. Brian Greeno, you gave me priceless ideas and content feedback. Your dream and creative instincts have been invaluable to this book.

Last, I want to acknowledge the contributions of Hampton Allen of Encore Productions for your unique and brilliant designs of the book's cover pages. You are indeed an artist of the highest level.

I am grateful to all these people for their contributions to this book. It would not have been possible without them.

Thomas J. Feely

Prologue
January 30th, 2025: Tampa, Florida

Tully Stone, the last man on Earth, sat alone in his room, staring at the blank wall. He had been alone for years, ever since the great plague and nuclear war had wiped out humanity. He had long since given up hope of ever seeing another person again. Today, he was sitting in his room, reading a book, when he heard a knock at the door. He froze. He couldn't believe it. Could it be? Was there someone else out there? Tully slowly got up and walked to the door. He put his ear to the door and listened. The older adult in his early 70s could hear someone on the other side, but they were too quiet to make out what they were saying.

He took a deep breath and opened the door. He stood there, frozen, staring at the person on the other side. It was a woman. She was young and beautiful, with long, flowing dark hair and piercing brown eyes. The woman smiled at him. "Hello," she said. "My name is Catherine." Tully stared at her in disbelief. "Catherine?" he asked. "Is that your name? That was my wife's name" The woman nodded. "Yes," she said. "It's a good name, don't you think?" Tully smiled. "Yes," he said. "It's a splendid name."

Catherine stepped forward and hugged him. Tully hugged her back tightly. He had never been so happy to see another person in his life. "I'm so glad you're here," he said. "I thought I was the only one left. Catherine" smiled. "You're not alone anymore," she said. "I'm here now." Tully and Catherine stood there for a long time, holding each other. They were both so happy to have found each other. Finally, Catherine broke the silence. "We should go inside," she said. "It's getting cold out here."

Tully nodded and led the woman inside. They closed the door behind them and locked it. They were finally safe.

Suddenly, a loud clang jolted Tully to sit upright, eyes open, wondering where he was, when Catherine yelled from the first floor of their home,

"Tully, time to get up, old man!" Tully sat in a fog, wondering what had just happened until he realized he was having "that dream" once again.

Catherine, and her husband of 25 years, Tully Stone, have been "hunkered down" in their suburban Tampa, Florida home, for the last ten days, ever since the second civil war broke out. It is the second to last day of January, but it seems to Tully like it has been months, or more accurately, a year since life was "normal." The elderly couple, Tully, now 72, and Catherine, 62, have saved up enough food and supplies to get through another week, possibly two weeks if they are careful. Tully knows they must venture out soon to replenish their nearly empty pantry and fridge, but that thought seems terrifying. The stores, virtually everywhere in Florida, have been savaged by looters so that nothing remains in them. In the rural countryside east of their home, Tully had heard from his neighbors if he took only back roads into the countryside, he could buy fresh fruits and vegetables from people who had stands set up in their front yards and on the corners of the roads, so that is what they plan to do. Tully knew they could only travel during the daytime, as it was mayhem everywhere after dark, despite the national curfew that the government ordered. Tully and Catherine have continuously seen in the news media that those who venture out do not dare try to drive on major roads or highways, even if the road maintenance crews cleared the burning vehicles. Rioters throw rocks and cement blocks at every passerby from the overpasses, then raid the smashed vehicle with their crude but deadly weapons. They are also painfully aware that the pandemic alone has taken millions of lives in our country since it began five years ago. Because of its ever-mutating nature, each mutation fuels a fresh surge worse than all the previous surges. They have observed that vaccines seem to dampen the infection rates for a time, but the new variants only neutralize the effects of the vaccines. Catherine and Tully, putting their trust in the CDC and other medical experts, took each new vaccine when made available. So far, they both felt extremely fortunate to have been spared the horrible effects of the Covid-19 variants.

Catherine often succumbs to uncontrolled tears, as she lost so many loved ones, on her side of the family, to this epidemic. Tully has been luckier, as his side of the family has been spared death, but some family members are still in grave danger of dying from the virus, if not at the hands of the

THE CROWNING: CULMINATION OF THE NATION

mobs. Tully is deeply grieved for their devastating losses now that this recent civil war has begun. He dwells on how, ever since January 20th, 2025, just ten days ago, their lives had transformed dramatically. However, before that fateful day, it did not seem possible things could have gotten worse, yet that day tragically transformed the entire world.

Catherine would often say to her husband, "I am grateful for the things we have not yet lost. We still have power in our home, and we still have internet access and even cable television. Tully agreed with that but knew that cable news had already undergone major changes. Tully pointed out that "Every news outlet, except for one, has been canceled, declared illegal, and shut down. Social media on the internet has suffered the same fate; the plug has been pulled. The current administration has blocked all social media and news media websites originating in other countries. Even the dark web has been quiet, but it still exists if you know how to reach it." Tully knows exactly how to do that. "There is no way of knowing if we will ever return to the way things were before all hell broke loose", Tully said to Catherine, "I have wondered if the U.S. itself will survive, and if so, what will that look like? Everything we ever dreamed about, or ever assumed about our future lives is in jeopardy of extinction. It makes me scream at the top of my lungs, "How could this have happened?"

Catherine listened quietly, her eyes downcast. She knew Tully was right. The world they had known was gone, and there was no going back. But she also knew that they couldn't just give up. They had to find a way to survive and rebuild.

"We can't let this defeat us," she said finally. "We have to keep fighting. For ourselves, for our children, for the future."

Tully nodded. "You're right," he said. "We have to keep fighting. No matter what." They sat in silence for a few minutes, each lost in their own thoughts. Then Tully spoke again. "I am going to save our family from being destroyed if it is the last thing I do! Catherine gave Tully a knowing smile and said, "Let's start by finding some food, we have almost run out."

Chapter 1.
Nation In Crisis
January 30th, 2025: Tampa, Florida

Tully retired from his career in education nine years ago, after forty-three years as a high school teacher, guidance counselor, and 47 years of coaching. It was a career reminiscent of his father and oldest brother, Bryan, who coached for 53 years.

Three of Tully's sons continued the family's coaching tradition. Coaching was in the 'Stone' blood. Each Stone family member had a remarkable athletic career, most of whom played at least one sport in college. Tully played three sports, as did Bryan. Still, none were more successful than James, Tully's oldest living son, who excelled in the NFL for fourteen seasons after playing in the Big Ten. The entire family was very competitive. Tully, 48 years removed from his senior year in college, still worked hard to keep in shape and competed in several sports with men in his age range. At 72 years old, Tully's frame shows his years, but he maintained the ability and motivation to compete with his friends in the sports he loved for most of his life.

Tully sat in his makeshift office, just off the living room, on the first floor of his two-story home. He sat nervously in front of his somewhat dated laptop. It was Thursday evening, and his knee pumped vigorously up and down as he fidgeted in anticipation.

Tully had opened windows to every search engine he could find, all lined up in little "minimized" boxes, with two words typed into the search box. He prayed these two simple words would take him to his virtual destination. Tully checked the clock on the computer and his cell phone for the twentieth time as 6:00 pm. edged ever closer. Those two words, separated by a period, could mean the difference between rewriting history to ensure the rise of tyranny or preserving historical facts to spur the fight for freedom.

THE CROWNING: CULMINATION OF THE NATION

Finally, as the clock ticked over to 5:59 pm, Tully began the execution of his plan. He rapidly opened each search engine, some well-known, like Google and Bing, and others more recently created in the internet's underground. With the clumsy swiftness of a 72-year-old, Tully clicked the ENTER key as each of his prepared windows popped open. With each press of the key, those two words flew at the speed of light through networks worldwide. Ironically, he had picked up these words through the 'word-of-mouth network. Now he would finally see if the letters TRUTH.Life bears fruit.

As Tully set the last search engine in motion, he bounced back to the beginning to search for the truth. One by one, he checked, waiting for the search to reach its conclusion. Tully felt his heart pound as he read the ominous words: 'The 'URL' you have entered has a permanent fatal error and does not exist.' Tully's disappointment was overwhelming, and tears filled his eyes as each search engine delivered the same fateful message. He hesitated to bring up the last window, afraid of what it would mean if he saw those hated words again. The results from the final search engine appeared on his screen when he clicked the mouse. He wiped his eyes as his emotions rapidly shifted from despair to hope as he saw the bold and simple word: 'Truth'.

Tully stared at his screen in disbelief and shock for a good 10 minutes, dumbfounded that he had broken through the 'Great Transition' to a government-controlled news media that prohibited any form of dissemination of news in any medium that the Official Government News Agency did not generate. This "OGNA" controlled all forms of information, televised reporting, print news, and virtual news. All cable news networks, newspapers, local news, and internet-based forms of communication have been declared illegal and shuttered. Tully wondered how long this new underground internet site would remain "live" before the OGNA pulled the plug and arrested everyone involved. Viewing this site was against the government's declaration and could lead to imprisonment. He wondered if this virtual breakthrough was merely a cruel practical joke perpetuated by the OGNA or, worse, a clever way to find and trap consumers of outlawed news sources. Suddenly, the word "Truth" dissolved into the background as the silhouette of a man appeared. The profile transformed into a familiar figure wearing round glasses. A man of dark skin and a slight build spoke while Tully listened and watched intently, his heart beating quickly.

"Good evening, I am Chester Colt, formerly of NBC Nightly News. This is January 30th, 2025, and you are witnessing the first broadcast of Truth".

Tully could hear his heart pounding and excitement surging through his body. He felt goosebumps running up and down his spine for the first time in years. 'It was so good to hear a trusted voice once again', he thought. Tully hung on every word. He heard Chester Colt speak in a deep and sober voice, one he often used when the news was grave.

"As many of you undoubtedly have witnessed firsthand, the situation in the United States is dire. Fires are destroying thousands of buildings in every major city in the country as rioters clash with police, the National Guard, and the U.S. Army. We have become a 'nation in crisis.' This is the 4th week of the violent rioting pitting groups of citizens from all ends of the political spectrum against each other and the armed forces controlled by the new government. The death toll from what the government calls "civil unrest," but most are calling civil war, is only surpassed by the death toll from the pandemic. Considering the pandemic is in its 5th year, and the current civil crisis is only at day 10, we can only speculate where the total final death tolls may reach.

The government has resorted to commandeering over a hundred thousand semi-trucks to transport dead bodies to the railroad yards. They are then carried away by train to national cremation sites. Though you won't hear about this campaign to dispose of countless deceased U.S. citizens from Cerberus News, the only official news agency approved by the OGNA, millions of cell phone videos are recorded by citizens, showing these efforts to eliminate the memory of our loved ones who have perished.

Originally, we believed it was the National Guard, which is under the control of the executive branches of state and federal governments, that had requisitioned the trucks and provided the troops to carry out the transportation of the dead bodies. Still, there have persistent and credible rumors that there is another entity involved. Some rumors identify the organization as new private paramilitary troops that serve only at the command of the President. We have not verified if these rumors are accurate,

THE CROWNING: CULMINATION OF THE NATION

and we will report to you as more information is vetted and proves to be factual.

"To answer the questions you all have been asking, 'How did we get here? How did this happen? What is the Truth?' We have assembled a relatively small team of courageous journalists, authors, historians, and eyewitnesses, all of whom are in hiding, all of whom will soon have warrants for their immediate arrest, and all of whom are risking their lives by appearing on this broadcast to lend us their knowledge, and to answer those very questions. There is always the strong possibility that this broadcast will be shut down mid-broadcast. Should that happen, be patient and keep your ears "glued to the railroad track" to listen for words on reconnecting with us. We will not give up on this campaign to preserve the truth. Somehow, we'll always make our way back to you. That is our promise."

Colt paused for a second to draw us in closer, and in a very serious tone said, "Record this broadcast through its entirety and save it somewhere safe. The more copies of the 'Truth' exist, the harder it will be to eradicate the actual history."

Tully knew he had to do something. He had to find a way to preserve the broadcast so that future generations could learn from the mistakes of the past. But how?

He had little time. The violence was getting worse, and it was only a matter of time before it reached his doorstep. He had to act now.

He looked around his house, searching for anything that he could use to record the broadcast. But there was nothing. He had no tape recorder, no video camera, no nothing. Tully was about to give up when he saw it. He realized there was software already loaded on his laptop that would record whatever played on his computer. After a brief search, he found that old software and booted it up.

The broadcast was coming in clear. He could hear the reporters' voices describing the violence and chaos around them.

Tully started recording. He knew that this was important. The report was their history. It was the story of how this all came about, how it happened, and perhaps how it all ends.

He recorded until the broadcast finally ended. Tully knew he had done the right thing. He had preserved the broadcast so that future generations could learn from past mistakes.

But he also knew that this was just the beginning. There was still so much more to do. Tully had to find a way to get the broadcast out to the world. He had to make sure that everyone knew what had happened. Tully didn't know how he was going to do it, but he was determined to find a way. He had to. The future of the world depended on it.

Hearing Chester Colt's opening words, Tully felt a strange mixture of dread and a renewed inkling of hope. He did not know dead bodies were being hauled in 18-wheelers to be loaded onto trains, all to be destroyed at crematoriums designed for mass cremations. It brought back to Tully the visions he had from the movies of the Nazis during World War II, disposing of the bodies of deceased Jews in the concentration camps. *How is this possible*? Tully wondered to himself. *Is this 21st-century America or Germany in the 1930s*? New Year's Eve was a time of celebration and fireworks just a year ago. In 2025, it was marked by the constant sounds of gunfire, sirens, and angry shouting overwhelming the cries of despair. Tully's focus returned to Chester Colt as the broadcast continued.

"We will start this historical documentary by attempting to answer the first question, 'How did we get here?' To answer how we got to this place in our history, I am going to begin the search for the truth by going to our first guest, who, like all our guests, is going to great lengths to keep his whereabouts hidden. All presenters will broadcast from bare rooms, giving no clues about their location. Even we don't know where they are, which is by design. Let me introduce a historian and noted author, Dr. Randolph Lawton.

"So, Dr. Lawton, please put into perspective for us, considering recent events, what transpired that brought about the tragic circumstances the nation is currently experiencing?"

Dr. Lawton calmly explained, "The Founding Fathers drafted the United States Constitution, heralding in a remarkable and revolutionary new form of government, the world's first 'Democratic Republic.' The 'Great Experiment' had begun. Unfortunately, the way the Electoral College evolved throughout the years created a potential weakness in the way we elect

THE CROWNING: CULMINATION OF THE NATION

the executive branch. This weakness was exposed in the election of 2020. Following that election, the outgoing President, Donald J. Trump, attempted a coup to remain in power, despite losing the election by over 7,000,000 popular votes and 74 electoral votes. That event, though unsuccessful, paved the way for things to come in the following four years, leading to the next presidential election in 2024. The stage was set for the 'Second Civil War.'

Three years later, in March 2023, the former President, Donald J. Trump, while still under investigation for his role in the attempted coup, made a speech to The Conservative Political Action Conference. In the speech, Trump made what would be an ominous prediction of what just took place a few weeks ago when he said, "In 2016, I declared: I am your voice. Today, I add: I am your warrior. I am your justice. And for those who have been wronged and betrayed: I am your retribution."

Trump claimed that he and his followers are "engaged in an epic struggle to rescue our country from the people who hate it and want to absolutely destroy it... We are going to finish what we started. We started something that was a miracle. We're going to complete the mission; we're going to see this battle through to ultimate victory. We're going to make America great again."... "We have no choice. This is the final battle."

The event the entire world witnessed on January 20th, 2025, just ten days ago, was the culmination of Trump's pledge, made two years earlier. Despite losing in the Republican primaries, Donald J. Trump was declared and installed "President of America." He has overthrown the three branches of the government, but this chapter is not over. The revolution against this newly appointed dictator resulted in a new Civil War in the United States and all the nations in the Americas. Our history is still being written daily, and our job here on this program, Truth, is to ensure it is reported and preserved accurately."

"Thank You, Dr. Lawton. We appreciate your courage and contributions to this project to preserve genuine history."

Tully felt a burgeoning respect for the brave newscaster, enlightened and impressed by how Chester Colt had connected the dots right on cue, but he was not done yet. Colt saved his best for last.

"Now I will introduce Malcolm Nance, an intelligence and foreign policy analyst who served in the U.S. Navy for 20 years. As a U.S. Navy specialist in Naval Cryptology, Nance was involved in many counter-terrorism, intelligence, and combat operations. Welcome to the Truth, Malcolm. We are honored to have you join us and are grateful for your 20 years of service."

"Thank You, Chester. I am very excited to be a small part of this critical endeavor. It allows me to provide a little perspective from my research into the massive amount of documentation on this topic."

"Malcolm, without question, you have become one of, if not the leading expert on this subject in the U.S. I have barely scratched the surface of the books, reports, articles, and films you have either authored or co-authored on this subject. In this documentary, we will barely come close to adequately summarizing some of what you have learned and shared with the world. So let's start with a straightforward question. Historically, what was the purpose of the Soviet Union, back during the Cold War, and later Russia, for getting involved in the politics of democratic countries, specifically, the U.S.?"

Nance paused, contemplating his answer, then said, "One of the greatest dreams of the old Soviet Union was to put a highly suggestible American ideologue into power who would do the bidding of the Kremlin for nearly a century. Russia wanted to change American policy so that the economy and alliances with NATO would be so damaged; the Soviet Union would become the preeminent superpower in the world. The idea of a Kremlin-controlled president in the U.S. would live on after the death of the Soviet Union. In 2012, the plan was launched to subject the 2016 United States election to a massive cyber-influence operation, possibly in coordination with the Trump campaign. It extensively started with hacking the Democratic National Committee's servers to steal hypothetical information to knock Hillary Clinton out of the running for President of the United States. The plan would eventually work to the benefit of Russia's chosen candidate, Donald Trump."[37]

Chester Colt leaned closer to Nance as if to ask a highly sensitive question. "Was this kind of interference a commonplace occurrence?"

Nance replied emphatically, "On November 8th, 2016, the American presidential election culminated into what could arguably be called the most significant intelligence operation in the world's history. In the Russian attack on the American election, a strategic adversary influenced enough voters,

THE CROWNING: CULMINATION OF THE NATION

through manipulation of the internet, to get their preferred candidate chosen and convinced over 40% of the American population that they (Russia) had nothing to do with it. I was determined to track down other information to illustrate where Russian intelligence used cyber warfare to influence elections, referendums, and political opinion to their advantage. My investigation shows that Russian Intelligence has used these advanced malware suites to attack other nations for almost a decade. As far back as 1987, Russia saw Trump as a potential asset. That the Russians established a plan to hijack the perceptions of the American public and steer it to the benefit of Donald Trump to make him President of the United States is now without question.

"One could allow that he may have been an unwitting asset when he sent his first tweet in 2012 promising to make America great again, but by 2018, it was clear, he was no longer unwitting. In the parlance of an intelligence professional, he is a witting asset. In the case of Donald Trump, the Russians had long known that he was, in fact, one of the worst deal-makers in the world. He was on a near-constant quest for money. None of his inheritance or many endeavors, from Trump's steaks to Trump wines, could bring him to the level of respect he thought he deserved. He always fell back on real estate. Russia made up a significant part of his portfolio. This makes Trump such a perfect target to be influenced by a foreign power. Trump exercises no impulse control, and this makes him easily manipulated.[37]

"A good human intelligence officer could handle a person like Donald Trump where he or she would get the person to do his or her bidding unknowingly. While he, the poor victim, remains unknowledgeable about who he or she works for and the real aim of the spy's mission in intelligence work. These are called 'unwitting assets.' If an asset figures out that his spy is handling him, but the rewards make it worth his while, he becomes a 'witting asset.'

The Republican party had dedicated itself for eight years to destroying any positive action by President Barack Obama. Hillary Clinton, his Secretary of State, was likely to be the Democratic Party's front-runner and even more likely to be the next President of the United States. Putin's hatred of both was the key motivating factor that caused him to intervene. But luck was on his side in 2016 because all the actors and stages the Russian Federation had cultivated over a decade were in place to effect a change more prominent than a U.S. President. Russia had taken a modest distrust of Hillary Clinton. It had used the Republican Party's argument, but Hillary's emails had turned it into a weapon. Russia capitalized on the repeated investigations into Clinton's emails found on a secure server in her secret service-protected home. It was an easy target when the election was done. America had fractured."

Colt interjected, "So what about the American President, elected in 2016? What category did he fit, and what purpose would he serve?"

"To Russia, Donald Trump started as a useful idiot and then became an unwitting asset, but quickly became a 'witting asset' once he realized Russia was working in his best interest. Trump's usefulness to Moscow was critical to their goal of breaking links between America and its traditional allies. He has lived up to that expectation within the first year of his presidency. He insulted virtually every ally, the neighboring country, the international treaty body, and all of Africa, the middle east, and Asia. Yet, Vladimir Putin held such sway over him it would take almost 15 months and a brazen chemical weapons attack for him to offer the first mild criticism. This sycophancy had an effect; by early 2018, as much as 65% of America was permanently alienated from Trump's administration, as it has become increasingly clear that he was determined to rule only for his 35% core constituency. No matter what, in Trump's view, anyone who did not vote for him is alien. Non-voters and opposition are unworthy of his attention. He wants to lead and reward those who elected him, and other policies have been designed to punish the major blue states that had the nerve to vote for Hillary Clinton. His only piece of major legislation, a massive $1 trillion tax cut to the ultra-wealthy, included many provisions which raised taxes on states like California and New York and cut them for the impoverished deep red states like Alabama and Mississippi. A figure like Trump was bound to come up in American history, a man who rigged the system for his benefit and rode the wave of populism." [37]

Tully reflected on this last expert's perspective and recalled reading a little-known account that came to light in a news report by Politico on June

THE CROWNING: CULMINATION OF THE NATION

24th, 2022, in an article they published titled 'New January 6th witness: Trump had mystery call with Putin' where they exposed that during a trip aboard Air Force One, a scheduled interview between Alex Holder, a British Filmmaker, and Trump was abruptly canceled. Holder recounted traveling with then-President Trump on Sunday, October 25th, 2020, three days after the second presidential debate and nine days before Election Day. That day, Trump flew from Washington to New Hampshire, Maine, and then back to Washington. But White House Chief of Staff Mark Meadows told Holder that something had come up and the planned interview was nixed. 'My memory is,' Holder told us, 'that the chief of staff came over and said that the interview couldn't happen today because the President was on the phone. And I believe, if I remember correctly, that he said that he was on the phone with the President of Russia, Vladimir Putin, which is why the interview had to be postponed.

Tully had mused to Catherine, "Those types of phone calls are way out of bounds for the established protocol for heads of state. This story, in my mind, is very suspicious, making me wonder how frequently it occurred. Calls on Air Force One would provide a certain amount of opaque shade for keeping the communication out of the official record and prying ears. Exactly what would be necessary for that kind of clandestine communication?"

Catherine nodded and smiled at Tully, but before she could respond, Tully's attention was transferred back to the broadcast when he heard the host's comforting voice.

Colt considered what he had heard, analyzing the words that influenced his next ominous question, "Can we stop it from happening? Do we have the weapons to counter these attacks on democratic countries and democracy?"

In a solemn voice, Nance looked Colt in the eyes and said, "Make no mistake, democracy in the era of Trump and Putin is in retreat and has been targeted for extinction. With the right amount of public awareness, determination, and dedication to the principles we hold dear and love, it can be stopped." [37]

"Before we sign off for the evening, I need to explain that our primary goal in these nightly broadcasts is just one thing, to preserve the truth about what has happened in the last ten years that brought us to these terrible and pivotal times. We will fight the new regime's attempts to alter history. Our greatest challenge is to stay one step ahead of the current government, which we know will leave no stone unturned in its efforts to shut this down. We must keep these broadcasts short as we know we are being hunted online every second we air. We must hold our cards close to our chest, with-holding who will be on all future broadcasts, for fear that will put a target on their back.

"Please return tomorrow night and each night after that at 6:00 pm Eastern time. If we were not "airing" our show that night, we would have been forced to move to a new location, but we would be back eventually, which is our promise. Good night and please stay safe."

Tully felt very impressed by the broadcast and grateful he had the good fortune to find it. Still, he did not know yet how crucial this endeavor was to preserve the events of the last decade would become, nor how much it would affect his life and the lives of millions of others. The setting sun in Tampa yielded its light to the night accompanied by the "tat" "tat" "tat" of guns, followed by the inevitable sirens of police cars and fire-rescue trucks in the near distance. Tully felt deep in his gut that it may be just a matter of time before those guns entered his neighborhood.

Chapter 2
A Desperate and Dangerous Time
Tampa, Florida
January 30th, 2025; 8:00 p.m.

Sitting at his computer, intensely mesmerized by the first airing of Truth, Tully felt a strong sense of reassurance knowing that Chester Colt, and others, are out there, somewhere, reaching out to them to give them an anchor to keep them from drifting off into the land of misinformation, lies, and the repression of true history. After sliding into his favorite recliner, Tully was reminded of the book he read as a high school junior with the simple title of <u>Nineteen Eighty-Four</u> by George Orwell, an English novelist, published in 1949, just four years after World War II had ended. Orwell wrote of a future world of one government rule. Orwell introduced many concepts needed to keep this social construct in tack, such as "historical negation-ism," also called "denial-ism", which is re-creating and distorting history.[1] He also coined the term "memory hole". A memory hole is the deliberate altering or elimination of documents, photographs, transcripts, websites, etc., for the purpose of giving the impression that something never happened. The first step to re-write history would have to be to eliminate those whose purpose is to report events and replace them with a government-controlled information stream.

With anticipation for the next broadcast, hopefully, the next evening as promised, Tully knew he had to, in the meantime, get on with the business of surviving another night. Catherine will be the first to sleep tonight while Tully stands guard with their only gun, loaded and ready, in his lap. As the night will be upon them shortly, they both make sure every door is double locked, every window is shut with drapes drawn, and all lights are on. They wanted to make it clear to invaders, or the police, that people

---

[1] https://en.wikipedia.org/wiki/Historical_negationism

were living here. The many homes vacated are quickly broken into and taken over by squatters. Tully will switch places with Catherine at 2:00 am so he can sleep until sunrise while she "holds the fort." Catherine and Tully were both thankful that just a year ago, they had replaced their windows and doors with hurricane-proof windows and doors as they give them an added sense of protection, although they did not know they would protect them from a human storm. Each night while standing guard, Tully would mentally rehearse what he would do when that time comes when someone tries to break into their home, or worse yet, a mob of invaders. Tully turned on the T.V. to watch the shows that had been given governmental approval. There are fewer cable networks available than there were just a month ago, but many of the remaining stations' air reruns are still available to watch. If he wants to watch the news, there is no local news and only one national news outlet, Cerberus World News. Tully watched that first to see what they had to tell the audience, as it is the only way to find out about government announcements and decrees. There is scant mention of the riots that are going on in every city in the country, except for reports about the military's progress in eliminating the violence. The Cerberus World News announcers profusely praise the newly appointed President Trump for taking swift and severe measures to detain all rioters, with many being killed. They paint a picture of President Trump being the savior of the "Americas," protecting all peaceful citizens from the "traitors, looters and scum that threaten our existence." There is no mention of the welfare or whereabouts of all the politicians, former Presidents, and all members of the Judicial and Legislative branches that were arrested immediately after the takeover. Catherine asks Tully incredulously, "Why do you bother watching that garbage? You know it is all lying propaganda." Tully replies, "I am following the philosophy of Sun Tzu, "Keep your friends close; keep your enemies closer." I need to know what the government is saying, so I know what we need to avoid, and when it is time to leave." Catherine, alarmed by the suggestion, asked "Leave? Where would we go?" Tully thought hard about her question, and then finally replied, "I do not know, but I do know we will need to be one step ahead of our enemies, and we can't do that if we remain in the dark."

The entire U.S. Stock Market has been in free fall from the new administration's first day. Following weeks of the worst stock market crash in

THE CROWNING: CULMINATION OF THE NATION

American history, the news stopped; there has simply been no news about the market or the economy. It is as if that no longer exists. Rumors are floating around about a total reconstruction of our monetary system to an entirely virtual-based currency controlled by the government so that the value of the currency can only be altered by governmental decree. Still, that rumor has remained just that, a rumor. So far, Tully and Catherine have the cash they saved that can buy food and supplies from individuals, at least until the cash runs out or is declared worthless by the government. Feeling glum, Tully settles in for another long night, and he can hear the sirens and the gunfire, right on schedule. Little did Tully know how massive the ever-growing riots were becoming throughout the country. He said a prayer that they would make it through the night with no trouble. He sat on his favorite easy chair, quietly listening intently to the gunfire and police sirens, trying to calculate the distance from their home based on the direction and volume of the sounds. Tully's mind turns to his memories of the annual Stone family reunions each summer. All his sons, their wives, and kids all come together to join the larger Stone family for an entire week of athletic competitions, card games, and lots of sharing of their stories from the previous twelve months. Tully and his brothers, Bryan, Alan, and John, and their families started this tradition in the early 1970s and have been doing it for the last 50 years. "Stone Week," as they called it, was the highlight of everyone's year. Tully wondered if that could ever possibly happen in the future. The nation, and the entire world, have changed dramatically in just the last ten days, and nothing was guaranteed any more.

Suddenly Tully's cell phone notifies him of an incoming text. He knew from recent experience it was one of his sons. The text is from Patrick, the fourth-born son of the six boys in his life. Tully's first-born son, Shane, died twenty-four years ago. He was born with a severe brain disorder leaving him profoundly retarded, with cerebral palsy and a severe seizure disorder. Doctors predicted he would not live past 18 months old, but he got such great care and loved that he survived for twenty- six years. "He was the lucky one", Tully would tell Catherine, "lucky to have completely avoided the last five years and whatever is ahead of us in our future." Patrick asked cheerfully, "Hey, Dad. How are you and Catherine doing?" Tully replied, "Ok. Just manning my post for the night." Patrick admitted, "Ya, me too.

Today, I grabbed some barbed wire off one of my closed construction sites and wrapped it around my house. Tully retorted, "Nice. Did you save some for us?" Patrick answered, "Sorry, there was just enough for one house, besides I could never get it to your home in Tampa." Tully chimed, "No worries, I've still got my gun." Patrick warned his dad, "Stay awake and ready. They will come for our homes and food as soon as everything else runs dry." "I could not be more ready," Tully asserted. That was not true, but Tully did not want Patrick to worry about them. Pat and his wife, Colleen, have had a rough time over the last five years raising two daughters during Covid. Tully would thank God they have been quick to get themselves and their daughters vaccinated, as they have contracted Covid three times but have fought it off each time. His home construction business was completely shuttered, as nobody could think about building a home now. He earned good money while the economy was booming, but most of his profit was invested in new projects that would never be completed because of the halt of literally everything. Banks are closed, distributors are shut down, and stores are burned. The irony of Patrick's survival is that he was always the biggest risk-taker and daredevil of the six boys, but now he has survived because of an abundance of caution. Tully understood Patrick, as he saw many of the same qualities in Patrick that he knew he had when he was a young man. They both were major risk-takers (which made them excellent athletes despite their diminutive stature), and they both drivingly needed to seek excitement and adventure. Like his Dad, Patrick was an exceptional athlete earning NCAA All-American honors three times in college football. His road to those honors was not smooth, requiring Patrick to relentlessly pursue his hard-fought dreams by overcoming monumental obstacles. Patrick, like his Dad, had an older brother that excelled in athletics by not only playing in college but James, Patrick's oldest brother, also excelled in the NFL, so Patrick was always trying to measure up to his older brother's accomplishments. Tully felt so bad for Pat and Colleen's two daughters for giving up everything young people have a right to experience, but at least they are alive and healthy. Patrick was an amazing Dad to his daughters. That role changed Patrick's outlook on life. Life in their world had suddenly shifted from the pursuit of happiness and prosperity to a desperate and dangerous time where the best one could hope for is survival, a goal that

THE CROWNING: CULMINATION OF THE NATION

would be put to the test beyond anyone's comprehension of how difficult that would become. Tully worried for his grandchildren the most. How could any of them ever experience the traditionally biggest moments of their lives; their first date; the senior prom, winning a sports championship for their high school, going to college, getting married, even having children? "How can anyone enjoy the things we have all taken for granted? "Will life ever go back to what was normal?" Tully would ask Catherine. Catherine, always the optimist, replied to those rhetorical questions, "Things will all be fine very soon." It's hard to imagine how she could have been more wrong than this.

Chapter 3
Shadowland
Tampa, Florida
January 31st, 2025

Catherine, like Tully, had been previously married before they met each other. Catherine's first husband, a large and driven man named Thad Powers, worked for a national corporation with offices in every major city in the United States. They lived for ten years in New York when Thad earned a promotion to vice president overseeing operations in the southeast. After selling their condo in New York, he moved first to Fort Lauderdale, Florida, to find a home there before Catherine joined him. Thad purchased for the couple an old house built in the 1920s that was in a magnificent neighborhood on the water. The home was in severe disrepair through decades of neglect, offering the couple a chance to renovate and "flip it" for a hefty profit. When Catherine arrived in Fort Lauderdale, she was overwhelmed by the daunting massive tasks that the home demanded before they could consider selling the property. Still, she vowed to renovate the house after work and on weekends, as her husband Thad worked 60-70 hours a week at his new job.

The third night Catherine spent in her new-old home, Thad never came home after work. Catherine stayed up all night calling around, frantic that something had happened to her husband. Her efforts of locating him or learning about his welfare went unanswered until about 8:00 am the following day when Thad showed up to grab a shower and change clothes before going back to work. He told Catherine he had to work through the night, but Catherine was unconvinced, noting that he seemed well rested. With that innuendo, Thad slammed his fist into Catherine's right temple, causing Catherine to become unconscious with a massive lump on her temple and an ever-swelling black eye. When she awoke, she opened her only

THE CROWNING: CULMINATION OF THE NATION

usable eye to see what appeared to be heavy fog. As her vision became slightly better in her left eye, she realized it wasn't fog she was seeing, but heavy smoke. She was propped up in a chair and had a burned-out cigarette in her fingers. Catherine did not smoke, but Thad was a heavy smoker. Thad had scattered cigarette butts on the floor beneath her chair and around her feet. Through the smoke, she could see into the kitchen. Heavy flames climbed the walls and consumed the drapes. Flames had also destroyed the living room, and she sat between the two rooms in the dining room. She pulled herself to her feet and found her way through the heavy smoke, past the growing flames, feeling her way out the front door. She ran over to a neighbor's house, who, after answering the door, called 911. The Fort Lauderdale Fire Department saved the place. Still, the blaze severely damaged the kitchen and living room, and smoke damage found its way into every room on the first floor. The police, confirming her story, and documenting Catherine's injuries, arrested Thad and charged him with attempted murder and arson.

Six months later, Catherine was introduced to Tully by mutual friends. Her dark, hypnotic eyes, incredible natural Mediterranean beauty, and infectious laugh instantly swept Tully away. She seemed at peace with her post-Thad life. She spent every waking hour working on repairing and refurbishing her classic 1920's era southern home. Tully would come over on weekends to lend her a hand, and together they forged a strong relationship that three years later resulted in matrimony. They both had found their forever love and never looked back. Catherine was a woman of great strength from a Greek family who was no stranger to hard work and self-reliance. Catherine's father came alone to America from Greece as a 16-year-old boy. He built a business from scratch that supported his entire family. Andonios, Catherine's father, told Tully, in his imperfect Greek accent, many years later, "I come to America in 1956, to the New York port after thirteen days of traveling by sea on Queen Federica, with no English, no money, and I got to work, sewing for the Tremont Clothing Company in Boston. Andonio would explain to whoever asked, "I met my future bride, Elaine, at St. Johns Church in Boston. I saw her sitting by herself, a very nice-looking 20-year-old Greek girl, and asked her for her phone number. At first, she resisted, but I was relentlessly persistent." After a year, Andonios quit the factory job and opened his own vegetable business that prospered for the next 50 years. Catherine gained that same tenacity and added to it her unyielding optimism. Like her father, she was a 'force to be reckoned with,' consistently unyielding. To Catherine, Tully was the exact opposite of her first husband. She found Tully to be a kind, caring man who unconditionally loved his six children (all boys). Catherine happily accepted the role of stepmother to the six boys, which was only sometimes a smooth path to navigate. Still, it eventually worked out as everyone got to know, love, and respect her. She eventually became the ideal grandmother to the grandkids that came along a few years later. The kids and grandkids all came to refer to her as "Yaya," and she fit the role perfectly.

Tully needed to keep busy all day, a frigid day for a Tampa, Florida morning. Still, he could not stop thinking about the 6:00 underground broadcast he prayed would continue this evening. Behind Tully and Catherine's home is a vast forest preserve bordered on the north by the Hillsborough River, providing the preserve's western border. Tully has been working for the last month to create a hidden trail to give them an escape route if needed. The challenge is to make the path invisible to everyone, not to provide an avenue for people to come to their homes undetected by that very trail Tully created. About halfway along the makeshift pathway, a stream cuts pretty deep into the wood's floor. Tully constructed a small wooden bridge that would allow the traveler to get over the stream, then hid it nearby, covered by palm leaves and debris. He took great pains to ensure the undetectable trail appeared like more untraveled woods. To mark for navigation, he used wooden twigs and put a fluorescent orange and green dot on each end to point the way, then placed each one on the path. Hence, it was only visible to someone who knew where to look for them. They were his beacon, yet, they remained nearly invisible. Deep down in his gut, Tully instinctively knew that this secret passageway would someday save their lives.

When 6:00 pm arrived, Tully was again at his computer, ready, except that he knew this time which search engine worked the last time, so he was prepared to start with that one first. To his great relief, it worked. The word "TRUTH" soon was front and center on his screen. Tully was back, and so was Chester Colt as the host! Colt exclaimed, "Good Friday evening, the last day of January, and I am Chester Colt bringing you the Truth. Last night, in our inaugural broadcast, we spoke with a historian to give some background

THE CROWNING: CULMINATION OF THE NATION

to understand how this Civil War of 2025 came to pass. We will see later in our journey to find the Truth of how that history applies to the events that unfolded in the last eight years."

Tully's pulse quickened, and his hands became slightly sweaty. He expected with excitement the 2nd installment of this history-preserving endeavor. Tully felt he was a part of the rogue project now that he could record the show himself. Colt said, "Tonight, we will focus on how conspiracy theories were weaponized to create a political climate that will achieve the political goals of those who propagate those theories.

We are connecting tonight with a journalist who has spent much of his career chronicling many conspiracy theories throughout our history. He is Adam Sewer, formerly of The Atlantic. Good evening Adam, and thank you for being on our program tonight." Adam Sewer replied, "Thank You for having me, Chester. It is good to be here, but I am far away from you, hiding, which is definitely not pleasant." Chester Colt replied, "We all understand what you are experiencing, as we all have been doing the same thing. Adam, you wrote an expose in the May 13th, 2020 issue titled: Birtherism of a Nation: You proposed that the conspiracy theories surrounding Obama's birthplace and religion were much more than lies. They were ideology." Adam Sewer noted, "Yes, that article was a part of "Shadowland," a project about conspiracy thinking in America."[2] Chester Colt mused, "In that article, you said, and I quote, "Birtherism is not trying to explain some purportedly mysterious phenomenon…Birtherism was, from the beginning, an answer looking for a question to justify itself. Explain to us how perpetuating this conspiracy theory enabled Donald Trump to win the primary leading up to the election of 2016."[2]

Adam Sewer responded, "Well, Chester, as I wrote in that piece, "Birtherism" was a statement of values that expressed allegiance to a particular notion of American identity, one that became the central theme of the Trump campaign itself: To Make America Great Again. Trump won the Republican primary and united the party, partly because his run was focused on the psychic wound of the first black presidency. He had humiliated and humbled Obama."

Chester Colt questioned his guest, asking, "So how did Trump use that conspiracy theory during his term of office, or was it just something that ended in 2016, and everyone moved on? " Looking at the Trump administration's efforts to diminish the power of minority voters, imprison child migrants, ban Muslim travelers from entering the country, and criminalize his political opposition, it could be more accurately described as the governing ideology of the United States."2 Colt reacted saying, "So it never really mattered if it was true or not? All that mattered was that the outrageous lies stoked the innate fears and prejudices of a sizable subsection of our country?" Sewer explained, "In Obama's case, the lie that he was born in Kenya, making him ineligible to be the President, the lie that he was a Muslim, as was his father, and the implication that since he was secretly a Muslim, Obama was also supportive of terrorists because all Muslims are terrorists. It is all about "branding." How do your "brand" your image, name, or policies? For Trump, every issue, every antagonist, every accuser, every critic could be dealt with by re-branding the public's perception of them."2

Colt concluded with "Thank You, Adam, for sharing your knowledge and your perspective, it helps to understand the strategy of using lies to create shadowy illusions. That is all for tonight. We have been alerted that the government is closing in on our current location, so we will be closing the shop and relocating before they arrive. Please stay safe and return to the Truth. We promise to return as soon as possible."

Tully, during his time standing guard, thought about his neighbors. Some had left for what they felt would be safer places to live, only to be replaced by squatters. These previously homeless families never came out of their newly possessed homes, living in the dark shadows, without electricity or running water, but Tully would sometimes see their faces, blankly staring out the windows before closing the shades. Catherine and Tully's best friends, right next door, Wally and Pia, swore to stay in their home "come hell or high water". They were comforted in knowing the two families were still there to help each other out. Other than that, there was no mingling of neighbors as paranoia prevailed; doors stayed locked and sometimes were barricaded to prevent an unwanted incursion.

Chapter 4
Until the Storm Has Passed
Tampa, Florida
Saturday, February 1st, 2025

The chilly morning arrived after another sleep-deprived night of standing guard for four hours and trying to sleep the other four hours. Catherine looked relieved when Tully came into the living room. Catherine said there was not much happening outside that she could hear, and then she went back to bed. Tully rummaged through the kitchen and pantry, looking for something that might resemble a breakfast, settling on oatmeal. Tully was grateful that they still had power, although there were daily rolling brownouts that occurred at seemingly random intervals. He knows it will be time, soon, to venture out in search of staples. The fear of what might be out there waiting for them to come along is eventually overtaken by hunger and the desperate need to survive. They decided they could probably postpone the potentially deadly trek another week. Tully felt a sense of peace at the sight of Catherine pouring a giant mug of coffee and passing it to her husband, then sat outside in their backyard garden to enjoy the serene morning, watching the cardinals, finch, and woodpeckers compete over the bird seed.

Suddenly, both their phones blared out that horrible sound indicating some sort of emergency was being broadcast. Tully grabbed his phone, which read, "Emergency. Dangerous conditions exist requiring all citizens to shelter in place immediately. Lock doors and windows and stay indoors." Tully's first instinct was to go to the best view of the sky where he could observe it. The sky remained blue, and the wind was non-existent. At that moment, he heard the local sirens go off. They were not the same sirens he had heard when tornadoes were nearby, but a siren more ominous and eerily familiar. Tully remembered, as a child, hearing those same sirens every first Wednesday of the month signaling they were having an atomic bomb test and the public had to move to their atomic bomb shelters.

Tully ignored the warnings as curiosity overtook his good sense. Watching the skies for some sign of what might happen, Tully observed a set of three fighter jets flying in a 'V' formation, followed, a minute or two later, by what seemed like twenty armed military helicopters. Taking up the rear were six medical ambulance helicopters. They were all headed toward MacDill Air Force Base, near downtown Tampa. This was proof that something big was happening nearby, and Tully returned to the safety of their home, locked the doors and windows, and took up arms (his sole gun) to await whatever may follow. Suddenly, Tully's cell phone rings and he rushes over to pick it up. "Hello," Tully said." Grace, Tully oldest granddaughter, a young blond-haired, blue-eyed nurse in her early twenties, said, "Hi Grandpa, it's Grace." Tully, excited to hear Grace's voice, "Hi Grace, how is it going there?" There is a long pause showing Grace is trying to compose herself before speaking. "We're hanging in there. Chase, Pam, and Suzy are helping fortify our home. They have been solid through this." Chase, Pam, and Suzy are Tully's grandkids and Grace's younger siblings. Chase is a 21-year-old senior in college and a football player with NFL dreams. Pam is an 18-year-old college freshman, and Suzy is a high school junior with college offers already for soccer and volleyball. Once all schools shut down in-person learning two months ago and returned for the fifth time to all remote classes, Chase and Pam came home to live with their parents, James and Suzanne, who both fell terribly ill with Covid shortly after the kids returned home.

Tully inquired, "What is the news about your parents?" Grace hesitated, then answered, "Um, well, the intensive care nurses say they are both still stable. No significant changes to report. They are still on the ventilators. I am so scared, Grandpa." Tully, feeling great empathy for what they must be going through, yet needing them to hold it together, said, "I know, Grace, but you need to be the strongest person there. You are your sibling's rock now. I wish I could be there for you, but travel is not safe or advisable." Grace reacted, "I know you do, Grandpa. I wish you could too, but that is out of the question. It is way too dangerous to be outdoors, even for a few hours. I have to go to the hospital today, which scares me. What would happen to Chase,

THE CROWNING: CULMINATION OF THE NATION

Pam, and Suzy if I never made it back home?" "Just make sure that never happens, Grace. Don't take any unnecessary chances and don't travel alone." Tully warned. Grace promised, "Grady will be with me. We won't ever travel without each other. We have had all these strange sirens going off here, and I don't know what they mean." Grady is Grace's husband, they got married while still in college, about four years earlier. They are truly a beautiful couple, both with blond hair and very good-looking. Grady has climbed the corporate ladder rather quickly. He has that kind of personality that draws people in and develops a rapport with everyone quickly, and Grace is about as sweet and kind as any person you know. In only three years, she finished college and nursing training to become an RN. Tully always thought of Grace as the sweetest, most sincere little girl, who, as the eldest child, was a perfect role model for her two younger sisters. She lived her strong faith and always made her parents proud. When Tully visited Grace, she was a senior in high school. He witnessed her compete on the volleyball court and the soccer field. Tully soon realized Grace had a very competitive and extremely tough character that was hidden by her sweet character. Grace was, in fact, a fierce warrior on the playing field. She was a tenacious competitor that never gave an inch to anyone. She was also a natural-born leader who led her team to a state championship in its third year. James served as the head coach, explaining their instant success as a team. Grace exhibited the same qualities her father had when he played the same sports. The family referred to that set of ultra-competitive traits as "being a Stone," and Grace was no exception. She was a "Stone" on the field of competition.

Tully told Grace, "We have heard the same sirens here, too. There also have been a lot of military jets flying over us here in Tampa. Something big is going on. Have you seen them where you are too?" "Yes, but they are north of us, near Phoenix. What do you think that means?" Grace asked. Tully answered, "I don't know. I would ask Michael if I could reach him, but he isn't answering his phone, nor is Paul."

Michael and Paul are their two youngest sons, and both boys serve as officers in the military. Paul is a pilot in the Coast Guard stationed in Miami, Florida, while Michael serves in the Air Force in their military intelligence division.

Tully explained, "There seems to be a communications blackout with anyone in the military. I have not been in contact with either Michael or Paul since before January 20th. Grace, be sure to tell your parents I am praying for them every day, even if they can't a close eye on their progress. I know they will make it. They are robust and sturdy people and live a very healthy lifestyle, which will help them fight this virus off and overcome it. Bye, Grace, stay safe, and call me every day." Grace said while fighting off her tears, "I will, Grandpa. I love you both!" Tully told her, "Love you all, Grace; thanks for calling."

As Tully hung up the phone, that dreaded feeling of total helplessness returned to his consciousness. The distance between Florida and Arizona seems to have quadrupled in the last month. He can't imagine what those kids are going through, with their parents unable to be there for them, and instead, they are fighting for their own lives alone. He concludes, once again, that he has no other option than to continue to pray for James and Suzanne's recovery and trust that their kids will remain strong and safe and make wise decisions in their parent's absence. Tully says out loud, to himself, as if he were talking to Catherine, "They have been raised well, so I am certain they will keep each other as safe as possible," subconsciously trying to convince himself of that fact.

Tully turned on the T.V. to watch the news show, Cerberus World News, hoping to find out what was happening worldwide. War was breaking out in locations worldwide, as massive troop movements were occurring in Europe, Asia, and Russia. The Cerberus World News reporter informed the audience that in the U.S., the Air Force and Navy were moving their assets into a "defensive posture" as a precautionary measure and that around the nation, the National Siren Systems were being tested in every city, as well as the newer cell phone National Alert Systems. He assured the audience that these actions were precautionary and had no reason for alarm. Changing subjects, he began reporting on the nation's internal struggle with continued violence and rioting in virtually every city in the nation. Local and State police, the National Guard, and the U.S. Army were deployed in the hardest-hit cities under Martial Law, declared by the President last month. A national curfew continues because the worst of the riots occur after dark. The reporter urged

THE CROWNING: CULMINATION OF THE NATION

all Americans to, as much as possible, stay home with doors and windows locked at all times until the "storm has passed."

Tully thought to himself how ironic it is that the news anchor would refer to this nation's wide chaos as a "storm," considering the events that have transpired to create this mayhem. Tully told Catherine, sitting next to him he believed what the reporter was disguising, through his positive spin, was that the "Navy and Air Force were withdrawing from NATO countries and other European, Middle Eastern, and Asian allies. Those assets are vital to our ally's survival against invasion from Russia or China. Without them, they cannot defend against certain destruction or surrender." Reaching for his cell phone, Tully again called his son, Michael. Catherine frowned and asked, "Are you calling Michael again? Don't you think if he could answer, he would have by now?" Before Tully could reply, Michael said, "Hello, Dad." Tully looked over at Catherine with an 'I told you so" expression on his face. "Hi Michael, I have been trying to reach you for over a week. How are you doing?" Michael, sounding tired, said, "I'm sorry, Dad, it has been crazy here, and I have been working 24/7 all week." Getting right to the point, Tully asked, "I heard on Cerberus World News that the Navy and Air Force had shifted to a defensive position. Does that mean they are withdrawing from the two theaters of protecting NATO countries and our allies in Asia?"

"Dad, you know I can't talk about that. It is all highly classified. I'm sorry, Dad." An awkward silence followed until Catherine spoke up and said to Michael, "Hi honey, how are you feeling?" "Exhausted." was Michael's monotone reply. Catherine asked, "How is the weather up there?" After a brief pause, Michael reports, "It remains cloudy, never seems to change. It is getting warmer, however", he added. Catherine asks, "Have you seen any birds returning from their winter migration yet?" Michael's voice got a little more upbeat, saying, "Yes there are a lot of birds and ducks gathering at the shoreline." "That's something positive," Catherine replied, " you need to get some sleep. Take care, and stay in touch with us." "I will," Michael promised. "Goodnight."

Catherine hung up the phone and turned to her husband, saying, "You need to learn how to communicate with Michael." Tully looked puzzled and said, "All we learned from the conversation is that it is cloudy and getting warmer." "No, Tully. He told me that the Navy and Air Force had been withdrawn from all foreign war fronts and brought home. The "cloudy, never seems to change" reference meant that the Air Force and Navy are not aligned with the Trump government, at least not yet."

When he said, "the birds and ducks are migrating to our shores," he was telling us that the generals and admirals have brought their assets home to our shores. Perhaps to prepare for a domestic battle, or to protect against foreign invasion. I assume the Army and National Guard are under Trump's control. However, the other three, including the

Coast Guard, are still loyal to President Biden, and possibly the recently elected President, who has not yet taken the oath of office, because he is missing." Tully, looking shocked, said, "You got all of that from your weather chat with Michael?" Catherine smirked knowingly, patted Tully on the head, and said, "You must learn his coded language. He wants to protect his family but has to follow the rules, which is a wobbly tight-rope to walk."

At 6:00 pm, Tully was once again ready for the "Truth," the underground broadcast designed to preserve for the historical record what has happened in the last ten years of American history. He now felt a strong sense of civic duty to help preserve the facts of our history from being hindered by sinister sources. Tully had downloaded the software they recommended in an earlier broadcast that allowed him to record the digital broadcast and save it on his portable hard drive. He had that software running when today's broadcast began. A very familiar face appeared. A face Tully recognized immediately as Sheldon Smithson, formerly of Fox News and later CNBC. "Good evening, and welcome to "Truth." As you know, to keep this historical documentary alive, we must keep our whereabouts secret and be incredibly flexible, changing both location and presenters often so as not to allow authorities to track us down. It is my turn to take the metaphorical baton and run with it. I am very fortunate to have one of the most highly regarded historians in the nation with me for this broadcast. He is a nationally recognized authority in the history of the United States, having earned the Pulitzer Prize for his many books and papers on American political events. A graduate of Oxford, he has served as the Department Head at three different Ivy League Schools, Harvard, Yale, and Columbia University, and was a Rhodes Scholar. We welcome you to this broadcast, Dr. Vaughn Woodman, Ph.D. Woodman responded, "Thank you for that kind introduction,

THE CROWNING: CULMINATION OF THE NATION

Sheldon. I felt great relief when you contacted me about this endeavor. I have always fought the battle between historically factual information and misinformation that comes in many forms and from many sources."

Smithson added, "It was a great personal sacrifice you agreed to join us in this project, as this means you have to go underground for an unknown period of time, as the rest of us have done." Woodman confided, "Ethically and morally, I did not have a choice. I have worked my entire career to bring clarity and fidelity to the historical record. Believing, as I do, that it is under grave threat, I knew I had to do something. Your platform has made that possible when it would not be possible through conventional ways. Knowing that thousands, perhaps eventually millions of people will not only be watching this broadcast but also recording it for the preservation of the historical reality, unvarnished by politicians, foreign bot farms, and social media campaigns to spread misinformation and lies."

Smithson told the audience, "That brings me to an important reminder for our audience. As we conceived this project, we all vowed only to present proven factual events leading up to the present. The standards for presenting past events in this documentary must be extremely high and without prejudice. Everything declared worthy of inclusion on "Truth" must be devoid of speculation and inference and vetted for unsubstantiated information, even if we suspect it is true. It must be proven through first-hand accounts, written or spoken words that are recorded by the speaker or author, and collaborated by reliable witnesses." Woodman concurred, adding, "That is why I have joined this team and this effort. As a historian, I must follow those principles and share those commitments." Smithson reminded the audience, " In the initial broadcasts, we tried to give the audience some important perspective, historically, to understand better the events we will describe going forward. As much as possible, we will keep the events in chronological order to better comprehend the cause and effect of the events that transpired." Smithson, turning to his guest asks, "Dr. Woodman, where do you recommend we start? What was the first significant event leading to what is coming?"

Woodman reported, "I would say foremost, that there is good reason to hope that we will come out of this crisis with Democracy still in tack. I believe this storm will pass. To give you a synopsis of events, the best place to start is the events leading up to former President Trump's first impeachment by the House of Representatives. Without going into all the specific details, it is historically correct to say that President Trump will go to great lengths to win re-election by trying in 2019, to get Ukraine's president to investigate a leading domestic political rival, Joe Biden. It shocked that any President on the United States would use the power of his office to solicit interference from a foreign country in the 2020 election. However, we did not know how far he would go to remain in office. A little over a year later, that knowledge became apparent."

Smithson asked, "Dr. Woodman, I realize this incident resulted in an impeachment of Trump, his first of two during his first term in office, but was that the "north star" event that predicted the events of 2024 and this first month of 2025?

Dr. Woodman responded, "It was just the 'tip of the iceberg' of what was soon to follow. I think the pandemic, caused by the Covid-19 virus, and how the Trump Administration dealt with the crisis was even more impactful on the election of 2020 and predictive of the oncoming storm."

Smithson advised, "Our time is up, Dr. Woodman. Thank you for your expert insight and ask to have you continue sharing your knowledge with us as we travel this journey together to explore how this nation came to be on the brink of its demise." "Thank you for giving me this opportunity. I pray daily that this Democratic Republic will survive this crisis," Dr. Woodman confided.

The program concluded for the night. Tully was left with a feeling of encouragement that Dr. Woodman thought there was still a chance we may come out of this, the "Great Experiment," with Democracy remaining in tack. "We desperately need that kind of hope," he thought. Tully was cognitively aware of the realities of the current situation in the country, seeing the riots and the extreme social unrest in the news. Still, he had not yet experienced it firsthand. That was about to change; they were finally out of food.

Chapter 5
That Day Has Come
Tampa, Florida
Feb. 2, 2025

"Tully, I think that day has come. You need to head out in search of food. Our pantry and refrigerator are both almost empty", Cathy said. They had talked about this day for months, often debated how best to do this, and finally settled on the best plan. Tully would make the journey into the countryside alone. He sat at the kitchen table to eat a can of tuna and washed it down with black coffee while planning his first trip out in search of food. Tully studied a Google map on his phone to map out the safest route while still increasing his chances of finding food for sale. Checking his wallet to see what denominations of cash he had in it, he found six $5 bills, a $10 bill, and a $20. He wondered if $60 would buy very much, then added two more $20 bills, hoping that $100 would be enough. Tully did not want to bring too much cash as he did not want to risk losing it to a desperate thief. He contemplated whether he should bring their gun with him or leave it here with Catherine. Tully kept the gun at home, as it is the only one they had, and if the robber took his money, he would most assuredly also take their gun, leaving them with no weapon. Instead, Tully grabbed a knife to be his sole means of self-defense.

You don't have to drive very far to get out into the rural area to the east of their home. It is a smattering of modern homes recently built between much older and smaller homes that date back a good forty years or more. Tully had driven these roads so many times in the past that it seemed perfectly safe, but as he drove those roads today, he noticed a lot of abandoned cars, often burned out, without wheels, stored in the front yards of the older homes. They all seem inhabited, but there was no telling if they were occupied by their owners or squatters. The new homes were walled off by iron fences, and some had boarded up their windows. No cars were parked in their yard. Probably, they were safely stored in a garage.

Tully drove for about 30 minutes when he spotted a home with a sign posted that simply read, "vegetables and fruit 4 sale". As he pulled over, parking on the side of the road, a bearded man walked out the door dressed in jeans and a dirty long-sleeved shirt. He looked at Tully suspiciously, so Tully said to him, in the cheeriest voice he could muster, "Good afternoon, Sir." There was no reply, except the man glared at Tully and surveyed Tully from head to toe. " I am here to buy some of your produce," Tully announced. "Strip." the man ordered as he pumped his double-barrel shotgun.

"My God," Tully thought to himself, "what did I get myself into?" Tully's heart started pounding while staring at the two large holes at the front end of the shotgun, aimed at Tully's chest. Tully had a chilling flashback from a scene in the old 1972 movie, Deliverance. Out loud, Tully asked, "Excuse me?" The bearded man demanded, "I got to know if you have any weapons on you first, so strip to your underwear." "I am not here to rob you, Sir. I just want to buy some of your food." Tully declared while gesturing to his "4 sales" sign. "If you want food," he said, "You will have to strip first. I can't take no chances these days."

Throwing caution to the wind, Tully did as he asked. Standing there in his briefs, the man seemed satisfied Tully wasn't packing a gun. "Ok, you're good; put your clothes back on and follow me." Tully did just that in a hurry, then walked behind him as he led Tully around his home to the backyard, where he had an old greenhouse. Stepping inside, Tully could see he had grown and harvested a lot of produce. The bearded man helped Tully carry two large bags filled with fresh food. Tully paid him whatever the man required for the food, and he still had $10 left. Knowing $10 would not get much more, Tully headed back home quickly. Crossing Highway 301, a Sheriff's car pulled up behind Tully's pickup, and then the Sheriff's car lights flashed red and blue, with no siren. Tully pulled over and waited for the officer to come up to his car window. He got out and closely checked Tully's truck. Tapping on the driver's side window, he gestured for Tully to roll down the window.

"Good afternoon Sir." Tully said, once again trying not to show his nervousness. "License and registration," the Sheriff said back. Tully fumbled

THE CROWNING: CULMINATION OF THE NATION

through his wallet to find the requested documents, then handed them to the police officer as ordered. The Sheriff took them with him as he went back to his car. Tully waited, with some anxiety, for what seemed like an eternity, until the Sheriff finally returned. "What is your purpose for being out here?" the officer asked. "I needed to buy some food because my wife and I ran out." Tully said as his voice cracked from his nervousness. "Any luck finding any?" he asked. Tully wondered to himself why the lawman wanted to know, but replied honestly. "Yes Sir. I bought some produce from a man a few miles from here." "Do you remember the address?" he asked. "It was a farmhouse on Skewlee Road. The house was gray. I did not see the number of the house. Would you like an apple?" Tully kicked himself mentally, adding that stupid apple question. He looked at Tully, then cracked a smile, not a big grin, just a hint of a smile. "No, but thank you. You look like you need it, and I am sure that you have to pay a lot for it." He handed me back my documents and said, "You need to get home before 6:00. The curfew is being enforced strictly now." "I will, Sir, thank you." With that Tully started his car and drove west. Tully arrived home well before 6:00 and Catherine greeted him with the first sign of happiness he had seen on her face in months. She saw the bags of food and helped carry them in while asking all about the experience. Tully told her about everything that happened, but she was already planning, in her mind, how to make these fruits and vegetables last the longest.

By 6:00 Tully was at his computer waiting for the screen to come back to life. Right on time the word, Truth, appeared on the screen. The very face Tully was expecting appeared, "Good evening, this is Sheldon Smithson, and welcome to the next edition of Truth. I have to start out this broadcast with some very disturbing news. Chester Colt was taken into custody, during the night by a Swat Team. I cannot mention where this took place, but we have confirmed he has been arrested. We wish our colleague the best. We have no idea what has happened to him since, nor exactly what he has been charged with, but that is easy to guess. The same potential fate looms over all our heads, but we assure you we will not surrender. This program is much more than just delivering news, but a far greater purpose, to preserve the factual record of our recent history. You, our audience, play a very crucial role in that all-important endeavor, by recording and saving each of these segments. We are delighted that the number of people watching these broadcasts is multiplying by leaps and bounds each day. We can only hope and pray that most of you are preserving the Truth for all our fellow citizens to have for whatever our future holds." Tully's heart was pounding in his chest at the thought of what might happen to Chester Colt. He closed his eyes and said a brief prayer for the man he only knew from watching him in the news. "Tonight, we have asked our guest from last night's show to return to pose to him another important question. As a precaution, we are going to shorten each of these broadcasts. The longer we stay live, the more time they have to find the source of this broadcast." "Welcome back, Dr. Woodman, and thank you again for sharing your knowledge with us." "I am honored to be a part of this, and I am so very sorry about Chester Colt," Dr. Woodman commented. Sheldon Smithson said, "In the interest of brevity, let's get to our question for today. Dr. Woodman, we gained significant insight into former President Trump's motivations last night by exploring the events that led to the first of two impeachments in his first term of office. Was there any other event during those four years that gave us a peek at the forces at work in his mind?" Dr. Woodman explains, "Well, the Helsinki Summit between Trump and Putin was a watershed moment. On July 16, 2018, President Trump met with his Russian counterpart Vladimir Putin in the Finnish capital, Helsinki. The two world leaders spent two hours speaking alone. The only other people in the room were their interpreters; even key administration officials later said they did not know the full details of what was discussed. After their meeting, the two leaders began a 45-minute news conference that would be remembered as one of Trump's most controversial, with the U.S. president casting doubt upon the findings of his intelligence agencies and telling reporters that Putin had given him an "extremely powerful" denial of claims that Russia had interfered in the 2016 U.S. presidential election. During the meeting, reporters asked both Presidents some poignant questions that produced interesting answers. One of those questions came from Jeff Mason of Reuters."

Jeff Mason from Reuters asked, "President Putin, did you want President Trump to win the election, and did you direct any of your officials to help him do that?" Putin's reply stated, "Yes, I did. Yes, I did because he talked about bringing the US/Russia relationship back to normal." Dr.

THE CROWNING: CULMINATION OF THE NATION

Woodman explains, "This was an explicit confirmation of Putin's desire to have Trump be President of the United States. The next logical question would be, 'Why?' While that raised eyebrows, the next question from Jonathan Lemire from AP asked, "President Trump, you first. Just now, President Putin denied having anything to do with the election interference in 2016. Every US intelligence agency has concluded that Russia did. My first question for you, sir, is, who do you believe? My second question is, would you now, with the whole world watching, tell President Putin — would you denounce what happened in 2016, and would you warn him never to do it again?"

Trump's intoned refutation was, "So let me just say that we have two thoughts. You have groups that are wondering why the FBI never took the server. Why haven't they taken the server? Why was the FBI told to leave the office of the democratic national committee? I've been wondering about that. I've been asking that for months and months, and I've been tweeting it out and calling it out on social media. Where is the server? I want to know, where is the server and what is the server saying. With that being said, all I can do is ask the question. My people came to me, Dan Coats came to me and some others said they think it was Russia. I have President Putin. He just said it's not Russia. I will say this. I don't see any reason why it would be, but I really do want to see the server. But I have confidence in both parties. I really believe that this will probably go on for a while, but I don't think it can go on without finding out what happened to the server. What happened to the servers of the Pakistani gentleman that worked in the DNC? Where are those servers? They're missing. Where are they? What happened to Hillary Clinton's emails? 33,000 emails gone — just gone. I think in Russia they wouldn't be gone so easily. I think it's a disgrace that we can't get Hillary Clinton's 33,000 emails. So I have great confidence in my intelligence people, but I will tell you that President Putin was extremely strong and powerful in his denial today. And what he did is an incredible offer. He offered to have the people working on the case come and work with their investigators with respect to the 12 people. I think that's an incredible offer. Okay, thank you."

Dr. Woodman argued, "This convoluted answer, which just seemed to wander from an attempt to divert the subject to old but frequent topics of Trump's, such as Hillary Clinton's emails and some mysterious missing server to deflect away from the clear question, being "who do you believe?". Undoubtedly this was a very provocative question, but the second was more of a direct challenge to Trump when Lemire asked, "Would you now, with the whole world watching, tell President Putin — would you denounce what happened in 2016 and would you warn him never to do it again?" Trump's only response to his challenge was when he said, "My people came to me, Dan Coats came to me and some others and said they think it's Russia. I have President Putin. He just said it's not Russia. I will say this. I don't see any reason why it would be. A few weeks later, Dan Coats, who was the Director of National Intelligence, was asked about the meeting in Helsinki. Director of National Intelligence Daniel Coats was asked what he knew about the Trump-Putin summit." "I'm not in a position to either understand fully or talk about what happened in Helsinki," Coats responded. Woodman continued to explain saying, "Coats has made his concerns known both about the lack of preparedness and Trump's conduct in a news conference after the Helsinki summit. "Obviously, I wished he had made a different statement," Coats said, "If he had asked me how that ought to be conducted, I would have suggested a different way."

Dr. Woodman expounded, "It became apparent to me from this episode of Trump's first term that Trump distrusted his own Intelligence Agencies, and also that he had an affinity for Putin that was hard to understand, much less explain. This theme becomes crucial in understanding the events in 2020 and 2021."

Feeling tired, Tully closed his eyes and drifted into thoughts about his family. Not unlike most grandparents, Catherine and Tully's lives revolve around the intertwined well-being of their children and grandchildren. Simply being with them during those precious moments can be the elixir that keeps them alive and happy. Tully pictured the days of summers past when the family gathered for a week of activities and social interaction. The joy he felt being visited every morning by his sons as they stopped by Tully and Catherine's cabin for coffee before heading out on the golf course for an early morning round of nine holes. But in this alternate universe, they have found

THE CROWNING: CULMINATION OF THE NATION

themselves, where the way things used to be, are being transformed into the accelerant of tragedy, the most cherished moments of their existential beings are about to be ripped to shreds.

Chapter 6
Just Bad Luck
Tampa, Florida
February 3rd, 2025

Monday morning brought a beautiful dawn, not as chilly as the previous days had been, and the eastern sky promised a sunny day. Tully spent the morning walking on his secret trail with his Golden Retriever on a leash when Tully's cell phone rang, with a special ringtone called "Sherwood Forest". Its horns announced to him that his 3rd son, Anthony, is calling. Tony, as everyone calls Anthony, lives on a ranch he calls "The Stone Farm" in which he and his family raise horses, donkeys, pigs, chickens, ducks, and rabbits. The farm is 13 acres, of which 8 acres is a forest preserve. His home and barn are on the other 5 acres.

Tully answered the call saying, "Tony! How are you doing?" Tony replied, "I'm OK. How about you and Catherine?" "We have food now! Couldn't be any better," Tully jested. Tony inquired, "What did you find?" Tully exclaimed with glee, "Fruits and Veggies." Tony informed his dad, "You need to get some protein. Why don't you try to make your way here so I can set you up. We have more eggs than we can possibly eat." Tully exclaimed, "I'd like that. Let's plot a safe route to get to your home." Tony advised, "I will work on that for you and send you the directions. There are some roads around here that have been totally blocked off and are impassable. I wish I could bring the eggs to you." Tully heeded, "No. That would be a terrible idea. When you got back home, you would not have an animal left on your property. You need to stay there with your wife, Tommy, and Sheila." Tommy is Tony and Marie's 12-year-old son, and Sheila is their 10-year-old daughter. Marie almost had succumbed to the Covid virus two years earlier, however, after a very brave and difficult battle, she miraculously survived. Unfortunately, she suffers from "Long Covid". Two years after coming home

THE CROWNING: CULMINATION OF THE NATION

from months in ICU, Marie experienced extreme fatigue, headaches, and shortness of breath. She has never regained her sense of smell or taste. Tony does all the "heavy lifting" around the farm, prepares the meals, and serves as the kids' classroom teacher. They can't leave their property since this insane mayhem began. He stays up all night sleeping with one eye open on the back porch throughout the night. The biggest threat is not the wild hogs, nor the coyotes that often wander on the property at night, but human thieves looking for a meal by stealing whatever animal they can get their hands on. Sheila is a cancer survivor and has been cancer free for 3 years now. She was diagnosed with "stage 5" when she was four years old, but thanks to great parents, chemo, and St. Jude's Hospital, she defeated the insidious disease.

Tully asked, "How are the kids doing?" Tony responded, "They're doing very well. They are a big help here on the farm. Marie and I have them doing their school lessons every Monday through Friday during school hours to keep a normal schedule in tack. Tommy is doing high school subjects, now that he can progress at his own pace, and Sheila is progressing better than earlier, now that she is finally accepting that I am her teacher, instead of her Mom." Tully questioned, "Do you have them online with the school yet?" "Not yet, I still don't have access to the internet and have no idea how long that will take to get back up and running. Fortunately, I was able to get the books and materials I needed from the school to last a full year, before they shut their doors," Tully reported.

After a moment of silence, Tully informed Tony, "Catherine and I will drive down to the farm as soon as you get to me the recommended route. We will leave early in the morning in order to spend some time with you before leaving in the afternoon." Tony exclaimed, "Great. The kids will be really excited to see you both. I will text you the best route." "We can't wait to see you four. Give them our love, Tony" Tully implored. "I will, Dad. See you soon," said Tony.

They all know that a trip, which Tully and Catherine have made hundreds of times before this all began, will now be very dangerous. The trip will be taken, not so much for acquiring the fresh eggs, as much as seeing Tony, Marie, and the kids, making the risk worth it. A week went by before Tony sent that text. He explained he had to contact many friends to get a current picture of the road situation. With that information, he was able to create a route he felt was the safest, although, instead of it being a 40-mile drive, this route added up to about 60 miles because of the many detours. Catherine insisted they leave the next morning, as she could not wait another day without seeing her grandkids. Tully reluctantly agreed as he had a bad feeling about the journey.

That evening, right at 6:00 pm Tully went back to the "Truth" website to see and record their broadcast. He decided he would make a copy of each broadcast on a separate thumb drive and give it to Tony to watch after the kids are in bed. Right on cue the word "Truth" appeared on the screen. Tully shouted out to Catherine to join him, but she had no desire to watch a show about things that already happened, preferring instead to see something she found more entertaining. Tully hit the record button on the screen and settled in to watch the documentary. He saw the familiar face of Sheldon Smithson who said, "Good evening, this is Sheldon Smithson, and welcome to the next edition of Truth. Today I have set up an online team meeting with one of what were the nation's top health officials, who had worked with the Trump administration on the pandemic response. We are going to explore how that response played a significant role in where we are today. We want to make clear, for the historical record, all the variables that led to the events we are experiencing today. Our first guest is the famous investigative journalist, Bob Woodward who is sharing his unique knowledge, coming to us through a pre-recorded video during an interview by Steve Paikin on The Agenda.[45]

Woodward started working for The Washington Post as a reporter in 1971 and now holds the title of associate editor. Woodward's first book with Bernstein, All the President's Men, became a #1 national bestseller in the spring and summer before Nixon resigned in 1974. Recently he co-authored three books with Robert Costa, Fear, Rage and Peril; a trilogy covering the four years of Trump's administration, from 2016-2020. Most recently Woodward published another book called Trump Tapes. Responding to a question by the host, Steve Paikin, listen to Woodard's epic response."

"Here's the problem. You're talking about democracy in this, (Donald Trump) doesn't understand democracy, but significantly, at the same time, he does not understand the presidency and the obligations of the President. And, in the United States, the President is, under the constitution, such

THE CROWNING: CULMINATION OF THE NATION

a central player in the government...if it was a crime, what he did, on the mishandling of the coronavirus. I think he put the country in moral free fall. If it was a crime, this is the indictment, because it turns out, he would say things to me, or this early 2020, the last year of his presidency, say, "Oh yeah, the virus is coming. I always tried to play it down. I don't want to panic people." I thought, well, this kind of surprised him. But because I had the luxury of time, I could spend weeks and weeks digging into the White House. And on the tapes, you hear Trump's National Security Advisor coming in early in January, January 28th, for a top-secret briefing. And Robert O'Brien says to him, Mr. President, the virus is coming. It is going to be the biggest national security threat to your presidency. His deputy, Matt Pottinger, who'd been a Wall Street Journal reporter in China for seven years during the SARS epidemic, had golden sources in China. And they told him, they said to him, this is going to be out of control. It is going to be a firestorm. It's going to be like the Spanish flu pandemic, that killed 650,000 people in the United States. We're now at 1.1 million; million! And I mean, think of it. Trump knew this, and he lied and covered up and concealed it for months and months. And I mean, just think if he'd done, I, I once asked him, what's the job of the president? He said, "to protect the people." He failed totally to protect the people... But I mean, here's the stunner. Trump is meeting with the doctors, the experts, and I'm talking to them. They're saying he won't pay attention. He won't listen. He's off. He's, got these virus deniers in the meetings. On April 5th, I called him, and I say, you really need the doctors. And they know you are not listening. We need a World War II-style mobilization of the country. And I go through the list, and I think Trump is going to do something. And he didn't, and he did nothing.

I said, "What's the plan? " And he said, "We'll have a plan in 104 days. If I put it out now, no one will pay attention". One hundred four days and I realize that it's election day. He was obsessed with being reelected. That's all he cared about. That is the tragedy. That's the moral free fall. You cannot do that. Now, at this point, we all knew about the virus. There was nothing I could do to tell people, but I could put it together in the book and say, this is who he is."[45]

Smithson declares to the audience, "Finally, I would like to steer this discussion to get the perspective from our historian, Dr. Vaughn Woodman PhD.

Dr. Woodman, how do these missteps by the Trump Administration regarding the handling of the pandemic, affect the election of 2020?" Dr. Woodman acknowledged, "Well Sheldon, in all likelihood, had the pandemic not happened, Trump was a lock for re-election. The economy was strong and that, historically, has boded very well for an incumbent to win re-election. However, unfortunately for Trump, it happened, and the growing fears of the voters, combined with the lockdown of the economy in almost every state, followed by the severe drop in the stock market all combined to rewrite the outcome of the election."

Smithson, refuting what he just heard, said, "You make it sound like it was just bad luck that caused Trump to lose to Joe Biden in 2020. Is that all it was, bad luck?" Dr. Woodman insisted, "No, no, not at all. Trump's inept handling of the national crisis did him in. He calculated he had to continue to appease his base. In so doing, he came into conflict regarding the messaging of every aspect of the mitigation efforts, wearing masks, testing for infection by the Covid-19 virus, and even getting the same vaccines he so desperately wanted to be created and distributed before the election, even though that was later sabotaged. Throughout the first year of the pandemic, his words and actions screamed out to the nation that there was nothing to see and nothing to fear there. He even grabbed onto whatever quackery treatment or medication that was promoted on cable news and social media and promote it as a cure for Covid-19, despite the objections of his medical experts. Trump created the very mistrust that doomed his re-election. He was his own worst enemy. The near panic that enveloped the country when the first few lives were lost because of Covid-19 was eventually replaced with "Covid fatigue," a term that could be described as widespread apathy toward the over 1.2 million American deaths. A split along political party lines developed that made the same weapons to fight this deadly plague, masks, social distancing, and even the vaccinations that the science created; all became symbols of liberals plotting to destroy American freedoms.

Smithson concludes, "We need to close this discussion for tonight, but we will continue to explore why the Trump administration's handling of the

THE CROWNING: CULMINATION OF THE NATION

pandemic affected the election of 2020 and all the events that followed on tomorrow's program. We wish you all a safe night tonight. Please join us tomorrow night to continue discussing how the pandemic cost millions of lives and changed the course of history."

Tully was worried about the nation's dilemma, with a pandemic the country has not dealt with in over a hundred years, which would eventually kill well over 1 million Americans and 7 million worldwide. It was bad enough that we had to quickly learn how to combat a lethal virus without the tools needed for such an epic battle. We also faced the tidal wave of conspiracy theories regarding its existence, deadly efficacy, and various disease-combating methods. What should have been a formidable challenge, fought by our army of scientists and medical experts to save lives, became a political game of dodgeball, where even our top experts were turned into villains and thrown out of the arena.

A week passed before the directions Tony researched were received and put to use. Armed with his step-by-step plan for getting safely to his farm, Catherine and Tully set out early in the morning for the journey, a trip that they would forever regret making.

Chapter 7
Blinded by the Flames
10 Miles South of Tampa
Feb 10th, 2025:

Driving the route provided by Tony to get to Tony and Marie's home, Tully noted to his wife, "What is normally a 45-minute trip, today will take a good 90 minutes." Along the way, they observed there were many cars in yards, and in the ditch next to the road that was black from fire, tires gone and the interiors turned to ash. Homes were filled with people, but there was no way to tell how long they had lived there because as soon as a home was abandoned, another homeless group of people would break in and take it over. It surprised both of them to see so many people sitting on the sides of the roads, observing them as they drove by them. They were not begging for a handout, but it seemed as if they were assessing what we might offer them if we were stopped. Tully's spine tingled with a cascading chill that flowed to his arms and legs. Catherine said, "It feels like we have suddenly driven into an impoverished foreign country. Is this what Haiti was like when you went there for Tony's mission?"

"Yes", Tully said quietly, "except the Haitians seemed friendlier". They finally got to Tony's farm. Tully honked his horn to get Tony's attention while he was walking his horses. Tony came to the gate and punched in the code to allow the gate to open. Tony had reinforced their fence around his property with barbed wire. Tully thought to himself that he must have worked for weeks on that fence.

Tony greeted Tully and Catherine cheerfully saying, "Hi Dad and Cathy! I am glad you made it safely!" "Hey there son, it's good to see you," Tully replied. Catherine added, "We had not seen you or the kids since Thanksgiving, which was just before all hell broke loose" "Yaya! Papa!" Tommy and Sheila screamed in unison as they came running from the front

THE CROWNING: CULMINATION OF THE NATION

porch to their car. Tully smiled, as the fact is "Yaya" (their name for Catherine) always came first. They totally adore her and Tully was "second fiddle" but that never bothered him a bit. Catherine had no children of her own, and she was crazy enough to marry a man who already had a family of six boys. Basically, Tommy and Sheila have three grandmothers and two grandfathers, and they love them all, but it is undeniable that they have a favorite, Catherine.

Catherine hugged the kids as hard and long as Tully had ever seen her do before. She had tears in her eyes that Tully and Tony knew were tears of joy. "I missed you both so very much," she said. Sheila looked her in the eyes with a big smile and said, "I missed you to the moon and back!" Tommy, not wanting to be outdone, said, "I missed you to Pluto and back!" They each pulled her by each hand to go into the house to see their rooms. Tony and I walked to the barn so he could give the horses their hay. "How are you doing, Tony?" Tully asked. Tony dismissively responded, "Me? I am fine." His reply was not very convincing. "I still miss her healthy self," he admitted. Tully assured, "Marie is an amazing woman, Tony. She defeated Covid, just like Sheila defeated cancer. She is a good Mom and no one can replace her. Remember that old saying, "This too shall pass. I promise it will."

After a brief pause, Tully continued, "You and Marie are doing a great job keeping these kids so safe and happy, well, as happy as two young kids can be under the circumstances. Tony responded, "Dad, we are doing our best." Tully retorted, "You deserve a Nobel Peace Prize, for what you two have done here." Tony vouched, "The kids have been a great help. Tommy wants to "man the fort" at night so I can sleep, but I don't want that for him. He is still just a kid, and that is way too much to ask of him. Marie desperately wants to take a shift, but she is just too weak."

Tully concurred, "Ya, I think you are right. Also, Tommy is only eleven years old, and he needs to be a kid." Tony nodded his head in agreement and the two walked in silence for a minute when he quietly said, "Why don't you and Catherine come live with us here, Dad? We would make a great team." Tony declared with an upbeat expression. Tully thought for a minute then said, "You know that is not a bad idea. I will discuss it with Catherine after we leave for home. I would need to bring our dog, Brandy too." Tony, encouraged by the possibility, smirked and said, "Of course, always room for another dog!" Brandy is their Golden Retriever who has already outlived her expected life span, now at 16 years old.

Tully and Catherine spent a glorious day with Tony, Marie, and the kids. They were finally packed up for the return trip later than they planned, with three dozen chicken eggs in the trunk. They headed out the gate at 4:30 pm, with barely enough time to get home before the curfew. The two retraced their steps home, with Catherine serving as navigator, and Tully driving, while Catherine used her phone for navigation. Suddenly they came to a roadblock. A large truck was blocking the intersection on their route. It appeared to be abandoned and there was smoke coming from the engine. Tully asked Catherine to find an alternate route from where they were, knowing that this request is not in her skill set, but unless they switched places, she had to be the one to solve this problem. "Turn left," she said. Tully followed her direction and turned left. They drove about a mile and then came to a dead end. Having no choice they turned around and went back to the blocked intersection. The truck was now fully engulfed in flames. Tully maneuvered around the truck and kept going in the same direction they were headed. They now were in uncharted waters. As they progressed, they came to a place in the road where many people were gathering. Catherine realized it was getting late and they would not make it home before the curfew. As they came up to the crowd, the mob stepped into the road in front of them, then filed more people behind the car as well. Within seconds of stopping they were surrounded by people, who started pounding on the hood and trunk and yelling for them to get out, something Tully and Catherine knew would be their demise. Catherine got this look of mad determination on her face. She told Tully to keep going. "Drive through the mob," she said. Tully didn't reply but started inching forward. The pounding got harder and louder and now they were pounding on the roof of the car. Suddenly a bottle of liquid splattered on the windshield and flames engulfed the front of the car and the windshield. Blinded by the flames Tully just kept moving forward, slowly but steadily. Catherine shrieked when the Molotov cocktail exploded on the car, but she quickly regrouped and just repeated to Tully to keep going, which he did, slowly, while not running anyone over.

When Tully cleared past the mob he sped up to escape. Tully looked over at Catherine. She was slumped over with her forehead resting on the car's dash. It was then Tully saw the dark red bloodstain on the back of her shirt. Tully stopped the car and gently lifted her by the near left shoulder. She had been shot in the back and the bullet had exited her body at her chest. She was making gurgling sounds out of her mouth and blood was coming down her chin. "Hold on Cathy!" Tully shouted, "Hold on! I am going to get you to a hospital."

Tully hit the gas and raced as fast as he could toward the city of Brandon, where he knew the Brandon Regional Hospital was on Oakdale Ave. Tully pulled up to the emergency entrance, to find police surrounding the hospital at every entrance. When he got to the front door Tully shouted, "My wife's been shot. Please help!" One police officer ran inside while the other opened up the passenger door. Two orderlies rushed out with a rolling bed. They put her on the gurney. "Park your car in the underground garage," the other police officer instructed. "We guard that garage as well." Too worried about Catherine, Tully forgot to thank the officer. After finding a place to park Tully ran into the emergency waiting room. "Where is she?" he shouted. A nurse came up to him and said, we took her straight to surgery, she has lost a lot of blood. Wait here and we will come out when there is news of her condition." Obediently Tully sat down, speechless and in shock. Tully realized he had her blood on his hands and asked if he could wash it off somewhere. The nurse walked him to the men's room. Tully waited in that waiting room for over 14 hours before a Doctor came out to talk to him. It was the longest 14 hours of his life. He prayed his heart out during that time. A doctor emerged from the operating room. "Mr. Stone?" he asked. "Yes, how is she?" Tully asked apprehensively, dreading the answer he feared he would hear.

"She is stable, the bullet pierced her lung, but fortunately it missed her heart completely. Her lung collapsed, but she is a sturdy woman. I believe she will recover. She will need to remain here for a few more days before you can take her home. Your wife will need to remain in bed for at least a week, maybe even two. She can't get up, not even use the bathroom until she is healed and the threat of blood clots is gone. Go home and rest now, then prepare her room for a long and difficult stay. Normally, we would keep her here throughout this process, but under these conditions, we don't have the beds to keep anyone for over a day or two. Three at the most," the Doctor reported.

Tully, feeling immense relief, replied "Thank you, Doctor. Can I see her now?" "Just for a minute or two, she is sleeping and under heavy sedation." the doctor explained. After spending some time by Cathy's bedside, and praying, privately, tear-filled prayers of thanks to God, Tully left and made his way home.

When Tully got home he jumped into the shower where he finally felt safe and alone enough to let out his emotions, weeping tears of multiple raw emotions, all coming out at once. Tully realized he came so close to losing, not only his wife but also his true "best friend forever". He understood, for the first time, how much his life would instantly change if she passed away. After getting into his pajamas, he went into his office to turn on the computer. Tully had missed the "Truth" the last two nights and wondered what important historical information of our nation's worst crisis in its history since the (first) Civil War. Tully instinctively knew he needed to get his mind off the events of the last two days, and diving into the "Truth" would be the perfect way to accomplish the escape from the nightmare he had just experienced.

As the word "Truth" dissolved into a silhouette of a man, Tully quickly realized the host tonight was not Sheldon Smithson, and Tully worried for Sheldon's safety, concerned he might have been a victim of the same fate that fell upon Chester Colt.

"Good evening, this is Bryce Waldron. You all know me from my decades of journalism working for Fox News, followed by CNN. Continuing the salvation and preservation of our recent history in this nation has now fallen upon my shoulders. As you may recall, I not only interviewed key players in this history, but on one specific occasion, I was a part of it. That incident is just one episode in the story we are about to chronicle about the election of 2020 and the events that followed that election. Events that were the launching platform for what has just occurred leading up to the election of 2024 and the Civil War that followed which we all, painfully, are aware is ongoing today." Tully knew painfully that the life of the most treasured person in his life, Catherine, was hanging in the balance, at this very moment, as he listened to Bryce Waldron's words. Words that after today's events, take

THE CROWNING: CULMINATION OF THE NATION

on a whole new reality on a personal level. He refocused on the host and his message as if he were speaking directly to Tully.

Bryce Waldron continued saying, "I want to establish the background of events that gave significant clues as to the mindset of the President as a lead up to this monumental nationally televised debate. The first clue of racist tendencies by then President Trump came with the signing of Executive Order 13769, titled "Protecting the Nation from Foreign Terrorist Entry into the United States", labeled as the "Muslim ban" by critics, or commonly referred to as the Trump travel ban. Critics referred to it as a "Muslim ban," because President Trump had previously called for a temporary ban on Muslims entering America,and because all the affected countries had a Muslim majority. Later, other orders (Executive Order 13780 and Presidential Proclamation 9645) were signed by President Trump and superseded Executive Order 13769. On June 26, 2018, the U.S. Supreme Court upheld the third Executive Order (Presidential Proclamation 9645) and its accompanying travel ban in a 5–4 decision.

The second major tipoff was the white supremacist rally in Charlottesville, Virginia when the president spoke to reporters that day in August 2017. Two days after the death of a young woman protesting against a massive white supremacist rally in Charlottesville, Virginia. Trump stood in the lobby of Trump Tower in Manhattan and speaking about the protesters, which included left and right-wing groups, and declared, "I think there is blame on both sides," "You had some very bad people in that group," Trump said, referring to the white nationalist groups rallying against removal of a Confederate statue. "But you also had people that were very fine people, on both sides."[6]

Now I am going to take us forward to Sept. 29th, 2019. This was the first debate between the incumbent President, Donald Trump, and his opponent, former Vice President Joe Biden. The debate in which I was the moderator, was marred by incessant interruptions and insults. In the final moments of the debate, I asked what turned out to be a pivotal question. Here is the transcript of that exchange, as best as we can decipher it with all the "over-talking" that occurred throughout the debate." Bryce Waldron then put on the screen the transcript of the debate for the viewers to read while Waldron read the words out loud.

"You have repeatedly criticized the Vice-President for not specifically calling out Antifa and other left-wing extremist groups, but are you willing tonight to condemn white supremacists and militia groups and to say that they need to stand down and not add to the violence and a number of these cities, as we saw in Kenosha, and as we've seen in Portland," Waldron said to Trump.

Trump countered, "I would say almost everything I see is from the left wing, not from the right wing, but what do you, what do you…" Waldron interjected, "What are you saying?" Trump demurred, "I'm willing to do anything. I want to see peace." Biden quipped, "Do it. Do It! Say it!" Trump demanded, "Do you want to call them? What do you want to call them? Give me a name. Give me a name…" Biden blurted "Proud Boys." Trump then boldly commanded, "Proud Boys, Stand back and stand by. But I'll tell you what, I'll tell you what, somebody's got to do something about Antifa, and the left, because this is not a right-wing problem. This is a… this is a left-wing problem."

Biden retorted, "Antifa is an idea, not an organization." "You gotta be kidding," Trump muttered. Biden exclaimed, "That's what his FBI director said." Waldron turns back to Trump declaring, "No, no, no we're done. We're done, sir. Moving on to the next…"

Biden, feeling bolstered by Trump's frustration exclaimed, "Everybody in your administration who tells you the truth. (You say) 'there's a bad idea'. I tell you what, you have no idea." Trump retaliated, "Antifa is a dangerous radical group. They will overthrow you if you let them."

Bryce Waldron, speaking to the online audience of Truth remarked " The old saying, "Hindsight is 20-20" is very fitting because in hindsight we now know that Trump's words "Proud Boys, stand back and stand by" turned out to be much more than just a debate strategy, it was, in actuality, a notice of an upcoming call to action that went out to not only the Proud Boys but also the Oath Keepers, another white supremacist group with over 38,000, members and the "Three Percenters", militia groups in the U.S. and Canada that consider themselves "patriots" opposing the tyranny of government (except for while Trump was president), as well as thousands upon thousands

THE CROWNING: CULMINATION OF THE NATION

of others "patriots" not affiliated with one of these organized groups. Trump's notice of a call to action, was later followed by the actual call to action after the election and before the January 6th, 2020 insurrection. To give us some understanding of this exchange, I am bringing to our discussion tonight Leila Fadel, who is a national correspondent for NPR based in Los Angeles, covering race and identity. As a national correspondent, Fadel has consistently reported on the fault lines of this divided nation. She flew to Minneapolis amid the pandemic as the city erupted in grief and anger over the killing of George Floyd. She's reported on policing and race, on American Muslim communities, and on the jarring inequities the coronavirus laid bare in the healthcare system. Her "Muslims in America: A New Generation " series, in collaboration with National Geographic, won the prestigious Goldziher Prize in 2019. Welcome, Ms. Fadel, and thank you for agreeing to be here tonight." Fadel replied confidently, "Thank you for inviting me, Bryce. I am privileged to participate in such a noble effort." Waldron queries, "Help us understand the dynamics of the right and left-wing groups."

Leila Fadel explains to the audience saying, "President Trump did not explicitly condemn white supremacy and right-wing militias during the debate, despite an invitation from you, Bryce, serving then as the moderator, claiming that the "left-wing" is more responsible for violence than the "right wing. When you asked Trump, "But are you willing, tonight, to condemn white supremacists and militia groups and to say that they need to stand down and not add to the violence in several cities as we saw in Kenosha, and as we've seen in Portland? Are you prepared to specifically do that?" Trump responded: "Sure, I'm prepared to do that. I would say almost everything I see is from the left wing, not from the right wing. I'm willing to do anything. I want to see peace." Both you and Joe Biden asked him to "do it." And then, Trump singled out one group with a statement, "Proud Boys, stand back and stand by".

Waldron posed, "Most Americans, before that debate had scarcely, if at all, heard of the Proud Boys or for that matter any of the other white supremacist groups by name. Give us a little background on them, please" Fadel explained, "The Proud Boys, a group labeled by the Southern Poverty Law Center as a hate group, was involved in the Unite the Right rally in

Charlottesville, Va., in 2017, which attracted several white supremacist groups. Members of the Proud Boys are known for using white nationalist memes and anti-Muslim and misogynistic rhetoric. The FBI had then elevated the threat level of racially motivated violent extremists in the U.S. to a "national threat priority" that year. In testimony to the House Homeland Security Committee, FBI Director Christopher Wray said most domestic terrorism threats and violence comes from "racially motivated violent extremism," mostly from people who subscribe to white supremacist ideologies.

Wray described Antifa as an ideology, or a movement, rather than an organized group and said the FBI was investigating some cases involving people who self-identify with Antifa. But he said the protest-related violence doesn't appear to be organized or connected to one group. Protests for racial justice have turned violent but were mostly peaceful."[4]Bryce Waldron concluded by saying, "Thank you for that clarification, Ms. Fadel. We have reached the limits of our time; it would be dangerous to remain on air for too long. We will be back tomorrow night, at 6:00 pm so please return here and please keep recording and saving these documentaries for the historical record. Good night."

Tully was exhausted, both physically and mentally, from the day's events, and knew he needed to sleep, but his inescapable worry for his wife would make sleep like trying to capture your own shadow. Bags formed under Tully's eyes, making him look even older than usual. Despite his acute anxiety, he would be made even more distraught if he knew then that he could never return to the hospital he had entrusted with the fate of his soul mate.

Chapter 8
She is Going to Die Soon
Tampa, Florida
February 11, 2025

After what seemed like a fortnight of tossing and turning, caused by nightmares about the events of the last 48 hours, Tully finally gave up trying to sleep and got up before dawn to make coffee. Feeling exhausted, and looking bedraggled, Tully waited anxiously for the morning so he could call the hospital to check up on Catherine's condition. The clock on the kitchen wall finally read 7:00 am and Tully could wait no longer. He grabbed his cell and called the number the hospital personnel gave him. The hospital operator put the call through to the nurses' desk on Catherine's floor. An oddly cheerful floor nurse answered by saying, "Hello, 3rd floor, this is Nurse Adams, how may I help you?" Tully replied, "This is Tully Stone, Catherine Stone's husband. How is she doing?" Nurse Adams responded, "She is sleeping quietly right now. We gave her a sedative about 4 hours ago so she should sleep for another 3 or 4 hours. Her condition is listed as stable, but she has great difficulty breathing so while she is under, we put her on a ventilator to assure she is getting enough oxygen." Tully, confused, asked, "A ventilator? Does that not mean she is in serious condition? Nurse Adams responded with a calm voice saying, "Well, we don't go to that extreme unless it is necessary. The doctor felt it was definitely necessary. Hopefully, she can come off the ventilator soon." Tully asked, "What time can I come in to see her?" Nurse Adams rebuffed that suggestion saying, "I am sorry, Sir. Since the riot began, the hospital has not allowed visitors to see our patients because it is too dangerous to travel here and we want no more victims of violence than we already have now."

Tully reacted with alarm and asked, "I can't see her at all. What about bringing her home? I will need to travel to you to pick her up." Nurse

Adams rebuffed that as well, "No, we don't want you to risk that. We will use an ambulance, with a police escort to bring her to your home." "Will that still happen in three days?" Tully asked in a worried tone. The nurse responded unemotionally, "We shall see. It all depends on how her recovery is progressing. If she is in serious condition, we will keep her here, but if she is stronger, or if *she is going to die soon*, we will bring her to her home. Should that happen, you will be contacted by the hospice to arrange for their services to be delivered in your home."

The only words Tully heard were "She is going to die soon" which landed on Tully's skull like they were made of cement. He was momentarily speechless, but after a long silent pause, he continued, "Thank you. I didn't realize just how serious this is until now. I hope you don't mind if I call you from time to time?" "Absolutely, call as often as you need to. I will also call you if anything changes," the nurse affirmed. Tully, distraught by the bad news and the horrifying possibility of losing his beloved wife, summoned the discipline to say simply, "Thank you, I appreciate it more than you can know."

Tully sat in silence for the next hour, trying to process what he had just learned. He knew he had to prepare their bedroom for her convalescence, or perhaps for the last days of her life. The thought of her passing away was something he never really contemplated before. Catherine was ten years younger than Tully, and she was always in great health, so Tully always assumed Catherine would outlive him. The realization that she may not recover from this was slow to be assimilated into Tully's conscious reality. Now he had to be strong for her and for the family. Tully decided it was time to notify the family of what had happened. After thinking through his options, he decided the best way to let the family know what had happened and the serious nature of the situation, so Tully wrote them all an email so they could all read the same words from him and receive notification close to the same time. Tully recalled that James and Suzanne would not be reading emails soon, if ever, but he included them. Tully sat down and carefully composed the email. As he wrote, he was already expecting what he knew would be their immediate reaction, acute distress, so tears run down his cheeks. His love for each of them made imagining them reading the news unbearable, yet, he reminded himself he needed to be strong, and positive. After emailing, Tully went about preparing the bedroom for her arrival. He

THE CROWNING: CULMINATION OF THE NATION

also prepared a spare bedroom, once occupied by all his sons at different times, for himself to sleep in, while being close enough to hear Catherine should she call out for help. Just a few minutes after emailing, Tully's phone signaled Tony was calling back. "Hi Tony, I assume you just read the email", Tully said. Tony sounded as if he was in shock and asked, "How did this happen, Dad? I feel this is my fault." Tully rebutted, "No Tony, this is not your fault at all. The route you had planned was perfectly fine, but the mob must have caused that route to be blocked by a burning truck in the intersection. We got ambushed when we tried to find an alternative route."

"I want to go see her today," Tony insisted. "Sorry Tony, the hospital won't allow any visitors at all, not even me; it's too dangerous, " Tully advised. Tony mused "What can I do to help?" "Pray. That is the best thing you can do for her. She is in expert hands," Tully noted. Tony declared, "We all will pray, I promise." Tully acknowledged, "I know. I have much to do now, so let me call you later." "Ok, Dad. You take care," Tony said, and the two hung up.

Patrick also called Tully shortly afterward, and the conversation was like the one with Tony, except that Pat wanted to know why Tully and Catherine were on the road. Tully explained the plan, but Pat did not seem satisfied that they should have taken that risk "for a few eggs". Tully thought to himself how ironic this criticism is coming from the "Grand Poohbah" of the "No Fear Stone Club" (a fictional" club" Tully created to motivate his children to attempt things they found to be scary). Patrick just did not grasp the true motive for making that trip, which was to see the grandkids, and Tully did not want to go there with Pat. Pat's home is two hours away from Tampa, so visits to them were not as frequent. A trip to Pat's house during these riots would be nearly impossible, and extremely treacherous. Interstate-4, between Tampa and Orlando, was virtually impassable. Pat eventually got over his initial outrage, slowly transforming it into a sincerely empathetic and concerned son. The call ended with Pat and Tully reaffirming their love for each other and for Catherine. Tully went about the business of preparing the rooms, in case Catherine would be brought home.

While he changed the sheets on the beds, Tully's mind drifted to his two youngest sons. Both Paul, serving in the Coast Guard while stationed in Miami, and Michael, serving in the Air Force, and based in Ohio, wrote reply emails back to extend their love and support. Tully knew fully that for those serving in the military, phone calls and text messages were not currently permitted, and even emails, while allowed to be received and sent, were being closely scrutinized before they could be released to the recipient of the email. The military administration was keeping a tight lid on what information was flowing from the military to the civilian population, and vice versa. Those service members outside the U.S. could not speak, even by email, with their families, while the other stateside members were allowed closely scrutinized, and often partially censored emails.

Tully knew from following the reporting on Cerberus World News that the war in Europe and also the war in Asia, now in its third year, has all the military on high alert. The military involvement in these battles was only to support NATO countries, by sending equipment, and not as an outright U.S. effort to engage our military forces. Now, based solely on the recent conversation with Michael, translated by Catherine, we know the American troops are being brought home. Ever since the attack by Russia, invading Ukraine, first in 2014, then again on a much larger scale in 2022, and China's takeover of Hong Kong and Taiwan, the world has been in absolute chaos. The desire of both countries to expand their territories was met with profound objections from the free world, and often military resistance, however, with limited success. None of those efforts were ultimately effective in stopping the aggressors. The threat of a nuclear war, often insinuated in speeches and news pressers, by officials of the protagonists, paralyzed the full-scale efforts to halt the military expansion into neighboring countries. Russia and China have occupied and asserted control over seventeen formally sovereign nations. Tully felt as if there seemed no end to their hunger for dominance of all of Eurasia, the Middle East, and Oceania. With each new invasion into yet another national domino, falling into their steel bear trap, the world moves one step closer to World War III. Although the public was not aware of the inevitability of World War III, nonetheless it was coming.

Chapter 9
Take Back our Country
Tampa, Florida
Evening of February 11th, 2025

Tully was suddenly awoken from a badly needed nap by the sound of knocking on his front door. He rubbed his eyes and slowly got up to see who was knocking. When the door opened, there was nobody there. As he closed the door, he spotted a small paper bag on the ground. He picked up the bag to see it was from Walgreens. He thought to himself, 'I didn't know they were making home deliveries. I thought they simply shuttered like everyone else." he opened the bag to find a typical bottle of prescription pills. He shook the bottle to hear the rattle of something inside. He looked inside the bag for the usual instructions that always accompany medications and found with a note carefully tucked inside the folded instructions. The message read, "Dad, on this thumb drive you will find the truth behind the Truth. When you plug it in, a pop-up box will ask for the password. I can't take the chance to provide that here, or anywhere else. The password is the name of my imaginary friend when I was 5 years old. Only you and Catherine would know that answer." That was it. It wasn't even signed, but there was no doubt who sent this package, Michael. Tully opened the medication bottle to find the thumb drive Michael had referenced. It had a familiar A.F. logo on it validating Tully's conclusion about who sent this mysterious package. The problem was, he had no recollection of Michael's imaginary friend. The only hope of ever seeing what is on the thumb drive is if Catherine recalls the name, and she is totally unreachable at the moment. Hopefully, she is sleeping soundly at the hospital. Tully took the thumb drive, put it back into the medicine bottle, stuffed the bottle with cotton, and put it in his medicine chest.

Just then, right on time, 6:00 p.m., and with his distinctly recognizable voice, the host began the evening edition of Truth saying, "Good evening, this is Tuesday, Feb. 11th and I am your host, Bryce Waldron. Welcome back to the Truth. Before we introduce our guest tonight, I have some devastating news to share with you all. My heart is heavy as I must share that today we learned that Chester Colt is dead. After he was taken into custody, he was taken to an unknown facility to be questioned. We don't have any details, but the official statement announcing his death only said that he has died of 'natural causes'. Chester Colt has served faithfully as a journalist his entire career, and those of us that have worked alongside him, as I am sure his audience, will surely miss this truly noble man." A long moment of silence followed, then Bryce Waldron turned to the camera and said, "We are on a mission; we believe it is one which may change the course of history, by simply reviewing the historical record without altering history. We must preserve the facts of what has happened faced with the current government's "alternative facts" and their version of the history they want to establish. To you, our audience, we remain in your debt, for your diligence in returning each night and recording these documentaries to guarantee the "Truth" is preserved. Tonight I want to introduce you to our guest, a seasoned intelligence expert, Malcolm Nance, the nation's leading authority in Russian propaganda, who will inform us about how the Russian government could wage a war against our country without even firing a shot.

In previous appearances on cable news, Malcolm noted that President Donald Trump and his fellow Republicans seem to have taken up the "playbook of Russia" and created their own propaganda machine. Nance said that the plot Russia concocted in the early 2000s, the "Gerasimov Doctrine", handed Trump and his team the plan. Nance explained it was a tactic Russians used where they combined an information warfare strategy, comprising flooding a country with so much misinformation that a country would eventually welcome an invasion without a war.

Nance began his expert analysis by saying, "Thank you, Bryce. I too am shocked and feel great sorrow for losing a great man and journalist, Chester Colt.

What the Russians did in the years leading up to the 2016 election is they created an information bubble in which the Trump campaign was friendly

THE CROWNING: CULMINATION OF THE NATION

and then, the Trump data team took that information, including stolen information from the Democratic National Committee, and created their own information sphere. Once the Russian bubble popped after the 2016 election, the Trump team took the ball and ran with it. The Russians barely had to do anything. The Trump team and their control over conservative television stations like Fox News and OAN enabled them to indoctrinate their own followers into believing some of the most insane things ever crafted. He talked about a kind of radicalization that gives Trump's supporters the confidence that their actions are not only patriotic but that "violence is the only solution and they're carrying out a second Lexington, a second Concord, 1776 2.0." [7]

Nance continued his account of the Trump supporter's view explaining, "They think they're restoring the United States, despite the fact they are physically attacking the United States, and believe me, the way that ammunition prices went up, before the 2020 election, on the public market, I think these people really believe they were going to affect the revolution at some point." [7] Waldron asks, "That 'playbook', as you call it, then was carried over and even amplified after the election of 2020. Do you agree with that assertion, Malcolm?" Nance responded, "Without a doubt. You heard it articulated in the testimony of many of those charged with the January 6th Insurrection at the Capitol. They sincerely believed that what they were doing was fighting for the salvation of the country, as their president literally told them so, for many months prior, and even in his speech at the Ellipse, just prior to the invasion of the Capitol when Trump said to the rally, "I want to thank you. It's just a great honor to have this kind of crowd and to be before you, and hundreds of thousands of American patriots who are committed to the honesty of our elections and the integrity of our glorious republic. All of us here today do not want to see our election victory stolen by emboldened radical-left Democrats, which is what they're doing. And stolen by the fake news media. That's what they've done and what they're doing. We will never give up, we will never concede. It doesn't happen. You don't concede when there's theft involved. Our country has had enough. We will not take it anymore and that's what this is all about. And to use a favorite term that all of your people really came up with we will stop the steal. Today

I will lie out just some of the evidence proving that we won this election, and we won it by a landslide. This was not a close election. Now, it is up to Congress to confront this egregious assault on our democracy. And after this, we're going to walk down, and I'll be there with you, we're going to walk down, we're going to walk down, anyone you want, but I think right here, we're going to walk down to the Capitol, and we're going to cheer on our brave senators and congressmen and women, and we're probably not going to be cheering so much for some of them. Because you'll never take back our country with weakness. You have to show strength and you have to be strong. We have come to demand that Congress do the right thing and only count the electors who have been lawfully slated, lawfully slated... and we fight. We fight like hell. And if you don't fight like hell, you're not going to have a country anymore. Our exciting adventures and boldest endeavors have not yet begun. My fellow Americans, for our movement, for our children, and for our beloved country, and I say this, despite all that's happened. The best is yet to come. So we're going to, we're going to walk down Pennsylvania Avenue. I love Pennsylvania Avenue. And we're going to the Capitol, and we're going to try and give them the kind of pride and boldness that they need to take back our country. So let's walk down Pennsylvania Avenue." [8]

Bryce Waldron elaborates by saying, "I understand from that speech at the rally how perfectly that fits the "Russian playbook", the campaign strategy you mentioned earlier, Malcolm. Thank you for that insight. We will be returning, in a later episode of The Truth, with an in-depth analysis of what actually happened on that momentous day. Before we do that, there are a few very important events to memorialize that led up to that day, events which are critical to understanding how this could have happened, not only the insurrection but all the events that followed the 2020 and the 2024 elections. We will have you back again, Malcolm, if possible. Thank you for your expert perspective."

Tully turned the computer off for the evening, but he then sat in silence reflecting on how this time in history had affected his immediate family. Tully recalled an impromptu debate that took place in July 2020, four months before that election, and six months before the resulting insurrection. The family had gathered for dinner at the cabin James had

THE CROWNING: CULMINATION OF THE NATION

rented for his family. The occasion was the annual Stone family reunion of the extended family, held in July each year. Each nuclear family either owned or rented their own cabin. After dinner, they gathered in the living room, overlooking the lake, and, as was customary, they began discussing politics, this year the topic being the upcoming 2020 election. The discussion remained very civil, with all parties explaining why they supported or opposed the candidates, which by now was clearly a race for the presidency between the incumbent, President Donald Trump, seeking reelection, and his feared opponent, Joe Biden. Tully recalled his final warning to the family when he concluded the discussion with, "The actual truth about what Trump is, who he is, and what he is, will be revealed if Biden wins the election. The test will be if Trump cooperates with a peaceful transfer of power or if he does not; to remain the President. My prediction is that he will not." Virtually everyone involved in that discussion, except for Catherine and Tully, expressed their belief that Trump would never interfere with the peaceful transfer of power to a new administration. "That is absurd", James insisted, "it has never happened before and Trump would never be that corrupt." That is how that debate ended, and Tully would remember that moment in his life, for the rest of his life, as the onetime he truly wished he was wrong because history would reveal the truth, just six months later.

Tully stayed up late into the night working feverishly to make sure the house was perfect for Cathy's return home. He had become obsessed with sterilizing everything that could put Catherine's immune system in jeopardy. He scrubbed down the bathrooms, kitchen, and every floor in the house with bleach. By the time he went to bed, he had been up for 20 hours. Early the following day his cell phone dings indicating an email has arrived in his inbox. Curiosity overwhelmed his need for sleep and he got up to read the email. It was from his 5th son, Paul, who flies "helos" for the U.S. Coast Guard. He wrote, "Hi Dad. Hope you are doing ok. How is Catherine doing? I am surviving, but we are working double shifts. I am flying for 12 hours straight, then resting for 8 hours, and then back in the cockpit another 12. This is not a normal schedule but these are not normal times. I can't go into the details of why as we are under 'strict information restraint orders' (S.I.R.O). I wanted to let you know all is well with me and I am praying for Catherine. Love you, Paul." Tully read and reread the email looking for clues

Paul might have been trying to communicate, but unable to say overtly. Paul has never been one to reach out for idle "chit chat", so the very fact he emailed today tells him Paul had something essential to communicate but had to do so in code. Tully responded to Paul with an upbeat reply that would not attract any unnecessary scrutiny from his superiors. Tully concluded the intense flying schedule must be a sign that the Coast Guard is doing more than search and rescue, but most likely, also reconnaissance against military intrusion into our protected waters off our east coast. Little did Tully know how accurate his hypothesis was to reality. The one thing Tully knew for sure was that Paul was still doing his job, and therefore, still healthy and alive, which gave him a temporary sense of relief. The endless fear of either Paul or Michael becoming casualties of the current chaos always simmered in Tully's subconscious mind. Those fears erupted into vivid periodic nightmares that jarred Tully into an abrupt awakening.

An hour later, Tully's cell phone signaled a call was coming in from his oldest granddaughter, Grace. "Hi, Grandpa! It's Grace!" "Good morning, darling. You sound in good cheer today, what's up," Tully replied. Grace chuckled, "You know me too well, Grandpa. Actually, I am calling with great news! The hospital called me this morning to tell me that Dad is doing better. They are going to take him off the respirator tomorrow, and see how he does." "Wow! That is great news, Grace," Tully exclaimed enthusiastically, then added, "How is your Mom?"

Grace changed her voice to a somber tone, "Well, her condition has changed little. Her pre-existing health issues are still causing the doctor's concern. She will remain on the respirator for now. The good news is that she is not getting worse." Tully tried to encourage Grace by saying, "Well, let's focus on the positive, your Dad is improving, and your Mom is holding her own, and that matters. I keep praying for them both. How are your sisters and brother doing?" Grace replied, "Chase and Pam are doing really well, but both are getting cabin fever." "How about Suzy," asked Tully, referring to Grace's youngest sister, Suzanne, named after her mother. Grace responded, "Not so well, she is torn up with concern about Mom and Dad, and being sixteen she is acting out her anger against the three of us." Tully, concerned for his granddaughter, asked, "Would you like for me to talk with her?" "I was hoping you would ask that, Grandpa," Grace said. Tully instructed, "Ask

THE CROWNING: CULMINATION OF THE NATION

Suzy to give me a call or text message. Tell her I called, but she was not available. Grace countered, "You know me, Grandpa, I can't bend the truth for anyone. I will ask her to call you." "Ok. That is fine. I will do what I can, if she calls me," Tully promised. Grace said cautiously, "I will do what I can on this end. Thanks, Grandpa." "Always, Grace. Good Bye, Tully said before he hung up. It was a great relief to Tully to hear his oldest surviving son was making significant progress. His biggest concern was that James and Suzanne could never come off of their ventilators. It was imperative that Tully give thanks for every step forward, instead of dwelling too much on those things outside of his control. Since Tully often advised those who would listen, to the importance of putting their faith in God and letting go of their own fears, Tully decided that this is precisely what he must do, although actually doing so is very difficult. Tully did not know how events transpiring on the other side of the world were going to make his commitment to putting his faith in God a thousand times more difficult.

Chapter 10
A Nuclear Option
Tampa, Florida
February 12, 2025

Wednesday morning Tully was up early after his second night of being on guard by himself, without Catherine's help. He had to adjust the plan to sleep and stand guard, in three 3-hour shifts. After two cups of coffee, he picks up his cell to check with the hospital on Catherine's progress. The nurse on duty informs Tully that she had a good night, rested well and the doctor will make rounds later in the morning. Tully inquires, "Is she still on a ventilator?" "Yes," the nurse replied, "but we hope that the doctor might decide to take her off of it today. We will need to make certain there is no internal bleeding or any infections before we can send her home. She is on strong antibiotics that should prevent any serious infections." Tully wondered out loud, "When she comes off the ventilator, will I be able to speak with her by phone?" "Initially she will not have a voice to speak with, so it may take a while before she regains that voice," Nurse Adams replied. "OK. Thank you. I will check in with you this afternoon," Tully advised. He was encouraged by the news he heard this morning and reminded of the good news he heard from Grace yesterday about Jame's progress. He should come off his ventilator today as well. 'Good news seems to come in pairs,' Tully thought to himself. He sat down to listen to Cerberus World News on cable T.V. to see what he had missed in the last few days. Tully discovered that the march of the two superpowers, Russia and China, has continued into new countries. China seems razor-focused on Japan as its next target after having North Korea join in with China to overrun South Korea. President Xi Jinping declared that there is only one Korea now, and the newly united country, Korea, has Kim Jon-Un as its new leader. Kim Jon Un announced that yesterday, Moon Jae-In was arrested for treason and will be

THE CROWNING: CULMINATION OF THE NATION

executed. A purge of all of South Korea's military and political leaders is underway. There was no mention of the United States in this broadcast, leaving Tully to wonder what had happened to our promises of protection to our ally of over 70 years.

In Europe, Russia had already taken over some countries formerly a part of the Soviet Union. The first, and most difficult to defeat was Ukraine, which was invaded, first in 2014 when Russia used a proxy army to invade and annex Crimea from Ukraine, and then with the invasion of all of Ukraine, which began in Feb 24, 2022, Ukraine, although not a member of NATO, had help from NATO as weapons to defend their country and imposing a vast array of economic sanctions. Ukraine became a NATO aspiring member in 2018. On February 7, 2019, the Ukrainian parliament voted to change its constitution to affirm its intention to join NATO and the European Union.

After the war in Ukraine in the spring-summer of 2022, Belarus, Georgia, Uzbekistan, Armenia, Azerbaijan, Kazakhstan, Moldova, Turkmenistan, and Tajikistan all returned to Russian control, almost without firing a single shot. Russia seemed poised to begin a major offensive in Europe. NATO declared all of Europe is under their protection and that any attack against any country in Europe will be met with their full force, and swiftly dispatched. Putin did not blink an eye when he responded, staring directly into the camera while on Cerberus World News saying, **"мы похороним тебя"**, translated from Russian meaning, "We will bury you!" (a phrase Tully recalled was first used during the Cold War by Soviet[1] First Secretary[2] Nikita Khrushchev[3] while addressing Western[4] ambassadors in Moscow[5] in 1956). The coldness and ruthlessness of that statement gave Tully the chills. He sensed that this time Putin was not bluffing. The inference, once again, was that nuclear warfare was still on the table if there was resistance, or even could be deployed preemptively.

1. https://en.wikipedia.org/wiki/Soviet_Union
2. https://en.wikipedia.org/wiki/General_Secretary_of_the_Communist_Party_of_the_Soviet_Union
3. https://en.wikipedia.org/wiki/Nikita_Khrushchev
4. https://en.wikipedia.org/wiki/Western_Bloc
5. https://en.wikipedia.org/wiki/Embassy_of_Poland_in_Moscow

The rest of the day was spent completing preparing the home for Catherine's arrival. Tully kept his mind on the tasks at hand in order to not worry about things he had no control over, especially those things happening in a unique part of the world. He recalled the adage, "Ignorance is bliss," and pretending to be ignorant may be as blissful as ignorance, so he would just pretend he didn't listen to the news and stay busy. But Tully could not help being reminded of his youth in the 1950s and 1960s when, during the post-WWII Cold War, every school and the public building had signs showing where the nearest designated "Atomic Bomb Shelter" was located, and as a reminder of the potential threat of nuclear war, every Monday at 1:00 pm, just after lunch, the Atomic Bomb Sirens would go off in every major city in the country. In schools, the children were then sent, walking in formation, to the designated bomb shelter to wait for the all-clear siren. For Tully's catholic school, St. Leo's in St. Paul, Minnesota, the bomb shelter was the indoor gym where the entire school crammed into, and sat on the floor in their designated spot. Tully never could understand, as a child, how that gym was going to protect them from an atomic bomb, or why it was so important to be sitting in a spot predetermined by a chart with everyone's name on it. When 6:00 pm arrived Tully was dutifully ready to record the nightly broadcast. His computer screen once again came to life.

Bryce Waldron began the introduction to this episode by stating, "Good evening, this is Wednesday, Feb. 12th and I am your host, Bryce Waldron. Welcome back to the Truth. Tonight we are going to address a pivotal moment in our recent history, one like so many other similar events in history that began with a brutal act of violence, by a person in authority, that so outraged the public that a cascade of violent reactions turned the nation into a time of crisis. This time the scene of the crime was in Minneapolis Minnesota, shortly after 8:00 PM on May 25th, 2020. To guide us through the significance of this event and the subsequent civil unrest that followed I have with us tonight, joining us remotely from their unnamed locations, authors Carol Leonnig and Phillip Rucker, who discussed this event in the book they co-authored, <u>I Alone Can Fix It; Donald J. Trump's Catastrophic Final Year.</u> Thank you both for agreeing to join us tonight." Carol Leonnig, replied first, "Thank you Bryce for inviting us. Phillip and I wrote the book to chronicle that fateful year leading up to and following the election of

THE CROWNING: CULMINATION OF THE NATION

2020, and thus we were doing exactly what your efforts are accomplishing on these docuseries, to find the facts and record them for the historical record." Waldron urged the Co-authors imploring, "Please describe to us what happened that late May evening, 2020, in Minneapolis, Minnesota."

Phillip Rucker reported, "George Floyd, a 46-year-old black man was handcuffed and pinned against the pavement outside of south Minneapolis convenience store. He pleaded for his life. He cried out for his children and for his mother. Floyd said 'I can't breathe' over 20 times. A white officer, Derek Chauvin, knelt on Floyd's neck for nine minutes, Floyd gasped "They'll kill me. They'll kill me". His pleas grew faint and then silent. His body went limp. Paramedics could not resuscitate him. Floyd, having struggled with addiction and unemployment, having contracted COVID-19 and survived, died under the knee of a police officer that night.[3]

Carol Leonnig felt the need to clarify adding, "The police had received a radio call about a man trying to pass a counterfeit $20 bill to buy cigarettes. Responding to the scene, a pair of officers noticed Floyd nearby with a friend inside his car and suspected they were doing drugs. They handcuffed Floyd who complained about being placed in a squad car. Two additional officers arrived on the scene. His arrest rapidly turned into a Savage show of force and brutality as Chauvin knelt on Floyd's neck and Floyd cried out again and again, I can't breathe. Horrified bystanders gathered, some recording video on their phones. The next morning, May 26th videos circulated widely online and people reacted with overwhelming revulsion. By that afternoon, the Minneapolis police department had fired all four officers involved. The city's mayor, Jacob Frye appeared near tears at a news conference. "It was malicious, and it was unacceptable," he said of Floyd's death. "There is no gray there." Video of Floyd's final breaths played on a loop in the media becoming indelible in the nation's conscience. Other black Americans who posed no threat had died at the hands of the police, including Eric Garner, Tamir Rice, Walter Scott, Philando Castillo, Alton Sterling, Stephon Clark, Brianna Taylor, and now George Floyd. Many Americans perceived an unending cycle of police brutality, and the last one, George Floyd's death at the hands of the Minneapolis police officers, was too much to tolerate any longer."[3]

Upon learning of these events, Tully quickly recalled how he first learned about them. Tully was at his cabin in northern Minnesota, a place he had purchased when he was only 31 years old in 1983, and spent much of his time in the spring and summer there ever since. His five sons all loved being there, as there was so much for them to do beyond just fishing. In the spring of 2020, Tully made his annual trek from Tampa to the cabin, an 1850-mile drive, to get it cleaned and ready for the summer. Late in May 2020, Tully heard on T.V. about the death of George Floyd, followed by reports about the escalating violence taking place in Minneapolis. Although it was only 200 miles away, it seemed like it was a very distant event, not affecting him or his family personally. Tully did not realize that Joe, his nephew, lived just a few blocks from the Cup Foods store where the murder took place. Tully was scheduled to teach a high school student field goal kicking, in Maplewood, a suburb of Minneapolis, before heading to the Minneapolis-St. Paul Airport to fly home to Tampa. He saw remnants of the riots that had occurred every night since the murder in Minneapolis during his journey to the airport on May 31st, after the lesson. Burned-out shops were surrounded by police barriers and streets were closed off by the police after looters pillage that block. People were on overpasses with signs declaring their outrage. The least angry signs read "Black Lives Matter", while others were disparaging the police. Tully felt a strong sense of relief when he boarded the plane for Tampa, erroneously believing he was getting far away from the erupting human volcano taking place in Minnesota. When he arrived, he called Catherine who had fallen asleep while waiting for his call. She, as planned, jumped into the car to go to the airport, to pick up Tully. Soon after Catherine leaves, Tully gets a call from Catherine who is in a full-blown panic! Tully recognized immediately that Catherine's voice was in her panic mode when she said, "I don't know where to go. There are police cars everywhere blocking Busch Blvd. and they are forcing us to turn right or left." Catherine had memorized one route to the airport but had no sense of direction, so she was disoriented by the detour. Tully calmly asked, "Where are you now? I will tell you how to get here." "I turned right on 56th Street, Catherine replied. Tully knew that meant she did not know where she was after that one turn took her outside her driving comfort zone. He instructed, "Ok, go up to Fowler Ave. and turn left. Go past the University Square Mall

THE CROWNING: CULMINATION OF THE NATION

and you will run into I-275. Go south on that and it will take you to the airport exit."

Neither of them knew what was actually happening in Tampa, and Tully was in fact literally, leading Catherine from the "frying pan into the fire" As Catherine approached the University Mall she could see people running in all directions. Cars in the mall parking lot were on fire and across the road in a smaller strip mall, a sporting goods store was in flames with the window broken and people running out of the door carrying boxes of sporting goods. Police cars quickly arrived and blocked the intersections to keep the traffic, including Catherine, from driving into the mayhem. Catherine, returned to her state of terror yelling into the phone, " I don't know where to go now! Where should I go?" The panic in her voice was increasing and Tully knew she would be in even more serious trouble if he could not talk her through this dilemma. Remaining calm and upbeat, Tully said, "Turn left on 30th St. then I will talk you through the rest of the way. While he was directing his wife where to go, he was already on his cell phone trying to learn what was happening in Tampa. There was no mention of the riot that was unfolding before Catherine's eyes. He used the Maps program on his phone to wind her through the neighborhoods, not the best neighborhoods, but at least they were without riots. He navigated her way to the airport. She had held it together and did not panic out of control. After she arrived, Tully took over the driving and chose an alternate route to get home that steered clear of the riots. When they got home and turned on the 10:00 news, they heard the reporting about the riots in Tampa, and in cities around the country. Catherine, upon entering their home, locked every door and window and grabbed a blanket to cover her up. Tully realized he had missed some of the program, Truth, while lost in that memory, so he returned his focus to the show being presented.

Carol Leonig stated, "That evening angry protesters took to the streets in Minneapolis to demand action for what they rightly called a police murder protests would erupt the next day in cities, across the country from Los Angeles to Chicago, to Memphis before long demonstrations were taking place practically everywhere on May 27th. Trump met with Bill Barr to review what had happened in Minneapolis. Barr told Trump the Justice Department was launching a civil rights investigation following the local authority's own investigation and went over the key questions. The legal team would seek to answer in deciding whether to charge the officers. Trump was visibly disturbed by Floyd's death. The President was agitated about what he believed to be obvious abuse. However, his emotions took a back seat to practical political concerns about the optics of his response."[3]

Carol Leonig expounded, "On May 28th, the third straight day of protests in Minneapolis, some of them violent, Minnesota governor Tim Walz activated the National Guard to restore peace to the Twin Cities, but protests continued. A large group of demonstrators surrounded the Third Precinct Police Station, forcing police to abandon the building, which was soon set ablaze by protestors. Crowds spilled into neighboring St. Paul, burning and vandalizing more storefronts and buildings in a commercial district. Not even the announcement that Chauvin had been arrested and charged with second and third-degree murder could calm the unrest in the streets. On May 29th. After watching television footage of the precinct station fire, Trump tweeted that the Minneapolis mayor was very weak and that the protestors were thugs who are dishonoring the memory of George Floyd. Trump then tweeted "When the looting starts, the shooting starts", a phrase that echoed the brutal crackdown on civil rights protests in black neighborhoods in Miami, in the 1960s."[3]

Phillip Rucker recalled on the evening of Friday, May 29th, the demonstrations literally came to the president's front yard in anticipation of civil unrest. In the nation's Capitol officials in Washington had taken some modest security precautions. The Justice Department brought in a few dozen US marshals and Bureau of Prisons officers who had been trained in prison riots to protect the departments, Pennsylvania Avenue headquarters over the coming weekend, the U S park police, which has jurisdiction over the national mall monuments and other federal lands in the city. And the secret service set up a temporary perimeter of the waist, top sections of metal fencing, resembling bike racks, a few yards out from the white house as the Northern fence line. This essentially created a buffer on Pennsylvania Avenue, the most exposed side of the 18-acre complex. Other than that, however, there was no planning for or expectation of the protests that would come that evening. The first crowds began gathering in small clusters

THE CROWNING: CULMINATION OF THE NATION

throughout the city that Friday evening at about five o'clock at 14th St. and Northwest, the epicenter of black culture in Washington, which was scarred by the 1968 riots, but had been reborn in the 21st century as a diverse, vibrant gentrified neighborhood. Roughly 200 people assembled peacefully, but noisily, some in the group chanted, "I can't breathe". And a speaker led the crowd and recited a list of names of unarmed black men and women killed by police."[3]

Carol Loenig described the scene saying, "Then the crowd marched south on 14th street toward the White House, as people floated into Lafayette Square in front of the White House, a small skirmish ensued between protesters, many of them, young people chanting "Black Lives Matter" and the park police and secret service officers. Some protesters tossed plastic bottles at the officers' heads. Police surrounded one man shortly after 7:00 PM. The crowd swelled considerably to the surprise officers that were now 500 people. Members of the crowd rushed to the perimeter of temporary fencing, many tugged at the metal racks and hopped over them, where they could, and in some spots, push them over entirely secret service officers radioed and alert a young man with dark hair and a yellow shirt had hopped over the fencing around the Treasury Building. The threat level at the white house was elevated from condition yellow to condition red indicating a breach that put the president in potential danger members of the president's security detail rushed up a flight of stairs to his private quarters and quickly guided Trump along with Melania and Barron down a narrow tunnel to the emergency shelter under the east wing, the secret service decision reflected the real danger of the trumps faced secret service officers would later remark that the forcefulness of the demonstrators that night was like nothing they had experienced before calling to mind clashes between police and Vietnam war protests in the 1960s."

Phillip Rucker revealed, "The next morning, May 30th. Trump also commended the secret service and a series of messages on Twitter. "I was inside watching every move and couldn't have felt safer", he wrote. The president added "a big crowd, professionally organized, but nobody came close to breaching the fence. If they had, they would have been greeted with the most vicious dogs and most ominous weapons I have ever seen.

That's when people would have been really badly hurt. Trump's suggestion of sicking vicious dogs on Black Lives Matter protesters evoked, ugly memories of police brutality and racism. This language coupled with a later tweet, blaming D.C. Mayor Muriel Bowser for the unrest prompted a scornful rebuttal from the black democrat. "There are no vicious dogs and ominous weapons". Bowser wrote on Twitter. "There was just a scared man, afraid, alone". The protests continued in Washington all weekend, including in front of the White House. And though they were peaceful during the day, at night, violence increased and several dozen law enforcement officers were treated for injuries. Downtown stores and office buildings were vandalized as was the Hay Adams Hotel on Lafayette Square. On Sunday night, protestors set fire to the basement of St. John's Episcopal Church and historic place of worship on Lafayette Square."3

Carol Loenig identified Trump's fear reporting, "On May 31st as protestors took to the streets in Washington for the third day straight, the New York Times reported Trump had been taken to the bunker two nights earlier, the report infuriated the President because he thought it made him appear scared and weak. Trump demanded to know who had leaked this news to Maggie Haberman and Peter Baker of the Times. He told Mark Meadows, "Mark, you have to catch whoever leaked that, they should be in prison. They should be tried for treason. This is treasonous." A few days later, Trump would deny what had happened. It was a false report. Trump said in a call in an interview with Fox News Radio's Brian Kilmeade. "I went down during the day and I was there for a tiny little short period of time. And it was much more for an inspection."3

Waldron inquired of Rucker, "So how did the events on Lafayette Square turn into a debate about the use of the military in handling civil unrest?" Phillip Rucker responded to the hosts' question by saying, "Trump gathered Meadows, Defense Secretary, Mark Esper, Joint Chiefs of Staff Chairman Mark Millie, and other top advisors in the oval office to plan an end to the protests. The President wanted to deploy the military, both in Washington and elsewhere in the country. Sitting in front of the resolute desk, facing the President, Esper, and Millie warned Trump that deploying active duty troops on American streets was almost never a good idea, especially not to handle

THE CROWNING: CULMINATION OF THE NATION

civil unrest. Millie's opposition to the use of military force domestically was well known throughout the Pentagon. From the back of the room, Stephen Miller piped up, though Miller had previously only worked as a congressional staffer and had zero military experience. He was valued by the President for his hard-edged nationalism and innate understanding of how to cater to Trump's political base. "Mr. President, you have to show strength," Miller said, "they're burning the country down". "So Stephen shut the f**k up". Millie snapped. "They're not burning the f**king country down." Then he turned back to Trump. The President's obsession with tapping the military might lead the Pentagon to keep at ready, data it had never needed before. So Millie could fight fire with facts. The Chairman's office got updated counts of the total number of law enforcement officers and national guard available in every major city in the United States. "Mr. President," Millie said, "There are 276 cities in America with over 100,000 people in them. We tracked this all the time in the last 24 hours." Millie said there were only two cities with violent protests so large that local authorities might have needed reinforcements. Otherwise, he said, there was some vandalism and some rioting, but they were handled by local police. Then he turned back to Miller. "Stephen, that's not burning the country down". Miller pushed back. "Let me get this straight", he said. "We're supposed to say, sorry, your city's being burned down, too bad. Your mayor doesn't want to do anything about it. That's our argument? We can't possibly take the position that the people are free to riot for as long as they want to in this country. This is a completely untenable position".[3] Still Millie's firmness made an impression on Trump who watched silently and eagerly as if the argument between his advisers were a pay-per-view fight on HBO."[3] Carol Loenig added, "Despite Millie whacking Miller's argument, deploying troops came up in a subsequent White House meeting. Trump asked why it couldn't be done. Protesters were looting stores and vandalizing buildings. The President reasoned they had to be stopped just like when troops were used in the 1960s to bring order to the streets." "Mr. President, it doesn't compare anywhere to the summer of 68", Millie said "It's not even close", Miller piped up again. "It's an insurrection!" he said. This time, the General didn't bother turning toward the young aide though. Millie had been sharp with Miller before he tried to stay calm with the President. Millie said, "You don't have an insurrection. When guys show up in gray and start bombing Fort Sumter, you have an insurrection. I'll let you know about it. You don't have an insurrection right now."

Waldron concluded the show with, "That is all the time we can afford tonight, actually I am afraid we may have gone too long. Thank you both for helping us understand these events and hopefully we can have you back again very soon."

Tully, immersed, and lost in the program's narrative, was suddenly jolted back to his personal reality. He began trembling with the overwhelming fear of the potential loss of his wife, his son, and his daughter-in-law, each of whom is hospitalized with life-threatening health crises. The worst-case scenarios haunted his conscience, yet, the next day he would be delivered the news that would change everything.

Chapter 11
What Do They Know?
Tampa, Florida
February 13th, 2025

Tully was jolted from his deep sleep by the jarring alarm on his cell phone. His eyes were foggy and he couldn't believe how long he'd been sleeping. The last thing he recalled was that he had been keeping guard in his chair near the back door, intending to go to bed at 4:00 am. He realized he had slept for six hours, probably the longest amount of sleep he had in weeks. Tully picked up his cell phone and called the hospital, asking to be put through to the nurses' desk on Catherine's floor. Nurse Adams answered the phone, "Good morning, third floor. May I help you?" "Good morning. I am calling to check up on Catherine Stone. How is she? Tully asked with a nervous voice. Nurse Adams asserted, "She had a good night and rested very well. Her vitals are showing positive progress. The Doctor was in around 6 and said she can be discharged tomorrow morning." "That is outstanding news. Will you still be bringing her home in an ambulance?" Tully asked, hoping for clarification. Still upbeat, Nurse Adams briefed Tully saying, "Yes Sir. That is standard practice for now. She will be bed bound for a week or two, and you will need to be prepared to take care of her. She will remain on antibiotics for another 10 days, more if needed, and will have a drip line providing fluids in her arm. The antibiotics will be in the fluid, no pills." Tully, still cautious, asked, "What if something should go wrong?" Nurse Adams reassuringly replied, "Call us anytime you are concerned. We will monitor her temperature, heartbeat, pulse rate, and blood pressure through a special monitor attached to her breastplate that is sending us her readings 24/7 through a special cell phone. If something goes wrong, chances are, we'll know it before you do and call you. We will call you tomorrow morning to give you an update, and a nurse will be with her on the trip to your home.

That nurse will fill you in on everything you need to know. Tully, finally feeling relief, said, "Thank you, I will be anxiously awaiting that call. Good Bye."

Tully spirits just rose to a level he had not experienced in a very long time. He kneeled down in prayer, thanking God, and every deceased relative he knew, thanking everyone for his prayers being answered. One more time, just to be safe, Tully sterilized everything he could find in their home that one might touch. He wanted to take no chances at an infection that could be prevented. That afternoon his cell phone rang and he answered it recognizing the number as belonging to Grace, but it wasn't Grace on the line. A very soft and very raspy voice said, "Hi Dad" Tully sat in silence for what must have seemed like an eternity, partly trying to figure out which of his five sons was on the other end. Tully, eventually realizing who it is, asked, "James? Is that you?" He had not heard his voice since before he went into the Intensive Care Unit.

James slowly drew a breath before saying softly, "Yes, I thought I'd call you". James said that each time, in the past, as the conversation began, so Tully knew it was really James. Tully reflected out loud, "I wasn't sure for a second, James, it didn't sound like you. Truth is son, I wasn't sure I would ever hear your voice again." James declared, "It's me, still alive and still kicking."

Tully, laughing with joy, joked, "Well don't kick too hard you might take out the doctor. How are you feeling? "Horrible," James testified, "but better than I felt for the last three weeks. I better not talk too long, my voice won't take it."

Tully expressed his gratitude by saying, "I understand. I can't tell you how much I am so grateful that you have pulled through. It is those Stone genes, we are survivors, and God's answer to my prayers for you both." "Now we have to get Suzanne through, she doesn't have the Stone genes," James remarked. "She will make it through, I promise. You both took great care of your health, throughout your life, so she must be strong too, Tully assured James. "Well, perhaps, but we made one major mistake. We didn't take the virus seriously enough." Tully argued, "The only thing that matters now is to get you two back to full health. You need to rest now, James. Thanks for the call."

THE CROWNING: CULMINATION OF THE NATION

James said, "Thanks Dad, I will." James gave the cell phone back to Grace. Grace, still exuberant, said, "Isn't that the best news yet, Grandpa?" "It sure is. Thank you, Grace, for putting him on the phone, it made my day. Catherine will come home tomorrow also," Tully announced. Grace replied, "That is wonderful, Grandpa! I am so glad. I will check in on Mom soon. I'll let you know how she is. Bye Grandpa." Tully was elated at the good news, twice within a single day. The rest of the afternoon was filled with peace and hope. Tully believed that these were signs from God that all was going to get back to normal soon. Perhaps by summer, he mused, we will all be able to travel again, and the Stone annual family reunion will go on as it has for the last 50 years.

That evening, Tully "tuned" back into the Truth broadcast, which began at 6:00 pm sharp, once again. Tully clicked the link to record the show and settled back to listen to the program. Bryce Waldron addressed the audience with the usual opening remarks saying, "Good evening, this is Wednesday, February 13th. My name is Bryce Waldron, and I will be your host tonight. Welcome back to the Truth. Tonight we are going to expose the actual election of 2020 between the incumbent, President Donald J. Trump, and former Vice President, Joe Biden. To guide us through this election and the actual events that took place leading up to that presidential election, we have tonight three election experts, Kate Shaw, Jennifer Mercieca, and Jan Leightley and Representative Joaquin Castro. In October 2016, just weeks before the general election of 2016, Trump wanted to cast doubt on the results by tweeting, "The election is absolutely being rigged by the dishonest and distorted media pushing Crooked Hillary - but also at many polling places - SAD," providing no evidence for the claim. This isn't the first time Donald Trump has questioned the legitimacy of a U S election in 2016 when he won the electoral college but lost the popular vote. Trump claimed without evidence that millions of votes were cast illegally.

Even after the election ended and Clinton had lost and conceded victory to Trump, the President didn't stop lamenting over the election he had won. He quickly made the claim that he also won the popular vote over Clinton, which is something that did not happen. "In addition to winning the Electoral College in a landslide, I won the popular vote if you deduct the millions of people who voted illegally," Trump said. The President lost the popular vote to Clinton by nearly 3 million votes, and there was no evidence of voter fraud then, just as there is no evidence of voter fraud in 2020," Waldron explained. "Representative Castro, let me begin with you. In the 2nd Impeachment trial of Donald Trump you pointed to one Twitter post from May 24, almost six months before the election of 2020, in which Trump wrote the election will "be the greatest rigged election in history." You followed up with this question, "How could he possibly know it would be the greatest rigged election in history six months before the election happened?" You cited two other tweets from June and July 2020 where Trump again predicted the election would be fraudulent. Were President's Trump's words worthy of anyone's concern? Was he just blowing smoke," asked Waldron. Castro responded, "Again, just big words with nothing to prove them...But he wanted to make his supporters believe that an election victory would be stolen from him and from them. And this was to rile up his base, to make them angry." Waldron shifted to his second guest, Jan Leightley, stating, "I think we can all agree that Democracy in the United States, depends on free and fair elections and hinges on the peaceful transfer of power." Waldron opined, "When Trump proclaimed during the debates, "You know, that I've been complaining strongly about the ballots and the ballots are a disaster, get rid of the ballots, and you'll have a very transparent, I have a very peaceful, there won't be a transfer of... frankly, there'll be a continuation" he was proclaiming war on mail-in ballots as those using them voted later and he calculated he would not be getting many of those votes. Jennifer Mercieca, Waldron's third guest, fielded Waldron's cue by saying, "I think what he was trying to do is prepare the nation again, sort of setting the groundwork for these arguments that he's going to have later to say, you know, the Supreme court should decide whether we should continue to count these ballots. He's preemptively doing that in 2020. So he is laying the groundwork for an argument that says 'I didn't lose, they cheated.'" Waldron added, "Trump said, and I quote, "Well, we're going to have to see what happens. You know, that I've been complaining very strongly about the ballots and the ballots are a disaster. Get rid of the ballots, and you'll have a very transparent, have a very peaceful, there won't be a transfer of... frankly, there'll be a continuation." Jan Leightley responded, "Whether Trump means it or not, either way, it is anti-democratic because it throws the whole electoral process into doubt,

THE CROWNING: CULMINATION OF THE NATION

and it uses compliance, gaining strategies rather than persuasion to try to convey his message." Waldron mused, "President Trump ramped up his rhetoric on voter fraud and focused much of his attention on mail-in ballots, saying "...because what they're doing is a hoax with the ballots. They're sending out tens of millions of ballots, unsolicited, not where they're being asked, but unsolicited. This is going to be a fraud like you've never seen."

Kate Shaw, who up to this point had remained silent, spoke up saying, "I think it is clear that there is no evidence that widespread or systematic absentee voter fraud is a real phenomenon. The conservative heritage foundation actually took a look at this recently and found that over 20 years and over 200 million mail-in ballots cast, they could only identify 143 instances of absentee ballot fraud. So it's just not a problem at any scale. And when it comes to mail-in ballots, you know, they do have the mechanisms in place to check the ballots that are being returned to ensure their accuracy. President Trump has largely polarized the issue of absentee voting. He has cast doubt about voting by mail for months. And I think that that message has resonated with his voters." Jan Leightley agreed, and added, "There's been a lot of talk about how the election outcome will be de-legitimized or called into question. If we don't have all of the votes counted on election day, which is really a fallacy when elections are called, whether they be for the House or the Senate and in the presidential race, they are called based on the vote that is already recorded. With the number of outstanding votes to come in and a set of typically provisional ballots that still have to be counted, no one is elected on election night."

Jennifer Mercieca contended, "Donald Trump is an expert at "weaponizing" communication. He's constantly using threats of force or intimidation, like saying he's going to sign up poll watchers that make you feel like, you know, things are really scary." Waldron added, "As when Trump said, "Either way, when, when, not if, when you see shenanigans, please report it to your authorities. The real authorities are watching and the authorities are watching." Jan Leightley heeded, "Much can happen between November and December to legitimize the outcomes, to clarify any possible errors and to show that the United States has a vigorous electoral system that can produce elections that have some level of legitimacy for the majority of Americans. Donald Trump has primarily used conspiracy theory rhetoric when he talks about the election in 2020, conspiracy rhetoric is a self-sealing narrative, which means that logic and evidence are not allowed to count against the conspiracy. And if you say, well, no, that actually the evidence shows that this doesn't happen very often at all. There is no mail fraud, for example, the conspiracy says they're hiding the truth from you."

Kate Shaw recalled the events explaining, "Trump took to his favorite platform, just moments before major media outlets had projected Biden the winner in this year's election, and falsely tweeted, "I WON THIS ELECTION, BY A LOT!" That tweet was flagged by Twitter because Trump was not declared the victor and because for months since his rally on Aug. 17 in Oshkosh, Wisconsin when he famously said, "The only way we're going to lose this election is if the election is rigged." Trump has been attempting to cast doubt on the American electoral process. Trump continued to attack mail-in ballots and absentee ballots well into the fall months so that when the ballots were to be tabulated, he could cast doubt and speculate that he was the victim of fraud because of the vote-by-mail system. On Twitter, the day after Election Day, as Biden's lead was becoming more clear in several states, Trump tweeted, "They are finding Biden votes all over the place — in Pennsylvania, Wisconsin, and Michigan. So bad for our Country!" Waldron continued the topic by saying, "The next days, the President made the claim that he has always said mail-in ballots are not to be trusted. "I've been talking about mail-in voting for a long time. It's—it's really destroyed our system. It's a corrupt system. And it makes people corrupt even if they aren't by nature, but they become corrupt; it's too easy. They want to find out how many votes they need, and then they seem to find them. They wait and wait and then they find them," Trump said two days after Election Day. As mail-in ballots continued to be counted, states like Pennsylvania showed a clear Biden lead."

Shaw continues by saying, "In the days after Election Day, Trump continued to make falsehoods on Twitter, which the social media platform quickly flagged. "WATCH FOR MASSIVE BALLOT COUNTING ABUSE...REMEMBER I TOLD YOU SO!" he tweeted, claiming that ballot harvesting took place and he was right about the potential of it happening. Trump has stuck to this playbook for years; however, his claims have never prompted a meaningful change in the election process. This time,

THE CROWNING: CULMINATION OF THE NATION

the President is taking his claims through the legal system[1] with no evidence to back them up. Meanwhile, the campaign is continuing to raise money for the battles, as it's clear the President isn't willing to give up quickly." Bryce Waldron knew time was up. He said, "That is all for tonight. Thank you, my treasured guests for sharing your expertise with us, and to our audience. We are planning a special broadcast for our next segment in which we will expose the truth about the players and the planning behind the coup attempt in 2020 and early 2021. I only ask that you continue recording our segments and come back each night at 6:00 P.M."

The following day Tully was up early awaiting the call from the hospital. He had done everything he could think of to prepare for Catherine's arrival and subsequent care. At 7:00 his phone rang with the hospital number showing on the caller ID. A burning sensation in Tully's stomach felt as if an ulcer had formed overnight. Nurse Adam's voice was atypically upbeat, "Mr. Stone? Are you ready for your wife to come home?" Tully instantly felt an enormous relief from that question. He knew it meant she definitely was coming home today, and he was more than primed and eager! "If I were any more ready, it would be illegal." His attempt at a lame joke fell on the floor like a lead balloon. Nurse Adams forced a fake laugh and said: "Well, that is good, I think." She will leave here within the hour and, as we promised, a nurse will be with her to show you how to do everything you need to do to take good care of her. Tully responds, "I appreciate that, thank you. I will be at the door waiting." He hung up and moved his chair near the front door to watch for the ambulance and police escort. When they arrived Tully was out the door before they even stopped and parked. Two attendants and the nurse brought Catherine out of the ambulance on a gurney. When Catherine's eyes found Tully's smiling face, she grinned and her hand reached out to grasp Tully's hand. Tully realized how weak she really was by the lack of strength in her grip, but he was overwhelmed with joy by the knowledge that she was home and alive. After two hours of getting Catherine situated comfortably and instructions on her care and how to do everything, the crew left. Tully experienced a momentary panic because of the realization he was, in the future, responsible for her recovery. Whether he had what

---

1. https://abcnews.go.com/Politics/election-2020-trump-campaign-election-lawsuits-stand/story?id=74041748

it takes to continue to improve her health seemed a distant possibility to him. He had not had to take care of someone this helpless and dependent on him since his first son, Shane, was alive. Tully thought of that experience, which lasted several decades, and realized he had been prepared well for this challenge, because of that chapter of his life. That realization made him feel peaceful and confident. Catherine had fallen asleep and was resting quietly now. Her monitors were beeping rhythmically giving Tully the sense that all was good and the hospital personnel was watching over her like guardian angels. As Catherine slept, Tully did not want to make any noise that might wake her up, so he texted all of his extended family about her arrival at home. Everyone, almost immediately texted back their relief, joy, and excitement, followed by a myriad of questions. Tully was silently on the phone answering their questions for hours. He promised himself that next time it would be a group chat instead of dozens of individual conversations. Catherine woke up later in the afternoon. She was thirsty and seemed uncomfortable. She was too weak to speak complete sentences so she told Tully what she needed in short phrases and single words. She was keeping an upbeat demeanor, despite her obvious pain and discomfort but, he thought, 'That is her, always positive'. Within about an hour, after all her needs had been met, she drifted into a deep sleep that would last all night. Tully eased into his guard chair listening to the rising sounds of the civil war, the gunshots, the sirens, even if you listened hard enough, the far-off voices of people shouting, but what they are saying is impossible to make out, except for the undeniably sense of despair and anguish. Tully looked up into the darkening sky and noticed a flock of large birds, all flying in the same direction. "What did that mean?" Tully wondered. "What do they know?"

Chapter 12
Internal Divide
Tampa, Florida
Feb. 14, 2025

With Catherine sleeping soundly, Tully went into his office and turned on the computer. He remembered the promise made by the host, Bryce Wallace, that today's program would be "special" so Tully was pleased that he would not miss the show.

Bryce Waldron began the broadcast by saying, "Good evening. This is Friday, February 14th. My name is Bryce Waldron, and I will be your host tonight. Welcome back to the Truth. Tonight we are bringing back Dr. Vaughn Woodman, Ph.D. We welcome you to this broadcast, Dr. Woodman." Dr. Woodman answered Waldron saying, "Thank you, Bryce. It is always rewarding to further the understanding of how our past shapes our present and future world. "Dr. Woodman," Bryce Waldron inquired, "Let's begin with the first few days and weeks after the election in November 2020. Give us the significant events and efforts that were unfolding to disrupt and interfere with the peaceful transfer of power from the Trump presidency to the Biden presidency." "I think the place to start is with the "Freedom Caucus" in the House of Representatives," explained Dr. Woodman, "how deep these bonds between some of the Freedom Caucus members and these efforts to "stop the steel" really were, at the time immediately following the determination of Joe Biden as the winner. There was a lot of coordination between Mark Meadows, Trump's Chief of Staff, formally a freedom caucus colleague, and other members of the Freedom Caucus and the White House staff, specifically Stephen Miller and Kaylee McEnany, concerning how best to perpetuate these unfounded conspiracy theories that Donald Trump has won the election. Two days after the election is called for Joseph Biden, on November 9th, there's a meeting at Trump's campaign headquarters in Virginia. Stephen Miller, Ronna McDaniel, Chairperson of the Republican National Committee, and others, talked about how they were going to communicate that Trump still could remain President. In particular, Jim Jordan and Scott Perry played a key role in shaping that messaging. Besides Perry and Jordan, the top officials of the White House were present, including Meadows, Stephen Miller, top Trump advisor, Bill Stepien, the campaign manager, who was named the White House political director, and Kaylee McEnany the white house press secretary. As a result, a strategy was developed that Trump's congressional backers could use to deliver their messages: claiming there was an election fraud; announcing legal actions that Trump and his acolytes would take, using allegations of rampant voter fraud. Later, McEnany dispatched the communique, "the election is not over", she said, "far from it." Neither Jim Jordan nor his spokesman said he was involved in a coup to overturn the election; the meeting was simply to "discuss media strategy."

"Dr. Woodman," Waldron, quickly getting to the core subject, probed, "would it be historically and factually accurate to say that there was a conspiracy to nullify the election of 2020 and that conspiracy involved the President of the United States, some members of Congress, the White House, including the President's Chief of Staff?" Dr. Woodman bluntly asserted, "By definition, whenever the President of the United States has his Chief of Staff; sitting members of Congress; possibly the Department of Justice, and the political apparatus of that sitting president, trying to negate a free and fair election to keep him in power, it's a failed authoritarian coup. In this case, this was a coordinated collaborative effort between the executive branch, loyalists in the legislative branch, and outside political players to overturn an election for the singular goal of keeping the current president

THE CROWNING: CULMINATION OF THE NATION

in office, who had lost the election." Waldron countered, "What actually occurred, shortly after the election of 2020 that provides you proof that this was an attempted coup?" Dr. Woodman was quick to respond to Waldron's challenge explaining, "Let me try to describe to you the key events that took place in chronological order, as much as possible, that we know from testimony under oath, massive amounts of records and documents, copies of text messages from key players and other considerable empirical evidence that is indisputable. We need to start with the totally legal strategy of going through the court system to seek judicial remedy. Immediately following the election, the Trump campaign filed lawsuits in battleground states where the race has been extremely close. (Dr. Woodman shared his PowerPoint presentation with the audience showing the following slides covering the legal court battles while reading the slide content):

Slide 1: On Nov. 4, the day after Election Day, the campaign filed a lawsuit alleging that observers were not allowed to "meaningfully" watch the vote count in Philadelphia County. A Pennsylvania judge on Nov. 5 granted the Trump campaign's request to observe Philadelphia poll workers as they process the remaining mail-in ballots. The city of Philadelphia promptly filed an appeal to the state Supreme Court to overturn the decision.[13]

Slide 2: On Nov. 17, the Pennsylvania Supreme Court rejected the Trump campaign's claim that election officials had failed to provide campaign observers "meaningful" access. The court, on a vote of 5-2, found that election officials followed the law in providing the Trump campaign sufficient access to the workers who were opening mail-in ballots. Pennsylvania simply has no requirements that say how close the observers need to be placed to watch the process, the court found.[13]

Slide 3: Trump campaign v. Kathy Boockvar and County Boards of Elections

The Trump campaign sued in state court on Nov. 5 alleging that Pennsylvania Secretary of State Kathy Boockvar illegally extended a deadline for mail-in voters to supply any missing ID requirements from Nov. 9 to Nov. 12. A judge ordered the Pennsylvania State Department to further segregate any mail-in ballots with missing voter ID information provided after Nov. 9. In a rare legal win for the Trump campaign, on Nov. 12, an appellate judge ruled Boockvar lacked the authority to issue guidance to change the deadline, and enjoined the state's boards of elections from counting any ballots that have been segregated.[13] Waldron interjected stating, "This was one the only win secured by the Trump legal team out of the 62 cases."

Dr. Woodman concurred, "Yes that is correct. We will not be going through all 62 cases, as it would take hours, but overall, case-by-case judges rejected the claims of Trump's lawyers. A few examples include when Trump's lawyers took their complaint about election[1] observers being denied sufficient access to watch the processing of ballots, U.S. District Judge Paul Diamond appeared startled when the lawyers then acknowledged that the observers had, in fact, been permitted within 15 feet of the poll workers. "I'm sorry, then what's your problem?" said Diamond.[14] In Georgia, a judge rejected the campaign's effort to force Chatham County to separate and account for late-arriving ballots over a concern that the county may mishandle ballots, an allegation based on an incident involving one out-of-state poll worker involving just 53 ballots. The judge said he saw "no evidence" to back up the claim.[14] And just hours later, a Michigan judge denied the campaign's effort to halt absentee ballot counting in Macomb County, Michigan, home to Detroit, over allegations that Trump campaign observers were not given "meaningful access" to observe the process."[14]

Dr. Woodman recalled the Michigan Judge Cynthia Stephens said while looking over the evidence presented by the president's lawyers, which alleged a poll watcher had been instructed to back-date late-arriving mail-in ballots to make them count. "Come on now, What I have, at best, is a hearsay affidavit."[14] Dr. Woodman continued this chronicle by proclaiming, "A judge in Nevada denied an effort to toss out signature-verification machines in Clark County, home to Democrat-stronghold Las Vegas, based on what the campaign said was "lax procedures for authenticating mail ballots. U.S. District Judge Andrew Gordon said he didn't think the Republican Party arrived in court with "sufficient evidence" to support its claims.[14] Of the 62 lawsuits filed disputing the presidential election, 61 failed, and decisions have come from both Democratic-appointed and Republican-appointed judges.

---

1. https://abcnews.go.com/alerts/elections

THE CROWNING: CULMINATION OF THE NATION

As Jonathan Karl wrote in his novel Betrayal; "Recounts and challenges are part of the democratic process. Trump legitimately had a right to seek election audits and to go to court in states where he believed the rules had not been followed. In a few instances, it was not entirely unreasonable to argue that changes to election rules had been hastily and improperly made. But when those efforts failed, Trump turned to a new tactic, something so brazenly anti-democratic that no losing presidential candidate, let alone an incumbent president, had ever seriously contemplated. He went directly to Republican-led state legislatures and asked them to throw out election results in their states and choose the winner themselves. There was a thin thread of legal basis, sort of for this effort in article two of the constitution, which gives state legislatures the power to determine the manner for choosing their state's electoral votes. On November 20th, Georgia certified Biden as the state's winner after counting the ballots three times; in an initial count after the polls closed on election night; a machine recount, and a recount of all 4.9 million ballots by hand. In terms of Trump's hopes for challenging the election results, the certified result in Georgia was another nail in a coffin that had already been hammered shut. And announcing the results of the hand recount Georgia's Republican, Secretary of State, who had been a Trump supporter said, "I live by the motto the numbers don't lie. Brad Raffensperger had done his job as a public official, even as he ratified the defeat of the candidate he had supported."[15] Bryce Waldron affirmed, "The planning process by the Trump White House and outside actors continued through November and into December with some highly unusual fireworks, would you highlight some of those rather heated discussions Dr. Woodman?" Dr. Woodman, describing the explosive events that followed explained, "Certainly, in the Oval Office on Friday, November 18, 2020, President Donald Trump convened a heated meeting that included lawyer Sidney Powell and former national security adviser Michael Flynn, that began largely as a spontaneous confab, but transformed into shouting matches when some of Trump's aides reacted to Powell and Flynn's outrageous suggestions about trying to overturn the election."[16] Quoting from his notes, Dr. Woodman continued, "Flynn suggested Trump could invoke martial law, but others in the room forcefully pushed back and shot it down. White House Chief of Staff Mark Meadows and counsel Pat Cipollone, also pushed back intensely on the suggestion of naming Powell as a special counsel to investigate voter fraud allegations. Powell has focused her conspiracies on voting machines and has floated having a special counsel inspect the machines for flaws."[16] Dr. Woodman went on by saying, "A serious internal divide formed within Trump's campaign following the election with tensions at their highest between the campaign's general counsel, Matt Morgan, and Trump lawyer Rudy Giuliani."[16] "Acting at President Trump's direction, Giuliani had called the Department of Homeland Security's Ken Cuccinelli and asked if it was possible for DHS to seize voting machines. Cuccinelli, the senior official performing the duties of the DHS deputy secretary, told Giuliani it wasn't within the authority of the department's cybersecurity agency to seize voting machines. Though the campaign distanced itself from Powell, Trump urged others in earshot to fight as she has..."[16]

Waldron questioned, "How close did Flynn and Powell come to convincing Trump to invoke martial law, to confiscate all the voting machines, possibly even hold a rerun of the election?" "Well," Dr. Woodman declared, "first they already had an Executive Order Trump had signed in 2018 giving him the power to do all of those things. It was called Executive Order 13848—Imposing Certain Sanctions in the Event of Foreign Interference in a United States Election, and should there ever be any event of foreign interference in an election then these powers could be invoked, thus the need to claim that had happened by claiming a foreign power, albeit Italy, China, Iran, Venezuela or even the Vatican, all floated as potential culprits for corrupting the voting machines. The argument presented by Sidney Powell and Michael Flynn to convince Trump that the military should see the voting machines was a core part of their case. They argued a foreign country attacked us from a foreign country, altering the number of votes cast. Therefore, the military must intervene. Fortunately, White House Counsel Pat Cipollone fought against this, and Homeland Security's Ken Cuccinelli informed Rudy Giuliani that they did not have the authority to do so. Attorney General Bill Barr, when pushed by Trump to carry out the same plot to seize the voter machines, told Trump, in no uncertain terms, he would have no part in that scheme. Trump even held meetings with members of two State Legislators, Michigan, and Pennsylvania, asking them to seize their state's voter machines; however, they also refused."

"Please, Dr. Woodman," Waldron implored, "go into that in more detail, I had never heard of this before." Dr. Woodman confirmed, "Sure, this was November 20th, 2020. This was happening while Trump decried the Michigan election results, insisting he must have won that state, and it must have been stolen from him. It's two and a half weeks after the election. Trump was not only disputing Biden's victory in Michigan, but he was publicly trying to pressure local election officials in Michigan counties that went for Biden, that they shouldn't certify the election results in those counties. Trump invited a whole delegation of Republican lawmakers from Michigan to come to the oval office and meet with him personally. It was believed at the time that he had invited those Republican lawmakers from Michigan to rope them in on this scheme to pressure them, to go back home to Michigan and somehow use their authority as state lawmakers to undo the Biden victory in the state of Michigan, but later it was revealed that Trump pushed them to seize their states voting machines so they could be examined for potential hacking and corrupt manipulation of the votes. Those lawmakers spent nearly two hours with Trump inside the White House that day. After their white house meeting, those two Republican leaders who had their faces projected on the outside of the hotel put out a statement saying they had no information that would change the outcome of the election. The same goes for a nearly identical meeting that Trump held with Republican lawmakers from Pennsylvania, five days later. He brought a group of Pennsylvania Republicans to DC. In those separate oval office conversations, Trump addressed the idea of the seizure of voting machines in Pennsylvania and Michigan. This was one more prong of the planned plot, enacted and directed personally by the President himself.[17] We know there was at least one person in local law enforcement in Michigan who tried to carry out Trump's scheme that the voting machines needed to be seized. The lawyer for the Sheriff of Barry County, Michigan wrote an email to Sidney Powell, "My client, the Barry County Sheriff called me, and I instructed him to put the (voting) machines and the ballots in the evidence room. He's done that. We're trying to get the same thing to happen next county over in Kalamazoo. I don't know if we can get the Sheriff in Kalamazoo to seize voting machines and ballots in that county, but if we could, a comparison of the machines could yield some potential forensics, attaching the unofficial results tabulation for Barry County. Again, my client has apparently taken all the machines and ballots into evidence." The attorney for that sheriff put it in writing, to Sidney Powell, that they had confiscated the voting machines and the ballots in Barry County, Michigan, demonstrating the influential power of simply suggesting the public take action through social media and specifically "tweets"."

Bryce Waldron declared, "Thank you, Dr. Woodman, for that very informative chronicle. Once again, our time is up for tonight. We will be back again tomorrow night to continue this important historical journal. Thank you for recording these segments and be sure to save your recording on multiple devices. Until tomorrow, I wish you a good night.

Tully turned the computer off, processing the information of the events just described, and felt a sense of amazement that this could have actually happened in the country, the United States, as he dreamed nothing like this was remotely possible. What Tully also did not know was that soon the dangers posed by a violent and lawless new world would sink its fangs into yet another member of his family.

Chapter 13
They're All Gone
Tampa, Florida
February 15th, 2025

The long night seemed to drag on forever, for Tully. Between listening for signs of civil unrest in the surrounding neighborhood, and checking in on Catherine every hour, Tully stayed awake all night long. He was thrilled to have Catherine finally resting at home, but Tully also felt enormous pressure to keep her healthy and safe from danger. By dawn, he had already consumed an entire pot of coffee which might account for his jitters. Cathy had slept reasonably well but her breathing was very labored, interrupted frequently by coughing fits. Each time she coughed, Tully rushed to her side to be certain her tubes did not become dislodged. At around 11:00 am Tully's cell phone rang and Tully knew it was Tony on the line. "Good morning Tony, How are you doing?" asked Tully. Tony responded, "Not too well, Dad. I have a very serious problem." "What happened?" Tully asked, alarmed by the severe tone of Tony's words. Tony confided, "I was taking care of the horses this morning, while Tommy was target shooting with his BB gun he received for Christmas. He ran into the barn to tell me he had seen a turkey at the edge of the woods. I told him to shoot it so we can have turkey for dinner and I kept on working, shoeing the horse. When I came out of the barn, Tommy was gone. I called for him and then started walking through the woods, but I got no reply from him. Sheila and I started searching the woods, but he was nowhere to be found. I need help to look for him. I have called the police but they can't help as they are tied up with rioters. What can I do?" Tully, shifted into his problem-solving mode saying, "I wish I could rush there but I can't possibly leave Catherine. I will call around to ask my friends if they can lend a hand. Also, if I can find a nurse to stay with Catherine, I will help as well."

Tony replied, "Thanks, Dad. Patrick is coming over, all the way from Orlando, but with the way traveling is these days, it may take him many hours to get here." "Don't worry, I will find you help. Keep your cell phone on you so we can get in touch with you while you are searching for Tommy, Tully advised. "Will do, Dad", Tony murmured, "Text me who will come so I will know who they are and that they are friendly."

Tully immediately called every friend he had in his contact list within 50 miles of his home. Most could not, or would not help. Finally, he got through to his old friend Charlie Stretch. His name is fitting as he is about 6'5 and is a very fit man in his early 60s. Charley did not hesitate for a second to volunteer. He had never met Tony, but that did not matter to him. He would gladly risk his life to save another. Tully gave the contact information and address to Charlie who promised to leave immediately.

Tully's next call also paid off. He reached out to a friend he had not talked to in a very long time, Pastor Ron. Ron was physically the exact opposite of Charlie. While Charlie is a tall white man with little body fat, Ron is short, black, and has a very round physique. What was important, however, was their character. Despite the danger of traveling, even the shortest trips could bring disaster, both were more than willing to lend a hand. Within minutes they were both headed to Tony's ranch home. Tully's next call was to his friend and next-door neighbor, Wally. His real name is Wallace, but he hates being called that so Wally it is. Wally and his wife, Pia, are "salt of the earth" people, who, besides being next-door neighbors, were also Tully and Catherine's closest friends. Wally is a red-headed Scottish lad of 80 years old and Pia is 100% Italian. The two of them seem to know everybody in Tampa. Whenever Tully needed an expert for some project, he could count on Wally to know who to call. Tully wanted to find a nurse to stay and care for Catherine so he could join the search party for Tommy. Wally promised to call right back with the name of a nurse who could stay with Catherine. As promised, within minutes, he called Tully back. Wally was excited to report, "Good news, I not only found you a nurse, but I found you a doctor too. They will both be there this afternoon." Tully was shocked at the news and responded, "A doctor? How did you manage that?" Wally replied, "Easy, I called Vinnie (Wally's son who is an Emergency Room Doctor at a local hospital, and who is also married to a doctor), Becky

THE CROWNING: CULMINATION OF THE NATION

(Vinnie's wife) is coming over and bringing her friend, who is a nurse, with her. The nurse can take over while Rebecca works from our house next door, via her laptop. Vinnie is off of work today so he is going to Tony's home now to help with the search." "That is great news Wally, thank you", Tully exclaimed.

Wally, delighted in his ability to help, responded, "Of course. Call me if you need anything else." By 2:00 that afternoon, Dr. Becky Sampson and her nurse, named Joy, arrived at Tully's front door. Tully explained to Catherine, who was awake now but feeling pretty dreadful, why he had to leave her in the doctor's care and nurse. Worried more for her grandson than herself, Catherine told Tully to drive safely and carefully, then quickly find Tommy. Tully took a similar route to Tony's home as the one he took before. He drove by the truck that had blocked the road, which had been gutted by the fire and later pushed to the side of the road. Careful to not go down the road that had been the scene of the ambush causing Catherine's injuries, Tully arrived at Tony's ranch without incident. It was already 3:00 in the afternoon and it would get dark in another three hours. Tully saw six cars parked in the yard by the house and knew that they were the vehicles of the volunteer search party. Marie emerged from the back door of their home to greet Tully. She had obviously been crying as her eyes were red and swollen, but now she had the look of determination. "Thanks for coming, Dad. Your friends have already arrived and Tony took them into the woods to begin the search. My job is to give you this walkie-talkie and coordinate the search parties." Tully gave his daughter-in-law a big hug, took the walkie talkie and asked, "Which way did they go?" Marie pointed in a westward direction and said, "They left about 10 minutes ago so you should be able to catch up to them. They are spread out with about 50 feet between them." Tully promised Marie he would stay in touch. Marie spoke into the radio saying, "Tony, your Dad has arrived and is on his way to catch up to you." "Roger, thanks Marie" was Tony's reply.

Tully put on his boots, secured his gun in the holster, just in case, and headed off into the woods, which he was aware he had never explored before. Listening to the voices of the other rescuers in search of Tommy, Tully picked his way through the woods that had no foot trails. After about an hour, he finally found the search party spread out about 50 feet apart and walking in a westward direction. Tully found Tony leading the group, repeatedly calling out for Tommy. Tony gave his dad a big hug, a hug born from apprehension and fear for his child's life, and told him they had found nothing yet, not a single sign that Tommy had even been there. "I'm really worried that it will be dark soon and it may get cold tonight. Tommy was not dressed for cold weather," Tony acknowledged. His voice was on the verge of cracking into tears, but he was using all of his strength to keep it together. "Don't worry, we will find him, Tully assured him, "He has to be here somewhere." The sound of Marie's voice yelling out Tommy's name stood out as much more urgent, more filled with fear, yet louder than all the men's voices. Despite her handicap and weakness caused by the devastating effects of Long Covid, Marie's "Momma Bear" instincts and a strong surge of adrenaline gave her the strength to plow through the heavy brush in the forest, while using her normally weakened and hoarse voice to bellow Tommy's name.

The group continued their methodical march through the forest, calling out Tommy's name, then listening carefully for a reply. There was never a reply, not a sound except for the eerie call of the crows, observing the intruders from the branches of the surrounding tall trees. Finally, they came to the end of the preserve which was bordered on the west side by a dirt road. The group moved their line down about a hundred yards to the north then start back towards the ranch house going east. As they walked down the dirt road Charlie leaned over and reached into a nearby brush and pulled out a BB rifle. He handed the gun to Tony and asked if this was Tommy's gun. Tony did not hesitate to answer, "I'm afraid it is." "Why do you say that?" asked Pastor Ron. Tony explained, "Tommy loved that gun, it was his prize possession. I can't imagine him leaving it anywhere, on purpose. Charley noted fresh car tracks on the dirt road and mused over what that could mean, but he decided not to cause Tony any more concern than he already was experiencing, so he kept that observation to himself. The group continued with their plan of staying spread out as they walked back through the forest in an easterly direction. By the time they reached the ranch house it was getting to be dusk, and the temperature was dropping. Tony went to the barn to see if Tommy had returned there. Upon returning from the barn, he was pale and had a look of near panic on his face. Tully noticed the wide-eyed expression on his son's face and asked, "Tony, what's wrong?"

THE CROWNING: CULMINATION OF THE NATION

"They're all gone! The animals, the horses, pigs, chickens, all of them are gone," Tony announced in a monotone voice that came from shock. Stunned, everyone in the search party stood in silence trying to process what had happened. Finally Tully stressed emphatically, "We need to continue our search for Tommy. How many flashlights do we have? I have one in my trunk. I'll go get it." Not waiting for a response from the others, Tully walked out to his car and opened his trunk. Suddenly, he heard a vehicle on the road in front of Tony's home and Tully turned to look in that direction. A dark-colored van, with dark-tinted windows, stopped on the road in front of Tony's home, sat motionless for a moment, then it took off with its wheels squealing sharply from spinning tires sending black smoke behind the van. As the van vanished, and the smoke dissipated, a silhouette of a young boy stood motionless on the road from where the van had stopped. Tully ran toward the boy who stood there with a gray hood over his head. Tully knew almost immediately, this must be Tommy! He screamed at the top of his lungs, "Tommy! Tommy! I am coming! Tully reached the frozen scared boy and pulled off the hood. It was indeed his grandson, crying from fear, but very much alive and physically unharmed. They hugged like never before, the hug of a life saved, the hug of fear, overcome. Tully opened the front door and walked in with Tommy holding his hand. Tony and the team of friends stood there in disbelief for a few long seconds. Tony exclaimed, "Tommy! Oh my God, thank the Lord!" Tony rushed to his son and picked him off the ground. Being in his daddy's arms once again brought such relief from the trepidation that Tommy could not talk but just sobbed and squeezed his daddy's neck with all the might an eleven-year-old could muster. Tony started crying as well, tears of joy and the release of all his angst.

After hearing what had happened to Tully and Catherine, the last time they went home from here, the group all decided it would be prudent to spend the night at Tony's house and wait until morning to head back to their respective homes. While discussing the events of this portentous day, the group concluded Tommy had been lured away from the home and kidnapped in order to cause Tony to leave his homestead unprotected while searching for his son. They all agreed with the motive for this plot was to steal the animals he had in his barn. Tully theorized they must have rolled in with trucks and trailers, during the rescue party's search in the woods for Tommy, to load all the animals up and take them away, probably to be used for food. "These were not homeless people, this was done by people with trucks and trailers," Tully surmised. Tony agreed, and vowed to file the police report the next day, for whatever good that would do. That night, the group turned on Tony's computer to watch the night segment of The Truth. Charlie, who was a die-hard Trump follower, was skeptical of the entire story being told on Truth, while Pastor Ron was simply unaware of its existence, but all politely listened to the broadcast in absolute silence. For years now, Tully and Charlie vigorously debated every political event concerning Trump's presidency and the 2021 insurrection, yet, miraculously, their friendship remained untarnished by the discourse.

Bryce Waldron began the show with his usual opening remarks saying, "Good evening, this is Friday, February 15th. My name is Bryce Waldron, and I will be your host tonight. Welcome back to the Truth. I want to let you know upfront that tonight's segment will be my last, at least for now. We believe it is unsafe for me to continue broadcasting from this location, so by the time you are watching this broadcast, I am already "on the lam" as they say. We have pre-recorded this broadcast, thus this is the first of these that is not aired live, and we apologize for that but we determined we needed to "get out of dodge". When the authorities arrive at this location, I will be far away. Joining us tonight via Skype, is a historian, in her own right. She is a Rhodes Scholar who has authored many books regarding the contemporary history of the powerful conglomerates of the oil industry and also political corruption in American history. She is the authority on the topic we are addressing tonight. We would like you to welcome our guest scholar, Regina Mangione.

Regina Mangione exclaimed, "What a wonderful, and I am sure, over-flattering introduction, Bryce. Thank you for that. I want you to know I have been following this endeavor since you began and am so very honored to be a part of the salvation of the Truth." Bryce Waldron declared, "Let me get right to the topic for tonight. You are here tonight because you have been at the forefront of the research into the facts about the scheme to send into the National Archive, and all the other required recipients, documents purporting to represent duly elected electors from states that narrowly were won by Joe Biden. This is one more prong of actions in the plan to carry out

THE CROWNING: CULMINATION OF THE NATION

the coup to disrupt the peaceful transfer of power in 2021. Please tell us all about that effort to misrepresent those states to the Electoral College.

Regina Mangione reported, "I hope I can fully capture the magnitude and boldness of this diabolical plan, Bryce. I will do my best. In November 2020, a lawyer for the Trump campaign in Wisconsin received a memo setting out the rationale behind an outrageous plan to overturn the results of an election by putting in place alternate electors and slates. Two memos, one on November 18 and another three weeks later, share the distinction of being among the earliest known proposals for preparing alternate electors. Those memos contributed to Trump's adoption of a crucial strategy with profound consequences for him and the nation. Despite losing the election, Trump and his friends are trying to keep him in power by falsifying the outcome. All along, part of the plan was to send fake electors to Congress in at least seven states that Biden won which were pro-Trump Republicans. They created and signed fake certificates, identifying themselves as the real true presidential electors in their respective states. These certificates were created and sent to five states by Republicans, but the submitted certificates contained slightly distinct language in two additional states. In those two states, they re-worded the template, so that they claimed they were just a backup in case Trump overturned the election. Five of the state's certificates just claimed to be the real electors when they actually weren't.

A massive, coordinated effort had been conducted across several states. To use the fake electors instead of the real electors to overturn Biden's election, the Trump campaign coordinated the effort to get these fraudulent slates of electors in front of Vice President Pence on January 6th. Rudy Giuliani coordinated a strategy to approach Republican legislators in certain states that former President Trump had lost and urge them to reclaim their authority by submitting an alternate slate of electors that would support former President Trump by directly appointing electors who would vote for Trump.

Pennsylvania State Senator Doug Mastriano, who later secured the Republican nomination for Governor in Pennsylvania, told Steve Bannon, while on air, all about his plan to introduce a resolution in the state legislature that would allow them to seat a phony slate of Trump electors by introducing a "Resolution, going to say, we're going to take our power back. We're going to seat the electors. Now we got it. We're going to need the support of the leadership of the House and Senate. We're getting there on that, but we need to act like... Steve Bannon interrupted to clarify saying, "You're saying you're going to get a joint resolution to actually go forward. And the Republicans control the House and Senate to go forward to, to basically take the power back from the secretary of state and put it in the state legislature to put forward the electors." Manstriano replied, "That is exactly what we're going to do". Mangione continued her description of events, "Kelly Ward, chairperson of the Arizona Republican Party, was another prominent player. The plotting started with Donald Trump just a few days after the election as the votes were being tallied. Ward texted the chairperson of the Maricopa County Board of Supervisors on November 7th, "We need you to stop the counting". Kelly Ward also perpetuated false allegations of election fraud. She also sent fundraising messages about the "stolen election." Kelly Ward also acted as an elector to meet with Congress and eventually transmit alternate Electoral College votes to Congress. This made her one of the fake electors as well. She admitted signing the phony document that was sent to Congress and the national archives in a public statement when she said (Regina Mangione pauses momentarily, then plays a recording of Kelly Ward speaking publicly on December 15th as the transcript of the words appears on the screen) "December 14th, the true electors for the presidency met yesterday. Yes, the Republican electors, we gathered together. We took a vote for President Trump and for Mike Pence for president and vice president. We have transmitted those results to the proper entities in Washington, DC for consideration by Congress. We believe we are the electors for the legally cast votes here in Arizona."

Regina Mangione, resuming her description of the plot explains, "Fake documents were actually created by them to appear as certifications of their status as electors. This was filmed and posted online on Twitter by none other than the Arizona Republican Party. The voice you will hear is that of the chair of the Arizona Republican party, Kelly Ward, who is reading the certificate language to the other ten Republicans, all of whom, including Kelly Ward herself, signed the document": Kelly Ward speaks on the video: "We, the undersigned, being the duly elected and qualified electors for the President and Vice President of the United States of America, from the state

THE CROWNING: CULMINATION OF THE NATION

of Arizona, hereby certify the following; for President, Donald J. Trump of the state of Florida, number of votes 11; for vice president, Michael R. Pence from the state of Indiana, number of votes," 11

Mangione clarifies explaining, "The certificates all have the same format, the same font, the same spacing, and almost the same wording. At least seven states submitted these documents with fake electors for Trump after this effort became public about a year later when the National Archives released the thousands of boxes of White House documents to the House Committee. Five of the seven were all identical and purported to be the real electors, while two, including Pennsylvania, were unique in content and were offered with verbiage showing that in the event a court ruled in favor of changing the outcome of the election for their state, giving the election to Trump, they would, in that case, be the electors to cast their vote for Trump. Michigan's Secretary of State, Jocelyn Benson reported about the attempt in their state that "nothing happened in isolation. Everything was connected from the moment our unofficial results were released 24 hours after the polls closed. And then subsequently almost every day after that there were attempts to harm the full certification of the results and interfere with that certification at the local level and at the state level. And, and then, when we met at the Capitol, the state Capitol on December 14th, we had individuals actually show up outside claiming that they should be let in because they were the actual electors. So, all of these things are happening at the same time."[19]

Mangione played another video clip of Boris Epstein, a lawyer for the Trump campaign regarding this plan. "Yes. I was part of the process to make sure there were alternate electors for when, as we hope the challenges to the seated electors would be heard and will be successful." Regina Mangione expands the storytelling to the audience, "In order to avoid testifying to the January 6th investigation, one of the Trump officials invoked his Fifth Amendment right against self-incrimination. This Justice Department official is Jeffrey Clark, a former judge and a former official of the George W. Bush Justice Department. After working for the George W. Bush administration, he returned to the Justice Department in 2018. His first day as head of the Civil Division of the DOJ was September 2020. In December, after Attorney General Bill Barr's departure, Jeffrey Rosen and his deputy, Richard Donahue, were pushing back on Trump's attempts to use the Justice Department to undermine the election. They were unaware that Mr. Jeffrey Clark had been introduced to President Trump by a Pennsylvania politician. Clark had told the President he agreed that fraud had affected the election results. Clark met privately with Trump, then he drafted a document. It was a letter intended for Georgia's Governor, Brian Kemp, the Speaker of the House, and the President Pro Tem of the Senate in Georgia. It was drafted for Rosen and Donahue to sign as the top two authorities in the Department of Justice. The letter said in part, "The Department of Justice is investigating various irregularities in the 2020 election for President of the United States. At this time, we have identified significant concerns that may have affected the outcome of the election in multiple states, including the state of Georgia. While the Department of Justice believes the Governor of Georgia should immediately call a special session to consider this important and urgent matter. If he declined to do so, we share with you our view that the Georgia General Assembly has implied authority under the Constitution of the United States to call itself into special session for the limited purpose of considering issues pertaining to the appointment of presidential electors."

That draft letter was dated December 28th. Donald Trump and Jeff Clark want Acting Attorney General Rosen and his deputy to publicly declare that the election in Georgia was contaminated by fraud and that the Georgia General Assembly had the right to send its own electors to Washington using the power given to them by the U.S. Constitution. According to Deputy Attorney General Richard Donahue's contemporaneous notes, Trump was already pressing Acting Attorney General Rosen and Donahue, telling them to just state that the election was corrupt for the rest to be handled by me and the Republican Congressman.

In order to bypass Jeffrey Rosen and his deputy, Richard Donahue, as well as the rest of the Justice Department, Trump tried to appoint Jeff Clark as Attorney General so Jeff Clark could sign that letter himself, and send it. In a private meeting with Trump, Clark tells Mr. Rosen, the Acting Attorney General, that Trump plans to replace Rosen with Clark. Clark will most likely try to stop Congress from certifying the electoral college results. Clark apparently persuaded Trump to appoint him the Attorney General so that he could sign that letter, which likely would have precipitated a constitutional crisis. Imagine, the U.S. Justice Department formally notifies the states with the signature of the US Attorney General they shouldn't send in their electors because your state is experiencing genuine issues with voting. In fact, if that letter had been sent, it would have been as radical as General Flynn's other idea to use the Insurrection Act to send out the National Guard and seize the voting machines to force a rerun. Such a drastic move by the Justice Department would have been draconian." Mangione stated, "In Georgia, and several other states, the Justice Department believed that both a slate of electors supporting Biden, and a separate slate of electors supporting Trump, cast a ballot on December 14th, and both sets of ballots were sent to Washington DC to be opened by Vice President Pence. Besides proclaiming that these were the duly elected electors from those states, several people who would have been Trump electors from those states, if Trump won, were replaced with other Republicans who were willing and signed these documents. Nearly every state that did this swapped Trump electors with these other Republicans before sending in the forged documents."

Bryce Waldron declares to the audience, "This is the perfect time to bring in another guest to help us understand the gravity of those events to our democracy. He is U.S. Representative Jamie Raskin. Congressman Raskin was a constitutional law professor at American University Washington College of Law for over 25 years before becoming the U.S. representative[1] for Maryland's 8th congressional district. As a congressional representative, Jamie Raskin served as the lead impeachment manager for the second impeachment of President Donald Trump and later as a member of the January 6 committee in 2021-2022. Congressman Raskin, as an expert of constitutional law and someone literally on the front lines, please help the audience understand the extent of President Trump's involvement in inciting the insurrection."

Jamie Raskin gets right to the core issue and said, "Well, all of it flows out of the 'Big Lie'. Of course, if you start with the premise that Donald Trump won, then of course, you're going to need to go out and certify these fraudulent electors. And we should note that a lot of Republicans refused to participate in it, and refused to participate in essentially a fraud on the

1. https://en.wikipedia.org/wiki/United_States_House_of_Representatives

public. If it's a crime for people to go into the ballot box and impersonate a voter for one vote, what do you call it when people come forward and say their electors represent the whole will of the state? And they know that that is fraudulent. Trump wasn't just inciting an insurrection; he was working to organize a coup against democracy." Bryce Waldron presses Congressman Raskin, asking him, "Many in our audience may not have the same understanding of that word, coup as you may have. Can you explain why you call this a "coup against democracy? Jamie Raskin explains, "Yes, absolutely. This would definitely have been the first American coup, specifically, it would have been what political scientists call a "self-coup"., whereas a sitting executive in power overthrows the electoral process and constitutional order to prolong and continue his reign. Trump had orchestrated the violent dimension of the January 6th assault on the government, partly to show his rabid popular support to Mike Pence, Mitch McConnell, and others who were appalled by his plan and who stood in his way. He wanted to scare them both politically and physically. But of course, there were a lot of Republicans who supported either explicitly or implicitly the inside strategy related to the electoral college and the contingent election."

Bryce Waldron concludes the evening broadcast by saying, "Thank you Congressman Raskin and Regina Mangione for those fascinating disclosures of the lengths people went to bring about the overturning of the election of 2020. We will continue with this chapter in our recent history, tomorrow night and Regina Mangione will continue to be our expert guide for Part 2 of the events leading up to Jan. 6th, 2020. Remember, both segments were pre-recorded as we are moving our operations to new and undisclosed locations. Thank you all for faithfully recording each of these segments. With millions of copies of this historical documentary in circulation, the Truth will be impossible to be purged from the historical record. — Napoleon Bonaparte once declared, "History is the version of past events that people have decided to agree upon." We must all commit to preserving our history as it actually happened, not how some wish to reshape and rebrand it. A quote by Wanyanwu says, "History will only remember those that remembered it and the best way to make history is to read history."

It is time now to say farewell for tonight. Please return here every night at 6:00 pm, for our next segment of Truth."

THE CROWNING: CULMINATION OF THE NATION

Having had no sleep for the last 48 hours, and exhausted from the events of the day, Tully crashed on Tony's couch, with his friend, Charlie Stretch trying to sleep on an air mattress, on the floor. "Could you believe that garbage?" asked Charlie, always a denier of any wrongdoing by Trump and his cohorts. Tully smiled, he expected nothing else from Charlie, and said, "Charlie, I can't believe we actually elected that garbage." With a disgusted snort, Charlie rolled over and said no more. Tully, feeling a sense of peace, slept through the night, the first full night's sleep in over a month, a badly needed respite, in this time of national chaos and turmoil. However at peace Tully was that night, he will soon learn that danger exists in many forms.

Chapter 14
You Are Not Replaceable
Riverview Florida
February 16th

The next morning, Tully, his back stiff from sleeping on Tony's couch, was woken by the sound of an incoming text. He groped around looking for his reading glasses, then finding them discovered the text was from Grace. It read, "Great news Grandpa, today Dad is actually coming home from the hospital! He is being released this afternoon. Grady and I will bring him home. The hospital is overwhelmed right now with patients so they are letting him go home earlier than usual." Tully's heart began pounding from the news. He joyously replied, "That is awesome news, Grace!" Then Tully warned, "Please be careful driving there and back. Try to get home before dark." "We will," Grace acceded, "I will let you know when he is home safe and sound. He will be in a wheelchair for a while and using oxygen tanks to support his breathing until he gets stronger." Tully, still very concerned, asked, "What about your Mom? "She's not being released yet. She is still on the ventilator and her condition has not improved, Grace reported. Tully's last text to Grace read, "We will pray for her, Grace, and for your Dad. Thanks for the news." After what happened to Catherine and Tully, in Florida, Tully worried about Grace and Grady traveling to the hospital, and then home with her Dad still very weak. Compounding that fear is the lack of progress by Suzanne. He knew that the longer she stays on that ventilator, the worse the prognosis for survival. Tully thought about how he will have his hands full taking care of Catherine. Dr. Rebecca, who is caring for Catherine in Tully's absence, reported to Tully that although Catherine can't get out of bed yet, and her cough is deep and painful, she is slowly improving. Catherine also got a good night's sleep and was actually hungry for breakfast. Tully was grateful that she was in excellent hands, yet

THE CROWNING: CULMINATION OF THE NATION

he felt an urgent need to get back home quickly, so he dressed, had a cup of coffee, and left 'Tony' and Marie's home as early as he could. The ride home was thankfully uneventful, unlike the last time he made this same trip. "What a nightmare that was," he thought to himself. He could not get his mind off of James and Suzanne, who were fighting for their very lives. The constant worry about them was a dark cloud hanging over Tully's head, and his gut told him they were still in grave danger from the virus.

With the help of the attending nurse, James got dressed in his gray slacks and white button-down shirt at the Oasis, the hospital in Phoenix where James and Suzanne were being treated. James was tired but mostly excited to be going home. Grace and Grady arrived right on time to pick up their dad who was waiting in a wheelchair. Grace and Grady were very careful to get their dad into the car without a mishap, noting that James clearly struggled from a complete lack of strength and stamina. He relied heavily on the oxygen tank during the stress-filled trek back home. James told them, in short phrases between breaths, how glad he was to see them, how much he missed all of his kids, and how deeply worried he was for Suzanne. He did not mention to them, however, his greatest fear, that he would never again see his wife of 27 years, alive because he did not want them to worry more than they already are now. When they pulled into their driveway, they all instantly knew something terrible had happened! The garage door was pried open and James's prize possession, his Porsche was gone. When Grace and Grady got out they discovered that some of their belongings kept in their garage were also stolen. Grace stayed with James while Grady ran into the house to check on Chase and the girls. After a few minutes, Grady and the girls came out to the driveway, but Chase was not with them. Grady looked pale as he reported, "Chase took his truck and went after the thieves!" James suddenly saw the girls, Pam and Suzie, crying simultaneously out of both fear for Chase and joy for their dad that he was back home after being hospitalized for a whole month. They both ran to their Dad and hugged him while sobbing uncontrollably. The tears he witnessed, from his two youngest daughters, brought on his own tear-saturated eyes, and together they wept and hugged. James kissed both of their foreheads with a father's most profound love. He then turned to Grady and ordered, "Get your truck (long breathless pause), we need to go after Chase." "You can't go anywhere,

James," Grady insisted, "I will go alone". James learned Chase had driven to the location of his Dad's car by using a tracker app James had installed on Chase's cell phone to track the car's location and the route the car used to get to that location. Grady only needed to log into the same app, then follow the same route to find where the car was taken and hopefully find Chase nearby. Chase's journey had led him through the worst neighborhoods of Phoenix, all places neither Chase nor Grady, had ever ventured before as these places were the "barrios" of the poorest and most crime-ridden neighborhoods in Phoenix. The buildings appeared to be destroyed by fire and were clearly the remnants of extensive recent looting. No buildings appeared to be occupied, yet the streets were filled with people sitting on the curbs and the steps of abandoned buildings. Chase had parked a block away from a warehouse that his app showed his Dad's Porsche was parked inside when his cell phone rang with "Grace " appearing on the screen. "Hi Grace," Chace said in a very muted voice. Before saying anything to her brother, Grace turned to speak to her Dad and to her family, back in the driveway at their home, "I just called Chase's phone and he answered it! I'll put it on speakerphone." James said to Chase, "What are you doing, son?" Chase defensively tried to explain to his father, "They stole your Porsche Dad, and they tried to break into the house. I shot through the door with your gun and that scared them away, but I had to get your car back. I am tracking the car with the app on my cell phone. I know where they are, Dad and the police can't, or won't help." James was too weak to raise his voice in anger, so he tried to summon all the forcefulness he could saying, "No Chase. I don't give a damn about that car! It is you I care about. You must leave them and come home immediately. We need you here." Chase, feeling the adrenaline from the dangerous situation, replied, "But Dad, I am close. They are inside a building just a block away from me." James drew from all the remaining energy he had to demand, "No Chase. I order you to come home. The car is insured, you are not replaceable. We need you here." Grady, who had not yet left the home, interjected saying, "Do what your Dad says, Chase. Come home." Chase realized he was outnumbered, and he would never disobey an order from his father, even if it meant saving his father's favorite car, conceding, "Ok, I will be home in about 30 minutes."

THE CROWNING: CULMINATION OF THE NATION

Chase hung up and reluctantly turned his truck around and headed for their home. When he arrived, James was already in his bed, breathing with the help of the oxygen tank. When Chase walked into his room, with the three daughters surrounding his bed, James whipped off the oxygen mask and gave Chase a big smile. They hugged for at least two minutes, tears flowing down both of their cheeks. Grady, standing in the back of the room, was worried that the thieves would be back, but this moment was not the time to bring that up. This was time for a long-awaited reunion. James was home, and the girls, Chase, and Grady were safe, everyone except for Suzanne. Suzanne's pulse was getting weaker, and she was losing her will to live. They had given her every form of medication they had to fight off the virus, but her body was losing the battle. Her doctors felt it was just a matter of time and debated moving her to Hospice. That decision would be made in consultation with her family, on another day, perhaps tomorrow.

Back in Tampa, it was mid-morning when Tully had himself returned to his home, he profusely thanked "Dr. Becky" and her friend/nurse, Joy, for their incredible sacrifice in unselfishly taking care of Catherine during Tully's quest to help Tony and his crew to find Tommy. Dr. Becky and Nurse Joy both had children of their own to get back home to, so they quickly left in order to be home before dark, and all that night-time in the city brings out. That evening, with Catherine sleeping quietly, Tully turned on his computer and navigated back to the dark web to hear the "Truth" once again. As was his habit now, he dutifully started the recording app to capture the program and save it for the historical record. Right on cue the word, Truth, appeared on the screen, followed by the familiar voice of Bryce Waldron, saying, "Good evening, this is Sunday, Feb. 16, 2025, and I am your host tonight, Bryce Waldron, bringing you the next edition of the Truth. As you may recall, we pre-recorded the last segment, as well as tonight's segment, so consider this a continuation of the history of the days just prior to the Jan. 6th Insurrection and Coup. We have with us Regina Mangioni, who told us about the attempt to introduce a second set of electors in order to persuade Vice President Mike Pence to overthrow the election results. Regina, last night you introduced us to one of the main characters in the coup attempt, Jeffrey Clark, who you told us conspired with President Trump to have himself installed as the Attorney General of the

Department of Justice, replacing Acting Attorney General Jeffrey Rosen and his deputy, Richard Donahue. I know he was just one of the cast of characters scheming with President Trump to disrupt the Transfer of Power, for what would have been the first time in history. Tonight, Regina, you are tasked with telling about the other planners involved in actively working to prevent Congress from certifying the electoral college votes by the states. Let's start where we left off, with Jeffrey Clark. What stopped him from fulfilling his and President Trump's plan? Regina Mangione replied, "Thank you, Bryce. The short answer is that the pushback against this plot was massive. Jeffrey Rosen and Richard Donahue both threatened to resign, rather than quietly step aside, and there could be a mass resignation in the rest of the Department of Justice personnel if this plan came to fruition. In addition, the White House Attorney, Pat Ciplione, also made it clear he would resign as well. Trump knew that this would be worse than the "Saturday Night Massacre" that helped to sink Richard Nixon's presidential ship. As much as he wanted to elevate Jeffrey Clark to the top position in the Department of Justice, allowing Clark to send his letter to the state legislators, he calculated the fallout from this political nuclear bomb was too much for him to bear. Trump stood down, for now, but he would not relent in his pursuit of maintaining the power of the presidency. To answer your broader question, let me walk you through the other key participants in the desperate last-minute effort to change the outcome of that election. The first one I want to discuss is a man no one knew very well prior to this time, John Eastman. John C. Eastman was the founding Director of the Center for Constitutional Jurisprudence, a public interest law firm affiliated with the conservative think tank Claremont Institute.[20] He was also a former professor and dean at the Chapman University School of Law and was a former law clerk to Supreme Court Justice Clarence Thomas.[20] During December 2020, Eastman represented President Donald Trump by filing an intervention motion in Texas v. Pennsylvania, which was filed directly with the high court by Texas Attorney General Ken Paxton, in which the state of Texas sought to nullify the voting processes and, as a result, at least four other states' electoral college results. Eastman's brief included an array of unfounded claims and asserted "It is not necessary for Trump to prove that

THE CROWNING: CULMINATION OF THE NATION

fraud occurred," and asserted it was enough to show that elections "materially deviated" from the intent of state lawmakers, adding, "By failing to follow the rule of law, these officials put our nation's belief in "elected self-government" at risk."[20] Two days later, the Supreme Court declined to hear the case, finding that Texas did not have standing. It did not address the merits of Texas's claims.[20]

In late December 2020, Trump and some of his supporters, such as former National Security Adviser Michael Flynn, promoted the idea of the "Pence Card", a legal theory by which then-Vice President Mike Pence had unilateral authority to reject electoral votes from states deemed to be fraudulent.[22] The theory originated with a two-page proposal tweeted to Trump by Flynn associate Ivan Raiklin on December 22. Under the theory, Pence was entitled to declare that state certificates from contested states hadn't been received and that he is authorized to receive new certificates.[22] Trump retweeted Raiklin's post urging invocation of the "Pence Card" on December 23, the day specified in statute, but Pence did not respond[22]

On December 24, 2020, the Trump administration called John Eastman asking him to write a memo "asserting the vice president's power to hold up the certification" of the presidential election.[20] Eastman circulated a two-page outline and memo to the Trump legal team several days later, followed by a more extensive memo later.[21] Eastman called the vice president "the ultimate arbiter" of the election in his two-page memo.[20]

In Eastman's memo, he explained his plan to prevent Joe Biden's election as president by claiming that there were disputed electors. He hoped that Mike Pence would say, ' There is a dispute about whether these seven states have legitimate electors. Therefore, they are being returned to the States. The electors on these alternate certificates obviously were not legitimate, but this was at the core of Eastman's strategy.

While being subjected to criticism, Eastman asserted in October 2021 that the memos were not his beliefs but he had written them at the request of "somebody in the legal team". He also pronounced that a scenario in which Pence would reject ballots was "foolish" and "crazy," further claiming he had told Pence during their Oval Office meeting that his proposal was an "open question" and "the weaker argument."[20] In a video taken secretly and made public that same month, Eastman suggested he believed that Pence's actions served Washington politics. Someone posing as a Trump supporter asked "Why do you think Mike Pence didn't do it?" Eastman responded that "Mike Pence is an establishment guy" who fears that Trump is "destroying the inside-the-Beltway Republican Party."[20]

On January 2, 2021, Eastman joined Trump, the President's personal attorney Rudy Giuliani, and others in a conference call with 300 Republican legislators from Arizona, Michigan, Pennsylvania, and Wisconsin to brief them on allegations of voter fraud, with the aim of the legislators attempting to decertify their states' election results.[20] That same day, together with Giuliani and Boris Epshteyn, Eastman appeared on Steve Bannon's podcast and promoted the idea that state lawmakers needed to reconsider the election results.[20] On January 5, 2021, Eastman met with Vice President Mike Pence in the Oval Office to argue that the vice president has the constitutional authority to alter or otherwise change electoral votes.[20] According to Eastman, he told the Vice President that he might have the authority to reject electoral college votes, and he asked the Vice President to delay the certification.[20] Pence rejected Eastman's argument and instead agreed with his counsel, Greg Jacob, and conservative legal scholars and other Pence advisors, such as former Vice President, Dan Quayle. Trump, however, insisted that Pence had the authority to accept or reject electoral states, and continued to request him to reject electoral votes from states with alleged fraud; however, on January 5, Pence informed Trump he did not believe he had any such authority.[22]

Trump said to Pence, "If these people said you had the power to overturn the election wouldn't you want to?" Pence responded curtly, "I wouldn't want one person to have that authority." Trump persisted, "But wouldn't it be almost cool to have that power?" "No, I've done everything I could, and then some, to find a way around this. It simply is not possible," Pence asserted uncharacteristically sternly. Trump exclaimed with increasing volume and agitation, "No! No! No! You don't understand, Mike. You can do this. I don't want to be your friend anymore if you don't do this. Do you want to go down in history as a patriot, or a pussy?"

That evening, Trump called over to Giuliani and then to Bannon, who were both at the Willard Hotel. Trump told Bannon that Pence had been "very arrogant" when the two discussed the matter earlier in the day."[17] Bryce Waldron pivoted the discussion by saying, "Let's dwell a little deeper on Steve Bannon for a moment regarding his role in the events leading up to the insurrection. You may recall, Regina, in yesterday's segment of this broadcast Jamie Raskin referred to the "three rings" of the coup. Specifically, he said, "The innermost central ring was what I called the "ring of the coup" in my mind; here is the bull's-eye center of the action." Was Steve Bannon, a private citizen, formerly one of Trump's advisors, in the inner circle he calls the "ring of the coup"?

Regina Mangione contended, "By my calculus of the construction of the apparatus that planned and conducted the attempted coup, I agree with what Congressman Raskin described yesterday, but I would add one important ring to his description. I would divide the "inner circle" ring into two distinct rings that are interacting with each other closely, but holding two distinctly different roles. The first ring, the exterior ring of the "ring of the coup" comprised those who are part of the communication team. They are the primary conduit to the outer two rings. They developed a powerful and very effective social media and podcast machine that worked to build their following and direct their audience to carry out their bidding. This was how they were whipped up into a frenzy, both before the election, and leading up to the Jan. 6th insurrection, the thousands of people that descended upon the capital on Jan. 5th and 6th. Let me walk you through the major players within this ring and what they did to affect the desired outcome, which was incredibly successful from their point of view. I would have to begin with the man I believe was the mastermind of this strategy, a man that has implemented the same, or similar campaigns in past elections, Roger Stone, while Bannon was one of the most prominent members of this team, carrying out Stone's scheme. Roger Stone, a long-time Trump associate, and confidant, deployed "Stop the Steal" during the 2016 presidential election. Stone's campaign was organized "first to defend Trump's Republican primary nomination, then to contest a Hillary Clinton win that never materialized."[28] Stone revived the phrase in 2020, intensifying their efforts to pressure state and federal officials to reverse the results of the election. Several prominent Republican leaders aligned with Trump, and embraced and promoted the movement, as they had before. The movement became responsive whenever Trump seized and promoted the "Stop the Steal" campaign."[28]

In his podcast, "War Room" Bannon claimed that then-Vice President Mike Pence had "many alternatives" to certifying the Electoral College results on January 6. He mentioned Giuliani and Eastman in his January 2nd show, saying that Giuliani was trying to prevent the election's certification in the Senate.26"We're hurtling towards a constitutional crisis.... (that) is going to be complicated and it's going to be nasty," he said. Bannon also predicted that Trump's "first term is ending with action, and his second term is going to start with a bang."26

Then, on January 5, Bannon had a lot to say about what he thought would happen the following day. Bannon told listeners, "It's not going to happen like you think it's going to happen, OK. It's going to be quite extraordinarily different. And all I can say is: Strap in, the 'War Room' posse. You have made this happen, and tomorrow, it's game day." Bannon predicted that a constitutional crisis was "about to go up, I think, five orders of magnitude tomorrow" and said, "We're going to go through a couple of three very turbulent 24-hour periods."26 In a tweet, just hours before 1:00 AM on January 6th, the day of the insurrection, "If Vice President @Mike_Pence comes through for us, we will win the Presidency," he claimed. "Many States want to decertify the mistake they made in certifying incorrect & even fraudulent numbers in a process NOT approved by their State Legislatures (which it must be). Mike can send it back!"

Regina Mangione paused her description of the events in order to catch a breath, hoping the host would jump in to give her a break, but to no avail, so she proceeded with her reporting, "On January 6, Eastman, formerly functioning as the White House expert on the Constitution, spoke alongside Giuliani at the "Save America" rally that preceded the 2021 storming of the United States Capitol and asserted without evidence that balloting machines contained "secret folders" that altered voting results.[23]

Here is the transcript of John Eastman's speech on January 6th, 2021 (the words began streaming across the computer screen with the voice of John Eastman speaking).

"...pending before the Supreme Court that identifies in chapter and verse, the number of times state election officials ignored or violated the state law in order to put Vice-President Biden over the finish line. We knew that there was a fraud, traditional fraud that occurred. We know dead people voted, but we now know because we caught it live last time and in real-time how the machines contributed to that fraud. And let me, as simply as I can explain it, you know, the old way was to have a bunch of ballots sitting in a box under the floor. And when you need more, you pull them out in the dark of the night. They put those ballots in a secret folder in the machines sitting there waiting until they know how many they need. And then the machine after the close of polls, we now know who's voted and we know who hasn't. And I can now, in that machine, match those unloaded ballots with an unvoted voter and put them together in the machine. And how do we know that happened last night? In real-time, you saw when it got to 99% of the vote total, and then it stopped, the percentage stopped, but the votes didn't stop. What happened? And you don't see this on Fox or any of those stations, but the data shows that the denominator, how many ballots remained to be counted. How else do you figure out the percentage you have? How many remain to be counted? That number started moving up? That means they were unloading the ballot from that secret folder, matching them, matching

THE CROWNING: CULMINATION OF THE NATION

them to the un-voted voter, and wallah; we have enough votes to barely get over the finish line. We saw it happen in real-time, last night. And it happened on November 3rd as well. And all we are demanding of Vice President Pence, is this afternoon, at one o'clock, he let the legislatures of the states look into this, so we get to the bottom of it, and the American people know whether we have control of the direction of our government or not.

We no longer live in a self-governing Republic, if we can't get the answer to this question. This is bigger than President Trump. It is the very essence of our Republican form of government and it has to be done. And anybody that is not willing to stand up to do it does not deserve to be in the office. It is that simple." Trump allies, led by Rudy Giuliani, had persuaded partisans in five swing states to submit signed certificates falsely claiming they were "duly elected and qualified" members of the Electoral College.

Vice President Pence knew that Trump's attempt to cling to power was about to fail, because he had to do what he believed was what the Constitution demanded. The problem was that the sitting president and allies had hyped up fake electors for weeks, so Pence had to deal with that as well. Relying on crackpot legal theories created by Trump's closest allies, especially John Eastman, Trump wanted Pence to introduce those illegitimate electors on Jan. 6 and use them to block Joe Biden's victory, throwing the election back to the states, or to the House.[34]

Vice President Pence was instrumental in drafting the specific language he used during the session of Congress on Jan. 6th disrupted by Trump's mob aiming to prevent the counting of the Elector from taking place. The new language Pence used simply articulated established laws and rules governing the counting of electors. Constitutional experts and policymakers have traditionally only recognized as legitimate those who are certified by state authorities - like governors and secretaries of state. In his remarks, Vice President Pence wanted to make that clear. Vice presidents normally begin the counting of electoral votes by indicating that votes will be counted "after ascertaining that the certificates are regular in form and authentic." Pence added one additional sentence to this explanation that the preceding vice presidents did not.[34]

Not only would each certificate he introduced to be "regular in form and authentic," he said but they would be the ones that "the parliamentarians have advised me is the only certificate of the vote from that state, and purports to be a return from the state, and that has annexed to it a certificate from an authority of that state purporting to appoint or ascertain electors."[34]

Mangione was speaking unabated with renewed confidence, so she proceeded with her account of the events, "Later, during the Capitol storming, when Pence was forced into hiding, Eastman exchanged emails with Greg Jacob, Pence's chief counsel. Jacob wrote to Eastman, " "I have run down every legal trail placed before me to its conclusion, and I respectfully conclude that as a legal framework, it is a results-oriented position that you would never support if attempted by the opposition, and essentially entirely made up. Thanks to your bullsh*t, we are now under siege." Eastman replied by blaming Pence and Jacob for refusing to block certification of Trump's loss in the election, writing, "The 'siege' is because YOU and your boss did not do what was necessary to allow this to be aired in a public way so that the American people can see for themselves what happened."

Jacob answers next by dropping a bomb: "The advice provided has, whether intended or not, functioned as a serpent in the ear of the President of the United States, the most powerful office in the entire world. And here we are."

With that, Bryce Waldron stated, "That concludes our segment today. We will be back again tomorrow night. Please return to us tomorrow and please stay safe."

Tully turned off the computer and settled into his chair to stand guard for the night. Catherine was sleeping soundly, with those machines the hospital set up to monitor her vital signs. He was, as yet, unaware of the events that took place in Phoenix, Arizona to James and his family. Sometimes temporary ignorance is a gift when our need to control the amount of stress in our lives is critical. This was one of those times for Tully, however, transitory.

In a computer-filled secure war room at Wright Patterson Air Force Base in Montgomery, Ohio, a landline phone rings, startling the only person in the room. "Captain Stone," the officer said answering the call on the phone that never rings. "How may I serve you?" "Captain Stone, I was told you would man the fort which is why I am calling you now." Michael stood to attention and said, "Yes Sir."

"Captain, can I call you, Michael?" "Of course, you can, Sir," Michael replied in a rigidly military style of speech. "Michael, you are going to need to learn to relax around me. We are going to be spending a lot of time together soon, and I would prefer you were less formal with me, so I can be myself around you. "Yes Sir," Michael replied. "Michael, come on man, from now on cut out the 'Sir' and just call me Joe." "Yes Sir, uh, I mean Joe," Michael replied, still nervous and formal. "Michael, you have been a rock through all of this chaos." "Sir, you are not replaceable." "Nonsense, Michael. No one is irreplaceable, not even me. What we are doing, we are doing to preserve our nation, our democracy." "I understand, Sir, and thank you for the compliment. I was fortunate to have been raised by wonderful parents who taught me how to be strong, like a stone. Pun intended." "I can't wait to meet them, Michael." "I can't wait to meet you, Sir. The plans are coming together, and Project Exodus is progressing on the timeline we established." "Good to know, Michael, that is why I called. Keep up the great work. We have to keep this completely top secret." "I understand Sir. The only person who knows on my end is my brother, Paul."

"Great, Michael. I will call you again as we get closer. If you run into any roadblocks, let me know. I still have some clout and can open doors that were slammed shut." "Yes, Sir!"

Chapter 15
Looks Like We're Under New Management
Tampa, Florida
February 17, 2025

It was an especially chilly morning on Monday, Feb. 17th when Tully was suddenly woken by Catherine calling for Tully from their upstairs bedroom. Tully, alarmed by the urgency in her voice, despite being a man in his seventies, leaped to his feet and rushed upstairs bounding like a spry teenager, skipping every other step as he climbed the stairs. Breathing hard because of the sprint up the stairs Tully opened the bedroom door, to find Catherine sitting up in her bed. She was soaking wet with a look of disgust on her face. "Take me to the bathroom, I need to take a shower." Catherine demanded.

Tully explained as sympathetically as possible, "The Doctor said you had to remain in your bed for a few days, honey." Catherine demanded impatiently "Take me to the bathroom, now!" Catherine's voice was strong, and her determination even stronger. Tully decided it was useless to argue with her. After unplugging everything Catherine was wired to, he carefully helped her to her feet, and they slowly, arm in arm, walked into the bathroom. No sooner did they get into the bathroom when Tully's cell phone rang. It was the hospital calling, and Tully knew they would not be happy. Tully explained to the hospital nurse on the line the urgency with which Catherine demanded to be taken to the bathroom. The nurse was not pleased and scolded Tully to call them before doing anything like that again. She instructed Tully to call back to let them guide Tully through setting up the monitors. Catherine's wounds seemed to heal nicely, and Tully changed out the bandages after she took a shower. He believed his wife was back, feisty and bullheaded as always. Safely back in her bed and finally re-wired to all the monitors Catherine dozed off. Tully used that moment to call Grace to check

THE CROWNING: CULMINATION OF THE NATION

up on her Dad. "Hi Grace, it is Grandpa. How is your Dad?" Grace was especially chipper when she said, "He is doing well and sitting up without the Oxygen mask on, so he can talk on the phone, I'll put it on speakerphone now." Tully said, "Hi James, how are you feeling? "I feel like crap, Dad, but a lot better than I felt while in the hospital," James replied before pausing to take a couple of breaths from his mask. "There, I was in sheer agony." Tully, trying to keep things positive said, "Thank God you made it through that ordeal. Now we need to get your wife back home too. How is Suzanne doing now?"

Grace responded to her dad saying, "We have a meeting set up for this afternoon so we can discuss that with the doctors caring for her. We'll let you know what they tell us. Grady, Chase, and I are going to meet with them, so Pam and Suzy will stay here with Dad. We will fill you in after the meeting," "Please do," Tully requested. James, sounding fatigued, said, "I need to rest now, Dad. Have Grace tell you about yesterday." Tully replied, "Ok James, get some rest. I will call you tomorrow."

In the conversation's course, Grace detailed everything that had happened to the car, including Chase's efforts to track it down and recover the stolen vehicle. When Tully heard the whole incident, he was shocked, then he expressed his gratitude that Chase listened to his dad and came home. "If he'd gone into that warehouse," Tully said, "he could have easily been killed." Her thoughts were the same, and she concurred with the likely outcome. "That could have been tragic," she replied. Tully's rest of the day was spent caring for Catherine. He fixed her dinner, and she slowly ate the entire meal. At 6:00 Tully turned on his computer and found his way back to the Truth website. Bryce Waldron, once again, stood before the camera. "Welcome back to the Truth. Tonight is part 3 of a three-segment documentary, led by our expert, Regina Mangione. We pre-recorded all three segments before we departed from this location, to find a new home to broadcast from. Tonight's broadcast is being aired on Monday, February 17, 2025. Welcome back, Regina. Also back with us tonight is Congressman Jamie Raskin. Regina, please talk about the days of Jan. 6th through the words of those that actually were there, experiencing this unprecedented event firsthand.

Regina Mangione, in her usual professional and scholarly demeanor, said, "Yes, and thank you for giving me this opportunity." Without waiting for a reply from Bryce, Regina plowed forward saying, "Ali Alexander and Amy Kremer, who was listed as the point of contact on the rally permit, organized the rally at the Ellipse to begin at 9:00 a.m. January 6, along with Dustin Stockton and Jennifer Lynn Lawrence. The latter two had planned for a second rally at the Supreme Court that same day. Between the two rallies, demonstrators would have to walk Constitution Avenue past the Capitol, although neither rally had a permit for a march.

While rally-goers ended up swarming the Capitol, the rally at the Supreme Court never took place. The question became, who planned and who promoted sending the mob to the Capitol instead, and for what purpose?" Jamie Raskin, who was also one of the expert guests on the show added, "It's important for us to understand exactly what the relationships were between the official rally organizers and the White House and the violent insurrectionists who launched the violence on that day."

Bryce Waldron informed the audience that, "Ali Alexander previously maintained that he had worked with GOP congressmen to plan the rally on Capitol Hill on January 6. The Republican Reps. Paul Gosar of Arizona, Mo Brooks of Alabama, and Andy Biggs of Arizona were all involved in the rally before the riot. Alexander stated as much in Periscope videos in December 2020." Mangione responded, "That's correct, and Mo Brooks was one of the first speakers at the rally held at the Ellipse that morning. His fiery language helped set the tone for what came next. Here is a clip of his speech that morning of Jan. 6th." Mo Brooks was standing on the stage near the White House speaking to the ever-growing crowd. In the speech, he said, "Today is the day American patriots start taking down names and kicking ass," the six-term Republican shouted to the assembled protesters. "Our ancestors sacrificed their blood, their sweat, their tears, their fortunes, and sometimes their lives... Are you willing to do the same?"

Mangione continued her narrative of that cold January morning explaining, "The day before the Jan. 6 rally, Mo Brooks tweeted Trump had "asked me personally to speak and tell the American people about the election system weaknesses that the Socialist Democrats exploited to steal this election." During the siege of the capitol Brooks tweeted "Tear gas dispersed in Capitol Rotunda," Brooks then wrote in a tweet posted from his iPad. "Congressmen ordered us to grab gas masks under chairs in case we have to leave in haste!"

The 'Bonnie and Clyde of MAGA World', Dustin Stockton, and Jennifer Lynn Lawrence worked toward the goal of preparing House members to object to the electoral certification on the House floor and to take part in diverse events scheduled to protest the election.[29] Both Stockton and Lawrence claimed they were among a group that had concerns about an event dubbed the "Wild Protest" organized by far-right activist Ali Alexander that was staged outside the building as the vote was being certified. According to Stockton and Lawrence, that wariness was because of Alexander's links to militant groups and the potential consequences of bringing people who were "angry" about the election to the Capitol steps as the certification was taking place.[29]

"The people and the history books deserve a real account of what happened," Stockton explains. The truth, according to Lawrence, is this: "Violent sh*t happened," she says. "We want to get to the bottom of that." Stockton and Lawrence earlier teamed up with Kremer to organize a rally in Washington on Nov. 14, 2020. That event featured a drive-by from Trump in the presidential motorcade. That night, there were clashes between Trump supporters and counter-protesters. A high turnout of pro-Trump supporters inspired Kremer to launch a nationwide "March for Trump" bus tour with Stockton and Lawrence. In addition, they say, they were encouraged to take part in protests challenging Trump's election loss hoping they might win Trump's help with the fallout from the 'We Build the Wall' debacle. In December 2020, as the tour rolled around the country, Stockton and Lawrence say they got a call from Rep. Paul Gosar (R-Ariz.) and his chief of staff, Thomas Van Flein. According to Stockton, Van Flein claimed he and the congressman had just met with Trump, who was considering giving them a "blanket pardon" to address the "We Build the Wall" investigation.[29]

The Jan. 6 Ellipse Rally would have been the culmination of the bus tour, featuring a speech from multiple members of Congress and Trump himself. According to Stockton and Lawrence, it was planned to support the objections to electoral certification that were taking place that day on the House floor. They expected Trump and other leaders to present definitive detailed proof of election fraud as the crowd remained on the Ellipse, where security procedures were in place.[29]

Rudy Giuliani spoke at the Ellipse and said: "Who hides evidence? Criminals, hide evidence, not honest people. So over the next 10 days, we get to see the machines that are crooked, the ballots that are fraudulent. And if we're wrong, we will be made fools of. But if we're right, a lot of them will go to jail. So Let's have a trial by combat!"

Trump spoke for well over an hour about stuffing the ballot box and the rigged vote along with his familiar complaints about the media overlooking his crowd size, the "radical left," and "cancel culture." "All of us here today, do not want to see our election victory stolen by emboldened radical left Democrats, which is what they're doing, and stolen by the fake news media. That's what they've done and what they're doing. We will never give up. We will never concede. It doesn't happen. You don't concede when there is theft involved. Our country has had enough. We will not take it anymore. And that's what this is all about. And to use a favorite term that all of you people really came up with. We will stop the steal. We demand that Congress do the right thing and only count the electors who have been lawfully slated, lawfully, slated. I know that everyone here will soon be marching over to the Capitol building to peacefully and patriotically make your voices heard. Today we will see whether Republicans stand strong, for the integrity of our elections, but whether or not they stand strong for our country. Our country, our country, has been under siege for a long time. Now it is up to Congress to confront this egregious assault on our democracy. And after this, we're going to walk down and I'll be there with you. We're going to walk down, we're going to walk down anyone you want. But I think right here, we're going to walk down to the Capitol and we're going to cheer on our brave senators and congressmen and women. And we're probably not going to be cheering so much for some of them because you'll never take back our country with

THE CROWNING: CULMINATION OF THE NATION

weakness. You have to show strength and you have to be strong." Then, in the final 120 words of his speech, Trump declared, "We're going to walk down Pennsylvania Avenue... and we're going to the Capitol."[29]

"Many in the crowd got on the move as Trump concluded, and the barricades at the Capitol complex were first breached shortly before his remarks wrapped up. Fighting at the building between police and the former president's supporters would rage for hours, turning deadly.[29] Bryce Waldron suggested, "Let's listen to those that were actually at the insurrection and can give us a first-hand account of what they experienced on Jan. 6th. 2021. Let's begin with our esteemed guest, Congressman Jamie Raskin. Congressman," Waldron continued, "let me share with the audience the heartbreaking backstory for you and for your family. Just one week earlier, your son, who I know you were very close to, had passed away unexpectedly, so members of your family, your daughter, Tabatha and her husband, Hank, had accompanied you to the Capital on January 6th, as you all were still in mourning. Jamie Raskin replied in a soft voice, "Thank you, Bryce, that is correct, his name is Thomas Raskin, and he was a remarkable young man and was attending Harvard Law School. We were all devastated. Still, I felt it was my duty to participate in this important event when the peaceful transfer of power is finalized by the counting of the votes in the Electoral College. Here is what I experienced firsthand:

"Just before 1:00 PM, I collect my papers to head over to the floor. Tabitha and Hank, we'll follow shortly when an officer comes for them. I glance out the window onto the west front before leaving the office. Tabitha and Hank look out too. On the usually deserted western steps of the Capitol, the place where four years ago, Trump introduced the ominous image, "American carnage", to the world, a surly mob of thousands is now assembling. Pressing forward and against the fencing, jacked up by Trump's apoplectic pep talk from a rally he held outside the White House. "If you don't fight like hell", he told them, "you're not going to have a country anymore", upfront by fierce-looking Proud Boys, Oath Keepers, Three Percenters, Q-anon brawlers, and other shock troops of the extreme right. The crowd, in a matter of minutes, we'll begin to taunt, push, shove, punch, gouge, scratch, spray, smash, and harass the US Capitol Police Force kicking off four hours of savage, medieval-style violence, that will result in deep physical breaches of the Capitol. The insurrectionists and rioters will leave at least five people dead with several more to come by the suicide of officers and more than 140 officers wounded and injured. Many of them are hospitalized with traumatic brain injuries, concussions, broken arms, broken legs, broken ribs, broken vertebrae, black eyes, broken noses, lost fingers, broken necks, broken jaws, and post-traumatic stress syndrome in every manner of emotional and psychological damage. Of this unfolding rampage, we members of Congress assembling inside the Capitol, still know nothing.

I think back to a Black Lives Matter protest in DC on June 2nd when masks and helmeted national guardsmen in camouflage massed on the steps of the Capitol in a formidable, awesome display of force. I've not yet seen the national guard today, but I tell myself that they must be here somewhere, or else they've got to be on the way over.

A memo from Vice President Pence is passed out. This is a "make or break moment". Will Pence assert lawless new powers to deny Biden the presidency, or will he act according to the Constitution? I get a hold of the memo and speed reading, it is strikingly good news. Despite lots of genuflecting to the disseminators of the big lie, he says he will not be exercising unilateral powers he does not have to reject states' presidential electors or return them to the state legislatures for further action. It is not within his constitutional power. This is big. I breathe easier now, as any such act would have been a most dangerous flash point for constitutional confusion and political danger. Kevin McCarthy and Donald Trump wanted to block acceptance of Biden's electoral college majority and get Trump named president immediately, by 26 state delegations in a contingent of electors. Pence has just done democracy a giant favor by not lying and betraying the Constitution, although I am sure the vast majority of the public has no idea how important his little memo is. I do see just across the central aisle from me, Representative Liz Cheney, scrutinizing the memo, just as I have been doing, and she too seems to relax a bit. Vice President Pence has presided over with Speaker Pelosi behind him. No one objects to Alabama or Alaska, but then when Arizona is called, a slew of House Republicans, led by Arizona's Paul Gosar joins Missouri's Senator Josh Hawley and Texas Senator Cruz in objecting to Arizona's electors. So now the joint session recesses and we move

THE CROWNING: CULMINATION OF THE NATION

to meet in our respective chambers to consider the merits of this objection with each side of the debate, limited to an hour.

I am struck by the sensation that I am missing, perhaps we are all missing, what is really happening in or more precisely all around this proceeding. None of us can quite express it, but I am definitely feeling it. Strategic violence by extremist elements outside the Capitol is fusing with manipulative tactics inside the Capitol to try to coerce Vice-President Pence and Congress to overthrow the electoral votes in the states and force us into a contingent election. This synchronized coordination of bloodthirsty violence with extra-constitutional strong-arm tactics produces the radically as familiar, but nonetheless unmistakable feeling of a coup. We usually think of a coup as something happening against the President, but this would be a coup by the President against the Vice President, and Congress. has been focused on a strict interpretation of the arcane electro account act and that quaint 12th Amendment myopic in my grief polishing my speeches to a fairly well acting as if this were some kind of court argument at the end of which they wouldn't have prizes out to the best of all advocates, these legal and constitutional instruments truly set the table for our present conflict.

But in this extraordinary crucible struggle, the battle itself could be decided just as well by the deployment of raw power and deadly violence. General Michael Flynn, and Trump's other militaristic aides, have been talking openly, over the last many days, about imposing martial law to make sure Trump, the "real winner", stays in office for weeks and publicly urging Trump to deploy the military against hostile institutions and to rerun the election, to conduct a national re-vote, under direct military control. We've all heard rumors that high-ranking military people are afraid Trump will try to muster and mobilize the National Guard and federal troops against Congress and Vice President Pence, declaring martial law and canceling the 2020 election as fraudulent and corrupt.

I look around and everyone on the floor now is madly talking, texting, and pointing as strange and unprecedented sounds ricocheted loudly through the building. The mob is on the move within the Capitol. Now, after 2:00 PM, an hour into these proceedings and we are still only halfway done with our debate over the objection to Arizona's electoral votes, there are rapid reports circulating of bloody violence being waged against police officers. Texts flew in with graphic images of Capitol police being punched, crushed, mauled, sprayed in the face, speared with American flag poles, and accounts of the Capitol being breached and overrun. I see someone from her security team come whisper something to Nancy Pelosi. People began talking out of turn, even shouting openly. When representative Paul Gosar tries to speak. One of my democratic colleagues yells "Call off your damn stormtroopers" and my friend Representative Dean Phillips from Minnesota stands and shouts, "This is because of you!"

Someone sent me, now an iconic photo of the invading Insurrectionist casually carrying the Confederate battle flag in the rotunda. A three-minute walk from where we sit, right in front of the portrait of John C. Calhoun, the South Carolina, racist and slavery apologist. I cannot believe my eyes as the insurrectionist rebel, as it entered the Capitol, unlawfully, and brandished a Confederate battle flag in Congress, something that never happened once during the civil war. I look up to see Liz Cheney across the aisle, looking equally dumbfounded at the chaos engulfing us. She is tough as nails. I walk over and show her the picture of the guy with the Confederate battle flag, "Looks like we're under new management". She looks aghast and shakes her head. "What have they done?" she says. Someone gets up and tells us to put on our gas masks. I didn't even know we had gas masks, but there they are, under our seats wrapped in plastic. Members fumble so they wouldn't drop them, then ask how to put them on. When people get them working, the masks set off a buzzing noise. It fills the chamber like an elementary school, sounding the nuclear drill alarm from the last century. There is screaming and panic all around. I hear people phoning their wives, husbands, and children to tell them they love them. I hear someone up in the gallery, shouting to everyone to remove their congressional pins, so they will not be recognized as members. My colleague and friend, Susan Wilde, became ill on the floor, another colleague tells me it is a panic attack. All I can consider now is Tabatha and Hank. I am worried sick for them. They may be the only children of members in the Capitol today. I called Julie. She says, my daughter- and son-in-law are okay where they are, behind a locked door, barricaded with furniture.

I'm about to call Tabatha, and then boom! Boom! I hear the sound I will never forget. A sound like a battering ram, and what sounded like

THE CROWNING: CULMINATION OF THE NATION

a group of people. Members nearby press furniture up against the door and a number of us farther away run to the door, to help protect it, but we're quickly told to get back by Capitol police officers who rushed in and defended the entranceway with their guns drawn. The pounding at the door accelerates, and we can hear the sound of angry macho chanting out, they're chanting "Hang Mike Pence, hang Mike Pence" and "We want Trump. We want Trump". Some officials called upon us to evacuate right away. Calmly, everyone moves. Some people run to the speaker's lobby, carrying their gas masks. I look up to the gallery again to see our colleagues, who have been frozen in place on the Democratic side, now awkwardly, crouching, and sliding through the rows to make their way over the gallery, above the Republican side.

Meantime, the officers up there have locked all the doors to keep the rioters from breaking in, now presumably unlocking them to get our colleagues out. I feel strange about leaving them up there, but then again, who knows where we're going, where will any of us find safety on January six, a bloodthirsty mob of hundreds, as they entered the building outside the metal detectors. There was no security check, who knows what weapons they are carrying? It is hard to displace a thought. And I'm now looking for help to lead us downstairs and into the Capitol tunnels. The members talk madly on their phones. We're helping most of the members from the gallery have made it down the stairs and have joined their rapid stream of exit. I hear a Southern Republican Congressman yelling into a phone, "You screwed it up! Y'all screwed it up". My mind fills with swirling questions. Have we entered a violent power struggle on our side of the aisle? We have staked everything on popular sovereignty and the mechanisms of a democratic election. Trump and his enablers have forced us into a politically extremist place where the rule of law is trampled by violence. If the violence of Trump's own incited mob gets out of hand, he can easily declare a state of siege and impose martial law by activating the insurrection act.

But the question now, as we flee the capital from American democracies and all the enemy racist mob violence, is how our constitutional democracy can prevail over Donald Trump's party, which operates like a religious cult, and couldn't give a damn about the Constitution or democracy. They are working all the levers of control and violent coercion to keep their leader, his family, and his sycophants in power."[31]

Bryce Waldron concludes the segment by saying, "Thank you, Congressman Raskin, for that gut-wrenching description of your experience on that fateful day. We will come back to you later on, so please don't go anywhere. Next, we have a video to share with you showing segments of the testimonies of the Capital Police and Metropolitan Police, given on July 27th, 2021, that was on the front lines battling the insurrectionists that day, Jan. 6th, 2021. Please roll that video. The video began with a brief clip of Officer Michael Fanone testifying: "I recognize the fact that there were individuals that were trying to grab ahold of my gun. I remember one of them distinctly lunging at me, time and time again, trying to grab my gun. And I heard people in the crowd yelling, get his gun, kill him with his own gun. I no longer posed any type of threat, nor was I an impediment to them, you know, going inside of the building, yet they tortured me. They beat me. I was struck with a taser device at the base of my skull numerous times and they continued to do so until I yelled out that I have kids." Then the scene shifted to the words, "DC Police Officer Michael Fanone Full Opening statement on January 6th Attack at the U.S. Capitol" followed by Michael Fanone, dressed in his formal uniform, sitting at the table with his fellow survivors, preparing to address the members of Congress, and the entire nation. Michael Fanone said, "Thank you Chairman and members of this committee for inviting me to provide my eyewitness testimony of the violent assault on our nation's Capitol on January 6th, 2021. My name for those of you who don't know is Michael Fanone, and while I've been a sworn officer with the Metropolitan Police Department in Washington, DC for almost two decades, my law enforcement career actually began here in this building as the United States, Capitol police officer shortly after 9/11, in part, because of the 2001 attack on our country by terrorists, I felt called to serve as a Capitol police officer. I was proud to protect this institution and dedicated members of Congress and their staff who work hard each day to uphold our American democracy. I remain proud of the work of the United States, Capitol police, and MPD officers who literally commit their lives to protect the safety of each of you and all of us in this room, in our nation's capital.

THE CROWNING: CULMINATION OF THE NATION

After leaving the United States Capitol police, I became an MPD officer serving the residents of Washington DC. I have spent the majority of my nearly 20 years as a metropolitan police officer working in special mission units whose responsibilities include the investigation and arrest of narcotics traffickers and violent criminals.

I've worked both as an undercover officer and lead case officer in many of these investigations. In this line of work, it probably won't shock you to know that I've dealt with some dicey situations. I thought I had seen it all many times over. Yet, what I witnessed and experienced on January 6th, 2021 was unlike anything I had ever seen. Anything I'd ever experienced or could have imagined in my country. On that day, I participated in the defense of the United States Capitol from an armed mob and an armed mob of thousands, determined to get inside. Because I was among the vastly outnumbered group of law enforcement officers protecting the Capitol and the people inside it. I was grabbed, beaten, and tased, all the while being called a traitor to my country. I was at risk of being stripped of, and killed with my own firearm. As I heard chants of "kill him with his own gun". I could still hear those words in my head today. Although I regularly deal with risky situations on the job, nowhere in my wildest imagination did I ever expect to be in that situation or sitting here before you talk about it. That experience and its aftermath were something that not even my extensive law enforcement training could prepare me for.

I was just one of hundreds of local police who lined up to protect Congress, even though I had not been assigned to do that. Some had asked why we ran to help when we didn't have to. I did that because I simply could not ignore what was happening. Like many other officers. I could not ignore the numerous calls, numerous calls for help coming from the capital complex. I'm a plainclothes officer assigned to the first district's crime suppression team. But for the first time in nearly a decade, I put on all my uniform. When my partner, Jimmy Albright, and I arrived at the Capitol around three that afternoon, it was like an, excuse me. It was unlike any scene I had ever witnessed. Jimmy parked our police vehicle near the intersection of South Capitol Street and D Street in Southeast. And we walked to the Capitol from there, passing the Longworth House Office Building.

THOMAS J. FEELY

It was eerily quiet. And the sidewalks usually filled with pedestrians were empty. As we made our way to Independence Avenue, I could see dozens of empty police vehicles that filled the street, police barricades, which had been abandoned, and hundreds of angry protestors, many of whom taunted us as we walked towards the Capitol building. Jimmy and I immediately began to search for an area where we could be of most assistance. We made our way through the door on the south side of the Capitol, walking into the crypt and finally down to the lower west terrace tunnel. It was there that I observed a police commander struggling to breathe. As he dealt with the effects of CS gas that lingered in the air. Then I watched him collect himself, straightened his cap and trench coat adorned with its silver eagles, and returned to the line. That commander was Ramy Kyle of the Metropolitan Police Department.

And those images are etched into my memory, never to be forgotten in the midst of that intense and chaotic scene. Commander Kyle remains cool, calm, and collected, as he gives commands to his officers, "Hold the line!" He shouted over the roar. Of course, that day, the line was the seat of our American government. Despite the confusion and stress of the situation, observing Ray's leadership, and protecting a place I cared so much about was the most inspirational moment of my life. The bravery he and others showed that day is the best example of duty, honor and service. Each of us who carries a badge should bring those core values to our work. Every day, the fighting in the lower west terrace tunnel was nothing short of brutal. Here, I observed 30 police officers standing shoulder to shoulder, maybe four or five abreast, using the weight of their bodies to hold back the onslaught of violent attackers. Many of these officers were injured, bleeding, and fatigued, but they continue to hold the line. As I don't have to tell the members in this room, the tunnel is a narrow and long hallway. It is not the sort of space anyone would want to be pulled into hand-to-hand combat with an angry mob. However, the narrowness of the hallway provided what was probably the only chance of holding back the crowd from entering your personal offices, the House and Senate chambers. In an attempt to assist injured officers, Jimmy. And I asked them if they needed a break, but there were no volunteers. Selflessly, those officers only identified other colleagues

THE CROWNING: CULMINATION OF THE NATION

who may be in need of assistance. The fighting dragged on; I eventually joined the tactical line at the tunnel's entrance.

I can remember, I remember looking around and being shocked by the sheer number of people fighting us. As my police body-worn camera shows, thousands upon thousands of people seem to, to determine, to get past us by any means necessary. At some point, during the fighting, I was dragged from the line of officers and into the crowd. I heard someone scream. I got one, and as I was swarmed by a violent mob, they ripped off my badge. They grabbed and stripped me of my radio. They seized ammunition that was secured to my body. They began to beat me with their fists and with what felt like hard metal objects. At one point, I came face to face with an attacker who repeatedly lunged for me and attempted to remove my firearm. I heard chanting from some in the crowd, "Get his gun" and "Kill him with his own gun".

I was aware enough to recognize I was at risk of being stripped of and killed with my own firearm. I was electrocuted again and again and again, with a taser. I'm sure I was screaming, but I don't think I could even hear my own voice. My body camera captured the violence of the crowd directed toward me during those very frightening moments. It's an important part of the record for this committee's investigation, for the country's understanding of how I was assaulted and nearly killed as the mob attacked the Capitol that day. And I hope everyone will be able to watch it. The portions of the video I've seen remained extremely painful for me to watch at times, but is it essential that everyone understands what really happened that tragic day during those moments I remember thinking there was a very good chance I would be torn apart or shot to death with my own weapon.

I thought of my four daughters, who might lose their dad. I remain grateful that no member of Congress had to go through the violent assault that I experienced that day. During the assault. I thought about using my firearm on my attackers, but I knew that if I did, I would be quickly overwhelmed and that in their minds would provide them with the justification for killing me. So I instead decided to appeal to them, any humanity they might have. I said, as loud as I could manage, I've got kids. Thankfully, some of the crowds stepped in and assisted me. Those few individuals protected me from a crowd and inch me toward the capital until my fellow officers could rescue me. I was carried back inside. What happened afterward is much less vivid. I had been beaten, and unconscious, and remained so for more than four minutes. I know that Jimmy helped to evacuate me from the building and drove me to MedStar Washington Hospital Center, despite suffering significant injuries himself. At the hospital, Doctors told me that I had suffered a heart attack and I was later diagnosed with a concussion, a traumatic brain injury, and post-traumatic stress disorder. As my physical injuries gradually subsided and the adrenaline that had stayed with me for weeks waned, I've been left with the psychological trauma and the emotional anxiety of having survived such a horrific event. And my children continue to deal with the trauma of nearly losing their dad that day. What makes the struggle harder and more painful is to know so many of my fellow citizens, including so many of the people I put my life at risk to defend are downplaying or outright denying what happened. I feel like I went to hell and back to protect them and the people in this room, but too many are now telling me that hell doesn't exist or that hell actually wasn't that bad. The indifference shown to my colleagues is disgraceful!

My law enforcement career prepared me to cope with some of the aspects of this experience. Being an officer, you know, your life is at risk. Whenever you walk out the door, even if you don't expect otherwise law-abiding citizens to take up arms against you, nothing, truly, nothing has prepared me to address those elected members of our government who continued to deny the events of that day. And in doing so betray their oath of office, those very members whose lives offices, and staff members, I was fighting so desperately to defend. I agreed to speak here today and have talked publicly about what happened because I don't think our response to the insurrection should have anything to do with political parties. I knew what my partner, Jimmy, and I suited up for on January 6th. It didn't have anything to do with political parties or about politics or what political party any of you public servants belong to.

I've worked in this city for two decades and I've never cared about those things no matter who was in office, all I've ever cared about is protecting you and the public. So you can do your job in service to this country. And for those whom you represent. I appreciate your time and attention. I look

THE CROWNING: CULMINATION OF THE NATION

forward to the committee's investigation and I'm hopeful with your commitment, we, as a country, will confront the truth of what happened on January 6th and do what is necessary to make sure this institution of our democracy never falls into the hands of a violent and angry mob. We must also recognize the officers who responded that day, many unsolicited, and their countless acts of bravery and selflessness. It has been 202 days since 850 MPD officers responded to the capital and helped stop a violent insurrection from taking over this Capitol complex, which almost certainly saved countless members of Congress and their staff from injury and possibly death. The time to fully recognize these officers is now. Thank you again for the opportunity to provide my testimony here today." The scene on the video then switches to another survivor, Capitol Police Sgt. Aquilino Gonell:

Aquilino Gonell witnessed, "Thank you for the opportunity to testify regarding the attack on the U.S. Capitol on January 6th, 2021. It is with honor and heavy heart I come before you to tell you my story from a painful, firsthand experience, what happened that terrible day at the Capitol. I'm providing this testimony solely in my personal capacity and not as a representative of the US Capitol. It is imperative that the events of January six are fully investigated in Congress that the American people know the truth of what actually occurred, and that all those responsible are held accountable, particularly to ensure the horrific and shameful event in our history never repeats itself. I applaud you for pursuing this energetic, even though there's overwhelming evidence to the contrary, including hours and hours of videos and photographic coverage, (there) is a continuous, shocking attempt to ignore or try to destroy the truth of what truly happened that day, and to whitewash the facts into something other than what they all mistakenly reveal, an attack on our democracy by violent domestic extremists, and a stain in our history and our moral standing here at home and abroad.

When I was promoted to Sergeant three years ago, how I always took my oath seriously on January 6th, 2021, I fulfilled my oath once more, this was to defend the US United States, Capitol and members of Congress carrying out their constitutional duties to certify the results of the November 2020 presidential election.

To be honest, I did not recognize my fellow citizens who saw the Capitol on January six or the United States that they claim to represent. When I was 25 years old, and then a Sergeant in the army, I was deployed to Iraq for Operation Iraqi Freedom. From time to time, I volunteered to travel on IED-infested roads to conduct supply missions for U.S. and Allied forces and the local Iraqi population as well. But on January six, for the first time, I was more afraid to work at the Capitol, than my entire deployment to Iraq. In Iraq, we spent their armed violence because we were in a war zone, but nothing about my experience in the army or as a law enforcement officer prepared me for what we confronted on January six. The verbal assaults and disrespect we endured from the rioters were bad enough. I was falsely accused of betraying my Oath, of choosing my paycheck, choosing my paycheck over my loyalty to the U S Constitution. Even as I defended the barrier, the democratic process that protects everyone in the hostile crowd. Well, while I was at the low west terrace of the Capitol, working with my fellow officers to prevent the breach and restore order, the rioters called me a traitor, a disgrace, I, I, an army veteran, and a police officer, should be executed.

Some of the rioters have the audacity to tell me there was nothing personal, that they will go through me, through us police officers, to achieve their goal, as if it was breaking metal barriers to use as a weapon against us, although, they use more menacing language. If you shoot us, we all have weapons. We will shoot back or we'll get our guns, we outnumber you. They say join us. Or heard specific threats to the lives of the speaker, Nancy Pelosi, and also, Vice President, Mike Pence. But the physical violence we experienced was horrific and devastating. My fellow officers and I were

THE CROWNING: CULMINATION OF THE NATION

punched kicked, shoved, sprayed with chemical irritants, and even blinded with eye-damaging lasers by a violent mob, apparently who apparently saw us law enforcement officers dedicated to ironically protecting them as us citizens, as an impediment, to their attempt at insurrection, the mob weapons to try to accomplish their insurrectionist's objectives and use them against us.

These weapons, including hammers, re-bars, knives, batons, and police shields taken by force, as well as bear spray and pepper spray. Some rioters wore tactical gear, including bulletproof vests and gas masks. The rioters also forcibly took out batons and shields to use them against us. I was particularly shocked at the scene, the insurrectionist violently attacked us with the very American flag they claimed to seek to protect. Based on the coordinated tactics we observed and verbal commands, we heard that many of these attackers had law enforcement or military experience. The rioters were vicious and relentless. We found ourselves in a violent battle, desperate to attend, to prevent a breach of the capital by the interest near the integration stage. Metropolitan police officers were being pulled into the crowd. We have one right here, right next to me. As we tried to push the riders back for the breaching, the capital in my attempt to assist MPD officers, I grabbed one by the officer by the back of the collar and pulled him back to the police line. When I tried to help the second officer, I found some police shields on the ground that were slippery because of the pepper spray and bear spray. Rioters immediately pulled me by my leg or my shield by the gear strap on my left shoulder. My survival instincts kicked in and I started kicking and punching, as I tried and bang to gain the PD officer's attention behind, above me, they could not help me because they also were being attacked. I finally was able to hit the rioter who was grabbing me, with my baton and was able to stand. And then I continued to fend off new attackers, I think K rotating and attacking those again. And again, we're subject to what we were suggested was like something from a medieval battle. We fell, hand to hand, inch by inch, to prevent an invasion of the capital by a violent mob intent on subverting our democratic process. My fellow officers and I were committed to not letting any rioters breach the Capitol. It was a prolonged and desperate struggle. The rioters attempting to breach the Capitol were shouting "Trump sent us. Pick the right side. We want Trump".

THOMAS J. FEELY

I basically heard officers screaming in agony and pain, just an arm's length from me. I didn't know at that time that was Officer Hodges and he's here today to testify. I too was being crushed by the rioters. I could feel myself losing oxygen and recall thinking to myself, this is how I'm going to die, defending this entrance. Many of the officers fighting alongside me were calling for shields because their shields were being stripped from them by the rioters. I was one of the few officers left with a shield. So I spent the majority of my time at the front of the line."

Last, the words appeared on the screen: U.S. Capitol Police Officer Harry Dunn Opening Statement on January 6th Attack at the U.S. Capitol. Officer Harry Dunn, a large black officer, sat before the Congress and took a sip of water before he gave his testimony, Officer Harry Dunn said, "Chairman Thompson and members of the select committee. Thank you for the opportunity today to get my account regarding the events of January 6th, 2021, from my firsthand experience as a Capitol police officer directly involved in those events and still hurting from what happened that day. I provide this testimony solely in my personal capacity and not as a representative of the United States Capitol Police. Before I begin, I begin, I like to take a moment of my time to ask for a moment of silence for my fallen colleague, Officer Bryan Sicknick, who died from injuries he sustained in the line of duty, defending the Capitol of our beloved democracy. Thank you. I reported for duty at the Capitol as usual early on the morning of January 6th. We understood that the vote that certified President Biden's election will be taking place that day and protests might occur outside the Capitol. Where we expected any demonstrations to be peaceful expressions of first amendment freedoms. Just like the scores of demonstrations we had. We had observed for many years after roll call, I took my Overwatch posts on the east front of the Capitol, standing on the steps that led up to the Senate chamber. As the morning progressed, I did not see or hear anything that gave me cause for alarm, but around 10:56 am I received a text message from a friend forwarding, a screenshot of what appeared to be the potential plan of action. Very different from a peaceful demonstration, the screenshot board, the caption "January 6th, rally point Lincoln Park" and said the objective was the Capitol. It said amongst other things that Trump has given us marching orders to keep our guns hidden, it urged people to bring their trauma kits and

THE CROWNING: CULMINATION OF THE NATION

gas masks to link up early in the day in six to 12-man teams. It showed there will be time to "arm up". Seeing that message caused me concern. To be sure, looking back now, it seemed to foreshadow what happened later. At the time though, we had received no threat warnings from our chain of command. I had no independent reason to believe that violence was headed our way.

As the morning progressed and the crowd of protestors began to swell on the east side of the Capitol, many were displaying Trump flags. The crowd was chanting slogans, like "Stop the steel" and "We want Trump", but the demonstration was still being conducted in a peaceful manner. Early that afternoon, Capitol Police dispatch advised all units over the radio that we had an active 10-100 at the Republican National Committee nearby. "Ten one hundred" is the police code for a suspicious package, such as a potential bomb. That radio dispatch got my attention, and I started to get more nervous and worried, especially because the crowds on the east front of the Capitol or continuing to grow. Around the same time. I started receiving reports on the radio about large crowd movements around the Capitol, coming from the direction of the Ellipse to both the west and east fronts of the Capitol. Then I heard urgent radio calls for additional officers to respond to the west side and an exclamation, a desperate voice, those demonstrators on the west side had breached the fence.

Now it was obvious that there was a direct threat to the Capitol. I quickly put on a steel chest plate, which weighed approximately 20 pounds, and carried my info rifles sprinted around the north side of the Capitol to the west terrace and the railing of the inaugural stage, where I had a broad view of what was going on. I was stunned by what I saw and what seemed like a sea of people. Capitol police officers and Metropolitan Police officers MPD were engaged in desperate, hand-to-hand fighting with rioters across the West lawn. Until then I had never seen anyone physically assault Capitol police or MPD, let alone witness mass assaults being perpetrated on law enforcement officers. I witnessed the rioters using all kinds of weapons against officers, including flagpoles metal, bike racks they had torn apart, and various kinds of projectiles. Officers were being bloodied in the fighting. Many were screaming and many were blinded and coughing from chemical irritants being sprayed in their faces.

THOMAS J. FEELY

I gave decontamination aid to as many officers as I could, flushing their eyes with water to dilute the chemical irritants. Soon thereafter, I heard "Attention to all units, the Capital has been breached and rioters were in various places inside the building". At that point, I rushed into the Capitol with another officer, going first to the basement on the Senate side, where I heard an MPD officer needed a defibrillator. After returning outside to the west terrace to assist the officers. I went back into the Capitol and up the stairs towards the Crypt. There I saw rioters who had invaded the Capitol, carrying a Confederate flag, a red Maga flag, and a "don't tread on me" flag.

I decided to stand my ground there to prevent any rioters from heading down the stairs to the lowest terrorist entrance because that's where officers were getting decontamination aid and were particularly vulnerable. At the top of the stairs, I confronted a group of insurrectionists, warning them "Do not go back, go down those steps". One of them shouted, "Keep moving Patriots". Another displayed what looked like a law enforcement badge and told me "We're doing this for you". One of the invaders approached me like he was going to try to get past me and head down the stairs. I hit him, knocking him down. After getting relieved by other officers in the crypt. I took off running upstairs towards the speaker's lobby and helped the plainclothes officer who was getting hassled by insurrectionists. Some of them were dressed like members of a militia group wearing tactical vests, cargo pants, and body armor. I was physically exhausted, and it was hard to breathe and to see because of all the chemical spray in the air.

More and more insurrectionists were pouring into the area by the speaker's lobby, near the rotunda and some wearing Maga hats and shirts that said Trump 2020. I told him to just leave the capital. And in response, they yelled, "No, man, this is our house. President Trump invited us here. We're here to stop this steal. Joe Biden is not the President. Nobody voted for Joe Biden." I'm a law enforcement officer and I do my best to keep politics out of my job, but in this circumstance, I responded, "well, I voted for Joe Biden, does my vote not count? Am I nobody?" That prompted a torrent of racial epithets, one woman in a pink MAGA shirt yelled, "You hear that guy? This nigger voted for Joe Biden." Then the crowd, perhaps around 20 people joined in screaming, "boo f**king nigger!" No one had ever, ever, called me a nigger while wearing the uniform of a Capitol Police officer.

THE CROWNING: CULMINATION OF THE NATION

And the days following the attempted insurrection. Other black officers shared with me their own stories of racial abuse, on January 6th. One officer told me he had never in his entire 40 years of life, been called a nigger to his face and that streak ended on January six. Yet another black officer later told me he had been confronted by insurrectionists in the Capitol who told him, "Put your gun down and we'll show you what kind of nigger you really are." To be candid, the rest of the afternoon is a blur. But I know I went throughout the Capitol to assist officers who needed aid and help expel more insurrectionists. In the crypt. I encountered Sergeant Grinnell who was giving assistance to an unconscious woman who had been in the crowd of riders on the west side of the Capitol. I helped to carry her to the area of the house majority leader's office, where she was administered CPR. As the afternoon wore on, I was completely drained both physically and emotionally and in shock, and in total disbelief over what had happened. Once the building was cleared, I went to the rotunda to recover with other officers and share experiences from what happened that afternoon Representative Rodney Davis was there offering support to officers. And when he and I saw each other, he came over and he gave me a big hug. I sat down on the bench in the rotunda with a friend of mine who is also a black capital police officer and told him about the racial slurs I endured. I became very emotional and began yelling "How the blank could something like this happen? Is this America? I began sobbing."

Bryce Waldron, addressing the Congressman exclaimed, "Congressman Raskin, you created a powerful video to inform the Senate in the Impeachment Trial, from your research of what happened outside the chambers, and what was going on regarding the people who attended this event. Using video recorded by the rioters' own cell phones and the police's body cameras, you exposed this horrific day to show the undeniable reality of the violence.

Jamie Raskin responded, "Yes, Bryce. It was for most of those in the Senate, the first time they had seen how close the violence came to them personally. "The video began with Trump's repeated exhortations and incitements to the increasingly agitated mob. We will stop the steel. When you catch somebody in fraud, your labs go by very different rules. We won the election and won it by a landslide. And now we're going to walk down to the Capitol and I'll be with you. I hope Mike has the courage to do what he needs to do. If you don't fight like hell, you're not going to have a country anymore. Then it switched over to heart-pounding scenes of Savage violence and mayhem unfolding at the Capitol rioters overrunning the physical barriers. Helmeted insurrectionists assaulting officers with pipes and flagpoles protestors working to erect the gallows, all people screaming, "Fight for Trump and f**k you police. f**k you. And take the building. Take the f**king building" and "no Trump, no peace, no Trump, no peace". The video shifted to the battle inside where insurrectionists were taunting cops with face-to-face provocations. "We're listening to Trump," and "traitor Pence", "traitor Pence", and "then I'm going to slowly break it down, break it down", as rioters pounded on the doors of the House. Other scenes were etched in my mind, an insurrectionist yelling "is this the Senate?" "Where the f**k are they?" another yelling "That's what we need. 30,000 f**king guns in here", another shouting back into the mob. "We need fresh Patriots to the front" There was the heroic Capitol police officer, Daniel Hodges stuck in the doorway, screaming and in agony, as a rioter lifted his gas mask and sprayed him in the face with bear mace, the mob pressing forward and screaming in unison, "Heave hoh", rioters stealing police shields and using them as weapons. The scene then turned to Trump's pathetic tweeted video to his followers, two hours after the chaos began, clearly not disapproving, and still whining about his stolen election. 'Never has there been a time like this where such a thing happened, where they could take it away from all of us, from me, from you, from the whole country. He (Trump) then made a glancing effort to council peace, a day late and a dollar short, "Go home. We love you. You're very special. I know how you feel, but go home and go home in peace." Before it was all over the senators watched U.S. flags being used as weapons to spear officers. Insurrectionist urging his comrades to "look to the future, go home and storm your county buildings and take down every one of these corrupt mother f**kers." I watched the senators watching the footage. The Democrats were uniformly we're horrified and aghast, because members of Congress were inside when these events happened, all of us had missed the full magnitude of the "American carnage", Donald Trump unleashed outside on the perimeter of the Capitol and against our police officers downstairs, ended up en route to the chambers. The Senators, sheltered from the

THE CROWNING: CULMINATION OF THE NATION

bloodshed and did not know about the military character of a lot of the violence, the extremists marching in formation. Their arrival with dangerous chemicals, the coordinated poundings in beatings of officers, and the use of walkie-talkies to plan ambushes of our officers. Later that day, I must have heard a dozen times from Senators of all stripes, some variation on this statement 'I had no idea the violence was this terrible', or 'I never actually saw a Trump's speech before, and 'it's amazing how he ordered the whole thing, or I had no sense of how close we were to being apprehended or killed. The Senator's shock over the magnitude of the violence was inevitable given that we all had extremely limited perspectives on that chaotic day, but the video created a 360-degree Panorama of the battle in a coherent timeline of key events."[31]

Suddenly, Tully was abruptly returned to the present when he heard Catherine yell in a tone Tully had never heard before, "Tully! Tully! Tully!" Tully was surprised by the shrieking nature of Catherine's panic. He thought to himself, "What could be so wrong?" while he sprinted up the stairs.

Chapter 16
We Can't Just Give Up on Her
Tampa, Florida
February 17, 2025

Tully was startled out of the hypnotic trance he was experiencing while listening intently. While listening to Truth, he realized he had become mesmerized by the stories he had just heard, completely forgot where he was, and that his top priority was caring for Catherine. He replied to Catherine after her third and loudest call of his name, "Coming Cathy!" He bolted up the steps and entered the bedroom, again completely out of breath. Catherine was lying in bed looking at her cell phone with a look of concern on her face. Catherine said, "Did you read the text from Grace? She sent it out to the entire family." Tully answered, "No, honey, I was busy and did not see it. What does it say?" Catherine replied, "It says she, Grady and Chase are on their way to meet with the doctors caring for Suzanne at the hospital. She hopes they can bring Suzanne home soon to be reunited with the family, but worries that she has not yet even been taken off the ventilator. She is asking for our prayers." Tully asked, "Who is caring for James while they are gone?" "Pamala and Suzy are staying with him," Catherine responded.

Tully says grimly, "I wish they had left Chase or Grady, one of them, home in case those robbers return, or in case Grace and whoever is with her gets ambushed, and never returns home." Catherine was perturbed that her husband would even utter those words of gloom and negativism. She gave Tully a look that clearly communicated her displeasure with him, even if he was right, that look that only two people who have been together as many years as they have would immediately understand what she meant. Tully ever so slightly smirked at his wife, silently gesturing, in return, 'sorry'. They both understood the dangers of traveling, even just a few miles, in every city in the country. Neither of them, however, knew what the doctors had concluded

THE CROWNING: CULMINATION OF THE NATION

would be their message to Suzanne's family, that Suzanne's condition was not improving, and the demand for beds in Intensive Care was so great, that they could not justify having Suzanne occupy a bed that could save another's life. They had given up hope on Suzanne's chances of recovery.

At the hospital, the doctors invited Grace, Grady, and Chase into a large conference room, which Grace thought was rather odd as this room was reserved for the most important meetings of hospital elites. The doctors all knew Grace well, as one of their most respected nurses in the hospital, so they wanted to go the extra mile to delicately break the news to her and the others with her. Before Grace could say a word, she heard Chase ask if they could add James to the meeting by "FaceTime" calling him on the call using their smartphones. The doctors agreed and James, from his bed at home, was soon on the call with his children and the medical team. The Director of the Hospital, Dr. Horace Thompson spoke first for the group, "Mr. Stone (referring to James listening by the speaker), I first want to express our delight that you seem to recover well, and also from our entire team, how grateful we are that your daughter, Grace, is a valuable member of our staff. The job she has done here has been nothing short of remarkable, especially considering the extraordinary circumstances." Despite the praise, Grace felt a sudden fear that there was something awful Dr. Thompson was about to say. Just the fact that he was there in the first place, in Grace's view, was an ominous sign.

James responded to the introduction in a raspy and hardly audible voice, "Thank you Dr. Thompson. I am ever so grateful for the care I and Suzanne have received while in your care. (James takes a long take a breath from the oxygen tank)... and thank you for those kind words about Grace. Her Mother and I are very proud of her."

Dr. Thompson, being very direct, proclaimed, "Let me get to the purpose of this meeting. We all feel that your Mom can be best served by transferring her to a hospice facility that is equipped with everything she needs to be comfortable."

There was a long silence while those words were being processed. Finally, Grace broke the silence asking, "Are you saying she will never recover? Are you giving up on her?" Realizing he needed to be more empathetic, Dr. Thompson responded with his softer, kinder voice, "Yes, Grace, as hard as this is to say, that is exactly what we all have concluded." Chase asked everyone, wondering, "Dr. Thompson, I thought her condition was stable. When did her condition deteriorate?" "She is stable," Dr. Thompson replied, "She still needs the ventilator to breathe. While she has not gotten worse, she has gotten no better, and to be quite frank, well, her bed could be used by someone else with a better chance at recovery. And then he added, "I believe her chances are slim." Still raspy but with a louder volume, James exclaimed, "No! We can't just give up on her. No way! I won't agree to that! She is my wife and my children's mother." Grace, fighting hard to keep her composure, urged, "Dr. Thompson, let me ask you for one favor. Instead of moving Mom to a hospice facility, would you consider moving her to a private room care where she can be monitored? I will volunteer to take a temporary leave from my duties here to be her nurse full-time." Dr. Thompson looked around at the other doctors in the meeting, and all seemed to approve. Dr. Thompson agreed and assured, "Ok, Grace. We will move her from Intensive Care to a private room. You will be assigned to her care, but you will not take a leave from your duties as a nurse. You will be assigned to caring for your Mom as your duty. Mr. Stone, does that also meet your approval?" James affirmed, "Yes, yes, it does! Thank you!"

With that decision, the meeting adjourned, and Suzanne was moved to a private room that afternoon. She was still breathing with the help of a ventilator, but there was still hope, albeit very minute, for her recovery. Grace and her husband, Grady, stayed with her mom that afternoon, then went home for the night. The Hospital administration agreed her hours would be on duty from 7:00 am to 7:00 pm. She would go home to check on her father each night, then grab some badly needed sleep while other nurses on the night shift would attend to Suzanne. Grace was immensely relieved they had bought some time, hoping and praying for a miracle.

Grace again contacted the entire Stone family to fill them in on the news through a group text. The family agreed to add Suzanne to those they are already praying for through a "storming of heaven." Tully found his father's rosary beads and began immediately saying the rosary, a Catholic tradition he had done so many times in his youth. His family prayed the rosary after every dinner, praying while they all shared in the duties of washing dishes and sweeping the kitchen floor. Turning to the rosary in times of crisis was his natural instinctive response. This was surely one of those crisis events

THE CROWNING: CULMINATION OF THE NATION

warranting the ultimate weapon to gain God's attention for a miracle request. The last such crisis was when Tully and Catherine's granddaughter, Sheila, was diagnosed with cancer, and the disease was already at "Stage 5" at the time of diagnosis. The rosary was prayed by Tully every day for the next two years until Sheila was declared "cancer free." That was a miracle, so Tully had all the proof he needed as to prayer's fidelity to make miracles happen. Tully, while worried for Suzanne, felt optimistic that Suzanne's chances of recovery had dramatically improved because the family, while diverse in their religious denominations, all had their own way to pray, and would all be doing just that, "storming the heaven". This would prove to be needed more, going forward, than anyone knew.

Chapter 17
Peaceful Political Discourse
Tampa, Florida
Feb.18th, 2025

By the time the sun rose on Tuesday, Tully was already up fixing a healthy breakfast to serve to his wife, Catherine, who had a quiet night, getting a good ten hours of sleep. She wasn't ready yet to eat solid foods, so Tully made a smoothie out of the food he still had from his country run. When Catherine awoke, probably from the very loud noise made by the Vitamix blender, she was in a better mood than Tully had seen since before the shooting. Cathy was normally an upbeat person, one who only complained about Tully's habits that annoyed her, but little else. She smiled when Tully came into the bedroom armed with a green smoothie. After breakfast, Catherine wanted to shower, so Tully called the hospital who talked him through the disconnection process.

While helping Catherine prepare for her badly needed shower by helping her take off her tubes, wires and nightgown, Tully decided that this moment might be a perfect time to ask her the question he has been tortured to know for days. "Catherine, do you remember when Michael was five years old, and he had an imaginary friend?" Catherine was clearly puzzled by the odd question, but immediately responded, "Of course." "Do you remember what he called that imaginary friend?" Catherine looked perplexed, but humoring her husband responded, "Teddy, he was a talking pony, just like Mr. Ed."

Tully smiled at the memory of Michael running to the garage every morning to feed his imaginary pony and talk to him for hours. "That's it, Teddy", Tully explained. He finally had the password to the mysterious thumb drive!

THE CROWNING: CULMINATION OF THE NATION

Catherine was fatigued after her shower so she got fresh pajamas on and soon was napping peacefully. Clearly, she was on the mend. Tully went into the bathroom, opened the medicine chest, and pulled out the bottle containing Michael's thumb drive. Returning to his computer, he plugged in the drive and typed in TEDDY. An error message appeared saying that the password was incorrect. Frustrated, he returned to the bedroom where Catherine was sleeping and gently woke her up. "Teddy is not correct. Could it be a different name?" Tully asked impatiently. Groggy and irritated by the annoying questions when she only wanted to sleep, Catherine responded, "Go to my hobby room and look in the bottom drawer. I kept all of his drawings there. I remember he drew a picture of his pony he called Teddy." Tully did as he was instructed and found the crayon drawing. Below the pony was the word Tedy. A light turned on in Tully's head as he realized the name Teddy was spelled by 5-year-old Michael as 'Tedy." He was relieved and now has solved the puzzle. He decided he would see the contents of the thumb drive that evening when things were quiet and Catherine was awake.

Tully remembered he had not heard the rest of the program, Truth, the night before, so he went back to his computer and rewound the program to the spot where he was interrupted. The video picks up with Regina Mangione describing the Insurrection on Jan. 6th, 2021. "Later on, following Trump's speech, rioters broke through Capitol police barriers and broke windows, prompting the former president to tweet: "Mike Pence didn't have the courage to do what should have been done to protect our Country and our Constitution ..." That tweet only added to the anger fueling the mob.

According to Stephanie Grisham, a former White House press secretary, staffers watched the developing riots on television screens positioned throughout the West Wing. They were stunned by what was unfolding at the Capitol, but Trump remained so awestruck that he hit rewind and watched some scenes again. "Look at all the people fighting for me," Trump said, according to Grisham. As witnesses testified, Kieth Kellogg said the staff asked Trump to take immediate action to end the violence in the Capitol, but he refused to do so.[33] Sen. Lindsey Graham, R-S.C., then called Ivanka Trump, pleading that the president "ask people to leave." "We're working on it," she replied.

At that point, staffers acknowledged that despite efforts by Meadows, Press Secretary Kayleigh McEnany and Kellogg, the only person who could get through to him would be his daughter.[33] In response to the deluge of calls and texts from Trump allies begging him to end the violence, Ivanka Trump made at least two staunch efforts to reason with her father.

"Is someone getting to POTUS? He has to tell protestors to dissipate. Someone is going to get killed," a former White House communications official, texted. Ben Williamson replied, "I've been trying for the last 30 minutes. Literally stormed into the outer oval to get him to put out the first one. It's completely insane,"[33]

It was at 6:01 p.m. on that day that Trump issued his last tweet when he finally said that the 2020 election was "unceremoniously and viciously stripped away from great patriots who have been badly and unfairly treated for so long. Go home with love and in peace. Remember this day forever." [33]

Five hours after the insurrection erupted, the Capitol building was cleared of the rioters. Soon after, the House and Senate members returned to resume counting and certifying the Electoral votes. Mitch McConnell, the Senate Majority Leader, asked Mike Pence, who was presiding over the preceding, for permission to address everyone in the Capitol, and in the nation. What he said was the perfect summation of what happened that day and their resolve to fulfill their constitutional duties. Here is a video of that speech. Regina Mangioni started playing the video for all to see and hear:

Mitch McConnell, speaking on the floor of the Senate, said, "I want to say to the American people. The United States Senate will not be intimidated. We will not be kept out of this chamber by thugs, mobs, or threats. We will not bow to lawlessness or intimidation. We are back at our posts. We will discharge our duty under the constitution and for our nation. And we're going to do it tonight. This afternoon. Congress began the process of honoring the will of the American people and counting the electoral college votes. We've fulfilled the solemn duty every four years for more than two centuries, whether our nation has been at war or at peace under all manner of threats, even during an ongoing, ongoing, armed rebellion and civil war, the clockwork of our democracy has carried on. The United States and the United States Congress had faced down a much greater threat than

THE CROWNING: CULMINATION OF THE NATION

the unhinged crowd we saw today. We've never been deterred before, and we'll be not deterred today. They tried to disrupt our democracy. They failed; they failed. They failed to attempt to obstruct Congress. This failed insurrection only underscores how crucial the task before us is for our Republic. Our nation was founded precisely so that the free choice of the American people is what shapes our self-government and determines the destiny of our nation. Not fear, not force, but the peaceful expression of the popular will.

Now we assemble this afternoon to count our citizens' votes and to formalize their choice of the next president. Now we're going to finish exactly what we started. We'll complete the process the right way, by the book, and will follow our precedents and our constitution to the letter. And we will certify the winner of the 2020 presidential election. Criminal behavior will never dominate the United States. Congress. This institution is resilient. Our democratic Republic is strong. The American people deserve nothing less."

It took many more hours, because of the objections of Senators Hawley and Cruz to accepting the electors from Arizona and Pennsylvania, both of which prompted hours of separate debates in the two Chambers of Congress, but early the next morning, the electoral college was certified, and Joe Biden and Kamala Harris were declared the winner of the 2020 election.

Later, when the RNC Chair, Ronna McDaniel, described the insurrection as "peaceful political discourse," Mitch McConnell responded with this statement, "Well, let me give you my view of what happened on January the sixth, and we're all, who were not on the inside of the planning and execution of the insurrection, all declaring their disgust with the events of that historic and tragic day, what other significant events took place behind the scenes in the days following Jan. 6th? Regina Mangioni responded, "Well, Bryce, we realize that the entire world was shocked that this happened in the United States. Nothing like this has happened before since the Civil War. China became especially concerned that President Trump might use this event as a rationalization for a war with them to create a reason to halt the transfer of power in our government. Trump blamed the pandemic on China for over a year, calling it the "China Virus" and blaming its origins on the Chinese government. So, it seemed logical he would also blame the election results on China. If Trump needed a villain to start a war with, they believed they were candidate number one for that role.

Enter General Mark A. Milley, Chairman of the Joint Chiefs of Staff, the nation's highest-ranking military officer, and the principal military advisor to the President, Secretary of Defense, and National Security Council. General Milley sent an urgent message to his Chinese counterpart General Li Zuocheng, Chief of the Joint Staff of the People's Liberation Army, two days after the violent assault on the US Capitol on January 6th, 2021. The televised images of the unprecedented attack on Congress stunned and disoriented Li and the Chinese leadership. Then, to calm down the Chinese, Milley spoke on a secret back channel with General Li Zuocheng. Milley insisted the U.S. was not planning an attack. Milley hoped he had been successful in mollifying Li Zuocheng's fears, who would, in turn, reassure Chinese President Xi Jinping, but now, on January 8th, it was apparent China's fears had only been exacerbated.[24]

As military strikes have been launched in Iran, Somalia, Yemen, and Syria, it was clear to Milley that Trump could start a war. As outlined in the Constitution, the President had sole authority to employ the armed forces however he saw fit. A miscalculation or mistranslation could have cataclysmic consequences in an environment like this. A sweeping expansion of China's military was being conducted to reach the status of an almost superpower. The Chinese unveiled a five-times-faster-than-sound hypersonic missile, another groundbreaking weapon. Milley told senior staff it is possible to do some significant damage to a large industrial complex society like the United States through cyberspace or in space. And you could do that very, very quickly through some very powerful tools that are out there. China is developing all of this technology. China was staging military drills and sending planes toward Taiwan, a nation that it considered its own after years of American pledges to protect it. Taiwan alone posed a serious risk to stability in the South China Sea. Like never before, China aggressively established military bases on islands recently made by China and then challenged the U.S. Navy ships and planes, a staggering gamble.[24]

Milley told his service chiefs in the Army, Navy, Air Force, and Marine Corps to keep a close watch on everything. Paul Nakasone, Director of the

THE CROWNING: CULMINATION OF THE NATION

National Security Agency, was called by Milley to discuss the conversation he had with Li. It is the NSA's job to monitor global communications. Milley said, "Keep watching, scan, focus on China, but make sure the Russians are not exploiting the situation to make an opportunistic move." We're watching our lanes," Nakasone confirmed. Milley called CIA Director, Gina Haskell, and gave her a readout on the call with Li. "Aggressively watch everything 360" Millie said to Haskell, 'take nothing for granted right now. I just want to get through to the 20th at noon." Milley was determined to do everything, to ensure a peaceful transfer of power, in just twelve days.

Milley surmised that the attack that shook the world on January 6th, so tragic and brutal, might have been a sneak preview, or a gauge for something even grander, or more sinister. Chairman Milley spent the next twelve days trying to unravel the mystery of the January 6th riot. Milley told senior staff. "Neither I, nor anyone that I know of, including the FBI, or anybody else, envisioned the thousands of people who assaulted the Capitol. To basically, encircled the Capitol and assault it from multiple directions simultaneously, and to do what they did." Milley knew the internet chatter leading up to the attack lacked cohesiveness and did not supply the specific credible intelligence that could have prevented the tragedy.[24] Ultimately, Milley prevailed in accomplishing his objection to "land the plane" to its fruition on Jan. 20th, the day Biden was sworn in and Trump flew on Air Force One to his golf resort, Mara Lago, Florida, no longer the president, but still in possession of dozens of boxes of Classified and Top Secret documents, that by law were to be turned over the National Archives. Bryce Waldron then concluded the episode with, "Thank you Regina for all the expert knowledge you have contributed to this historical documentary. We will broadcast live tomorrow, from our new secret location. Good night. Stay safe."

That evening, when Catherine had just finished the meal Tully had prepared for her he said, "I received a thumb drive from Michael and have not seen the contents yet. I was hoping to view it with you. Are you feeling up to it?" Catherine replied, "Sure, it must be very important for Michael to go to all the trouble." Tully brought in the laptop and set it on the bed, inserted the thumb drive, and typed in the password, Tedy. A video appeared, clearly made on a cell phone with Michael's face in the preview icon. Tully pressed play to hear Michael's voice saying, "Hello Dad and Catherine. I hope you are recovering from your recent attack. Lindsey and I have been praying for you every day.

I will need you to destroy this thumb drive after you watched it. Don't just delete the video, but literally destroy the drive. That is very important. I want to keep you informed about what is really happening, so you can help me keep our family out of harm's way. Things are much worse than you are hearing in the news. Believe nothing you hear on Cerberus World News, that is pure propaganda and total B.S.

The program called Truth is historically accurate, but they don't know the actual things going on behind the scenes. I can't tell you everything, but there are a few things you need to understand. First, there is a cold war happening right here in this country. The key is who controls the military. General Milley has been removed in the middle of the night and replaced by a guy named John McEntee. He was Trump's 29-year-old body man who took control of personnel in the last days of the administration to become Director of the White House Presidential Personnel Office. McEntee has no military background, but he is in charge of the Army and the National Guard. He would be in charge of the Air Force, Navy, and Coast Guard, but those three branches of the service do not recognize Trump as the President, and remain loyal to President Biden. Trump has the FBI and CIA searching for Biden, who is in hiding. The President-elect, Ron DeSantis, has been arrested and is being held in a secret facility. We do not know yet where that is but we suspect it may be the same place where all the other members of Congress and the Senate are being held. I called it a 'cold war" because so far the branches of the services have not fought with each other, but that could change at any time. I am becoming convinced that this will lead to an all-out World War. The reason that has not yet happened is that Biden still has the nuclear codes. As long as he is not captured, we are at a stalemate. That is all I can tell you for now. Please remember to destroy this thumb drive immediately. Also, be very careful with this information. They could monitor your communications. Let me handle disseminating this information to our other family members. I don't want anyone getting arrested. Take care, and Catherine, I hope you heal quickly." With that, the video ended. Tully looked at Catherine, who was in complete shock, with tears forming in her eyes.

THE CROWNING: CULMINATION OF THE NATION

Tully yanked the thumb drive out and started leaving the room. "Good idea", Catherine said knowing precisely what Tully was about to do with the drive.

The leather reclining chair Tully sat in almost every night while standing guard was his favorite piece of furniture. Catherine bought it for him, replacing the ancient old chair he used for years. Sitting in the recliner, easing back into a comfortable semi-inclined position offered him the perfect relaxing posture that allowed Tully to reminisce about his past. He thought about his five living sons who Tully loved and gushed about with pride. James, Tony, and Patrick were the first three in the chronological hierarchy.

Paul and Michael came along later in Tully's life. Paul and Michael were three years apart and fought with each other throughout their childhood and teenage years. As children, both had confided to Catherine and Tully how much each resented the other. Ironically, after they went off to college and later became commissioned officers in the military, they grew very close, both serving as the best man at each other's weddings. Paul attended Columbia University and played football, while Michael went to the Air Force Academy, also playing football while majoring in Engineering and a minor in the Russian Language. Ultimately, Paul enlisted in the Coast Guard and later was accepted and graduated from the Coast Guard's Officer Candidate School. He trained for two years to become a pilot for the Coast Guard and was assigned to Miami to fly the "helos". Michael went to the Air Force Base in Anchorage Alaska where he started his career in Military Intelligence, where he continued his training in Russian and Modern Standard Mandarin, the official language of China.

Patrick, the younger of the first set of sons but 10 years older than Paul, was a successful businessman and a wonderful father to his two daughters. Patrick was a good kid, but he also was an adventurer, an extreme risk-taker, and had a love for "shenanigans", much like his father. He often got in trouble for the pranks he pulled on whoever was his next victim. The pranks were harmless, yet hilarious, and were the fodder for marvellous stories. Like his brothers, Patrick was an excellent athlete, eventually earning NCAA All-American honors while in college in football. How he transformed from his youthful self to the man he became as an adult can only be explained by one thing, a patient wife named Colleen. That patience would soon be put to the test.

THOMAS J. FEELY

Chapter 18
An Extraordinary Danger to the Nation
Orlando, Florida
February 19th, 2025

It was mid-morning on a cloudy day at Partick and Colleen's home in Orlando, Florida. The two lived in the home with their daughters, Elizabeth and Zoey, and two dogs. Patrick had built the home himself, as he had gained a stellar reputation as a master home builder, although he was self-taught. His father, and for that matter, all his relatives were not educated in the world of construction. Elizabeth, a college sophomore at FAU, was forced by the civil war, with all the violence it brought to college campuses, to remain at home. Her classes were all being held online with the professors also teaching from their homes. Elizabeth hated, with a passion, attending class virtually, as she had done for many semesters during her high school days because of the pandemic, but once again she had no choice. Zoey, age 14, also missed seeing her friends at school, and at her cross-country practices, but she felt more comfortable attending classes online. She did not have to deal with bullying by her classmates when she was remote learning, and that was a definite positive. Zoey, like her older sister, is a beautiful girl, but Zoey has always had to cope with her asthma. As long as she had her inhaler and used it daily, she could live an everyday life of a 14-year-old teenager, who loves distance running. She never complained or even hinted at feeling put out by her affliction, and the medical remedy is required. Zoey was, as Patrick called her, a "trooper", always cheerful and always sweet. She got that disposition from her parents, who were of true Irish descent and were always seeing the greener side of the countryside. But on this day, her parents, Patrick and Colleen were very concerned about Zoey's health. As much as they tried, and they have been doing everything possible, they could not find any way to replenish their supply of asthma medication. They were almost entirely out, and were panicking. Both Patrick and Colleen were on their phones calling every drugstore, hospital, and even random doctor's offices, trying to acquire the inhalers, to no avail.

Patrick called his childhood best friend, Dr. Vincent Sampson, whose parents were Tully and Cathleen's best friends and next-door neighbors since they moved into the neighborhood when Patrick and Vincent were both 8 years old. Vinny is an emergency room physician at Tampa General Hospital. Patrick declared to his lifelong friend, "Hey Vinny, I really need your help. We are about to run out of albuterol for Zoey. I can't find any pharmacy here in Orlando able to provide us with it. Please, can you help!" Vinny explained, "Well, albuterol is in short supply right now, but I'll see what I can do. Can you meet me this afternoon at my parent's home? I get off my shift at 2:00 and can be there by 2:30." Patrick was elated about finally getting some hope and replied, "That is awesome news, Vinny, I appreciate it so much. I will be there. It will give me a chance to see Catherine". Vinny concurred, "I want to check on her as well. We'll see you then." Patrick was ecstatic at the opportunity to finally get a supply of inhalers, just in time for Zoey. He hung up his phone and yelled the good news to Colleen who was with Zoey in her bedroom. He quickly jumped in his Range Rover and began his drive to Tampa calculating his arrival to be about 2:30, just in time to meet Vinny. He knew he could not spend too much time in Tampa. If he left there at 3:00 he should get back by 6:00 pm, just as the curfew requires. Patrick took the same back road route he used when he went to his brother's home to search for Tommy. When he got just outside of Lakeland, just an hour from his destination, he came across a detour that was not there the last time. He followed the signs, following the arrows, he realized this was going to make him later than he wanted to arrive. By the time Patrick arrived at the home of Vinny's parents, it was after 3:00, but Vinny was still there. Vinny handed over the package containing the lifesaving medication to Patrick and they both went next door to visit Tully and Catherine. Catherine was thrilled to see her son, and Vinny as well, as Vinny was like a son to both her and her husband. When they went on long family road trips to the cabin in Northern Minnesota, Vinny was always with them, just like another son in the family. The rendezvous between all of them was brief and emotional. Patrick gave Catherine, then Tully, a long hug and

THE CROWNING: CULMINATION OF THE NATION

said his goodbyes to everyone, reinforcing, once again, his gratitude to Vinny for delivering the albuterol. When he glanced at the clock, as he got into his SUV and started the Range Rover, he realized it was almost 3:30. He decided he needed to take the shorter route home by trying to navigate the I-4 Interstate, hoping that his four-wheel-drive SUV could maneuver around the masses of abandoned vehicles that had been sabotaged, pillaged for any valuables and usually set on fire. There were many semi-trucks and the bones of destroyed cars, on their sides blocking the roads altogether.

Patrick was driven by the fear that he would not get back home on time for Zoey, so he dodged the rubble and heaps of vehicles as he made his way eastward on the interstate going as fast as he could. He watched carefully for overpasses that still had people on them, presumably to do harm to any foolish travelers driving on this forbidden no-man's-land. As Patrick was going under these death traps, if he spotted a lookout on the bridge, he would stop his SUV, while directly under the bridge, pause for a few seconds, then after seeing a rock or cement block hit the pavement on the other side of the bridge, he would hit the gas to get away before they could reload. This strategy worked very well, but Patrick feared it was causing him to take too long to get home. Hoping to gain precious seconds, he hit the gas, instead of stopping, the next time he drove under an overpass. The next overpass came up at the intersection of I-4 and Highway 27 near Haines City. As Patrick approached, he saw the familiar lookout guys watching Patrick's Range Rover and shouting instructions to someone out of Patrick's sight. Patrick waited until he was about to go under the bridge and, as he planned, floored it. Just as he emerged at the east side of the bridge a loud crashing sound, as if he had been suddenly rear-ended, caused Patrick to bounce up and hit his head on the roof of the SUV so hard that he momentarily lost consciousness, and lost control of the SUV.

The Range Rover swerved off the interstate and plowed into the median just missing two other vehicles that were already destroyed. Patrick had sped up just before the crash so it was still traversing through the tall grass at a high speed when it abruptly hit a ditch which forced the vehicle to a sudden stop. Patrick recovered quickly from his state of being concussed. He opened his eyes to hear a loud ringing in his ears and blurry vision. He looked behind him to find a large hole in his roof. When he looked down, still stunned by the impact, Patrick noticed a cement block in the back seat directly behind his driver's seat. The cement block was caught by the backseat, which was severely damaged. The block missed Patrick's head by less than a foot.

Patrick's vision cleared, and he realized there was a crowd of screaming people running for the grounded Range Rover. Patrick knew he was in serious trouble and he needed to flee the scene before they surrounded his vehicle. He turned the key, but the engine would not start. They were getting closer and he could see sticks and bats in their hands. He pumped the pedal a few times and tried the ignition again. This time it turned over, and he could shift the transmission into drive and lurch out of the ditch that had stopped the car. Looking in the rearview mirror he could see the mob still chasing the SUV and throwing their bats at the car when they gave up running. Patrick could feel from the vibration that at least one of the front tires was flat from the sudden stop. Stopping to check out the tire was not an option. He would have to drive it as it was, flat tire and all. By the time Patrick reached his home the right front tire was gone entirely and Patrick was driving on the rim. He pulled into the driveway and rushed into his house with the albuterol in hand. Patrick kept the story to himself until he and Colleen were alone after the girls had gone to bed. It was not until that moment, telling the story for the first time, Patrick realized how incredibly lucky he was to have survived. Colleen, although grateful for his escape, scolded Patrick for taking such a colossal risk by driving on the Interstate. "Have you completely lost your mind?" she asked angrily. Patrick grinned with his best imitation of a leprechaun and said, "I almost lost my mind and my entire head." Colleen was not amused. He vowed he would never again take that chance. That night, lying in bed, Patrick worried about how he would get the next batch of albuterol. What Vinny was able to acquire for him was enough for about a month. "What then?" he asked himself out loud.

Patrick wasn't too eager to tell everyone, especially his parents how he almost got himself killed by taking an unnecessary and dangerous risk. He already had the reputation of being a daredevil, one he earned as young as two years old when he climbed a tree, or when he was four years old jumping off a 30-foot cliff into a lake in Arkansas, but this was different. This was reckless and Patrick knew it. Tully and Catherine were unaware of the nightmare their son, Patrick, just experienced after leaving their home.

THE CROWNING: CULMINATION OF THE NATION

Tully stayed by Catherine's bed until she fell asleep. She was definitely getting stronger and restless. Tully knows too well that she feels called to the breathtaking gardens she has developed over the years, to tend to her flowers. He also sensed that Catherine, being stuck in bed, is already getting restless and she wanted to get her past life back. After Catherine fell into a deep sleep, Tully texted Grace who has been staying with her Mom in her private hospital room. Suzanne was still on the ventilator and sleeping almost around the clock except for brief moments when she would wake up and look at Grace with soulful eyes. Tully typed, "Hi Grace. How is it going?" Grace responded "Hi Grandpa, Mom is sleeping a lot now. The ventilator is doing the breathing for her. I am getting worried now that she may give up the fight." "Why do you say that?" Tully asked. Grace explained, "Her eyes tell me that more than anything else. She is losing the emotion in her eyes. It's almost as if when she wakes up and she is disappointed she is still alive. Her pulse is getting slowly weaker and her blood pressure is declining." Tully suspected Grace was succumbing to hopelessness, so he stressed to Grace, "Keep talking to her, even if she seems asleep. She may hear your voice and that may give her reason to want to live. Tell her stories from your childhood, the things she would fondly remember. Make her want to see her family again. You can't give up and wait for her to improve. Keep her engaged in the fight. I will also do something for her." Grace wondered aloud, "Other than praying, what else could you do?" Tully acknowledged he lacked a plan saying, "I don't know for sure, but I'll let you know when I figure that out. We can't sit back and wait. Have your family FaceTime with her as well. She needs to hear their voices." Grace promised, "Ok Grandpa. I will try to make that happen." Tully raised his voice to emphasize his confidence saying, "Don't worry darling, I've got your back." Feeling encouraged by her grandfather's optimism Grace responded, "I've got this, Grandpa. I've got this!" She was trying to convince herself as much as her grandpa.

Tully was determined to find an option, no matter how implausible, so he immediately began searching the internet for information on Covid-19 treatments for the remainder of the afternoon. After several hours he found an article in a medical journal from 2021 about a life-support system called ECMO that can rescue COVID-19 patients from the brink of death. Children and adults with critical illnesses have been treated with extracorporeal membrane oxygenation (ECMO) for decades in select hospitals. This device temporarily replaces both the heart and the lungs, circulating the blood outside the body under constant medical supervision. For fear of harming their lungs, some experts were reluctant to place COVID-19 patients on ECMO at the start of the pandemic. Just less than half of COVID on ECMO patients survived at least 90 days in spring 2020, down from about 60% in spring 2020.[34]

The article was written by Dr. Barbaro, who wrote, "What we noticed right away is that the patients treated later in the pandemic were staying on ECMO longer, going from an average of 14 days to 20 days. They were dying more often, and these deaths were different," said Dr. Barbaro. "This shows that we need to be thoughtful about who we're putting on ECMO and when we're deciding to take patients off who aren't getting better. Across the U.S. right now, we have places where ECMO is a scarce resource whereas in Michigan it's not quite at that point, but we expect it might be."[34]

Tully learned, as he continued to research, that it can be challenging, especially during this national crisis, to transfer patients from distant states to an ECMO-capable hospital when there are many hospitals coping with numerous critically ill COVID-19 patients. In order to support each ECMO patient, a wide range of resources are needed, including the machines, tubing, and specially trained nurses, respiratory therapists, and other staff required to make it all work, not to mention teams of specially trained people, adequate blood supply, and other factors.[34] One place that had everything in place is at the University of Michigan Medical School. Tully thought to himself about the irony of that fact since both James and Suzanne attended the University of Michigan, which is where they met. James, from 1994 to 1998 also played football for the Michigan Wolverines and Suzanne was in the Pre-Med program. They were married in the summer of 1997 with both still having one year left to attend the University before graduating.

This was an option no one in Arizona had ever mentioned, as there was nothing like ECMO anywhere near them, and it is very difficult to even be

THE CROWNING: CULMINATION OF THE NATION

accepted as a patient. They had to become very selective who they choose to use the resource-intensive medical treatment. Tully picked up the phone and called James, hoping he was strong enough for this challenging conversation. James answered the phone, and his voice seemed to show he was feeling better, "Hi Dad". Tully queried, "How are you feeling?" James exclaimed, "I am getting stronger. I still have difficulty breathing, and need lots of sleep but I feel better today than I have in over a month". "You sound better," Tully affirmed. "That is the first time you said an entire long sentence with no breath of oxygen." James reported, "I spoke with Grace. She is anxious about Suzanne. We are planning a FaceTime call with her after dinner tonight. She told me you suggested this." Tully explained, "I think she needs to hear yours, and all your kids' voices. She needs to rekindle her feelings of love for everyone in order to invigorate her desire to be with you all again. You all need to talk like you all have done thousands of times at the kitchen table after dinner. Talk, laugh, sing, tell stories, anything fun. She needs to hear that. No one somber, everyone having a good time and wishing she will be home soon, to join the fun." James concurred, "Ya, I think we all need that."

It was time to run his new plan to possibly save Suzanne's life, albeit it being a "hail Mary pass", so Tully took a moment of silence to select his words carefully, then said, "Listen, I have been doing research and I found something that just might save her life. This is a treatment called ECMO, which has a 50% success rate with Covid patients that are on their deathbeds. It is much more than just a drug, it requires special equipment, and highly trained professionals running it so there are very few places you can get this treatment, but one of the leading institutions that offer it is the University of Michigan's Medical School. It might take some work but maybe we can get Suzanne approved for that treatment." James received the news favorably saying, "That sounds promising. We need to try our best. It might be her last hope. I'll call my U.M. contacts that still work there and see what they would recommend we do to get her accepted." "That is exactly what I had in mind," Tully declared, "You have the contacts from your five years there, and you remained active in alumni events, so maybe that history can help us now. I will talk to Grace about working with Suzanne's doctors to make a referral to them. They will need her medical records to determine if she is qualified." James was puzzled, asking, "Qualified? What do you mean by "qualified"? She is dying. How much more do you need to be qualified?" James was getting short-tempered, which he was inclined to do when things were outside of his control. Recognizing his son's impatience, Tully explained, "From what I read, they can only accept a few patients as it is very resource intensive and takes months to work, so they only accept those they feel offer the best chance for success."

Feeling both helpless and too tired to fight, James relented to his Dad's outlook, "OK, Dad. Thanks for your help. Let me know what her doctors say about it." "I will," Tully stated, "Grace, being a nurse there, is going to be an asset in making this happen. Maybe, because of her, they will go the extra mile for her. I will call you tomorrow, James. Keep getting stronger". "I will, Dad, I promise," James said before hanging up.

Tully finally felt like he was helping there, even though he could not go to Arizona, and that gave him a sense of satisfaction. He prepared Catherine's dinner, another very healthy smoothie, wondering when she would start requesting solid food. Catherine was staying awake longer, which was a sign that she was also getting stronger. She asked to watch the show, Truth with Tully, so Tully set the computer up in the bedroom so they could watch it together. When 6:00 arrived the computer was ready with the word, Truth, showing on the screen. That word remained on the screen with no other action for several minutes after 6 pm causing Tully concern that the government may have intercepted the broadcast, or captured the newscasters. Finally, the word Truth faded into the background and a familiar figure was standing before the camera. It was Chester Colt, who was the first host of the Truth and was rumored to have been caught and arrested.

Chester Colt declared, "Good evening, and yes this really is Chester Colt. I know and appreciate that my sudden disappearance caused most of you to fear the worst, however, rumors of my demise have been greatly exaggerated. I am fine and delighted to be back on Truth to bring to you the next chapter in our journey. I must not disclose too much for fear of putting my colleagues and this crucial project at risk of termination, but my hiatus, and the story of my death, was necessary, as my previous location was being exposed, I and my crew, were forced to go underground again to move to somewhere safer. We are safe now, at least for the time being, and will take the baton once again allowing my colleagues to use the time

THE CROWNING: CULMINATION OF THE NATION

to also move. Tonight, for the historical record to be accurate, we are going to report on the 2nd Impeachment Trial of former President Donald J. Trump. Only the third President in our nation's history to be impeached, Donald Trump is also the only one in our history to be impeached twice, and the first to face impeachment after leaving office. The Senate is charged by the Constitution to decide if the former president is guilty of inciting this assault that left five people dead. Most senators in the Republican party claimed that the Senate lacked the constitutional authority to conduct a trial against a former president before the trial began. As Trump is no longer the president when the impeachment trial takes place, what really was at stake in this trial is whether he is allowed to run for elected office again. On the eve of the trial, 150 legal scholars from across the spectrum of political opinions published an open letter affirming "that the Constitution permits impeachment, conviction, and disqualification of former officers, including presidents.[35]

What we will do to present, for the historical record, video clips of the most critical and pertinent arguments by both sides given during the trial. We begin first with the Senate majority leader, Chuck Schumer who spoke just prior to the start of the trial when he said, "The Senate has a solemn responsibility to try and hold Donald Trump accountable for the most serious charges ever, ever levied against a president. Those who say let's move on, that brings unity, are false. When you had such a serious invasion of the Capitol incited by a president... there must be truth and accountability."

Chester Colt reported "On the other side of the aisle, prior to the start of the trial in the Senate, Senator Rand Paul introduced a measure in the Senate regarding the constitutionality of holding the impeachment trial. Only five Republican senators disagreed with him, stating that the trial should take place, illustrating how steep the road was to conviction, especially considering the threshold needed to secure the conviction is 2/3rds. That means 67 of the Senators would need to vote in favor of conviction. The trial begins with Congressman Jamie Raskin giving the opening remarks."

Congressman Jamie Raskin, speaking to the Senate contended, "You will not be hearing extended lectures from me because our case is based on cold, hard facts. It's all about the facts. President Trump has sent his lawyers, who are here today to try to stop the Senate from hearing the facts of this case. They want to call the trial over before any evidence is even introduced. Their argument is that if you commit an impeachable offense in your last few weeks in office, you do it with constitutional impunity. You get away with it. In other words, conduct, that would be a high crime and misdemeanor in your first year as president and your second year as president, your third year as president, and for the vast majority of your fourth year, as president, you can suddenly do in your last few weeks in office without facing any constitutional accountability at all, this would create a brand new January exception to the constitution of the United States of America, a January exception, and everyone can see immediately why this is so dangerous. It's an invitation to the president to take his best shot at anything he may want to do on his way out the door, including using violent means to lock that door, to hang on to the oval office at all costs, and to block the peaceful transfer of power. In other words, the January exception is an invitation to our founder's worst nightmare. And if we buy this radical argument that President Trump's lawyers advance, we risk allowing January 6th to become our future."

Chester Colt interjected, "Raskin, the lead manager, played a video showing the horrific violence of the rioting at the Capitol along with a collage of many of President Trump's many speeches encouraging the crowd to march to the Capitol to "fight like hell". Raskin says to the Senators, "The president was impeached by the U.S. House of Representatives on January 13th for doing that, you ask what a high crime and misdemeanor is under our constitution? That's a high crime and misdemeanor. If that's not an impeachable offense, then there is no such thing. And if the President's arguments for a January exception are upheld, then even if everyone agrees that he's culpable for these events, even if the evidence proves, as we think it definitely does, that the President incited a violent insurrection on the day Congress met to finalize the presidential election. He would have you believe there is absolutely nothing the Senate can do about it. No trial, no facts. He wants you to decide that the Senate is powerless at that point. That can't be right. The transition of power is always the most dangerous moment for democracies. Every historian will tell you we just saw it in the most astonishing way.

THE CROWNING: CULMINATION OF THE NATION

We lived through it. And you know what? The Framers of our Constitution knew it. That's why they created a Constitution with an oath written into it that binds the President from his very first day in office until his very last day in office, and every day in between, under that Constitution. And under that oath, the President of the United States is forbidden to commit high crimes and misdemeanors against the people at any point that he's in office. Indeed. That's one specific reason. The impeachment conviction and disqualification powers exist to protect us against presidents who try to overrun the power of the people in their elections and replace the rule of law with the rule of mobs. These powers must apply. Even if the president commits his offenses in his final weeks in office. In fact, that's precisely when we need them the most because that's when elections get attacked."

Chester Colt added, "After, Joe Neguse, Congressman from Colorado, described the past historic precedents of cases where government officials have been impeached after they had left their office, establishing the necessity of holding officials accountable for their actions through the Constitutional power granted to the Senate of removal from office and disqualification of holding any government office in the future. He also explained how the Constitution does not say the removal must take place before disqualification can be declared, so if an offender is found guilty of the offense causing the impeachment, he can't escape being disqualified from future office by simply resigning before an impeachment trial occurs, or during the trial. Next, the floor was given to Congressman David Cicilline from Rhode Island. Here is part of what he said to the jury, "Mr. President distinguished senators. My name is David Cicilline. As I hope is now clear from the arguments of Mr. Raskin, and Mr. Neguse, impeachment is not merely about removing someone from office. Fundamentally impeachment exists to protect our constitutional system, to keep each of us safe, to uphold our freedom, to safeguard our democracy. It achieves that by deterring abuse of the extraordinary power that we entrust to our presidents from the very first day in office to the very last day, it also ensures accountability for those who harm us or our government in the aftermath of a tragedy. It allows us an opportunity to come together and to heal by working through what happened and reaffirming our constitutional principles. And it authorizes this body and this body alone to disqualify him from our political system.

Anybody whose conduct in office proves that they present a danger to the Republic, but impeachment would fail to achieve these purposes. If you created for the first time ever, despite the words of the framers and the constitution, a January exception as Mr. Raskin explained. Now, I was a former defense lawyer for many years, and I can understand why President Trump and his lawyers don't want you to hear this case, why they don't want you to see the evidence, but the argument that you lack jurisdiction rests on a purely fictional loophole, purely fictional, designed to allow the former president to escape all accountability for conduct that is truly indefensible under our constitution. You saw the consequences of his actions in the video that we played earlier. I'd like to emphasize in still greater detail, the extraordinary constitutional offense that the former president thinks you have no power whatsoever to adjudicate. While spreading lies about the election outcome and a brazen attempt to retain power against the will of the American people. He incited an armed, angry mob to riot and not just anywhere, but here in the seat of our government, in the Capitol, during a joint session of Congress, when the vice president presided, while we carried out the peaceful transfer of power, which was interrupted for the first time in our history. This was a disaster of historic proportions. It was also an unforgivable betrayal of the oath of office of President Trump. The oath, he swore, an oath said he sullied and dishonored to advance his own personal interests and make no mistake about it. As you think about that day, things could have been much worse. As one Senator said, 'They could have killed all of us'.

Now virtually every American who saw those events unfold on television was absolutely horrified by the events of January 6th. But we also know how President Trump, himself, felt about the attack. He told us here's what he tweeted at 6:01 pm as the capital was in shambles and as dozens of police officers and other law enforcement officers lay battered and bruised and bloodied. Here's what he said, "These are the things and events that happen when a sacred landslide election victory is so unceremoniously and viciously stripped away from great Patriots who have been badly and unfairly treated for so long. Go home with love and in peace. Remember this day forever." Every time I read that tweet, it chills me to the core. The President of the United States sided with the insurrectionists. He celebrated their cause. He

THE CROWNING: CULMINATION OF THE NATION

validated their attack. He told them, "Remember this day forever", hours after they marched through these halls, looking to assassinate Vice-president Pence, the Speaker of the House, and any of us they could find. Given all that, it's no wonder that President Trump would rather talk about jurisdiction and a supposed January exception, rather than talk about what happened on January 6th. Make no mistake, his arguments are dead wrong. They're distractions from what really matters. The Senate can and should require President Trump to stand trial. My colleagues have already addressed many of President Trump's attempts to escape trial. I'd like to cover the remainder, and then address the broader issues at stake in this trial. For starters, in an extension of his mistaken reading of the Constitution, President Trump insists he cannot face trial in the Senate because he's merely a private citizen. He references here the bill of attainder clause. But as Mr. Neguse just explained, the Constitution refers to the defendant in an impeachment trial as a person and a party. And certainly, he counts as one of those. Let's also apply some common sense. There's a reason that he now insists on being called the 45th President of the United States, rather than citizen Trump. He's not a randomly selected private citizen. He's a former officer of the United States government. He's a former President of the United States of America. He's treated differently under a law called the Former Presidents Act. For four years, we trusted him with more power than anyone else on Earth. As a former president who promised on the Bible to use his power faithfully, he can and should answer for whether he kept that promise while bound by it in office. His insistence otherwise is just wrong. And so, so is this claim that there's a slippery slope to impeaching private citizens if you proceed. The trial of a former official for abuses he committed as an official, arising from an impeachment that occurred while he was an official, poses absolutely no risk whatsoever of subjecting a private citizen to impeachment for their private conduct. To emphasize the point, President Trump was impeached while he was in office for conduct in office, period. The alternative, once again, is this January exception in which our most powerful officials can commit the most terrible abuses, and then resign to leave office and suddenly claim that they're just a private citizens who can't be held accountable at all. In the same vein, President Trump and his lawyers argue that he shouldn't be impeached because it will set a bad precedent for impeaching others. But that slippery slope argument is also incorrect. For centuries, the prevailing view has been that former officials are subject to impeachment, and you just heard a full discussion of that.

The House has repeatedly acknowledged that fact, but in the vast majority of cases, the House has rightly recognized that in officials, resignation or departure makes the extraordinary step of impeachment unnecessary, and maybe even unwise. As a House manager, Riley explained in the Belknap case, and I quote, "There is no likelihood that we shall ever unlimber the clumsy and bulky monster piece of the ordinance to take aim at an object from which all danger has gone by." President Trump's case though is different. The danger has not gone by, his threat to democracy makes any prior abuse by any government official pale in comparison, moreover, allowing his conduct to pass without the most decisive response would itself create an extraordinary danger to the nation. Inviting further abuse of power and signaling that the Congress of the United States is unable or unwilling to respond to insurrection incited by the President."

Chester Colt concluded, "Those words, spoken four years ago, in hindsight, were eerily prophetic to everything that would follow in the lead-up to the 2024 election. His warning that day by Congressman Cicilline was worthy of a Nostradamus caliber forecast: "The danger has not gone by, his threat to democracy makes any prior abuse by any government official pale in comparison, moreover, allowing his conduct to pass without the most decisive response would itself create an extraordinary danger to the nation". We will be back tomorrow night to cover the President's defense attorney's response in defense against the arguments presented by the Impeachment Managers."

Tully looked over at Catherine to see what her reaction to the broadcast was but he found her to be sound asleep. With that, he quietly retreated downstairs to begin his nightly sentinel duties. A couple of hours had passed quietly when the squeaking sound, made by opening the screen door of the lanais enclosing the pool in the back of Tully's house, woke Tully from a sleep he did not intend to be doing.

Chapter 19
Destitute and Homeless
Tampa, Florida
February 19th, 2025

The chair in his living room, which Tully sat in every night while on guard, was situated where he could see all three of the doors to the house. Tully watched quietly, while slowly reaching for his gun. A shadow of a figure moved stealthily to the back door by the patio. Another dark figure appears at the second door by the kitchen. Then a third shows up in the window of the front door. Tully's heart pounded so loud that he feared they could hear it beating. This was the first time that the horde of destitute and homeless had entered their neighborhood. Tully heard as all three of the violators tested the doors to see if they were locked. The handles were jiggled enough to find out that the locks were set. All three doors, recently replaced with hurricane-proof doors, had built into the doors a set of four locks in each door, and the hurricane-proof windows also were extra strong, rated for up to a Category-4 hurricane or E-4 tornado, so they should hold up well to an attempted break-in. Still, Tully was prepared, in case they penetrated the barriers, with his one semi-automatic Beretta. Tully had never been an enormous gun enthusiast. Other than two antique Russian hunting shotguns he kept in storage, which have not been shot in over 30 years, Tully and Catherine were opposed to having a gun in the house while it was occupied with children. With the kids all grown and living out of their home, they broke down and purchased the Beretta after the riots of the summer of 2020 came so close to their home. Now, was the first time that a gun became something Tully appreciated for the ability to protect himself and his wife. That fear of home invasion has just become a reality with three men literally at their doorstep. Tully breathed as quietly as possible, watching each of the doors while sitting in the dark. He wondered if he would have what it takes to shoot a person if forced to do so. Tully blocked that doubt from his mind by reminding himself he had to protect Catherine, at all costs, and if they broke in, he vowed to himself they would not survive. "I will shoot to kill," he thought to himself, remembering the advice he received from his retired buddies who had military careers, warning against the strategy of merely firing warning shots or shooting someone in the leg, both of which might still lead to being overwhelmed and disarmed by the criminals. Tully worried perhaps they had found his secret trail through the woods and followed it to their back door.

As quickly as the unwanted intruders arrived, they each quickly left after finding the doors were locked and disappeared into the night. Tully immediately called his neighbors to alert them of the invaders. They all were grateful for the call, even though it was in the middle of the night. Tully looked out the windows on all sides of the home but saw no sign of life. He brewed the coffee now, hours before daybreak, because he could never go back to sleep after that incident. He was grateful they did not cause a commotion that would have woken up Catherine. She needs uninterrupted sleep to recover from her wounds. Tully concluded they were just on a scouting trip, looking for abandoned homes, with no intention of breaking into an occupied dwelling. He realized he forgot to leave some lights on to let them know they were home. "Still," Tully surmised to himself, "you never know what someone would do if they were desperate enough". That may still happen one day. He needed to be better prepared. "What if they were armed with guns of their own?," Tully wondered. He turned on the T.V. to catch up on the news. The T.V. was already tuned into the only remaining news channel, Cerberus World News. Tully learned that the war in Europe and Asia, which the news commentators were refraining from referring to as a "World War" but "regional hostilities", continued to rage on and was slowly and systematically advancing by carving out small but strategic slices of land and cities, declaring that region as being "Independent" and requesting the "protection" of the invaders. With the U.S. in such disarray domestically, the current administration was unwilling or unable to get involved in those "foreign hostilities" choosing instead to use its military to regain control of the local cities domestically, which are all being destroyed by the violent clashes between the different warring domestic factions. The Troops overseas

THE CROWNING: CULMINATION OF THE NATION

were told to stand down and not engage in defending our allies, while at home the Army and National Guard were deployed to every major city in the country or were sent to bases near the southern border. "Nothing seemed to have changed on the world scene but the ground troops at home were being deployed suspiciously, " Tully concluded while talking to himself. He turned off what he considered being a pseudo-news channel and prepared breakfast for Catherine and himself. He had decided to not mention the visitors they had during the night to Catherine, for fear she would become frightened and Tully did not want her worrying about things she could not control.

Later that afternoon, on Wednesday, February 20, Tully got a text from Grace that read, "Dr. Thompson has agreed to refer Mom for the ECMO treatment at the University of Michigan's Medical School. He felt she was a perfect candidate as she had good health before getting Covid-19, and she is still relatively young. We will keep you informed about what they decide at UM." Tully replied, "That is great news!"

Tully called James to let him know about the news. James, however, already knew about it and was working the phone with his UM contacts advocating for her acceptance into the hospital. He sent a text back to Tully that read, "Can't talk now, on phone with my former head football coach, Lloyd Carr". Later, James called back, saying "Hi Dad. Thanks for understanding, I asked Coach Carr if he could help and he immediately made a call to the UM Department Head of the Medical School. He promised to watch for the referral and fast-track it to the Committee that makes those admissions decisions." Tully reacted with surprise, "Wow, you would think we were trying to get her admitted into the Medical School as a student. "James concurred, "I know, right? They are very selective of who they will accept for this treatment therapy, as you said. All we can do now is wait to see what they decide."

Tully inquired, "How is she doing now?" James observed, "I think she heard us last night when we were Facetiming her. We really lived it up and Grace said she seemed to open her eyes and was moving her hand as if to the beat of the music we were singing to. Grace said her heart rate increased during that call." "That sure sounds like she was trying to take part, " Tully reflected. "That is fantastic news. You all need to do that as often as possible. Let me know if you hear anything new." James informed, "I will Dad. I plan on getting up to walk around the house today. I need to move and get my stamina back." "Yes, that is exactly what you need to do. The golf courses miss you," Tully jokes. James began laughing hard, until he began coughing, "I miss them too, James declared." Tully enjoyed hearing James laugh until the deep cough reminded him of the seriousness of his condition. "I'll let you go now. Text me if anything happens." James replied, "Ok, will do, Dad."

More than a week passed with no word of Suzanne's admission status into the ECMO treatment at the University of Michigan's Medical School. Finally, on Friday morning, Tully's cell phone rang, and "James" appeared on the phone's screen. Tully wanted to remain calm, not wanting to get his hopes too high.

Chapter 20
Political Malpractice and other Illicit Behaviors
Tampa, Florida
February 28th, 2025

"Hi James, how are you feeling today?" Tully asked his older son. "Dad! They accepted her" James exclaimed with excitement in his voice, which Tully had not heard for many months. Tully, puzzled by which "her" he meant, asked, "Who, Suzanne?" James declared, "Yes! Suzanne! She is going to be admitted as soon as we can get her there. Chase, Grace, and I are going to drive her there." Tully was alarmed by this plan thinking about his trip home from Tony's home. Tully stressed, "Whoa, wait for a second there partner. You have been out of everyday life for over a month, I don't think you realize how hard, how impossible, it would be to drive from Phoenix, Arizona to Ann Arbor, Michigan. All Interstate highways are impassable and back roads are very dangerous. It could take you weeks to get that far, and your chances of making it at all would be very slim. James argued, "Dad, we have no choice but to drive. The airlines have closed off all commercial flights, and we explored hiring an air ambulance and they are not operating either." Tully noted, 'You were just released from Intensive Care and would still be in inpatient rehab now, under normal circumstances, rather than recovering at home. You're in no shape to be undertaking a very dangerous and very long trip." James urged, in an exacerbated voice, "I have to drive with them. Grace needs to be caring for Suzanne, so she can't drive, and Chase can't be the only driver. I need to drive with them." Tully thought for a minute about the dilemma, then said, "Give me one day to come up with an alternative plan. I will call you back either tonight or tomorrow." James, giving into his father's persistent insistence, relented, "Ok, that is all the time we can afford. We need to get her there as soon as possible. I'm really afraid if we don't hurry we will lose her." Tully, trying to assure James he would be successful, said, "I will call you back as soon as I have a plan." Tully immediately placed a call to Paul, Tully and Catherine's fifth son who is stationed in Miami. He is a pilot for the Coast Guard, trained, like all Coast Guard pilots, to fly a variety of small planes, and Paul is also an expert helicopter pilot, currently flying the Airbus MH-65 Dolphin, used for medevac, search and rescue operations and Airborne Use of Force missions. Tully explained to Paul that Suzanne is in a life-or-death situation. Paul asked a few questions first and then said he would go to his commanding officer to request an emergency family leave of absence. "I can't make a promise", Paul said" but I'll do my best to make this happen."

Tully did not know that Paul and Michael had stayed in very close contact with each other through backdoor channels that were secure from unwanted surveillance of their conversations. During Michael's training to become an Intelligence Officer in the Air Force, Michael worked at the National Security Agency, in their Central Security Service. To maintain military integration, Central Security Service coordinates and creates policies and direction on the missions including cybersecurity and signals intelligence. Because of this experience, Michael has access to secure and encrypted communication tools not available to anyone outside of the agency. Paul, in turn, was privy to the planning of operations within the Coast Guard, giving him an insider perspective of the events surrounding the changing roles of the Coast Guard, from a mission of primarily search and rescue, to being the eyes and ears along the coast.

The two brothers shared with each other their observations and developed a mutual commitment to save the nation from foreign infiltration, and their family members from becoming victims.

Tully called another friend, Manny, who served in the Air Force as a pilot. Manny flew for 30 years before retiring, and now works as a contractor for the same branch, flying occasional flights to Central and South America. Manny was more than happy to help. He owns his own Cessna 172 Skyhawk which he uses to train new aspiring pilots. Tully explained to Manny the situation and wondered if he could help. Manny explained he was scheduled to fly to Honduras the day after tomorrow, however, he offered to loan

THE CROWNING: CULMINATION OF THE NATION

us his Cessna. "I would need to have your son go up with me to show him the features and instrumentation of the plane. He may or may not be familiar with that plane." "I understand," Tully replied with a tinge of worry in his voice. Tully was concerned he could not get Paul here on time to have the instructional flight. "I'll find out if Paul can get away if he is given permission to leave his base." Tully hung up and just said a prayer that this plan would work out. Later, around 5:00 in the afternoon, Paul calls his dad and says, "My commanding officer gave me the emergency family leave. I can fly from Miami to Tampa tomorrow morning on a Coast Guard flight already scheduled to fly there." Tully exclaimed, "Awesome. Have you ever flown a Cessna 172 Skyhawk?" "Are you kidding?" Paul said laughing at the irony, "That is the exact plane I trained on for an entire year before getting my wings. I know that plane inside and out."

Tully remarked, "That is incredible. God has his hand in this. That is the plane my friend, Manny, is going to loan us. He wants to take you up for a test run tomorrow. He leaves overseas for his job the next morning. Paul instructed, "Pick me up at the Coast Guard Landing Strip at the Clearwater/ St. Petersburg Airport at about 9:00 am tomorrow morning. We can go directly to the hangar where he stores his plane so we can get that test flight done on time. I will work on flight plans from Tampa to Phoenix, then from Phoenix to Ann Arbor tonight. I have a lot of research to do tonight." Tully assured Paul, "I will be at the airport tomorrow by 9:00 sharp. See you there."

Tully knew he would have a hard time getting to that airport as it is on the other side of the Bay. There are several major roads with long bridges over Tampa Bay to get there but they too would likely be clogged with abandoned cars and trucks.

That night Tully called James and found that Grace was with James at the house. He told them of his "alternate plan," and how well it has fallen in place. He explained how this plan would get Suzanne to Ann Arbor far faster than driving her there, even if you had left by a car tomorrow morning. "I think we will get Paul to the closest airport, the Phoenix-Mesa Gateway Airport, by Sunday around noon. He is working on the flight plans now." James asked, "How many can the plane carry?" Tully spoke as persuasively as possible, "Four including the pilot," Tully responded, "that will mean two more can travel with Suzanne. I suggest those two be Grace and Chase.

James, you need to stay home and rest, you're still in recovery, and on medication." There was a long silence and Tully imagined they were all just looking for James to say something. James breaks the silence with a voice choked up from fighting back tears, "I need to be with Suzanne." Another long silence occurred until Grace, James and Suzanne's oldest child, said "Dad. Grandpa is right. You need to stay here and continue getting stronger. Mom may be there for a very long time. Chase should ride in the Co-Pilot seat. He is healthy, you are not. I will ride in the back with Mom." Chase added, "Dad, I agree with Grace and Grandpa. We've got this, Ok?" James, failing to hold back the tears, and unable to talk, simply nodded his head in reluctant agreement. Grace declared, "We're down for your plan Grandpa. I already got permission at the hospital to travel with Mom and stay with her for the duration of her stay, no matter how long it takes."

Tully clarified, "I will forward the flight plan to you all when Paul sends me it by email. Grace, you need to prepare your sisters to take good care of your Dad while you and Chase are gone. Chase, I need you to fly back to Phoenix with Paul, he will drop you off and you will need to have Grady pick you up and bring you back home. Grace, make sure Grady is on board with taking care of the family at your home." Grace stated, "No worries Grandpa, that goes without saying. He loves them very much, and is very protective." Tully concluded, "Ok, we are set. I will leave early in the morning to pick up Paul. I have to figure out how to get to Clearwater/ St. Petersburg Airport. It could take me hours to drive which normally would be 45 minutes. I need to check up on Catherine and bring her dinner. We will talk tomorrow. Love you all!"

Tully stumbled and almost spilled Catherine's dinner as he was walking upstairs. Catherine's face, when her husband walked into the room with her smoothie, reflected her disappointment in having another liquid shake for her meal. "What? You're tired of my cooking already" Tully quipped. Catherine shot back, "You call that cooking? You only need the blender to make that thing. Yes, I am tired of it after having three smoothies every damn day." Tully could tell she was not in a great mood, so he sensed that this is a time to tread carefully and choose his word wisely. He sat with her, caressing her left forearm while she used her right hand to hold the straw. "So, what would you like for breakfast tomorrow? He asked. "Toast and eggs please,

THE CROWNING: CULMINATION OF THE NATION

with jam on the toast", Catherine replied with a smile on her face. "Well, young lady", Tully exclaimed, "you're in luck, we still have both. I have used none of the eggs we brought home from Tony's home." "I am surprised those eggs did not break when we were attacked, " she said referring to the time she got shot through the chest on their way back home from Tony's house. Tony grinned and jokingly said, "Turned out the eggs were not as fragile as you are." Catherine laughed, which was the first time she had laughed since the attack that put her in the hospital. When 6:00 rolled around they had the laptop set up on the bed so they could listen to the broadcast. Catherine's interest was growing enough that she was staying awake through the broadcast now. She reminded Tully to turn on the recording software on the laptop. Tully took that as a sign she too was invested in preserving the historical record.

Chester Colt, the host that evening for the Truth began the show with, "Good evening and welcome back to this episode of the Truth. Today is Friday, Feb, 28th, 2025. It was three years ago, in late February 2022 that Putin launched the attack to overwhelm and occupy Ukraine with the goal of reuniting the former Soviet Union satellite countries to bring Russia back to being a world power. These historical events are important to give you the background on how the war in Europe began, a war that is in its third year today.

Tonight we are bringing back Dr. Vaughn Woodman PhD. You may recall that Dr. Woodman is a nationally recognized expert on the history of the United States, his many works on American political events earning him the Pulitzer Prize. Welcome back, Dr. Woodman." Dr. Woodman responded, "Thank you Chester for inviting me back. I am glad to see you are well. We were all very concerned for you." Chester Colt, ignoring the comment, plowed ahead to introduce his next topic, "Help us understand the events that took place on the domestic front, here in the U.S. after the 2nd Impeachment trial had concluded. Was there an undercurrent of political transition or posturing taking place that altered the landscape?"

Dr. Woodman took his glasses off and began cleaning them with his handkerchief while contemplating his answer. He finally said, "To understand what was happening in the U.S. we acknowledge it was not unique to the U.S. but actually happening in democracies all over the world.

THOMAS J. FEELY

Domestic factions have leveraged imperfections in democracies in order to continue promoting hate, violence, and unrestrained governance. In countries such as Russia, China, and Iran, authoritarian governments have become experts at subverting the principles and foundations meant to sustain freedoms and democratic ideals. China, Russia, and other dictatorial states have shifted world incentives to promote despotic approaches, which threatens the relationship between democracy, the affluence that comes from capitalism, protection, and freedom while fostering more autocratic forms of rule. They have developed powerful weapons in influencing social discourse, using social media, key media outlets, and authoritarian leaning political actors to alter the political discourse of the democratic country." Chester Colt sensed a disconnect occurring so he interjected, "I am going to go out on a limb here Dr. Woodman, and guess that 90% of the audience do not understand what you just told them. Would you summarize what you just said, please, in layman's terms?" Dr. Woodman appeared puzzled by what he thought was a perfectly clear description said humbly, "Sure, I'll do my best. Basically, what that means is that since the start of democratic governing came into being, the values that bind all democratic societies, mainly that all people are equal and self-governing by the people, is superior to governing by the few who have all the power. Since democracy spread around the world, autocratic governments have campaigned against them, and in the 21st century, the tools of that warfare have been social media, all forms of media outlets, and fostering politicians that will "carry the water" for the goals of the autocratic governments, with the goal to create chaos, foster hatred for minority groups, and create doubt about the very ideals of democracy, even the methods of elections are under attack. This led to World War II, and has continued around the globe for the last 75 years." Chester Colt inquired, "So, how does this global problem relate to the historic events of the last 5 years in the U.S.? Is there a connection?"

Dr. Woodman looked down, lowered his voice to a near whisper, and said, "Democracy's reputation and foundations have been severely damaged. Authoritarian countries such as China, Russia, and others have gained tremendous power, and democratic countries have seen their values undermined and shattered. Political malpractice and other illicit behaviors by politicians and other actors, who undermine the establishment that has

THE CROWNING: CULMINATION OF THE NATION

brought them to power, are subverting democracy from within. This was unquestionably most overt in the United States when, on January 6, rioters descended on the Capitol to overturn the presidential election results. But it did not end when the insurrection was over, nor when the Impeachment Trial was over, nor when the subsequent investigations into the Insurrection were completed. Quite the opposite occurred. The actors doubled down, passing voter laws designed to deter voting and change undesired results, fabricating emotional causes out of thin air, and fostering even greater hatred and bigotry on various innocent groups for problems the country is experiencing to blame on. Anything the playbook calls for in order to destroy faith in the country, its leaders, and even the democratic pillars of the country is founded. Even the scientists working hard to save lives in the face of the worst pandemic in well over 100 years, resulting in over a million deaths in the U.S. alone, were portrayed as corrupt characters with unscrupulous goals and purpose." Thank you, Dr. Woodman. As always, you have illuminated so very much for us. That will be all for tonight. We will be back again tomorrow, and each evening at 6:00 pm. EST. Please continue to record and save these programs. Good night."

In Miami, Paul opens a briefcase, pulls out a metal case the size of a pack of cigarettes, and opens it. He takes out a small sim card from the case housing dozens of more just like it. Paul picks up a very plain black cell phone, known as a burner phone, and installs the sim card. He taps the number 1 on the phone, and a phone on the other end rings. The voice on the receiving end says, "Hi." "Hey Mike, have you heard?" Michael responds, "Yep, your leaving in the morning. Just be very careful, I had to call in a big favor to get you cleared to make the trip, otherwise, you would never make it there." Paul responds," Glad to hear it, thanks!" Michael says, "Make sure you check into security before taking off. Remember, they are Cardinal fans." "Good to know", Paul responds and quickly hangs up, putting the phone in the briefcase after removing the sim card. He took the card and smashed it with a hammer. There were 19 more cards for future calls to his brother.

It was still very dark outside when Tully got up the next morning. He knew he had to get an early start, that Saturday morning, in order to meet Paul at the airport in Clearwater. He had charted a route, but there is only one way to avoid going over a bridge to get from Tampa to Clearwater and that was a much longer trip, going north over the top of Tampa Bay, then south to the St. Petersburg/Clearwater Airport. Tully knew there would be no way to get past the abandoned cars, buses, and trucks left on the bridges. He decided he had no choice except to take the longer route. As soon as the sun rose in the east, Tully set out on his extremely treacherous journey, unaware of the peril that lays ahead.

Chapter 21
Hovering a Bit Above Empty
Tampa, Florida
Saturday, March 1st, 2025

The curfew ended at 6:00 a.m. and that is the same time as the sun rose. At least this plan allowed for alternative streets to detour if a main road were cut off. Tully had not traveled in this direction since the citywide nightly riots began. The further west he made it, traveling through Tampa's west side, the more scorched earth he encountered. Tully wondered if the airport itself was even open for planes to land, but it was too late now to turn back. So many places Tully used to frequent for lunch or dinner were empty shells of burned-out buildings. Cars upside down or destroyed by fire had to be traversed like a downhill skier on a crowded mountain. As Tully made his way to the bay and eventually around the north shore, there were times he had to detour, but Tully always made his way back to the primary route. "Find a way, or make a way" was the mantra of one of the many great coaches, Coach Dominic Ciao, whom he had worked with during Tully's 47 years of coaching football. Never had those words seemed more appropriate, so Tully spoke them out loud every time he came to an impasse he thought was the end of the road. Saying those words, "find a way, or make a way" gave Tully renewed determination to make it to his destination on time. Tully's good friend and neighbor, Pia Sampson, agreed to take care of Catherine in Tully's absence. After two and a half hours of weaving through the debris and carnage, Tully arrived at the airport. He was relieved to see private and military planes coming and going, but Tully was not surprised that all commercial flights were grounded.

Right on schedule, at 900 hours, the Coast Guard plane flew in, landed and the passengers debarked from the plane on the tarmac near hanger 19. Perhaps the last to exit the plane, Paul emerged and started down the steps.

Tully had not seen his son in over two years and he was overwhelmed with the joy of seeing him in his military uniform. They hugged, albeit awkwardly, because Paul, at 6 feet, is much taller than his dad. They walked to Tully's car, while they talked excitedly about Paul's brief return to his home city. Paul asked about Catherine and Suzanne and James's health status. Tully replied, "Catherine is a really tough woman. It takes more than a bullet through her chest to stop her. She will be on her feet, and in her garden in no time. James is improving by what seems like leaps and bounds, based on what he is telling me. He sounds pretty good on the phone, but I wonder what the long-term impacts he will have to endure. Suzanne, well that is why you are here. She will need her portable respirator working throughout the flight. Manny, the owner of the plane you will use to fly her to Michigan is taking out two seats from the plane so she can remain prone." "How many seats does that leave?" Paul asked. "Just the pilot and copilot seat, I think. Hopefully, one more seat for Grace, who will take care of her Mom during the flight." Paul said "I have submitted the flight plans. I estimate we can get to Houston, Texas before needing to land to refuel, then we should be on our way to Phoenix, with another refuel stop in El Paso Texas. Grace, Chase, and Suzanne need to meet us at Phoenix-Mesa Gateway Airport. I will refuel again and we will depart for Michigan with a stop to refuel in Wichita, Kansas, and in Chicago Ill. If all goes according to plan, I can get her to Detroit by midnight. We will spend the night there and then return using the same route in reverse the next morning. How will we get Suzanne from Detroit to the University of Michigan's Hospital?" Tully smiled with satisfaction at hearing Paul's plan so carefully worked out and said, "That is James's job to figure that out. I believe he already has it worked out. He will call or text you with the info as soon as he has it confirmed."

    Manny met Paul and Tully at the local airport near his home in Wesley Chapel. It was late morning by the time they arrived, and Manny already had the plane fueled and ready to go. Paul gave Manny a salute when they first met, even though Manny was a retired Colonel in the Air Force and Paul was a ranked Commander in the Coast Guard. Paul wanted to show Manny the utmost respect, especially considering the incredible unselfishness proven by the act of loaning his new private plane to a complete stranger. Manny took both Paul and Tully up for a test flight to make sure Paul was

THE CROWNING: CULMINATION OF THE NATION

comfortable with the plane's instrumentation. Paul immediately put Manny's mind to rest, demonstrating complete mastery as a pilot. Paul explained to Manny that all of his training to gain his wings was on the same model plane. He was as comfortable flying this plane as he was with the helicopter he flew every day. The Cessna flew perfectly and Paul landed it with ease. He dropped Manny and his dad off at the airport and gave his dad a big hug before departing for Phoenix. Tully waived and yelled 'good luck' as Paul took off heading west toward Texas at about 12:00 noon. With no issues, Paul flew to Houston and landed at William P. Hobby Airport, then on to El Paso International Airport before eventually arriving at Phoenix-Mesa Gateway Airport. An ambulance pulled up to the Cessna and Grace, and Chase jumped out to greet their uncle Paul. The ambulance attendants, after the refueling had been completed, carried Suzanne into the back of the small craft and got her equipment all set up to keep her comfortable. They had given her sedatives so she would sleep through the voyage. After a short break for food, and using the facilities, Paul and Chase climbed into the cockpit while Grace squeezed into the back of the plane to be with her Mom. Grace did not complain at all about the confining and extremely uncomfortable space left for her for the long flight to Detroit. She was unquestionably very cramped, but she was more concerned about her Mom's comfort level than her own, and very grateful for this opportunity for this "hail Mary pass" for her mother's life.

Paul got the clearance from the control tower to take off and soon they had climbed to 9,500 ft. for the flight to Wichita Dwight D. Eisenhower National Airport. Chase had never flown in the cockpit before and was excited to have the chance to learn from Paul. "Why don't we go any higher? Wouldn't that allow us to go faster?" asked Chase. "Our challenge is to minimize the number of stops for refueling as each stop is going to take at least an hour or more before we are cleared for takeoff. Our first stop is Wichita Kansas. I figure if we cruise at 140 miles per hour at 9,500 feet, we should make it," Paul explained. "Should make it?" Chase asked with concern in his voice. "Yes," Paul said with a sideways glance in Chase's direction, "It will be very close, but we have a tailwind going east so that will help. The highest you should take this plane is 13,000 feet, but we will get more efficiency at 9,500 feet." Paul was pushing the envelope by cutting it so close, but he knew if he could make it to Wichita he could then fly with a refueled tank from Wichita all the way to Detroit Metropolitan Wayne County Airport, very near Ann Arbor, Michigan. He felt confident he could make it to both locations, saving the time a third stop would cost them. Chase watched the fuel gauge nervously as they proceeded to Wichita. After about two hours Paul looked toward Chase and said "We are about 50 miles from the airport, how is our fuel?" "Hovering above empty", Chase replied. "No sweat" Paul declared. Chase was sweating and silently began praying. Just as Paul could see the runway up ahead the needle had stopped bouncing and was pointing directly at the 'E' on the fuel gauge. Paul knew he could glide the plane in, if needed, from this distance, but fortunately for Chase, who now was a nervous wreck, gliding was not needed. The plane landed, with the engines still running and the propeller still turning. They had made it.

In the terminal, they took turns, one staying with Suzanne while the others used the facilities and got some food. When the plane was ready, loaded with a full tank, they started the engines and waited for the tower to clear them to take off. Once again, they climbed to 9,500 feet of elevation and continued their trek to Detroit. While in the terminal, Paul texted James the estimated time he expected to land in Detroit, right at midnight. James responded with the news that there will be an ambulance waiting for them at the airport, to take Suzanne to the hospital in Ann Arbor. The sky was clear, and the winds were still flowing in the right direction. They flew right over Kansas City, Missouri, and later just south of Chicago. Chase could see Lake Michigan as they flew right over the southern shoreline. The sun had set a while ago, so the lake looked like a giant black void with many bright city lights surrounding the lake providing the lake's outline. It was 11:30 pm when the lights of the runway of Detroit Metropolitan Wayne County Airport lined up with the nose of the Cessna. The landing went smoothly and Paul taxied the plane to the appointed gate. They had to wait about a half hour before the ambulance arrived to take Suzanne, along with Grace, to the UM Medical School's hospital. Chase gave his Mom a long hug, though she was still asleep from the sedatives, and wondered if he could ever hug her again. "You must get better, Mom. I need you. I love you, Mom" he whispered into her ear. Chase was sure she, ever so slightly, squeezed his

THE CROWNING: CULMINATION OF THE NATION

hand, but he could feel it, and he knew she was signaling back 'I love you too, son'. Paul and Chase found a quiet spot inside the terminal to lie out their sleeping bags and get some sleep for the night. It didn't take long before they were sound asleep.

Back in Tampa, Tully stayed awake until he got the text from Paul that they had arrived safely in Detroit and Suzanne was on her way to the hospital with Grace. With that news, Tully felt an enormous sense of relief, turned off his computer which had recorded the episode of Truth earlier that evening, and went to sleep in his chair in the living room. He would replay that episode in the morning, as he was too nervous and preoccupied to listen to it earlier. With his gun, safely at his side, he slept through the rest of the night, perhaps for the last time.

Chapter 22
Standing There, Helplessly
Detroit, Michigan
Sunday, March 2nd, 2025

The crisp cool Florida morning, with a haze in the air subdued to an unusually ruby red glowing sunrise which created an ambiance of tranquility that Tully had not experienced in a very long time. The night had been unusually quiet, allowing both Catherine and Tully to sleep through the night. Catherine was still asleep, and if the last week is any sign, she will sleep another two hours, at least. After pouring his morning coffee, Tully checked his phone for any messages. Paul had sent a text that read, "Chase and I will take off for Arizona in about 30 minutes. I will text when I have a cell tower connection." By the time Tully had read the text, Paul and Chase were already cruising at 9,000 feet and slowing climbing to 9,500. They had gotten clearance to take off about the same time as sunrise in Michigan. The route was the same as the prior day, only in reverse order, with Wichita Dwight D. Eisenhower National Airport the first stop on the flight plan. The skies were clear with visibility being 10 miles. Chase was following the route on a map and pointed out the Notre Dame campus when they flew over South Bend, Indiana. Paul had requested maximum fuel be put into the tanks so he would get to Wichita with more fuel to spare than they had in the tanks the day before. Chase, like Paul was concerned about the fact that yesterday they had a tailwind and today th,at wind was in their face, although the wind, even at 9,500 feet, was pretty weak. Paul kept a close eye on the gauge as they approached Kansas City. He landed at the Kansas City International Airport. He called their tower for permission to land, which he received without a wait because no commercial air travel was happening. It would take a while to refuel and they might lose an hour, but today, they got an early start so the urgency to complete the trip quickly was not so great. With a full

THE CROWNING: CULMINATION OF THE NATION

tank and fresh coffee, the duo was back in the sky continuing on to Wichita, just a 3-hour leg of the trip. Paul knew he would not make it back to Phoenix from Kansas City on one tank of fuel so he planned on refueling in Wichita. This leg was shorter, around 870 miles, and roughly a 6-and-a-half-hour flight. Before taking off, Paul sent a text to both James and Tully saying: "Should arrive at Phoenix-Mesa Airport around 6:00 pm." In return, he got a thumbs-up emoji from his brother, James, and a "Safe Travels" text from his Dad. The trip went smoothly as they flew over the far northwest corner of Oklahoma and into New Mexico. The route took them over Santa Fe and north of Albuquerque, New Mexico. They flew directly over a town called Grants, New Mexico when Paul noticed a very large column of dark clouds in the horizon. He made a call on the plane's radio to seek a weather report and the call was returned by the Sho Low Regional Airport. "Be advised there is a powerful storm between your location and this airport. It is at the Ramah Navajo Indian Reservation just east and southeast of the Zuni Indian Reservation. The storm is moving southwest toward St. John's, Arizona. This airport, Sho Low Regional is the closest airport in your vicinity. We suggest you turn south to a bearing of 220 degrees and climb to an altitude of 12,000 feet. When you reach the town of Quemado adjust your bearing to 265 degrees west. Then you will be on a course to our airport." Following those instructions to the letter, Paul navigated around the first column and was heading in the airport's direction in Sho Low, but as they approached that town the controller called in to warn them that a tornado warning was just issued for the area of the Sho Low Airport, and landing here would not be permitted until the warning is rescinded. "You can circle around Sho Low keeping a very wide path between you and these storm clouds, or you keep heading to your original destination. "Thank you Sho Low, we will move on to Phoenix." "Roger that", the controller replied. They continued the flight toward Phoenix-Mesa Airport, however, Paul was getting nervous about the fuel situation. The detour followed by the climb to 12,000 feet burned up enough of the tank's supply that he worried they may not have enough for the last few hundred miles. Chase was unaware of the predicament because he had fallen asleep. Paul nervously watched the gauge, but all the watching did not make a difference. They were over the mountains and desert of Arizona, and finding a safe place to land would be very difficult out here.

If he had to put it down, it would need to be a straight road that had no abandoned cars or trucks on it. Paul didn't notice any of the latter, but straight roads in these hills and mountains are not likely. He calculated if he could fly over the Theodore Roosevelt Lake, and then past the Theodore Roosevelt Dam he might find a long enough stretch of road on the Apache Trail also called County Road 88 as it travels right next to the Salt River. His map showed a stretch of road that appeared to be about three-quarters of a mile long just southwest of the Theodore Roosevelt Dam Overlook. He decided he was going to put it down there. "Chase, wake up!" Paul ordered.

Chase's head popped up as he looked perplexed and said, "What's Up?" "We are", Paul replied, trying to remain calm, "but not for long." Chase sat up straight in his co-pilot chair and said, "What's wrong?" Paul looked at him and then glanced at the fuel gauge. He did not need to explain, it was hovering over the "E" with a little bounce left on the needle. "We are about to fly over an enormous lake, then over a dam. After we make it over those, we can put this plane down on a road next to a river." Chase could see the lake up ahead, and sat there quietly, not saying a word. He wondered how deep that lake was and hoped he would never find out. Paul slowed the plane down as much as possible and flew as low as he safely could get the most out of the fuel they had left. They were over the water of the lake for about 3 minutes and then there was the biggest dam Chase had ever seen. Still, he remained silent and Paul was calling in a mayday to alert whoever would hear them where they were going down. "We will land in Pine Arizona on County Road 88. The coordinates are 33.664940, -111.169558. Repeat, we will land on County 88 at 33.664940, -111.169558." Just as they passed the Dam's Overlook, the Cessna Skyhawk's engine stopped. They had run out of fuel and now they were a glider. It is hard to turn when you have no engines, so Paul made sure he was aligned with the direction of the road. He could see the stretch of straight road running parallel to the Salt River. He gripped the controls so hard that his knuckles turned the same color as Chase's face, pure white. Almost silently they slowly guided right above the road. There were no vehicles they could see, so just like he had done on the last day of his fixed-wing training test to earn his wings, four years ago, he landed the plane with just a minor thud as the wheels touched down. They, and the plane, had returned to the solid ground with no damage. Paul immediately got on the

THE CROWNING: CULMINATION OF THE NATION

radio to notify the Sho Low Regional Airport, and anyone else able to receive the mayday call, that they had landed safely and needed to be rescued. No one replied.

Chase and Paul had no cell phone signal where they landed so they took out the maps that Paul had brought on the trip and looked at their options. They were located a few clicks southwest of the Roosevelt Dam Overlook. Their map showed two potential sources of fuel for the plane. The Apache Lake Marina and Resort were 12.5 miles to the southwest on the Salt River, and the Roosevelt Lake Marina on Roosevelt Lake was only 3.5 miles to the northeast. "Let's take the shorter route, that is a simple decision", Chase declared enthusiastically. Paul did not respond as he was studying the maps carefully. Finally, Paul said, "The problem is the roads that take us to the Roosevelt Lake Marina, are posted as "Restricted" and "Private" roads. We may run into roadblocks or even locked gates." After a considerable debate between the two, Paul caved into Chase's pleading to take the 3.5-mile option. They set off on foot for Roosevelt Lake Marina. Soon they came to a fork in the road. The map showed taking the left road of the fork would be a dead end as it stopped at the Roosevelt Dam. The only option was to take the longer right road off the fork which winded around tall hills of rock. After about 45 minutes of walking the dusty road in the desert heat during the hottest part of the day, they came across a warning sign that read, "Private Road. No Trespassing". Paul, once again looked at his map and noticed there were some trails called the Apache Trails that climbed into the desert hills. They were rugged and a considerable detour from the forbidden road. Paul and Chase started up the trails but soon changed their minds as they were a much harder climb than they bargained for, and by the length of the trails it appeared to be a long time to get a very short distance compared to the road. Returning to the easier road they decided it was worth the risk. A half mile further down the road, they came to a chain-link fence and gate blocking the road. A large padlock on a thick chain kept the gate secure from trespassers. Paul suggested turning back and going to the other marina instead, which now was about 14 miles away, instead of 12.5. Hearing that suggestion, Chase jumped on the gate and quickly climbed over the 6-foot-tall barrier. Now standing on the other side, he told Paul, "I'm really thirsty, we need to keep going. It is only about another mile away". Paul really didn't want to turn around either and was just as thirsty as Chase, but he had a terrible feeling about trespassing on private property. He should have listened to his gut. As soon as Paul had climbed the fence and they walked about 100 yards into the gated land, they were confronted by two men with rifles in their hands aimed directly at the two interlopers. They were Indian-Americans dressed in blue jeans and t-shirts. The taller of the two men, said, "You two are on our property. You need to turn around and march out the way you came." Paul looked at Chase who had a look of terror on his face, then said to the two men, "All we are trying to do is get to the marina. Our plane ran out of fuel so we need to buy some so we can get home." The two men looked at each other and the taller man said, "Where is your plane?" Feeling encouraged by this question Paul replied, "On county road 88 just south of the Roosevelt Dam Overlook." The shorter of the two men looked at the taller man, exchanging their thoughts by the look in their eyes rather than words or gestures. "How about you get in the back of our pickup and we will give you a ride to the marina, then back to your plane." Chase immediately responded "That would be so great! Thanks!" Paul could not shake the feeling in his gut that they were walking into a trap the men switched from being demanding to being very accommodating and it just did not feel sincere. 'Still', he thought, 'they have the rifles and we are on their private land'. The pickup was an old Ford that looked to be from the 40s or 50s. The paint was long replaced with just rust and it was a stick shift. Neither Paul nor Chase would have the skills to drive the stick shift. They had never even seen a clutch pedal before this. The two men sat in the two seats, and Paul and Chase climbed into the bed of the truck. They sat in silence while bouncing around on the bumpy dirt road. Paul wondered where they were being taken to when, to his relief, they turned a corner, honked their horn twice and the gate to the marina opened. The taller of the two men got out of the truck on the driver's side and said, "What kind of fuel does your plane need?" Paul replied, "The engine runs on 100-octane fuel, but we will need whatever is the highest octane they have. "They won't sell to you directly. If I bring them cash, I can get them to sell the gas to me, we can borrow their containers. How much cash do you have?" Paul and Chase were using cash for the fuel throughout the trip, so they had to dig into their wallets to see what they had left after the last fill up. Together, they had about $350

THE CROWNING: CULMINATION OF THE NATION

which Paul calculated would purchase about 50 gallons. He had been paying $6.00 per gallon and if the price here is similar 50 gallons would get them to Phoenix easily. "We have $350," Paul said, offering the money to the man. The man took the money without a word and walked away counting it. The other man remained in the passenger seat of the pickup with his rifle still in his hands. After about 20 minutes the taller man whistled and waved to his partner to bring the truck up to the docks. He slid over behind the wheel and drove the truck to a place that had a large gas tank with a valve and hose. They filled up six 5-gallon tanks and placed them into the truck. Paul looked at the man and said, "That is only 30 gallons, we paid for 50 gallons." The man grinned at him showing his lack of teeth and replied, "There are other fees for our time, gas, and giving you two mulattas a ride." He got in the truck and began driving back to the location of the plane. As they approached County Road 88, and turned the corner where the straightaway began, the place where they landed, Chase realized the plane was missing. They stopped where they knew they had left the plane. Paul and Chase walked around, looking over the nearby cliff to see if they could find it, but it simply had vanished. The two men turned the truck around and the taller man yelled, "Looks like you won't be needing the gas after all!" They hit the gas leaving Paul and Chase standing there, helplessly.

Chapter 23
Any Sign of Grady
Tampa, Florida
Sunday, March 2nd, 2025

In Tampa, Tully was waiting impatiently to hear from Paul and Chase. It was almost 3:00 pm on the east coast, which meant in Arizona it was nearly noon. He told Catherine, "They should be in Phoenix any minute now if they did not get delayed. I will let you know when they land safely. I am hoping Paul can sleep there and finish the trip back to Florida tomorrow morning." Catherine nodded her head in agreement while looking disapprovingly at the lunch he had prepared. It was a tuna sandwich made from the cans of tuna that had been in their pantry for years, but they had long since run out of mayonnaise, so he had substituted mustard. She took one bite and then spit it out with a look of horror on her face. "Can you just make me a peanut butter and jelly sandwich, please?" Catherine pleaded. Tully took the plate and went back downstairs to try again. His phone rang, and he saw it was James on the line. "Hi James, have you heard from them yet?" "No," James replied, "and I am getting really worried. You haven't heard from them either?" "Not a sound", Tully said. They sat in mutual silence, both fighting off the temptation to think about the worst plausible scenario, a plane crash. Tully feebly tried to change the subject. "I'm too worried to feel anything else right now," said James "I'll call you back when I hear from them, I don't want to miss a call from them." After delivering the PB&J to Catherine, Tully needed to take his mind off of the fate of his son and grandson so he sat down to listen to the news, tuning to the only source of current information, Cerberus World News. The broadcast was in English, but they mention frequently that it is being translated and broadcast in all the major languages around the planet. The news hosts were discussing the food shortages in almost every major democratic country in the world, but

THE CROWNING: CULMINATION OF THE NATION

from their reporting, there was no such shortage in China, nor in Russia. If Tully were to take this news source as gospel truth, he would quickly conclude that capitalists in the democratically governed nations were hoarding the resources for their own benefit, leaving the masses to suffer and die. Video of cities filled with starving masses of people played in the background. They also talked about the civil unrest in the U.S., showing videos of rioting and burning buildings, and highways with destroyed and abandoned vehicles making those roads impassable. They noted the U.S. administration had declared Martial Law and was enforcing strict curfews. International news highlighted the current battles in Europe and in Asia where both China and Russia were fighting to expand their controlled territories. NATO was defending its member countries, but they were significantly diminished in terms of their military effectiveness by the lack of U.S. participation. These "regional hostilities" were being met with fierce opposition by the populations of the countries being violated. It appeared like this situation would never end. China and Russia seemed determined to march on despite the resistance. Tully felt demoralized by the news, and he was completely disgusted by the U.S. position of dissociation and disengagement from foreign wars. After 30 minutes of the depressing newscast, he returned upstairs to check on Catherine. She had fallen back asleep after only eating a few bites of her sandwich.

It was high noon in the Arizona desert, and already the temperature was rising into the low nineties. Being early March and they were at higher altitudes, the weather would not get as torrid as it would have if it were summer, but this was unusually uncomfortable for an early spring day. Paul and Chase had set out on their journey to the Apache Lake Marina and Resort. They had already covered about 2 miles, leaving another 10 1/2 miles to go. They already were thirsty before they started out, but as it got warmer out, and they walked further, their dehydration was becoming worrisome. Paul complained, "I am getting a little dizzy, how about you?" Chase looked at his uncle, who was pale, and said, "Me too." Paul, at 32 years old, was 10 years older than his nephew. Both were in very good health, about the same height and Chase was still playing football in college in the same position as Paul played 10 years earlier. Chase was built with a little more muscle, while Paul was a little leaner, but both were physically strong. After another six miles and an hour and a half later, Paul stumbled, so Chase took Paul's arm and wrapped it over his shoulder to give him support. He estimated he had another four miles to go and hoped he could hold up with the extra weight on his shoulders. The last four miles, by far the hardest and the hottest, took a good two hours, but finally, they could see the buildings up ahead. When they arrived, a gate prevented them from getting into the compound. Chase yelled for help and after about 3 minutes, a man emerged from the main office and walked toward the gate. He was in no hurry, trying to find out the intruder's intentions. When he arrived at the gate, Chase explained what had happened and Paul, too weak to stand, had sat down on the ground while they talked. The man asked their names, and hearing Paul's rank in the Coast Guard, the man transformed from a suspicious doubter, to become sympathetic to their situations. He explained he had served in the Navy during the Vietnam War. He then unlocked the gate and let them in, helping bring Paul, still too weak to walk on his own, to the office of the resort and marina. In Phoenix James' cell phone chirped alerting him of an incoming call, and the name "Chase " appeared on James's screen. "Chase, I have been worried sick, what happened, the trip took much longer than you said it would?" Chase revealed, "The trip is not over yet. We had to land the plane on a road next to the Salt River. We had to walk to find fuel for the plane, then we got robbed and dumped where the plane had landed, but the plane was not there." "What!" James was confused by the rapid-fire way Chase was describing the events. "You lost the plane?" "It was gone when they took us back to the place the plane landed." Chase tried to explain, sensing his Dad was about to erupt in a fit of anger. "We had to walk another 12 miles to get to this resort. We are ok now." "Where are you?" James asked. 'We are at the Apache Lake Marina and Resort. We were only about 30 minutes from the airport in Mesa," Chase replied. James looked up the resort and marina on Google Maps. "You are 30 minutes away by air, but by car, it is 2 hours and 20 minutes away. Because of the mountains, it is 106 miles away. I'll have Grady take the truck and drive to you, to pick you up. Hopefully, he will get there before dark." Chase relayed the plan to Paul and the man who had taken them in. The man, whose name they later learned was "Red" O'Brien, is a short but stocky Irishman in his seventies, originally from Boston, who came to work at the Marina after his military service was over. He had been

THE CROWNING: CULMINATION OF THE NATION

the manager of the business for over 40 years now. Red advised the group while addressing James via the cell phone, "I highly recommend they stay the night and head home in the morning. They can stay the night here at the resort." James agreed and told them Grady would leave at the crack of dawn. Then Red graciously brought them to the resort's diner for a hot meal and a few beers. Paul used the resort phone to call his brother, Michael to tell him what had happened that day. Michael paced around nervously at his home throughout the night long after hearing the news. He was relieved his brother and nephew were safe, but knew this ordeal, caused by being short enough fuel to make it back to the airport, could completely sabotage his plan to save the country. Meanwhile, Paul and Chase slept like babies that night, exhausted from the ordeal.

Twenty-four-year-old Grady, James' son-in-law and husband to Grace was more than happy to rescue Chase and Paul from their ordeal. Grady got off to a rocky start in the relationship between Chase and Grady when Grady first started dating Chase's older sister. Throughout Grace's high school years, she dated Chase's best friend and football teammate, so when Grady entered the picture in Grace's senior year, Chase was distraught. Grady was eager to win over Chase, and he viewed this as a potential opportunity to accomplish a breakthrough. Leaving early on Monday morning, March 3rd, Grady was pleased to take James's new 2025 Ford F-450, which would handle the most rugged terrain with relative ease. He set out on the winding road called State Road 87, traveling northeast. James told him to "hang a right" when he passed a Carl's Jr. fast-food outlet on State Road 188. The terrain was desert mountainous, and the road was complete with many sharp turns winding through the hills. At Carl's Jr's, Grady stopped to pick up some food, but it had been closed for over a month, and no one was inside. Fortunately, Grady had packed food and drinks for all three before leaving his father-in-law's home, so he figured he would wait until he had picked them up before eating the food. Grady called Chase before going home to let him know he was on his way and to expect him in 2 and a half hours. Chase and Paul were up and ready after breakfast in the resort's diner. Paul had contacted the local Sheriff's office about the missing plane, which dispatched a couple of officers to get an official report from them. An hour later, the officers were at the gate to the resort, and Red walked out to let them in. They sat down with the Sheriff deputies, who seemed very suspicious, without actually saying so, of their story until they called in a request to reach out to the Sho Low Regional Airport to verify their contact with them. When the Sheriff's office operator called back and confirmed their interactions with the plane the day before, the officers changed their tone. "So, when you left the plane, you were walking toward the Roosevelt Lake Marina; what did you do when you came to the gate that said Private Road-No trespassing?" asked the sheriff. Paul glanced at Chase with a pained look and confessed, "We were desperate, and there was no other way there, so we climbed the gate and walked inside for about 100 yards when two men stopped us." The other officer asked, "Can you describe them?" Paul replied, "One was tall, about 6'2, dark skin and salt & pepper hair, and he looked to be about late 50s, and the other was shorter, about 5'8, and seemed to be in his 40s. They wore blue jeans, cowboy boots, and T-shirts. The shorter man was very stocky, and the taller guy was slender." Both sheriff officers looked at each other and nodded in agreement, "I think we both know who they are; the question is how they moved that plane and where it is now. We will start a search for it. In the meantime, you better get in touch with the plane's owner and have him call us so we can get the information we will need to identify it." Paul promised he would do that right away, a promise he wished he did not have to keep, but he knew he had to make that call. The policeman left, assuring them they would keep in touch when they finished their investigation. Two more hours have elapsed since the two officers left, and still no sign of Grady. Their attempts to reach his cell went straight to voicemail. They surmised Grady was in the mountains and could not get a signal but worried he might have gotten lost. Chase texted his Dad, "Have you heard from Grady? He is not here yet." "No" was the one-word reply from James. By 12:00 noon, they came to the mutual agreement that something must have happened to Grady. Red then offered to take them in his Jeep to look for him. Within minutes, they were on the dusty highway headed northeast on State Road 88 to the Roosevelt Dam, then turned northwest on State Road 188 toward the Tonto National Forest. The ride was jolting as the jeep seemed to have no shock absorbers and Chase hit his head on the roof several times, while they searched the ditches for any sign of Grady.

Chapter 24
The President is in His Cross Hairs
Tampa, Florida
Monday, March 3rd, 2025:

Back in Tampa, Tully is unaware of the recent developments in Arizona. The last he heard Paul and Chase were waiting for Grady to pick them up. Catherine was showing signs of recovery, her appetite had improved, and she was awake longer, even walking on her own to the bathroom. Tully had fixed her eggs and pancakes for dinner, which she seemed genuinely happy to eat. Tully read to Catherine a text from Grace that had been sent to the entire family. It read, "Mom has begun the EMCO treatment today. For those unfamiliar, extracorporeal membrane oxygenation (ECMO) temporarily replaces both the heart and the lungs, circulating the blood outside the body. The patient must be under constant medical supervision. She will be here for a few weeks at the very least. I am talking with her all the time, but she can't respond yet. Please keep praying for her and for me, Grace." After her dinner, Tully and Catherine sat on the bed together and turned on the laptop to watch the program "Truth" together.

"Good evening, and thank you for joining us once again for our nightly documentary to preserve the historical truth. I am your host Sheldon Smithson, once again receiving the baton to host this program. We are so grateful that so many of you are recording and saving these internet broadcasts to protect the truth for historical accuracy. This is Monday evening, March 3rd, 2025, and I have with me tonight our historian, Dr. Vaughn Woodman, Ph.D.

"Dr. Woodman, thank you for coming back on this program tonight."

Dr. Woodman, putting on his glasses, smiled and nodded before replying, "I am always honored to be of service to a cause as noble and critical as this one." Smithson asked, "We would like to shift our focus tonight to the events of the second half of 2022 and the first half of 2023, specifically the investigations that the Department of Justice, under Attorney General Merrick Garland's leadership, of the Jan. 6th insurrection before the midterm elections of 2022. Can you explain how the findings of the House Select Committee investigating the events and causes of the January six insurrection laid the groundwork for the Justice Department to bring a case to a Grand Jury?"

Dr. Woodman's expression revealed his judgment of the gravity of this topic, and his voice became somber. He began, "By the spring of 2022, the Department of Justice is reportedly expanding its investigation after having already indicted nearly 800 individuals who breached the capitol or supported the efforts to overthrow the government. Now, federal prosecutors are focusing on those who may have been responsible for pushing the big lie, people in positions of authority, examining not just what happened on January 6 but also what led up to it. Federal prosecutors convened a grand jury to investigate the events that preceded the attack on the Capitol and the VIP guests at Trump's January 6 rally at the Ellipse. First, the grand jury subpoenaed officials inside Trump's sphere of influence who helped to plan, funding, and executing the rally. Democrats, members of the public, and even the January six committee members advocated for holding key players responsible for the attack on January 6. They collectively pressed Attorney General Merrick Garland to announce their efforts publicly. Still, Garland and the entire DOJ kept their cards close to their chest, careful not to tip off their investigation findings. Grand Jury subpoenas allowed the Department of Justice to work its way up the criminal ladder to the insurrection's command structure by investigating the funders, planners, and organizers of the pre-insurrection pep rally at the Ellipse on January 6th.

A criminal investigation also was being expanded into the fake electors and not just into the fake electors themselves, but also into the Trump associates who perpetrated the fake elector fraud to preempt the results of the democratic elections. Grand jury subpoenas were issued by the Office of the Attorney General to people within former President Trump's orbit." Smithson added, "Merrick Garland told us his plan back in January 2022 when he told the public", "We build investigations by laying a foundation. We resolve more straightforward cases first because they provide the

THE CROWNING: CULMINATION OF THE NATION

evidentiary foundation for more complex cases. Investigating the more overt crimes generates linkages to fewer overtones. Overt actors and the evidence they provide can lead us to others who may also have been involved, and that evidence can serve as the foundation for further investigative leads and techniques. In the circumstances like those of January six, a full accounting does not suddenly materialize." I think Garland was letting us know no one is above the law, and his investigation will go where the facts lead them," Smithson concluded.

Dr. Woodman nodded affirmatively and responded, "Which of course was a clue that even the former President was in his cross hairs if they could prove he had knowledge that his claim of a stolen election was untrue, and he had the intent to disrupt the official proceedings that would complete the transfer of power to President-Elect Joe Biden with the goal of overturning the election. In a trial of the former President, all 12 jurors would need to dismiss the claim that Donald Trump had no corrupt intent for a couple of reasons. One, because he told his angry supporters on January 6th, "Your vote was stolen. Your election was stolen. Your president was stolen from you. And if you don't go down there and stop what's going on in the Capitol, you will no longer have a country anymore." And two, because Donald Trump knew it was a lie, which provides evidence of his corrupt intent. Bill Barr, the Attorney General told the President, "Your claim of the election being stolen was "B. S."; and three, there were those meetings in the oval office where Trump was telling Department of Justice officials, 'I don't care if there was no fraud, just say there was and leave the rest to me and my allies in Congress.' and forth, there is Christopher Krebs who served as the first Director of the Department of Homeland Security's Cybersecurity and Infrastructure Security Agency (CISA) and was nominated for that position by President Trump in February 2018.

Christopher Krebs, a longtime Republican, was fired by Trump by a Tweet on Nov. 17. 2020. The move comes just a few days after CISA and other federal agencies proclaimed the 2020 presidential election was the "most secure in history," with no sign votes were tampered with, lost, altered or "in any way compromised." Two leading election organizations issued a joint statement vouching for the integrity of the election."[39] Sheldon

Smithson jumped in to clarify by asking, "Each of these four points you spoke about proves that President Trump had cause and opportunity to know his "Big Lie" of the election being stolen from him was not true, how does that prove the case against him?" Woodman replied concisely, "Because his intent was a huge part of a prosecution of him by the federal government, in terms of his involvement in his role in the January six insurrection. Simply put, Donald Trump knew it was a lie, proving his corrupt intent. The other piece of the puzzle to convict former President Trump is to show his direct involvement in the planning of the events that led to the attack on Congress on Jan. 6th, and his lack of any meaningful actions to halt the attack on Congress and his own Vice President, Mike Pence. The testimony, records, and documents gained by the House Committee on January 6 provided a treasure trove of evidence of all those that took part at the highest levels of the Administration. That evidence became the foundation of Garland's case of sedition and treason in planning a coup to disrupt the transfer of power and keep the presidency by Donald Trump and his co-conspirators."

Sitting down behind a desk, Sheldon Smithson inquired, "During the Grand Jury Hearings, Cassidy Hutchinson, a former special assistant to the president and the chief of staff, when asked, under oath, which members of Congress were involved in calls about overturning the election, Hutchinson named Representatives Marjorie Taylor Greene, (R-GA.) Jim Jordan (R-OH.), Lauren Boebert (R-CO), Scott Perry (R-PA), Louie Gohmert (R-TX), Andy Biggs (R-AZ), Mo Brooks (R-AL), Jody Hice (R-GA), Paul Gosar (R-AZ), and Debbie Lesko (R-AZ). It took many more months of grand jury secret hearings, but finally, in December 2023, Attorney General Merrick Garland made what was probably the most significant announcement by any Attorney General in U.S. history. For the record, Dr. Woodman, tell us about that announcement." Dr. Woodman, sitting in a room with pictures of famous U.S. Presidents on the wall behind him, explained, "Yes, it was on December 15, 2023, that the Attorney General came on all the networks and announced the federal indictments of Donald Trump Jr. Steve Bannon, John Eastman, Jeffrey Clark, Peter Navarro, Mark Meadows, Rudy Giuliani, and former POTUS, Donald John Trump. Each of these eight men was charged with the same or similar crimes; defying two federal criminal statutes, conspiracy to defraud the United States, and

THE CROWNING: CULMINATION OF THE NATION

obstruction of an official proceeding, besides violating federal statutes about voter fraud and seditious conspiracy. Garland was a very cautious and meticulous prosecutor. He would not bring such grievous charges as these without the complete conviction that the evidence was irrefutable. He listed a second larger group of former President Trump's circle, including Senator Ted Cruz, Representative Jim Jordan, Representative Paul Gosar and Mo Brooks, and Kimberly Guilfoyle, the fiancé of Donald Trump Jr., Matt Gaetz, Marjorie Taylor Greene, and Madison Cawthorn (R-NC) who would be charged with lesser, but still severe felonies of aiding and abetting a conspiracy to obstruct an official preceding. Garland explained each person would be tried individually in federal courts all around the country. Many would be tried simultaneously unless they were settled by a guilty plea before trial. In a chilling final sentence, he invoked a theme he had been saying throughout the lead-up to this announcement, "We follow the facts and the law wherever they lead, and that's all I can say about the indictments, the facts will be delivered in their respective trials." Smithson concluded the program with, "Thank you again, Dr. Woodman. We will pick up the story tomorrow night at 6:00 pm. Please join us then for the next episode of the Truth." Tully looked over at Catherine, who was still watching the computer screen with an expression of disbelief. They recalled all these events that occurred just three years earlier but seemed like three decades earlier. So much has happened since, and these portentous events directly caused all of it. Catherine looked over at her husband and said, "Do you remember when you predicted to the kids that this would happen, and none of them believed you?" Tully knew she was referring to that evening in James's cabin during the Stone family reunion in 2020, when Tully told the family, "The real truth about what Trump is, who he is, and what he is, will be revealed if Biden wins the election. The test will be if Trump cooperates with a peaceful transfer of power, or if he does not, in order to remain the president. My prediction is that he will not." "I remember it well," Tully admitted. "I think about it often and truly wish I was wrong." "So do I," Catherine added. She then closed her eyes and went to sleep. They both were still unaware of what was happening in Arizona.

Chapter 25
The Vulture Looms
Tampa, Florida
Monday night, March 3, 2025

When Tully went downstairs to start his nightly vigil of guarding against intruders, he heard his cell phone ring. 'It must be urgent," Tully surmised because his family only calls if it is serious or an immediate response to something is needed. It was James's name on the screen, so he answered. "Hi James," Tully spoke with an upbeat tone, "How are you feeling? Are the boys back from Michigan now?"

James's voice showed a man with terrible news when he said, "It has been the day from hell, Dad." Before James could explain, Tully interrupted, "Is it, Suzanne?" "No, Dad, she is fine, well, considering her circumstances. It's what happened on the flight home and later. Just about 30 minutes before landing in Mesa, up in the hills near the Roosevelt Dam, Paul had to put the plane down on a road because they ran out of fuel. He landed safely, and Chase and Paul set out on foot to get more fuel for the plane to finish the trip. They walked onto private property en route to a marina and were held at gunpoint. The men took their money and then drove them back to the plane, but the plane was gone." "Gone? Like vanished?" Tully asked. "Yes, it vanished. They walked to a different Marina in the opposite direction, and when they finally arrived, they were met by a nice guy who managed the Marina and Resort. That was yesterday. Today, I sent Grady in my new truck to drive up and pick them up, but Grady never arrived, and no one has heard from him. He should have arrived there hours ago, but he is missing. Paul, Chase, and the manager of the Marina are in his Jeep searching the roads for Grady. So far, they have found nothing." "My God," Tully exclaimed. "I hope they find him well. He could have had an accident or mechanical failure up in the mountains." "I doubt it was a mechanical issue", James declared. "That

THE CROWNING: CULMINATION OF THE NATION

truck was new and had four-wheel drive and a full gas tank. Hopefully, he didn't have an accident, but if he did, we need to find him right away. It is unusually hot for this time of year. He could need medical attention." "What can I do?" Tully asked, feeling helpless once again.

James proclaimed, "All we can do now is pray. I am letting everyone in the family know by phone call. I called you first, so I need to make more calls. I'll text everyone if I hear any news. Cell phones are not working well up there, so I have to wait for them to get near a cell tower before they can send a message." Tully asked, "Does Grace know yet?" "No," James replied, and please don't tell her. She is worried sick about Suzanne, and she doesn't need to worry about her husband too. I'll tell her when he is found, healthy and well." Tully knew how protective James was of his girls, and those instincts are at play now with Grady's disappearance. He knew James was right not to add to the stress Grace was dealing with already in Michigan, so he no longer pressed that topic.

In the heat of the desert afternoon, Paul and Chase sat in the passenger seats of the Jeep driven by their new-old friend, Red O'Brien. They were on SR 188 close to the Tonto National Forest when suddenly Chase pointed to something and yelled, "Stop!" "What is it?" Paul asked. "I just saw something in the ditch. Back up slowly so I can find it again." Red put the Jeep in reverse, and they backtracked slowly. "There it is!" Chase yelled, and he jumped out of the Jeep while it was still moving to leap down the hill to the bottom of the ditch. Chase emerged with a baseball cap in his hand. "It's Grady's hat. He goes nowhere without this hat. The hat was red and black with an Arizona Cardinals logo on the front, the logo of the team James had played with for four seasons. James had given him that hat when Grace and Grady first dated in high school." "Well, that proves he was here, but where is the truck?" Red inquired without expecting an answer, which no one provided. They set off on foot to search the surrounding area, which, like everywhere else around these parts, were boulders, sand, cacti, and thorny brush. The only signs of life were the roadrunners running on the sand and an occasional curious prairie dog. A vulture loomed overhead, flying in large circles above them, which gave an ominous feeling of doom. After another two hours of searching the area, they found no sign of Grady or the truck. Red suggested they go home before it got too dark, and they would set out again first thing in the morning. Paul agreed, adding, "He might try to reach us by phone so we can get back to the resort where we will have connectivity." Chase wanted to keep searching, but he was overruled by the majority, so they retreated to the Resort and Marina. To keep their minds off their problems, Red talked non-stop on the way back about his days fighting in Vietnam. To Paul and Chase, who were not even born back then, in the sixties, talking about the Vietnam War was on par with talking about the wars fought by the Roman Empire or the Crusades, all boring ancient history, but they politely listened. At the Apache Lake Marina and Resort, Red O'Brien fixed another superb meal for his two guests. After dinner, Paul and Chase sat down on the docks overlooking the Salt River, and talked about all that had happened. Chase occasionally would try calling his brother-in-law, but the calls went straight to voicemail. At 8:30 p.m., Paul received a text message from an unknown number. He opens it up to read: "This is Sergeant Nichols of the Sheriff's Department. The plane has been located, and we arrested the men who had it. It has been moved to our hangar for safekeeping. We will need you to come in to give us an ID of the men we arrested, as we believe it is the same two men you encountered. Can you come in the morning?" Paul read the text out loud to Chase, and both started cheering so loud you could hear their echoes bounce off the mountains. Paul called the Sheriff back rather than send a lengthy text. He explained what they were doing because of their missing relative, and they needed to search for him first thing in the morning. The Sheriff said he would meet them where they found the hat. He and his partner would join in on the search, along with their police dog. "The hat will provide the scent the dog needs to help find your brother-in-law," he explained. They all agreed to meet at dawn to continue the search. The next morning, an hour before dawn, Red woke his two young visitors with breakfast already prepared. They wanted to return to the search area by sunrise to meet with the deputies and their canine companions. By 5:00 a.m. Tuesday morning, they were back in Red's black Jeep on their way back to the spot where they found Grady's hat, and by sunrise, they were there just as the deputies drove up. Rusty, their canine police dog, was anxiously ready to get to work. They gave the German Shepherd a good long sniffing of Grady's hat. Then they all headed off into the hills following the dog's lead. The dog's excitement provided evidence Grady was previously on the road

THE CROWNING: CULMINATION OF THE NATION

near where the hat was found, but he could not pick up a scent anywhere off the road. They roamed randomly on both sides of State Road 188, but no scent was found. After a thorough search of the area, the deputies decided further search was futile. "If he were in these hills, Rusty would have picked up a scent by now. I can only conclude he stopped here, then drove off in the truck after losing his hat," Sergeant Nichols declared. His partner, Captain Maloney, the ranking officer of the pair, was not so quick to draw the same conclusion saying, "Or, he was taken away from this spot by someone that ambushed him. Regardless, we need you boys to follow us back to the station where we can get you to ID the culprits who stole the plane from you and process the plane to be released to you." They agreed to the Sheriff's wishes and drove to the Sheriff's Station in Rye, just 20 minutes from the search zone. When they entered the main office, Paul was taken to a room with a large one-way window looking into an adjacent room. Soon, six men, all dark with dark skin, were escorted into the room behind the window and lined up in a straight line facing the window. Each was holding a number from 1 to 6, which looked similar to the descriptions Paul and Chase had given of their kidnappers. Paul looked them over carefully, although he immediately spotted the faces of the men that robbed them but did not want to seem impulsive. "Number 2 and number 5," Paul said with assurance. Next, Chase was brought into the room after Paul was placed in a waiting room. Chase looked at the men and smiled, "It is 2 and 5, I am certain." That was all the proof they needed. The officers immediately booked those two men.

"If you pay us for the fuel, we can fill your plane's tank with enough fuel to get you to Mesa safely, and you can take off right here on our runway," the Captain explained. Chase spoke up anxiously, saying, "We can't leave here without Grady. We need to keep looking for him." "We will do a larger sweep using our planes and helicopters. If he is out there somewhere, we will find him," Captain Maloney assured them. "I am a pilot for the Coast Guard; can I assist in the search? Paul asked. "No, that would not be permitted. I promise we will leave no stone unturned." Chase smiled, thinking to himself of the irony of using the word "stone," which was his last name. Grady's last name is Petrov, which in Russian means son of Peter, which also means stone. With those assurances and the reality that they were not given much choice in the matter, Paul and Chase paid for a full tank of fuel for the plane and proceeded with plans to depart, but not until they did one more search for Grady Petrov. Red O'Brien drove them back to the spot where they found the hat, and they continued on SR 188 going north, searching for anything they could find that might provide a clue. Three more hours of driving and walking the hills produced nothing new. Red decided they were running low on gas for the Jeep, so he drove the two back to the hangar, where the Cessna was refueled and ready for takeoff. Red promised to call the Sheriff for updates and pass on anything he heard from them, good or bad. Paul and Chase thanked Red profusely and offered to send him money for his hospitality and efforts. "I don't want your damn money," Red gruffly responded, then gave them a firm handshake. Paul then saluted Red, which made Red smile. They started the plane and completed their journey to Phoenix-Mesa Gateway Airport.

Later that afternoon, Tully's cell phone rings, and again the caller is James. "James, did they find Grady?" Tully asked. James responded with that same solemn voice he had used on the last call, "This only gets more bizarre by the minute. Are you sitting down?" "Yes, Tully replied impatiently, "what happened now?" James began by clearing his throat from the phlegm he still had from his illness, "Chase and Paul searched for Grady, with the police helping, but they found nothing. The police caught the crooks that stole the plane, and Paul is now flying it home to Mesa with Chase. So they are safe, and the plane is unharmed. But here is the bizarre part...." James coughed a few times and then caught his breath, choosing his words carefully, "Grady called me." "That's awesome, Tully exclaimed with excitement. "Where is he?" "We don't know where he is now. He told me he was stopped on State Road 188 by three white supremacist-type guys with guns and rifles. Grady also had a gun in the truck, but they had surprised him, so he could not get to it. He was forced out of the truck and they took his wallet, watch, wedding ring, and shoes. They drove off in my truck, leaving him to walk on the road without shoes, just his socks on his feet. They also have his cell phone and gun left in the truck. Grady walked for two hours in the heat. He was about to collapse from heat exhaustion when two I.C.E. officers appeared. They picked him up and took him to the I.C.E. detention facility. They had to determine if he was an illegal immigrant since he had no ID. He told me he was being interrogated by the officers, of which one was black, and the other

THE CROWNING: CULMINATION OF THE NATION

two were Hispanic. I.C.E. was trying to determine if he was an American citizen or someone who had come across the border illegally, so they asked him who he voted for in the most recent election. Grady felt threatened by the question and surmised that they would be friendlier to him if he told them he voted for the Democratic Party's nominees. He assumed because of their race that, they would be Democrats, so he lied. Then the next morning, some men from Homeland Security took him away. They interrogated him for hours, accusing him of being a terrorist spy. He was upfront with them, so when they heard his last name, Petrov, they accused him of being a plant from Russia, perhaps even born here in the U.S. but a Russian loyalist and trained spy. Grady tried to prove he was an American, even changing his story about his party affiliation and who he voted for, but that only made things worse. They allowed him one phone call before they moved him to a highly secure and secret location pending future investigations. They would not let a "foreign spy" slip through their fingers." James' voice was getting choked up as he spoke to the point he had to stop talking. Tully replied, "I can't believe this. How is this even possible? What kind of world are we living in? Do you have a plan?" James responded, "I called Grady's Dad. He is getting a hold of his lawyer to see what can be done. Beyond that, we don't know what can be done. I'll call back when Paul and Chase arrive home. I will have to go to the airport and pick them up". "Are you strong enough to do that?" Tully asked, worried about James. "We'll find out. I am not sending the girls out there after this happened." James did not know a critical fact (no one knew, not even Grady), that his colleagues at the KGB referred to Grady's father, Dmitry Petrov when he lived in Russia as "Dema the Butcher." He served the KGB as an assassinator of high-value targets. During the cold war, he, with his family, was assigned to live in the United States undercover. He was to be used, when needed, for a hit on dangerous politicians and other enemies who security guards, such as the Secret Service, closely protected. However, when he arrived with his family, he immediately sought asylum by surrendering to the Central Intelligence Agency. The CIA gave them a new identity, a job, and a home in Arizona. This was Dema's chance to start a new honest life, and he grabbed it and never looked back. Dmitry Petrov, Dema's new alias, whose English-speaking skills were well developed as a part of his training, soon climbed the corporate ladder to become a Vice President of Sales. Grady followed in his father's corporate footsteps. He knew his family was immigrants from Russia before he was born. Still, he did not know his father's former occupation, nor that their very survival depended on keeping their identity secret, always fearing the long arms of the FSB (formerly known as the KGB before the fall of the Soviet Union).

THE CROWNING: CULMINATION OF THE NATION

Chapter 26
Donald John Trump vs. The United States of America
Tampa, Florida
Tuesday, March 4, 2025

TRUTH once again appeared on the screen of Tully's computer, and Sheldon Smithson, as before, was in the forefront. "Good evening. Thank you for joining us for another episode of our documentary series striving to preserve historical facts. I am your host Sheldon Smithson, and this is Tuesday, March 4, 2025. Thank you so much for saving and recording these internet broadcasts to preserve the truth for historical accuracy. Dr. Woodman, thank you for returning to our program tonight. I enjoy having you as part of our program." Tully and Catherine were glued to the screen. Even though they had lived through these events just three years earlier, they often learned things in hindsight that was not known. Tully thought about how, three years earlier, life was pretty normal and pleasant. Catherine worked at her accounting position, working from her home office since the start of the Covid-19 pandemic. Tully was enjoying his life as a retired former school counselor and coach, frequently going to their grandchildren's soccer games and school events. They had always been 'news junkies' with a strong interest in politics and current events. That life seemed like a distant dream today, as so much has changed, especially since January 20th of 2025. Their fascination and dedication to watching and recording these broadcasts continue their past obsessive consumption of all things politically relevant. For their entire life together, in the past, they subscribed to two daily newspapers and read both papers in their entirety before going to work each day. The papers eventually gave way to electronic news, social media platforms, and the trappings inherent in those platforms. Tully was deep in

THE CROWNING: CULMINATION OF THE NATION

thought while reflecting on the political environment they have witnessed the last seven years. Out loud, he told Catherine his thoughts saying, "The political bias that becomes interwoven into the sources of the news, the ease of creating narratives that fit a political agenda, the use of analytics to manipulate entire segments of society to believe a certain way, the infiltration and manipulative power of conspiracy theories which become repeated by so many believers, both real and robotic, and even the use of incredibly realistic "deep fakes" that make anyone believe they see and hear things that are sophisticated fabrications. By the 2020 election, the nation was deeply divided by factions of the national conscience that saw the same events through completely different filters and came to opposite conclusions. Violence became an acceptable means of political and social discourse. The head of the RNC, Ronna McDaniel, even declared the January 6th Insurrection resulting in at least five deaths and hundreds of injured police officers as "legitimate political discourse." Norms of civility in public were destroyed, and the very fabric of the nation's character, the nation's ethics of right and wrong, were being challenged and altered. What was the fringe of a political party, the most extreme of the candidates to get elected to office, became more and more mainstream, more the norm, and their extremist rhetoric became not only acceptable but often continuously repeated by those formally considered moderates. "Alternative facts" were frequently cited as acceptable substitutes for the factual truth. The nation's definitions of family, gender, and morals were being polluted, with the media being the delivery system of the pollution. Chaos is the outcome, and by 2022 that chaos will be 'full speed ahead.' The Republican Party, in 2022 and beyond, challenged every election as illegitimate, even those in foreign countries, to where they appeared to advocate for the end of using elections to decide who keeps political power."

Tully realized he was talking to himself and shifted his focus back to the program Catherine was faithfully watching, with focused intensity, and ignoring Tully's ramblings. Dr. Woodman was speaking about the 2022 elections. Tully had missed some of what he had said but picked up the conversation with Woodman saying, "... The 2022 midterm elections turned out to be exactly what was expected, what was historically typical, a swing of control of the House of Representative, back to, in this case, the Republicans, but in the Senate, the Democrats maintained a narrow majority. Despite that political victory for the Republicans, for Donald Trump, it was a major setback because of the victories of several Republicans that Trump worked hard to end their political futures, most notably Brian Kemp, Republican Governor of Georgia, and Lisa Murkowski, Republican Governor of Alaska. Both had won their primaries despite Trump, "The Kingmaker", having worked hard to endorse a more loyal candidate than these two. Murkowski voted to have Trump impeached, and in Brian Kemp's case, he refused to help Trump overturn the 2020 election results in Georgia.

Those setbacks did not deter Trump from running for president in 2024, but he lost the powerful influence he held before the 2022 midterm election. With Republicans in control of the House in 2023, many revenge hearings were scheduled, including the call for Joe Biden's impeachment, as well as hated Republicans, including Liz Cheney and Mitt Romney, those Republicans that were not voting in sync with the Republican conference. The year 2023 was the year from hell. Anyone with a political megaphone, sitting in a position of power on Capitol Hill became unhinged in terms of their vitriol for the other party and each other. The more bombastic, the more outrageous, and the more attention it received. Now, the evolution of power in American politics is derived from being outlandishly shocking and spewing enmity and hatred towards others, directed at both natural groups of people or often imaginary threats. Creating and advancing culture wars over fabricated issues, issues that just do not exist in reality, but are quickly turned into dog whistles for rabid followers, is not a new strategy. We saw it throughout the last decade, but the power of social media turns it into a political nuclear weapon. This was done by Adolf Hitler against the Jews of Germany; and was done by then President Trump during his campaign and first term in office, citing the "Mexican rapists" that are invading our country, the hordes of criminals charging our southern borders from crime-infested "sh*thole" countries, and the very first move Trump made as president in 2017, the Muslim ban.

Overshadowing all the political chaos were the cases now being tried in the Federal courts against the small army of Trump's associates that had been indicted for the Jan. 6th Insurrection and the attempted coup. Every stall tactic imaginable was being employed in the hopes the cases would drag on

THE CROWNING: CULMINATION OF THE NATION

well into 2025 after a new president would be inaugurated. As was the DOJ strategy throughout Garland's tenure as Attorney General, the lesser charges would be tried before the most serious charges, building on the success of the earlier convictions. Those in Trump's inner circle were found guilty of some charges against them. Some of those accepted a plea bargain, and a few of them served time in jail, but their political futures were destroyed.

The culminating trial in pursuing justice would be the case of <u>Donald John Trump vs. The United States of America</u>. That trial was not scheduled to begin until the fall of 2024, with the 2024 presidential election to be held on the 5th of November, 2024. Since Trump was running for president in 2024, he believed if he could make it to then and win the election, he could halt the trial and use his power of pardon to end the 'witch hunt.'"

Sheldon Smithson interrupted Dr. Woodman's review of the events of 2024 by saying, "So let's talk about what was characterized as the 'biggest and most important trial in our nation's history', the trial of Donald J. Trump. Please walk us through some of the most important details of the Prosecution's case against Trump." Dr. Woodman took a long drink of water to prepare him for the detailed reply, and then he said, "Garland and his team started with the background to the election of 2020. The main lead prosecutor for the Department of Justice was a man in his 50s, which looked like a cross between John Wayne and Kevin Costner. His name was Gene Larson. Larson was 6'5 with a large square jaw, a full head of hair, and broad shoulders. His face seemed eerily similar to Kevin Costner's face. His voice was deep and commanding.

Larson declared, "Trump had laid the groundwork well before the election to make the same claims of voter fraud, in case he lost this election, an election he was sure he would win easily, based primarily by the enthusiasm and size of his rally's before election night. The President dispersed a series of outlandish claims void of evidentiary proof of election fraud both before and after Election Day to undermine the results. During this time, Trump enlisted a ring of close collaborators to develop and implement unparalleled schemes to, as Trump himself said, "overturn" the election fate. Among the results of this "Big Lie" campaign were the terrible events of January 6, 2021—a defining moment in what we now understand as nothing less than an attempted coup. In the months following the election, many credible sources, from the President's inner circle to agency leadership and statisticians, informed President Trump and Dr. Eastman that there was no evidence of election fraud. Fourteen months later, a federal district court judge, after reviewing the previously withheld emails to and from John Eastman, found that it was "more likely than not" Trump and his cohorts violated two federal criminal laws in their attempts to overturn the election. President Trump rejected the advice of his campaign experts on election night and instead followed the course recommended by an inebriated Rudy Giuliani, just to claim he won and insist that the vote counting stopped. Trump declared publicly, "This is a fraud on the American public, this is an embarrassment to our country... Quite frankly, we won the election". His refusal to accept defeat set the table for what was to come.

In the hotel suites around Washington D.C. and elsewhere, a seven-part plot to undermine and overturn the election was taking shape. Trump had taken the time to put together a new team of advisors under his command. Trump continued to beat the drums telling the American people that the election was, in his words, "a major fraud," and millions of Americans believed him. Donald Trump and his newly formed legal team repeatedly pushed a conspiracy theory about Dominion voting machines changing the votes, orchestrated by a deceased Venezuelan former dictator, or the Italian military changing votes via satellites.

Meanwhile, Attorney General Bill Barr, after conducting a thorough investigation using the vast network of the Justice Department, called Trump's claims "complete nonsense." President Trump's campaign advisors, his Department of Justice, and his cybersecurity experts, all reported, that Trump's claims of a fraudulent election were all fiction. For example, his White House lawyer, Eric Hirschman, said, "I thought the Dominion stuff was, I never saw any evidence whatsoever to sustain those allegations."

Prosecutor Larson called to the witness stand the top attorney for Mike Pence during his tenure as the Vice-President, Greg Jacobs, Pence's chief legal counsel. He was with Pence on Jan. 6 and participated in White House meetings about the former Vice President's role as Congress counted the Electoral College votes. During the two days before the Jan. 6th riot, Jacobs had taken part in a series of discussions with John Eastman about the legality of the scenarios Eastman was proposing, including those scenarios included

THE CROWNING: CULMINATION OF THE NATION

having Pence declare Trump the winner of the 2020 election or kick the matter back to the states by having Pence reject state electors. Mr. Larson opened his questioning of Jacob, asking him, "Mr. Jacob, you discussed and even debated this theory at length with Dr. Eastman. What was Vice President Pence's opinion on his constitutional role in the certification of the election results?" Jacob replied, "The Vice president's first instinct was that there was no way that any one person, particularly the vice president who is on the ticket and has a vested outcome in the election, could have the authority to decide it by rejecting electors or to decisively alter the outcome by, suspending the joint session for the first time in history, to try to get a different outcome from state legislatures. Then Eastman acknowledged his proposals would violate the Electoral Count Act, and I outlined further violations of the law Pence would be committing if he went along with Eastman's request."

Larson posed a second question to Jacobs, "Mr. Jacob, did Dr. Eastman say whether he would want other vice presidents, such as Al Gore after the 2000 election or Kamala Harris after the 2024 election to have the power to decide the outcome of the election?"

Jacobs smiled broadly when he said, "So this was one of the many points that we discussed on January 5th. He had come into that meeting trying to persuade us that there was some validity to his theory. I viewed it as my objective to persuade him to acknowledge he was just wrong. And I thought this had to be one of the most powerful arguments. "I mean, John, back in 2000, you weren't jumping up and saying Al Gore had the authority to do that. You would not want Kamala Harris to be able to exercise that kind of authority in 2024 when I hope Republicans will win the election. And I know you hope that too, John," and Eastman replied, "Absolutely Al Gore did not have a basis for doing it in 2000. Kamala Harris, shouldn't be able to do it in 2024, but I think you should do it today".

The next witness was the United States Attorney General during the Trump Administration. Gene Larson approached Barr after being sworn in, asking, "Mr. Barr, you have declared, many times, in the media, in your book, and in a sworn deposition before the January Six Committee members that your opinion of Donald Trump's campaign to convince the American public that the election of 2020 was stolen was, in your words, "bullsh*t," "nonsense" and "fantasy." For the record and the jury, please tell us what you thought about his claims." Barr paused a moment to chuckle to himself, then bluntly said, "There was never an indication of interest in what the facts were. I was somewhat demoralized because I thought, 'Boy, if he really believes this stuff, he has lost contact with — he's become detached from reality if he really believes this stuff.'"

Dominion Voter Systems sued Sidney Powell, Rudy Giuliani, and others for defamation. Powell lost all her counter-suits and was heavily sanctioned by a federal judge for bringing unfounded claims into court.[40] But there was a broader campaign to sway the public. Enter former CEO of Overstock.com, Patrick Byrne, who was lauded as "The Renaissance Man of E-Commerce." If Flynn is the movement's biggest persona, Byrne is among its most ardent supporters. In the wake of Byrne's alleged romance with a foreign spy, he resigned as Overstock's CEO and claimed the affair was part of an elaborate FBI sting. As Byrne stated at Trump's trial, "I think I can tell the whole story of all the events leading up to the events of January 6th better than anyone other." Byrne says that after the election, he teamed up with Flynn and Powell, which led to meetings with Wood at his plantation.[40]

The prosecutor asked Byrne, "In Antrim County, Michigan, a group of operatives showed up there in December 2020, and they ended up inspecting voting machines. What was your role in all that?" Byrne said, "These were all volunteers, and I was picking up the bill for all the hotels and the travel."[40] "And the team came in on a private jet. Are you the one that booked and arranged that?" the prosecutor inquired. Byrne responded, "Yes, I love it." Larson fires back, "Mr. Byrne, besides former President Trump, you seem to be the person most personally responsible for motivating the election fraud movement, and some would say for spreading disinformation. Do you think that's an accurate way to portray your role?" Taken back by the aggressive delivery of the last question, Patrick Byrne looks around the room, seeming to assess the seriousness of the moment. He finally answers saying, "I'm the one who's waking up Americans to this deep problem in our election apparatus. I figure if I am right, I am saving America. If I am wrong, then I have misjudged President Trump, and that's on President Trump."

THE CROWNING: CULMINATION OF THE NATION

The prosecutor turns away from Patrick Byrne, who is becoming more uncomfortable sitting on the witness stand of the biggest trial in history. He is facing the jury box, looking them in the eyes when he says, "Tell the court about the time you met with President Trump in the White House. Was that a meeting on the President's agenda that December 2020?" Byrne looks at the prosecutor back when he replies, "No, we didn't have a meeting scheduled with the President." Byrne says that on December 18th, he, Michael Flynn, and Sidney Powell went directly to the White House. "Mike (Flynn) got in touch with somebody who he had worked with, and that got us up to within about 20 yards or 20 feet, 30 feet of the oval office, and then Sidney (Powell) and I kind of hung around the offices until we saw President Trump walk by and we stuck our heads out and he recognized us and looked around and he said, "Hey, come on in". So we went down and walked in, and the four of us, including Mike Flynn, sat right there in front of President Trump across the Resolute Desk. We proposed that President Trump issue an executive order. We urged him to appoint Sidney Powell as a special counsel to investigate the election and to order federal forces to seize voting machines and inspect them for fraud. Mike Flynn knew of some National Guard units that were cyber specialists that could have been activated to do this. Flynn said, "I know that we like to keep uniforms out of elections, but this is a constitutionally unprecedented moment".[40]

"So, when you left the White House. What did you think was going to happen?" Larson asks. Byrne paused, considering his answer carefully, "I thought Sidney was going to become a Special Council at the White House, just focusing on this issue and that by Monday, people would go in and gaining the voter machine, imaging hard drives, and counting ballots." Gene Larson speaks directly to the jury, "That week Flynn appeared on the pro-Trump network Newsmax and suggested that the President could seize voting machines."[40] Gene Larson then requests a video of that interview be shown to the jury. The video shows Flynn who says in that interview, "Within the swing states, if he wanted to, he could take military capabilities, and he could place them in those states and rerun an election in each of those states. I mean, it's not unprecedented. I mean, these people out there talking about martial law, it's like, it's something that we'd never done. We've done... martial law has been instituted 64, 64 times!"[40]

Prosecutor asks the witness, "Just days before Congress was scheduled to certify Biden's victory, you, Mr. Byrne, you joined a large meeting in Washington DC. Tell the jury about that meeting". Byrne responds, "There was a very important meeting where some things were presented and there were senators and congressmen there, and people watching from Capitol Hill. What we were trying to accomplish was to ask Mike Pence to delay one week, and the state legislatures would meet again to reconsider their certification of Joe Biden in favor of President Trump.[40] "Was President Trump in on those calls? Did he speak with those senators and congressmen who were also on the call?"

Byrne did not answer. "Mr. Byrne, you are under oath, and let me remind you that there are many others on these calls, other witnesses who will testify if we call them in and put them under oath. Was the President included on these calls?" Still no answer from Patrick Byrne was given, who looked over at his attorney with a 'what do I say?' expression on his face. The attorney gave his client a very subtle nod. "Yes, he was on the calls. We were all sternly warned before and after the call to not reveal anything about the calls to anyone, including those who attended." The atmosphere in that courthouse was one of extreme trepidation on steroids. Prosecutor Larson asks, "Did you think Pence was going to execute on this? Byrne replied, "I was positive that afternoon. I got word that it was all going to happen, and I got word that evening that Pence had gone for it. And Pence was in, and Pence was going to do it. Still, I believed that the effort to challenge the election was on the verge of success. Byrne and Flynn took to the streets in Washington, riling up the crowds that had gathered to protest the certification of Biden's election."[40]

The prosecutor plays the next video for the jury, in which the night before the Insurrection, Mike Flynn was speaking alongside Patrick Byrne to the crowds gathering in Washington D.C. On it, Flynn, speaking to a riled-up crowd, declares, "The one thing that we can never, ever accept is to put up with a rigged election. That's the first thing. We feel freedom. We bleed for freedom, and we will sacrifice for freedom. (To the) members of Congress, the members of the House, members of the United States Senate;

THE CROWNING: CULMINATION OF THE NATION

those of you who are feeling weak tonight, those of you that don't have the moral fiber in your body, get some tonight because tomorrow we, the people, are going to be here. And we want you to know that we will not stand for a lie. We will not stand for a lie. God bless you. And God bless."[40]

Prosecutor Larson declares, "The stolen election myth, which all the team that met at L. Lin Wood's plantation had helped to finance; formed and spread and had become a powerful political weapon. Your honor, the prosecution calls Senator Ted Cruz to the stand." A loud murmur echoed throughout the courtroom, causing the judge to pound his gavel and demand, "Order! Order in the court! The court went silent as Senator Cruz walked to the witness stand and was sworn in. "Thank you, Senator, for joining us today. First, was the immunity deal we agreed upon coerced?" Senator Cruz leaned forward and said, "No it was not." Larson asks, "For clarification, you have agreed to testify today under your own free will?"

"Objection! Asked and answered," shouted the defense. "I'll allow," The judge replied.

Cruz responded with a simple, "Yes." Larson asks, "Senator Cruz, I remind you you are under oath. Did you ever say publicly, "It's not good, it's not good if Joe Biden becomes president to have half the country believe that, that he stole the election and it was illegitimate. That's not good for the next president or the next president or the next president."[46] "I did," Cruz responded.

"Did you also say publicly, "It is no surprise that Donald is throwing yet another temper tantrum or, if you like, yet another Trumper tantrum. Donald finds it very hard to lose."?[46]

"Yes, I did say that," said Cruz. "And did you state publicly, 'This man is a pathological liar?. The man cannot tell the truth, referring to Donald J. Trump?"[46] "Yes," Cruz admitted. Larson paused for dramatic effect, then asked Cruz. "Mr. Cruz, in late December 2020 and early January 2021, just prior to the January 6th insurrection, were you participating with other members of Congress to discuss ways to prevent the transfer of power to Joe Biden?" "Yes," was Cruz's reply. "And what was your opinion of the various schemes being discussed?" Larson asked. "All of the options that were being discussed, were problematic,"[46] Cruz replied. "How so?" Cruz explained, " It can't just be, you know, somebody tweeted this. It's gotta be demonstrable facts that can be laid out with evidence."[46] Larson looked surprised, glanced over to the Jury and asked, "Laid out? Laid out to who?" Cruz looked like a man who had been cornered and said, "A new commission was to be formed as soon as the House and the Senate failed to certify the electors. This would be the mechanism to force denying the certification on the sixth. "Larson pressed Cruz by asking, "So Senator Cruz, according to this plan you were advocating for, who would then decide who the next president would be?"

Cruz nervously cleared his throat before saying,"It would be the results of that commission."[46] The courtroom erupted, followed by the pounding of the judges gavel several times yelling, "Order! Order in the court!" Meanwhile, Prosecutor Larson took his seat indicating he was done asking questions. When order was restored, the judge asked the defense if they had any questions for Senator Cruz. "We do, your Honor."

Blankinship arose, approaching the witness, turned in the direction of the Jury and said, "Senator Cruz, thank you for coming here today. I would like to know if the immunity deal you were given and accepted to testify today, permit you to commit perjury?" "Objection!" shouted Larson. "Sustained. The Jury will disregard the last question." Blankinship continued his cross asking, "Did the defendant, Donald J. Trump, personally tell you to carry out these schemes you claim?"

Cruz looked over to the jury and said, "He told Representative Jim Jordan his orders, who in turn brought them to the rest of us." Objection, Your Honor, move to strike; the witness did not answer the question I asked him," Blankinship demanded. The judge responded, "The witness answered the question you asked. Just because you don't like the answer does not mean it should be stricken. The objection is denied." With that, the defense said, "We have no further questions for this witness, Your Honor."

Dr. Woodman paused his summary, took several sips of water, then explained, "The battle cries erupted outside the Capitol on January 6th, when about 300 Proud Boys and Oath Keepers members began their march to Capitol. The time was 10:30 am, long before Trump's speech at the Ellipse began. As the swelling crowd formed, chants began, such as "Hang Mike

THE CROWNING: CULMINATION OF THE NATION

Pence" and "Nancy, where are you, Nancy". Inside Congress on the Republican side of the aisle, where 147 lawmakers called for a rejection of Biden's election, Pence dutifully asked, "Is the objection in writing and signed by a Senator?".[40] The ten-minute phone call between President Trump and Representative Jim Jordan on the morning of Jan. 6th suggests that the 139 members of the House of Representatives who objected to the counting of the certified ballots were perhaps not simply making a protest vote but rather were part of a larger orchestrated Republican effort to steal the election. As Peter Navarro put it, Mike Pence was the "quarterback."

Prosecutor Gene Larson thanked and dismissed the witness before announcing, "Your Honor, I would like to call to the stand Representative Jamie Raskin." After Congressman Raskin was sworn in, Larson begins his examination of the Representative from Maryland's 8th Congressional District in the U.S. House of Representatives by asking, "Representative Raskin, for the record, before running for office, you served as a Professor of Constitutional Law at American University's Washington College of Law for over 25 years, is that correct?" "Yes it is correct," Raskin replied. "And before that you were a graduate of Harvard College and Harvard Law School? asked Larson. "That too is correct, replied Raskin. Larson adds, "And most recently, you served in Congress, among many other assignments and Committees, on the Select Committee to Investigate the January 6th Attack on the United States Capitol, true?" "True," replied Raskin. "And as a member of that Select Committee, you were privy to almost a million documents and over 800 witness testimony. Is that also true? asked Larson. Before Raskin could reply, the Defense attorney blurted out, "Objection, Your Honor; there is no way the witness could be personally familiar with that many documents and heard all of those witnesses!" The Judge retorted, "Let's hear from the witness before objecting to what you think he may answer." Raskin stated, "I was not personally reading all of those documents, not personally hearing all the testimony. Due to the volume of evidence and witnesses being deposed, the tasks were divided among different groups. I was, however, as were many of my colleagues on the Select Committee, synthesizing from the evidence what was significant to get to the answers we were seeking, so as a result of that process, I have a thorough grasp of all of the significant information garnered from the evidence and testimony." Larson continued, "So, let me ask you, Mr. Raskin, what do you know, with certainty, that took place after the Secret Service removed Mike Pence from the certification proceedings in the Capitol?"

Raskin explained, "Pence first went to his ceremonial office at the Capitol where he was protected by Secret Service agents, but vulnerable because the second-floor office had windows and those windows could be breached if the intruding thugs gained control of the building. Pence refused two requests from the agents in charge of his detail to evacuate the building, saying", quote, "I'm not leaving the Capitol"[44] "The last thing the Vice President wanted was the people attacking the Capitol to see his 20 car motorcade fleeing. It would only vindicate their insurrection.[9] The third time the secret service asked it was more of an order than a request. They move Pence down a staircase to a secure subterranean area where his armored limousine awaited." Raskin spoke with confidence and authority, "He was in a loading dock in an underground parking garage beneath the capitol complex, no place to sit, no desks, no chairs, and nothing. He was in this concrete parking garage and, you know, with his family and, I mean, this is the Vice-President of the United States. And he's like, hold up in a, in a basement. One of them is his chief of staff, Mark Short, showing him his phone. It's the tweet of Trump's saying, "Mike Pence didn't have the courage".[15 & 44] Raskin continued his testimony by saying, "So when his secret service agents, including one of them who had, was carrying the nuclear football with him, were chased out by this neo-fascist and they ran down to some still undisclosed, mysterious place in the Capitol, he uttered what I think are the six most chilling words of this entire thing I've seen so far. He said, "I'm not getting in that car".[44] Raskin concluded his statement by saying, "The secret service agents who presumably are reporting to Trump's secret service agents, were trying to spirit him off of the campus. And Pence said, "I'm not getting in that car until we count the electoral college votes." He knew exactly what this inside coup had planned for. Those who were going to do this were not a coup directed at the President. It was

THE CROWNING: CULMINATION OF THE NATION

a coup directed by the President against the Vice-president and against the Congress."

Sheldon Smithson summarized the bigger picture to the audience of Truth, saying "But, ultimately, Mike Pence did not comply. After a year of silence, Mike Pence, reacting to a Trump accusation that Pence should be investigated for "not overturning the election." Pence responded to Trump in a speech to Republicans. "This week, our former president said I had the right to 'overturn the election.' President Trump is wrong. I had no right to overturn the election," Pence said in an extraordinary public reproach of Trump during a speech at the Federalist Society.

Bryce Waldron picked up the story explaining to the audience, "In the months that followed, the stolen election myth continued to be perpetuated by Byrne and others. Their campaign once again focused on the local level, calling for an audit of the votes county by county.^{40} Their first stop was Maricopa County, Arizona, the county crucial to Biden's narrow victory in the state. As the largest funders of the audit, Byrne and Flynn spent more than $4 million to cover the cost, with Byrne's film crew being among the few who had access to the process. Over five months, a private firm hired by Arizona's Republican Senate, Doug Logan's Cyber Ninjas, conducted the election review. Many Republican lawmakers across the country visited the site hoping to bring it to their states.^{40}Ultimately, after four months of the "forensic audit" in Maricopa County, the results determined that Biden actually had about eight more additional votes than previously counted in all the other legitimate audits."

Sheldon Smithson thanked Dr. Woodson and promised the "rest of the story" of the biggest trial in U.S. history on their next broadcast. Tully turned off the computer and parked his tired bones on the chair he sat in a while on night duty. Of course, he knew the outcome of the trial, as everyone does, but he looked forward to hearing it told from the vantage point of a highly respected historian. He checked his phone to read a text from James, rejoicing that his son, Chase, and his brother, Paul, had safely made it back home. Paul would leave the next morning to return the plane and return to his post in Miami. Tully knew he would have to pick up Paul at one airport and bring him to another airport so he could complete his journey.

THOMAS J. FEELY

Chapter 27
The Verdict
Wesley Chapel, Florida
March 5th, 2025

Manny, the owner of the Cessna Tully had borrowed for the pilgrimage to Arizona and Michigan, called Tully to learn of the plans for returning his plane. Tully explained Paul was on his way, and as they spoke, he headed to the airport in Wesley Chapel, Florida.

"He should land there tonight around 10:00 pm," Tully explained. "How will your son get back to Miami?" asked Manny. Tully replied, " I plan to bring him back to St. Pete/Clearwater airport so he can hitch a military flight from there to Miami." Manny thought for a minute, then said, "Why don't I fly him to Miami first thing in the morning tomorrow?" Tully really loved that idea as the drive to Clearwater and back home is fraught with danger. He knew Paul could be stuck there for days trying to get a flight going to Miami, but, he didn't want to impose too much on Manny's generosity. Tully thought, 'we nearly lost the plane to thieves and the entire trip took far longer than he originally predicted '. "No, we can't ask that much from you. We all are so very appreciative of what you have already done for this family." Tully responded. Manny smiled and said, "I insist; your son is my brother in arms. I would be honored to fly him back to his base, besides; I want to ask him all about the trip, I heard it was exciting." Tully was relieved, so he replied, "Exciting isn't the word I would use to describe that ordeal. Horrifying is more appropriate." When Paul arrived at Wesley Chapel Regional Airport and learned of Manny's offer, he too was relieved. "I am already AWOL by a day now so getting back tonight would really help me out with my commanding officer." "Then we will leave now," Manny declared. Let's get this bird fueled up." Within an hour of landing, they were already back in the sky for the two-hour flight to Miami. Tully felt a little sad he didn't get to hug his son, or even see him, but was grateful to get him back to his post safely.

That evening Tully and Catherine got caught up in a discussion about the events of the last few days. They forgot to turn on their computer until it was already 6:15. Tully was mad at himself as he had hoped to have a recording of every minute of the historical documentary and hoped that it was delayed getting started. As Tully logged into the secret site and booted up the recording software, Catherine went downstairs on her own to get a hot chocolate for the two of them. She had gained strength and was strolling around the house at an increased pace, day by day. She was clearly on the mend. Before she got back the program was on, and all three of the hosts were on the show in different boxes, speaking from three different locations. They were in a discussion explaining to the audience why they were all in the broadcast together. Sheldon Smithson was talking first, "... we fear we may not be able to complete this historical documentary, to tell the world, the future world, about everything that has happened if we continue to broadcast each night. We know for certain that the authorities are closing in on our locations. It is a matter of hours before they will storm past our locked doors, arrest us, and shut us down for good. We decided instead of running away and setting up all over again somewhere else that we needed to deliver all the historical content in one longer broadcast." Bryce Waldron then spoke, and the screen switched to him as he continued the message, "So tonight we have brought back a few of our past guests who are the most knowledgeable about the events leading up to the start of America's second civil war. Our historian Dr. Woodman is back tonight, starting things off to walk us through the rest of the trial of the United States vs. Donald J. Trump. Other experts will take us from the trial's conclusion to the present, and we will have to culminate the series tonight. We hope you will all understand, and most importantly please preserve your recordings of the entire documentary in so many places that, by doing so you will assure the Truth will be preserved for eternity. When the rewritten alternative history is presented to the public, you will be armed with the truth. That will be our secret weapon. The Truth will reign."

THE CROWNING: CULMINATION OF THE NATION

Bryce Waldron continues turning to Dr. Woodman's image on the screen. "Dr. Woodman, in the interest of brevity, please give us the most critical portions of that long trial that led to the final verdict.

"Yes, Bryce, I will, as briefly as possible, I'll cover the highlights of the evidence brought to the jury. For the historical record, I think it is important to provide what was happening outside of the courthouse during the trial. Not only were there throngs of Trump supporters and Trump haters outside the Edward A. Garmatz United States Courthouse, a U.S. District Court for the District of Maryland where the trial was taking place but also in Federal and State Courthouses throughout the nation. Each state had to deploy its National Guard to protect the people and buildings from the angry mobs of protestors. This was a national protest unlike any ever seen before in our history. Competing factions of protestors broke into violent riots, and local police and the National Guard had to intervene to quell the rioters. Whoever was not protesting in the country was riveted to their T.V.s following the televised trial.

In order to establish beyond a doubt that there was a clear intent to disrupt Congress from certifying the electors that were purposefully planned including the violent insurrection, the Prosecution, led by Gene Larson called Donald J. Trump Jr. to the stand. After being sworn in, the eldest child of Donald Trump was asked, "Mr. Trump, on November 5th, 2020 did you send this text message to the president's Chief of Staff, Mark Meadows?" He then pointed to a large screen so everyone could easily read the text. The message said: "This is what we need to do. Please read it and please get it to everyone that needs to see it because I'm not sure we're doing it." Donald Trump Jr. barely read the text on the screen. He had already been through the drill during his own trial. "Yes," he answered blandly as possible as if to communicate the mundane nature of these messages. "The November 5 text message, sent two days before the election was called for Joe Biden, two full days before the outcome of the election. It outlines a strategy to overturn the election that is nearly identical to what allies of the former President attempted to carry out in the months that followed. Specifically, Trump Jr. previews a strategy to supplant authentic electors with fake Republican electors in a handful of states. That plan was eventually orchestrated and carried out by allies of the former President, and overseen by his then-attorney Rudy Giuliani.[41]

Text by text, Prosecutor Larson repeatedly projects onto the screen the text message and asks Donald Trump Jr. to verify that he was the person who sent those text messages to the Chief of Staff and, text after text, each time Trump Jr. answers with the one-word reply in the affirmative, "yes". Donald Trump Jr. had no choice. He no longer could portray himself as the brash renegade he loved to project, never scared of anything or anyone; bigger than life, like his father. Today he was a defeated man. He had no other choice but to admit the truth, not to mention his plea deal required he does so."

Dr. Woodman explains to the audience, "According to the text message he sent Meadows, Trump Jr. cited two key dates in December that served as deadlines for the states to certify their elections and compel Congress to accept them. Donald Trump Jr. seems to point to the dates as a potential vulnerability for leveraging by raising doubt about the legitimacy of the election results.[41] Trump Jr. specifically mentions suing and asking for recounts in order to prevent certain swing states from certifying their results, as well as having a handful of Republican state houses put forward slates of fake "Trump electors."[42] Trump Jr. argues in his text to Meadows that they should press their advantage by having Republican-controlled state assemblies "step in" and put forward separate slates of "Trump electors, "[41] "Republicans control Pennsylvania, Wisconsin, Michigan, North Carolina, etc we get Trump electors," Trump Jr. adds in one of his texts to Meadows. "Republicans could simply vote to reinstate Trump as President on January 6 if all those efforts failed", according to the Trump Jr. text.[41]

"And finally Mr. Trump, did you say in that text "We have operational control. Total leverage," "Moral High Ground, POTUS must start 2nd term now," asks Prosecutor Larson. Donald Jr. looked clearly embarrassed by this, but dutifully responded, "Yes, I did." Prosecutor Gene Larson turned to the jury and stated, "The text from Trump Jr. contains several layers of disclosure. This clearly shows how members of the Trump inner circle started discussing ways to overthrow the election months before the coup on January 6, and

THE CROWNING: CULMINATION OF THE NATION

before all the votes were even counted. Joe Biden will not be declared the winner of the election until two days later, on November seven."

Dr. Woodman explains to the audience of Truth, why this is so important to determining guilt, "After the 2020 election, Trump and his team of lawyers filed over 60 unsuccessful lawsuits in key states. None of them succeeded, failing to show evidence of widespread voter fraud to support their claims of a stolen election. Based on the same unfounded voter fraud claims, the team also sought various recounts. Several states conducted recounts in the months after the election, though none of them revealed any fraud substantial enough to have changed the outcome of the vote in any state. Every step followed the rough draft of a developing plan presented by the texts of Donald Trump Jr."

Dr. Woodman explains, "The plan that evolved was a very multi-pronged plan involving many people to make it all happen in a relatively short time. When Prosecutor Larson called his next two witnesses was the moment in the trial where President Trump's personal and active involvement in the coup plot was clarifying. When Ronna Romney McDaniel, the Chairwoman of the Republican National Committee testified was a pivotal moment. She responded to Larson's question when he asked her, "Ms. McDaniel, President Trump, and his campaign were directly involved in advancing and coordinating the plot to replace legitimate Biden electors with fake collectors, not chosen by the voters. They convinced these fake electors to cast and submit their votes through fake certificates, telling them that their votes would only be used if President Trump won his legal challenges. Ms. McDaniel, were you asked to take part in this effort?" "Yes," McDaniel replied. "What did President Trump say when he called you?" asked Larson. Ronna McDaniel drew a deliberately long breath, exhaled, and then said, "Essentially, he turned the call over to Mr. Eastman, who talked about the importance of the RNC, helping the campaign gather these contingent electors in case any of the legal challenges, that were ongoing, change the results. I think my role was just helping them reach out and assemble them, but my understanding is the campaign took the lead, and we just were helping them in that role."

The co-host of Truth, Sheldon Smithson proceeded methodically, for the historical record, to re-create the most significant testimony. He tells the audience, "Prosecutor Larson called to the stand his next witness, Rusty Bowers, the Republican Speaker of the House in Arizona. Larson started his questions with, "Mr. Bowers. I understand that after the election, you received a phone call from President Trump and Rudy Giuliani in which they discussed the result of the presidential election in Arizona. If you would, tell us about that call, and whether the former President or Mr. Giuliani raised allegations of election fraud."

Rusty Bowers replied, "Mr. Trump, President Trump, then President Trump came on and we initiated a conversation. He was asking that I would allow an official committee at the State Capitol so that they could hear their evidence proving a stolen election in Arizona and that we could take action thereafter. I refused. Trump countered with, "We have heard by an official high up in the Republican legislature, that there is a legal theory or a legal ability in Arizona, that you can remove the electors of President Biden and replace them. And we would like to have the legitimate opportunity through the committee to come to that end and remove that. And I said, that's something that's totally new to me. I've never heard of any such thing. And he pressed that, and I said, look, you are asking me to do something that is counter to my oath when I swore to the constitution to uphold it. And I also swore to the constitution and the laws of the state of Arizona, and this is totally foreign to me. And I would never do anything of such magnitude without deep consultation with qualified attorneys. And I said, "Mr. Trump, you are asking me to do something against my oath and I will not break my oath."

Larson then inquired of Speaker Bowers, "Why did you feel either, in the absence of that evidence, or with what they were asking you to do, would violate your oath to the constitution?" Bowers vouched, "First of all, when the people in Arizona, I believe some 40 plus years earlier, the legislature had established the manner of electing our officials or the electors for the presidential race. Once it was given to the people, as in Bush v. Gore illustrated by the Supreme Court, it became a fundamental right of the people. So as far as I was concerned for someone to ask me to deny your oath. I will not do that. It is a tenant of my faith that the constitution is divinely inspired, my most basic foundational belief. And so for me to

THE CROWNING: CULMINATION OF THE NATION

do that, because somebody just asked me to, even if that someone is the president, is foreign to my very being, I will not do it."

SMITHSON NOTED, "THE defense Attorney for Donald Trump declined to cross-examine Speaker Bowers. The next witness called by Larson was a woman named Laura Cox, the Michigan Republican Party Chair. Larson began questioning by asking, "Documents obtained by the select committee, show that instructions were given to the electors in several states that they needed to cast their ballots in complete secrecy because the scheme involved, fake electors, those taking part in certain states had no way to comply with state election laws, like where the electors were supposed to meet. One group of fake electors, even considered hiding overnight to ensure that they could access this as required in Michigan. Did they say who they were working with on this effort to have electors meet?"

Ms. Cox replied, "One of them said he was working with the President's campaign. He told me that the Michigan Republican electors were planning to meet in the Capitol and hide overnight so that they could fulfill the role of casting their vote, per law, in the Michigan chambers. And, I told him in no uncertain terms, that was insane and inappropriate."

Dr. Woodman pivots to highlight another facet being presented by the prosecution. "There were many moving parts, and as the meetings in posh Willard Hotel, just a block from the White House, where some of President Donald Trump's most loyal lieutenants were working day and night. "They called it the "command center," Dr. Woodman explained. Woodman continued his reporting by saying, "One of those loyalists involved in the planning joined the effort to drive as many people as possible to come to D.C. before Jan. 6th to create a massive force to pressure Congress. At nearly the same time Donald Trump tweeted out to his 80 million followers: "Big protest in D.C. on January 6th. Be there, will be wild!"

Dr. Woodman switched the screen to another video clip of House Representative Marjorie Taylor Greene, another Trump loyalist, and Q-Anon affiliate, who posted on her Facebook account, she said, "America reelected Donald J. Trump for four more years, you can't allow it to just transfer power "peacefully" as Joe Biden wants, and allow him to become our President because he did not win the election! It's being stolen, and the evidence is there. There's a large group of us, who are organizing an effort to object to the electoral college votes for Joe Biden in key states where there's real evidence that this election has been stolen. I am very conflicted, and what we're going to be doing on January 6th, and it's historic. And I feel it's very, very important January six, and you're able, there are going to be possibly a million or more people coming to Washington to be there for this historic event. It's critical for everyone to show up and show the nation who we are. We aren't the people that are going to go quietly into the night. We are not a people that are going to be thrust into socialism without stopping it."

Prosecutor Larson next recalls Donald Trump Jr. asking him, "As members of Stop the Steal emerged, right-wing activists such as Ali Alexander, a Republican operative formerly known as Ali Akbar, played key roles. They echoed President Trump's similar baseless charges of electoral fraud and conspiracy theories. Mr. Alexander and others seized on the Jan. 6th date, urging Trump supporters everywhere to converge onto the Capitol as Congress convenes to certify the electoral votes. Mr. Trump and his supporters were publicly framing this year's formality as criminal, fraudulent — even treasonous."[42]

"Objection," Blankenship blurted out, "The prosecution is testifying, is the question embedded in this theory?" "Mr. Larson," Judge Parker said in a scolding manner, "Where are you going with this line of questioning, get to the question, please, or I will have to hold you in contempt."

"Yes Your Honor," "I am about to ask my question now, please allow me to set the context of the question first so the question will make sense." "Very well, but get to the point quickly." Judge Parker ordered.

Prosecutor Larson returned to face Donald Trump Jr. and said, "Mr. Trump Jr. as the President's aides and supporters did what they could to forestall the inevitable, President Trump continued tweeting." Turning to the screen in the courtroom, each tweet appeared on the screen, as Larson read them aloud.

THE CROWNING: CULMINATION OF THE NATION

Dec. 27: "See you in Washington, DC, on January 6th. Don't miss it. Information to follow."

Dec. 30: "JANUARY SIXTH, SEE YOU IN DC!"

Jan. 1: "The BIG Protest Rally in Washington, D.C. will take place at 11:00 A.M. on January 6th. Locational details to follow. StopTheSteal!"

That same day, a supporter misspelled the word "cavalry" in tweeting that "The calvary is coming, Mr. President!" Mr. Trump responded: "A great honor!" The next day, Jan. 2, Senator Ted Cruz of Texas and eleven other Republican senators joined another Republican, Josh Hawley of Missouri — as well as over 100 Republican members of the House of Representatives — in vowing to object to the certification of Mr. Biden's election." "Objection!" Defense attorney Blankinship abruptly interrupted once again, shouting, "Your Honor, The prosecution attorney is continuing to testify. Is there a question somewhere in this speech?" "Sustained, get to the question now, Mr. Larson, or I will dismiss the witness and have you placed in custody," the Judge demanded.

"My question to you, Mr. Trump Jr., is: "Was this all done under the plan you created when you texted Mark Meadows on November 5th? Was all this a result of your efforts to promote these actions?" Silence fell over the courtroom while the prosecutor's words were percolating in Donald Trump Jr.s head. He finally responded, "I can't be certain everything that happened resulted from the plans I promoted, but they seemed to all follow my lead."

"Your lead? Mr. Trump, were all these ideas yours? Are you telling the court that you are the mastermind of the entire plot?" "Well, no, not exactly. Many other people contributed to it as well". "Like who, Mr. Trump, were these "contributors" to the master plan to overturn the election?" Not a sound in the courtroom could be heard. Even breathing seemed to stop at this moment. Nervously Donald Trump Jr. answers, "Like John Eastman and Jeffrey Clark." Knowing that these men had already had their day in court and their fates were sealed by their convictions, Trump Jr. knew by offering their names in his testimony was "old news" and would change nothing. Larson, raising his voice to an angry pitch, says, "And the President? Was Donald J. Trump, not a contributor?" Silence echoed throughout the room until Trump Jr. looked over at his father and with a sneer, he said, "He's always the boss, everything happens at his direction, he doesn't just contribute, he demands, he orders, he threatens, and if he doesn't get his way, he gets retribution." If 'looks could kill' Donald Trump Jr. would have been dead in the very next instant. Trump Sr.'s true feelings toward his son and his sons' toward him were revealed at that moment. The former president, Donald J. Trump, gave his son, Donald Trump Jr., the face of extreme disgust, disdain, and loathing. "Thank you, Mr. Trump. That will be all. No more questions, your honor, but I reserve the right to recall the witness at a later time." Turning to the defense counsel, the Judge, The Honorable Anthony Parker, asked, "Any cross, Mr. Blankenship? "Yes, your Honor, I have a few questions for Mr. Trump Jr." "Proceed," the Judge commanded. "Mr. Trump, in all the times you have spoken either in person or by phone, by text message or by email about the plans for overcoming the stolen election, in all those communications, did you ever hear your father take part in those plans?" Trump Jr. replied, "No, he never sends texts or emails. All his communication is an in-person conversation or by a phone call, and I did not hear him participate in any call that I was on." Thank you, Mr. Trump, that will be all." Blankenship said.

Judge Parker indicated to the Prosecutor that the ball was back in his court, saying simply to him, "You're up, Mr. Larson." Gene Larson stood up and declared, "The prosecution calls to the stand, Jason Sullivan."

Dr. Woodman, our historian on Truth, explains to the audience who this man is and why he is a witness explaining, "Jason Sullivan, is a Q-Anon supporter and a right-wing social media consultant, perhaps best known for his work with far-right political hatchetman and longtime Trump friend, Roger Stone. He instructed Stone to use so-called swarms of supporters on Twitter to amplify a political message. He was also subpoenaed as part of Robert Mueller's investigation into Russian interference in the 2016 election. But (in the trial of Donald J. Trump in 2024), he is coming into focus as part of the investigation into the insurrection itself. Sullivan was plotting the storming of the Capitol back in December 2020. And we know that because there were recordings of him doing precisely that."[43] Prosecutor Larson asks Sullivan, "Mr. Sullivan, what is your affiliation with Roger Stone?"

THE CROWNING: CULMINATION OF THE NATION

Sullivan responds, "Mr. Stone and I have worked together on many projects over the years." Larson asks, "Did he seek your help regarding the election of 2020." "Yes," Sullivan replied, "we both wanted to assist the President as we were convinced the election was stolen from him and from the nation." "And how did you go about assisting him?" Larson asked. "By advising Roger Stone and making the connection he needed," Sullivan answered with a temperament exuding cockiness. Larson drilled down on his next question, "Mr. Sullivan, I want you to listen to a recording we are about to play." Larson then queued up a recording that played for all to hear. "We've gotta be multiple front strategy, and that multiple front strategy, I do think, is to descend on the capitol, without question, to make those people feel it inside. Okay, so they understand the people are breathing down their neck, and we've had it, and they've had it. And we've got to be clear about it. No, I'm not inviting violence or any federal rights or anything like that. Still, we need to be loud and be like Jericho, okay,"

Larson continued with his inquiry asking, "My first question, Mr. Sullivan, is that your voice on the recording?" Sullivan replied with disbelief and confusion, "Yes, but how did you acquire that recording?" "Normally, Mr. Sullivan, I would not answer your question, but" (turning toward and addressing the Judge) "with Your Honor's permission, I would like to answer that question as it is pertinent to understanding the context of the recording you just heard. "I will allow it, " Judge Parker declared. Larson continued, "What we just played for you was provided to the Department of Justice by the January 6th Committee, who received it from a woman named Stacy Burke. She sued to overturn the election results, although that lawsuit was thrown out when a judge ruled she did not have standing to bring it because she was not registered to vote. Now that led Burke to one of Trump's lawyers, Sidney Powell.

"Objection, counsel is testifying again, Your Honor," Blankenship shouted. A clearly annoyed Judge Parker blurted out, "Overruled, continue."

Larson continued explaining, "Sidney Powell introduced Stacy Burke to a right-wing military-themed gang called the 1st Amendment Praetorian, an obscure far-right paramilitary group founded in 2020 that recruits military veterans and former police officers to provide security at right-wing events. They often served as hired security for Powell's friend, Trump's first national security advisor, Michael Flynn.[43] Apparently, the 1st Amendment Praetorians would serve as security for Ms. Stacy Burke. They moved into her home under the guise of protecting her from the deep state, a rotating group of middle-aged men invading this woman's home and staying there rent-free. Of course, the militiamen painted this as a favor to Stacy Burke. She says the men kept trying to take her cell phone when she repeatedly refused to hand over the phone, saying she had protected medical information on it from her previous nursing patients. Eventually, they left her with her phone. But before Burke recorded the call, you just heard Roger Stone's onetime aid, Jason Sullivan, plotting the insurrection. Mr. Sullivan, was that the first time you solicited security from a right-wing organization, and let me remind you, you are under oath?"[43]

Before Sullivan answers, Dr. Woodman explains to the audience, "Sullivan had already been convicted several months earlier of aiding and abetting the coup. He knew he had to tell the truth, as his sentencing was delayed until after this trial, so he had to be honest or risk a much stiffer sentence. Sullivan replies to the prosecutor's question saying, "I worked with Elmer Stewart Rhodes, the Oath Keepers, who has been charged with seditious conspiracy, for his role in planning the insurrection, including the so-called quick response team, which was prepared to bring guns to the occupied Capitol. I also worked with another far-right group, the Proud Boys, who were involved in the planning, along with Roger Stone, in the days before the attack. Roger Stone and I arranged for two of those leaders to meet in a garage the day before the attack."

Dr. Woodman describes how Larson dismisses the witness, and Blankenship declines to cross-examine him, then Larson calls for another witness, "Your Honor, I call to the stand, Sam Shamanski." Dr. Woodman explains to his audience that Sam Shamanski is the attorney for Dustin Thompson, who was found guilty of entering the capitol on Jan. 6th. He was first asked by the prosecutor, "I guess I should start with asking for your theory of the case legally, for your client. Why did you argue he was not guilty if in fact, he was inside that building in an unauthorized fashion and maybe took a coat rack as a souvenir?" Shamanski replied to the prosecutor's question, like one lawyer speaking to another over a beer, "This president,

THE CROWNING: CULMINATION OF THE NATION

(Trump), this gangster, (was) imploring a crowd of people whom he's groomed over the last year with his associates, to help him with his desperate, last-ditch effort to overturn the results of a lawful election. When you have the President of the United States grooming you to believe that the election was stolen."[43]

Dr. Woodman continued describing the witness' testimony, saying "Shamanski began quoting Trump's speech at the Ellipse, "Our democracy, our democracy is at stake, fight like hell, we're never going to concede. Its you get down to the Capitol, and I'll be right there with you or else an illegitimate president is going to take office" "So it's not hard," Shamanski said on the stand, "at least from my perspective, to understand how vulnerable, unsophisticated, politically speaking, people who've been fed this, this diet of B.S. would behave in accordance with their President's wishes, and, and that clearly impacts one's mental state. This can be the only explanation for otherwise law-abiding citizens with no record to convene in Washington, DC, and storm the holiest of holy spots in our fair capital. There's no other explanation. Zero. They were cajoled, groomed, and directed. Period." "Thank You Mr. Shamanski, that is all I have for you," said Larson. "The Defense," explained Dr. Woodman, had but one question for the witness. Unsurprisingly, he asked, "Mr. Shamanski, did Donald J. Trump, as President, ever personally ask your client to come to Washington D.C. on Jan. 6th, or for that matter, on any other day?" "No," was Shimanski's response. "The Defense has no further questions, your Honor."

Dr. Woodman examines the importance of the next two witnesses, telling the audience of "Truth," that "Larson calls for his next witness, Gabriel Sterling. Georgia Secretary of State. Brad Raffensperger appointed Sterling the COO of the Secretary of State's office after winning the 2018 election.

Gene Larson poses his first question stating, "Mr. Sterling, thank you also for being here today, I understand you became a spokesperson to combat dis-information about the election and the danger it was creating for elections officials. Tell us what you said that day on December 1 at a press conference." Sterling sat up tall and proud while he recalled his public remarks, "I said, Mr. President, it looks like you likely lost the state of

Georgia. We're investigating. There's always a possibility I get it, and you have the right to go through the course, what you don't have the ability to do, and you need to step up and say this, is stop inspiring people to potentially commit violence. Someone's going to get hurt. Someone's going to get shot. Someone's going to get killed and it's not right." The prosecutor looks straight at the jury and asks Sterling, "Did you believe that what you said that day was going to actually come to pass, as it did on Jan. 6?" Sterling replied to the prosecutor,, "I believed it was very possible that people were going to get hurt, perhaps killed, but I did not know it would take place in Washington D.C. at the Capitol." Larson follows up by asking, "After you made this plea to the president, did Donald Trump urge his supporters to avoid the use of violence?" "Not to my knowledge, " Sterling replied. Larson announces, "Your honor, I call to the stand the Republican Secretary of State of the State of Georgia, Brad Raffensperger."

After taking the stand and getting sworn in Larson says, "Mr. Secretary, the President references suitcases or trunks, filled with 18,000 ballots all from Joe Biden that were hidden under a desk and then dumped into the voting machines in the middle of the night. Were the objects seen in these videos, suitcases or trunks, or were they just, the ordinary containers that are used by election workers?" "They're standard ballot carriers that allow for our seals to be put on them so that they are tamper-proof, " Raffensperger replied. Larson followed, "Mr. Secretary, did somebody drop, drop a lot of votes there late at night?" "No. I believe that the president was referring to some counties when they would upload, but the ballots had all been accepted and had to be accepted by state law by 7:00 PM. So there were no additional ballots accepted after 7:00 PM, Reffensperger explained. "So Mr. Secretary, did your office investigate whether those allegations were accurate? Did 5,000 dead people in Georgia vote?" asked Larson.

Raffensperger answered, "No it's not accurate. And actually, in their lawsuits, they alleged 10,315 dead people. We found two dead people, and subsequent to that, we found two more. That's 4 people, not 4,000. Just a total of four, not 10,000, not 5,000."

Larson concluded, "So there's no way you could have recalculated, as Trump suggested on his call to you, except, by fudging the numbers?" "The numbers were the numbers," Raffenspurger argues. "And we could not

THE CROWNING: CULMINATION OF THE NATION

recalculate because we'd made sure that we had checked every single allegation. And we had many investigations. We had nearly 300 from the 2020 election." "After making a false claim about shredding ballots, the President suggested you may be committing a crime by not going along with his claims of election fraud. And after suggesting that you might have criminal exposure, President Trump made his most explicit 'ask' of the call when he said, "So what I want to do is this, I just want to find 11,780 votes, which is one more than we have because we won the state." Larson asks, "Was the President asking you for exactly what he wanted? One more vote than his opponent?" Secretary Raffenspurger, choosing his words carefully replies, "What I knew is that we didn't have any votes to find, to continue the look, we investigated, like I just shared the numbers with you. There were no votes to find that was an accurate count that had been certified. And as our general counsel said, there was no shredding of ballots."

Dr. Woodman speaking to the audience of the program, Truth, described the closest witness to Trump to give her testimony. Gene Larson announces, "The prosecution calls, Ivanka Trump." A loud stir in the courtroom occurred as Ivanka Trump came to the front of the courtroom and stood next to the witness chair. She was dressed professionally, but wearing a very expensive white designer pantsuit outfit. After swearing to tell the whole truth under penalty of perjury, she sat down in the witness chair. Prosecutor Larson started by greeting Ivanka Trump in a friendly manner and thanking her for her testimony today. Ivanka smiled graciously and nodded without saying a word. "Mrs. Trump, during the days leading up to and during Jan. 6th, 2021 were you working in the White House in your capacity as an advisor to the President?" Larson asked. "Yes Sir, I was," replied Ivanka. "Was your husband also working in the White House at that time?" "No Sir, " Ivanka replied, "He was out of the country in Saudi Arabia, but he was on his way back on Jan. 6th." Larson asked, "Were you aware of the planning for the Stop The Steal rally at the Ellipse on Jan. 6th? "Yes, I was not directly involved in the planning, but I could lend my thoughts about it to the planners."

"Were you aware that on the morning of the 6th, the police were called to the Ellipse location responding to a call for help with a very heated argument taking place between two of the event planners?" Ivanka explained, "I know about it, but I was not there when it happened. I heard about it when I arrived at the White House later that morning."

Larsen asked, "Did you learn about the reason for such a heated exchange, so heated that someone had to call for police intervention?". Ivanka replied, "Yes Sir, I learned it was a disagreement between two of the planners over who would be speaking at the rally. One of them was pushing for Alex Jones and Ali Alexander to be on the list of speakers and the other was adamant that they not be included. She felt those two would be too volatile." "How was it resolved?" asked Larson. "It was left up to the President to decide," Ivanka responded. Prosecutor Larson moved away from the witness chair and turned to face the jury, paused a moment before inquiring, "leading up to that day, in the days just prior to Jan. 6th, was there another debate among the planners taking place regarding the events of that day?" Ivanka shifted in her chair, looking uncomfortable for the first time, then replied, "Yes Sir."

"Would you tell the jury the nature of that disagreement", Larson questioned. Reluctantly, Ivanka Trump contended, "Well, from my understanding of the disagreement, the original planners had the rally goers proceeding from the Ellipse, after President Trump's speech, from the Ellipse to the Supreme Court Building to peacefully protest for the rest of the day. I believe they had secured a permit for that march. However, some people involved in the planning were advocating for the protesters to march to the Capitol instead, in order to air their grievances to Congress instead. It was my understanding that since there was no permit to go to the Capitol, that suggestion was dropped." "Who then made the call to pivot to the Capitol, instead of the Supreme Court building?" demanded Larson with an escalation in the volume of his questions. "I honestly do not know," Ivanka contended. Prosecutor Larson turned to a technician and instructed him to queue up President Trump's speech at the Ellipse, to the parts where Trump said, "We will never give up. We will never concede. It doesn't happen. You don't concede when there's theft involved," Trump continues, speaking on the video, "We want to go back and we want to get this right because we're going to have somebody in there that should not be in there and our country will be destroyed, and we will not stand for that," Larson explains, "The president also called for people to "walk down" to the Capitol to "cheer on our brave

THE CROWNING: CULMINATION OF THE NATION

senators. Just before concluding his remarks, Trump told attendees to "fight like hell" because if they didn't they wouldn't "have a country anymore."

Larson presents another clip of Trump saying, "I know that everyone here will soon march over to the Capitol building to peacefully and patriotically make your voices heard." and then, "So we're going to, we're going to walk down Pennsylvania Avenue. I love Pennsylvania Avenue. And we're going to the Capitol, and we're going to try and give... The Democrats are hopeless — they never vote for anything. Not even one vote. But we're going to give our Republicans, the weak ones because the strong ones don't need any of our help. We're going to give them the pride and boldness that they need to take back our country. So let's walk down Pennsylvania Avenue."

The prosecutor follows with a question to Ivanka Trump saying, "So Ms. Trump, when did you find out that the plans had shifted to send the protestors to the Capitol instead of the Supreme Court building?" Ivanka Trump looked Larson square in the eyes and with a somber and softer voice, she said, "When I heard the President's speech that day at the Ellipse." "So," Larson demanded, "Was it your father, the President of the United States, who sent the mob to the Capitol?"

Ivanka thought about the question for a long time, while the courtroom loomed in deafening silence waiting for her reply, "I don't know for sure, but his words in that speech told me he agreed with that plan, or he would not have told them to go to the Capitol." Prosecutor Larson then asked Ivanka "Shortly before 1 p.m., when Congress convened to certify the presidential election, Pence wrote a letter explaining that he felt his responsibility was to oversee the process and not insert himself, beyond allowing valid objections to be heard. Pence said he came to the decision after consulting constitutional experts. About an hour and a half after Congress gathered, Trump tweeted that Pence "didn't have the courage to do what should have been done." Rioters had already breached the Capitol, and some were attempting to get into House Speaker Nancy Pelosi's office. At this time did you go to your father to ask him to intervene in the insurrection?" Ivanka replied, "Yes." Larson then inquired, "What did he say to you?" Ivanka grumbled, "He paid little attention to me, which was not normal, he just blew me off while he was watching the insurrection unfold on his T.V. The president knew there was a violent mob at the Capitol when he tweeted at 2:24 p.m. that the "Vice President did not have the 'courage' to do what needed to be done." Larson interrupted Ivanka to add, "For the record, Trump's full tweet said that "Mike Pence didn't have the courage to do what should have been done to protect our Country and our Constitution, giving States a chance to certify a corrected set of facts, not the fraudulent or inaccurate ones which they were asked to previously certify. USA demands truth!" Did you think at this point that your father was making things worse with these words? Was he not throwing gasoline onto the flames?" Ivanka just looked down at her hands, tears visibly flowing down her cheeks as she nodded 'Yes'. "I will need an audible answer," Mr. Larson said in a softer voice reflecting his sympathy for her emotional distress. "Yes," Ivanka Trump said softly. Larson continued, "At 2:38 p.m., Trump called for people to "support our Capitol police and law enforcement." He added people should "stay peaceful" and that officers are "truly on the side of our country". Was that text the result of your first conversation with him earlier?" Ivanka quickly replied, "No, I had asked him again to stop this, so he wrote that text."

"Did that text change anything at the Capitol?" Larson questioned. "Not really, " Ivanka replied, as far as I could tell from watching the T.V. it was only getting worse."

"Trump tweeted at 3:13 p.m "I am asking for everyone at the U.S. Capitol to remain peaceful. No violence! Remember, WE are the Party of Law & Order–respect the Law and our great men and women in Blue. Thank you! Was that also done upon your encouragement?" "Myself and others, such as Kieth Kellogg and people who were calling him," Ivanka vouched.

THE CROWNING: CULMINATION OF THE NATION

"By now he was being bombarded with many people demanding he put a stop to it."

Prosecutor Larson probed a little deeper asking, "The Capitol riot unfolded, Trump attempted to call Senator Tommy Tuberville but first dialed Senator Mike Lee's phone number instead. It's unclear what Trump said to Tuberville, but the Alabama Republican said he told Trump they've "taken the vice president out," regarding the evacuation of Pence, and that "they want me to get off the phone." "Were you in the room when that happened?" "Yes," Ivanka replied.

Larson continued his questions with, "The former President Trump also told House Minority Leader Kevin McCarthy that the rioters were "more upset about the election" (than McCarthy was). Neither McCarthy nor Trump has confirmed the comment, although McCarthy confirmed that the two spoke. Were you a witness to this conversation also?" Ivanka countered "I only heard one side of that conversation, but I heard Dad, I mean, President Trump's side of that conversation. He said something similar to what you quoted." Larson contended "Three hours after the start of the incursion, actually over 3 hours, Donald Trump finally called off the dogs when he, at 4 p.m., 3 hours after the mob started clashing with police, Trump released a video on Twitter telling the crowd that he understood their "pain" and "hurt." Trump said in the video, "We had an election that was stolen from us. It was a landslide election, and everyone knows it, especially the other side. But you have to go home now," Trump continued, "We have to have peace. We have to have law and order... So go home. We love you; you're very special... I know how you feel. But go home and go home in peace." Was that caused by your words to your father? Larson asked Ivanka. "No, Ivanka insisted, "I was among many who were pleading with him to stop this, and he finally conceded." "Thank You, Mrs. Trump, for your candor and honesty." Ivanka looked at her father, who had a look of sorrow and deep hurt, the look of a man betrayed by the dearest and closest person in his life.

Prosecutor Larson's next witness was General Mark Milley, Trump's Joint Chiefs of Staff Chairman. "General Milley," Larson began with flamboyant theatrics, "Did President Trump, at any time on January 6, ask you to deploy any troops, the National Guard, or any other support to assist the struggling Capitol and Metro police?" Mark Milley replied in a matter-of-fact mode saying, "Vice President Mike Pence was the one who ordered National Guard troops to respond to the violence on Jan. 6, 2021, but I was told by the White House to say it was former President Trump. There were two or three calls with Vice President Pence. He was very animated, and he issued very explicit, very direct, unambiguous orders. There was no question about that," Milley said. "He was very animated, very direct, very firm. Pence ordered me to "Get the military down here, get the guard down here. Put down this situation", he added, referring to Pence. Milley also described his interactions with Trump's Chief of Staff, Mark Meadows, that day, drawing a stark contrast between those conversations with Pence. "He said: We have to kill the narrative that the Vice President is making all the decisions. We need to establish the narrative, you know, that the President is still in charge and that things are steady or stable, or words to that effect," Milley said, referring to what Meadows told him. I immediately interpreted that as politics. Politics. Politics. Red flag for me, personally. No action. But I remember it distinctly," he added.

Dr. Woodman summarized the rest of the trial, saying, "The trial then switched to the Defense team's case, which centered on the premise that Donald J. Trump truly believed that his election was stolen as he had so many people, including Rudy Giuliani, and Mike Flynn and many others telling him this. The theory is that if he truly believed the election was stolen, he could not be held responsible for his actions and that he was acting in what he perceived to be in the nation's best interest. The Defense Attorney, Blankenship, also contended that the planning of the insurrection was done behind Trump's back and without his knowledge or consent. He finished by reviewing his texts and other messages he sent to the rioters during the insurrection to put doubt into the notion that he was actually calling for violence, emphasizing the few times he used the word 'peaceful.'"

Chester Colt, the first host to lead the discussions on Truth, took the microphone to ask, "Dr. Woodman, Prosecutor Larson had been saving his star witness for last, a relatively unknown person to those of us who follow the players of the Trump White House. Cassidy Hutchinson, a 25-year-old aide to Mark Meadows, the Chief of Staff, and congressional liaison, was well known on Capitol Hill. She was an unswerving civil servant with an impressive resume serving Republican Senators and congressmen. Ms.

THE CROWNING: CULMINATION OF THE NATION

Hutchinson is a stunningly beautiful young woman with brown hair, strong yet nearly perfect facial bones and a very soft voice. Her height is taller than many men, but without being overly intimidating. After being sworn in to testify, Prosecutor Larson asked her to recall the evening of Jan. 2nd, asking her, "On January 2, 2021, Trump lawyer Rudy Giuliani met with Meadows and others in the White House, and afterward you walked him to his vehicle, is that accurate, Ms. Hutchinson?" "Yes, it is accurate," she replied shyly. "And do you recall your conversation with Mr. Giuliani that evening?" Larson asked, "Yes, I do. Giuliani asked me if she was excited about the sixth, and I said, Rudy, could you explain what's happening on the sixth? He responded something to the effect of "We're going to the Capitol. It's going to be great. The President is going to be there. He's going to look powerful. He's going to get the members. He's going to be with the senators. Talk to the chief about it. Talk to the chief about it. He knows about it." When I asked Meadows what Giuliani meant, I said, "Mark sounds like we're going to go to the Capitol." He didn't look up from his phone and said, "There's a lot going on, Cass, but I don't know. Things might get real, real bad on January six."

Dr. Woodman describes the next part of Hutchinson's testimony, saying, "January 5, Trump told Meadows to contact Trump confidants Roger Stone and Michael Flynn, both of whom Trump had recently pardoned after being convicted of crimes, to talk about the next day. Hutchinson says Meadows did that. Roger Stone was in Washington, D.C., where he was repeatedly photographed with Oath Keepers members acting as his bodyguards. The prosecutor's next question for Hutchinson was, "Is it true that Trump's associate Roger Stone attended rallies during the afternoon and the evening of January 5th in Washington, DC on January 5th and sixth?" "Yes, that is correct, " responded Ms. Hutchinson. "In fact, Mr. Stone was photographed with multiple members of the Oath Keepers who were allegedly serving as his security detail. "Yes, those photos have been made public," said Hutchinson. "As we now know, multiple members of that organization have been charged with or pled guilty to crimes associated with January 6th. Mr. Stone has invoked his Fifth Amendment privilege against self-incrimination." "Yes, as did General Flynn," Hutchinson pointed out. "Ms. Hutchinson," Larson said, "Is it your understanding that President Trump asked Mark Meadows to speak with Roger Stone and General Flynn on January 5th?" "That's correct. That is my understanding." "And Ms. Hutchinson, is it your understanding that Mr. Meadows called Mr. Stone on the fifth?" "I think Mr. Meadows completed both the call to Mr. Stone and General Flynn the evening of the fifth. "And do you know what they talked about that evening, Ms. Hutchinson?" "Well, I'm not sure because I could hear only Mark Meadows' side of the call, but I distinctly heard the words "Proud Boys" and Oath Keepers mentioned several times with regard to the events the next day," Cassidy Hutchinson explained.

Dr. Woodman reported to the audience that, according to Hutchinson, intelligence reports were already coming in by 8:00 in the morning of January 6 that some of those near the Ellipse, where Trump was to speak, was in body armor and armed with Glock-style pistols, shotguns, and AR-15s among other weapons. At 10:00, Hutchinson, Tony Ornato, the Deputy Chief of Staff, and Meadows talked of the weapons, but Meadows brushed it off, asking only if they had told Trump, which they said they had done. Larson then asks Hutchinson to walk them through the events of January 6th that she witnessed. Hutchinson took a sip of water to brace herself for the very painful briefing she was about to deliver. She braced herself for the hardest story she would ever have to tell and said, "I was in the tent behind the stage of the Ellipse with President Trump. I heard Trump urging the Secret Service to remove security magnetometers (metal detectors often referred to as 'mags') and let in people with weapons. He demanded the secret service allow the armed rally-goers into the rally because "they're not here to hurt me." Trump wanted the rally space to be full and "for people not to feel excluded, and he was "f**king furious" people were turned away. "I overheard the President say something to the effect of "I don't f-ing care that they have weapons. They're not here to hurt me. Take the f-ing mags [magnetometers] away. Let my people in. They can march to the Capitol from here," Hutchinson reported. "That is what Trump said just before delivering his speech at the Ellipse, where he said, "If you don't fight like hell, you're not going to have a country anymore." Larson then added, "And he knew for certain that the crowd was heavily armed for battle?" "Yes," Hutchinson responded. Larson then turned to the jury while asking his next question, "After his speech, what happened next?" Woodman opined that "Cassidy looked very uncomfortable as she dreaded answering this question

THE CROWNING: CULMINATION OF THE NATION

despite knowing it would be addressed. She shifted in her seat nervously and finally leaned back, briefly shut her eyes as if she was trying to visualize the events and she said, "When I returned to the White House, I saw Tony Ornato, who waved me into his office. Tony asked me if I had heard about the altercation that occurred in the President's SUV. He told me that Trump continued pressing to go to the Capitol following his speech to supporters at the "Stop the Steal" rally on the Ellipse. When Trump was told he would return to the White House instead of going to the Capitol that day, Ornato recalled Trump became irate. Tony told me that Trump lunged for the steering wheel, forcing Robert Engel, head of his Secret Service detail, to physically restrain him. The President said something to the effect of, 'I am the f**king president. Take me up to the Capitol now,'" Hutchinson said. She added that "While Tony relayed this story to me, Engel sat silent, looking very distraught."

Dr. Woodman paused for a second, providing Chester Colt an opportunity to offer a quick break from the broadcast to give him a chance to catch his breath. Woodman accepted the invitation, and Chester promised the audience to not go away as they would return in a few minutes. Tully and Catherine looked at each other in disbelief. They were not paying close attention to the events at the time they happened, just a few months earlier, so much of this testimony was newly learned details of the trial and quite shocking. "This really explains how the jury could come to the verdict they did", Tully declared to Catherine, who just nodded in agreement. A few minutes later, Chester Colt was back on camera. "Dr. Woodman, let's continue with Ms. Cassidy Hutchinson's testimony picking up at the same time the rioters had breached the Capitol". "Dr. Woodman responded by saying, "Prosecutor Larson's next line of questions began with him asking Cassidy Hutchinson, "Not long after the rioters broke into the Capitol, Describe what happened with White House Counsel Pat Cipillone." Cassidy Hutchinson nodded and, with a serious look on her face, responded, "I see Pat Cipillone barreling down the hallway towards our office, and rush right in and looked at me and said, "Is Mark in his office?" And I said yes. He just looked at me and started shaking his head and went over to open Mark's office door, and stood there with the door propped open. Mark is still sitting on his phone. And I remember Pat saying to him, "The rioters had gotten to the Capitol Mark. We need to go down and see the President now. And Mark looked up at him and said, "Trump doesn't want to do anything, Pat". And Pat said, "Mark, something needs to be done, or people are going to die in the blood's going to be on your 'effing' hands. This is getting out of control. I'm going down there. And at that point, Mark stood up from his couch, both his phones in his hand, and he had his glasses on. So he walked out with Pat. He put both of his phones on my desk and said, let me know if Jim calls. And they walked down, went down to the dining room. A few minutes later, Representative Jim Jordan called, So likely around between 2:15 - 2:25. I opened the door to the dining room, briefly, stepped in to get Mark's attention, showed him the phone to flip the phone his way so he could see it said Jim Jordan. I probably was two feet from Mark. He was standing in the doorway, going into the oval office dining room. They had a brief conversation. And in the crossfires, you know, I heard briefly like what they were talking about, but in the background, I had heard conversations in the oval dining room, at that point, talking about the hang Mike Pence chants. Mark hung up the phone and handed it back to me. I went back to my desk a couple of minutes later. Mark and Pat came back, I remember Pat saying something to the effect of Mark, we need to do something more. They're literally calling for the vice-president to be 'effing' hung, and Mark had responded, "You heard him, Pat. He thinks Mike Pence deserves it, He doesn't think they're doing anything wrong". To which Pat said "This is effing crazy. We need to be doing something more." Larson interjected asking, "Who did Mark Meadows mean by "they're" when he said, " He doesn't think they're doing anything wrong." Cassidy replied, "I understood "they're" to be the rioters in the Capitol that were chanting for the Vice-President to be hanged."

Dr. Woodman points out that at exactly 2:24, right after that meeting between Pat Cipillone, Mark Meadows and President Trump, Trump posted a tweet to his followers that read, "Mike Pence did not have the courage to do what should have been done to protect our country and our constitution..." a tweet which was the straw that broke the camel's back for a number of members of Trump's administration, who decided at that moment they needed to resign their positions. Dr. Woodman continued the saga saying, "Many people in Trump inner circle began sending texts and calls to Mark

THE CROWNING: CULMINATION OF THE NATION

Meadows, imploring him to get the President to call off the rioters, including Fox News personalities, Republican Congressman and Senate members trapped in a hideout beneath the capitol, even Trump's son, Donald Trump Jr. One of those congressmen, Mike Gallagher, also implored the president to call off the attack.

He tweeted out a video directed at Trump saying "Mr. President, you have got to stop this. You are the only person who can call this off; call it off. The election is over. Call it off. This is bigger than you. It's bigger than any member of Congress, it is about the United States of America, which is more important than any politician. Call it off, it's over." Although many people close to Donald Trump were urging him to send people home. He did not do so until later, much later at 4:17 PM. Donald Trump finally told the rioters to go home and that he loved them. Trump said in that video, "We have to have peace. So go home. We love you. You're very special. You've seen what happens. You see the way others are treated that is so bad and so evil. I know how you feel, but go home and go home and peace." Donald Trump was reluctant to put this message out, and he still could not bring himself to condemn the attack."

Dr. Woodman took a sip of water from a water bottle before continuing with his report. "What is really significant and completely unprecedented is that during the trial, the Republican primaries were playing out. Donald Trump was in the lead, but just barely. The Governor of Florida, Ron DeSantis, was giving Trump a very competitive race. By the time Trump's trial began, DeSantis had drawn the race to an even match. All other contenders had long since dropped out, turning the Republican nomination into a two-man battle. Trump continued to campaign throughout the trial, holding rallies at night in key states where the next primary was taking place. He was under strict orders from Judge Parker to keep the trial, and his thoughts on it off his lips while in public, while Ron DeSantis had no such restrictions, and he used that to his political advantage throughout his campaign.

Prosecutor Larson took his time to dramatically stand up and deliberately say to the court, "Your Honor, I have just learned of a critical witness, one who was at the center of all the events related to this trial, who has requested to give his testimony." "Objection! Your Honor, this is highly irregular, we have not been given notice of this surprise witness and demand the court refuse to allow such an egregious transgression," declared Blankenship. Judge Parker dictated that the two attorneys approach the bench for a quiet discussion of the last-minute addition. "Mr. Larson, who is this mystery witness, who is so critical that justice would not be served if he could not testify?" Parker asked with a hint of satire in his question. Larson replied softly to not be overheard, "Your honor, there is actually a witness that the jury absolutely must hear from in order for justice to be served. I assure you, your honor, when you hear his testimony you agree that justice has been served by the testimony."

Judge Parker looked over at the Defense Attorney, who simply shrugged his shoulders and said, "Let's hear what he has to say, but I reserve the right to cross-examine both witnesses." "Very well then, I will allow both witnesses to testify, but Mr. Larson if this is nothing more than theatrics, I will hold you in contempt of court." 'Thank you, your Honor. You won't be disappointed." Turning toward the back doors of the courtroom, Larson bellows out, "The Prosecution calls Michael Richard Pence." A loud gasp of shock projected from the courtroom, so loud it could be heard in the hallway. As the doors swung open, they revealed the former Vice President. Mike Pence walked to the witness stand with a demeanor of solemnity. With his right hand raised, he was sworn in, emphasizing the words, "So help me God" at the end of his oath. Larson walked up to the former Vice president and began, "Mr. Vice President, thank you so much for taking the time to testify today." Pence nodded affirmatively without responding. Larson continued, "Sir, on the days leading up to Jan. 6th, 2021, is it fair to say you were being pressed hard to play a role in the effort to change the outcome of the election of 2020?" "Yes it would," Pence replied. "I was under a full court press by the President and his attorney, John Eastman to reject the electors from certain states, which would have sent them back to the states, or possibly the election to the House of Representatives. After weeks of deliberation and consultation from multiple experts, I had determined that the Vice President did not have the constitutional authority to do what they demanded I do." Mr. Larson asks, "And were you being admonished by Trump for your refusal to sway the results of the election in their administration's favor? "I was." Pence replied.

THE CROWNING: CULMINATION OF THE NATION

"What did he say to you?" "He repeatedly told me not to "wimp out" — not to certify the results of the 2020 election. He would say, "If it gives you the power, why would you oppose it?" Also, he would add, "You can be a historic figure, but if you wimp out, you're just another somebody," Pence reported in a monotone and emotionless voice. He often told me, "'You're too honest,'" Pence said. "Hundreds of thousands are gonna hate your guts. ... People are gonna think you're stupid."[43 & 44]

Larson pressed on asking, "On the day of the insurrection, Jan. 6th, what did you think when you saw protesters at the Ellipse?" Pence responded by sounding more compassionate, "When I first saw "protesters standing peacefully," Pence said, I "felt compassion for all the good people who had traveled to Washington having been told that the outcome of the election could be changed. I turned to my daughter and sighed: 'God bless those people. They're gonna be so disappointed."[43 & 44]

Larson posed another question saying, "After the rioters breached the capitol, and you had to be taken out of the chambers to safety, how did you feel then?" Pence said in an assertive tone, "I was furious." Larson continued posing the query, "So you were taken to the basement, but you insisted on walking, rather than running, despite hearing the call for your name from the rioters?" "Yes," Pence replied, "I refused to drive away and insisted on walking, rather than running, to a safer space."[43 & 44]

Larson then walked closer to the Vice president and with a determination to bring the next point home with a dramatic pause, said, "Mr. Vice President, why was it you refused to get into the car that was part of your motorcade when you were instructed to do so by your Secret Service team?" Mike Pence looked down and cleared his throat before answering what would be the most shocking of revelations in the trial, "I refused to leave the building when my lead Secret Service agent, Tim Giebels, pushed for me to do so as protesters swarmed the building, some chanting "Hang Mike Pence. Seeing those people tearing up the Capitol infuriated me, but I would not leave. When we went to an underground loading dock, Mr. Giebels tried getting me into a car just as a place to wait, but I declined. I told my detail that I wasn't leaving my post," Mr. Pence said. "Mr. Giebels pleaded for us to leave. The rioters had reached our floor. I pointed my finger at his chest and said: 'You're not hearing me, Tim. I'm not leaving! I'm not giving those people the sight of a 16-car motorcade speeding away from the Capitol."41& 42

Mr. Larson leaned in closer to the witness and said, "I know your wife and family were also at the capitol that day. Was that the reason you would not leave?" Pence replied quickly, "Yes and no. I did not want to leave them in harm's way, but there was an even more important reason I did not want to leave. I knew that if I were driven away by the Secret Service that day, I probably could never return." A loud gasp emitted from the audience in the courtroom prompted Judge Parker to pound his gavel several times to regain order. Mr. Larson followed up with, "Why did you feel that way, Mr. Pence."

"Two reasons," replied the former Vice President, "First, in a private phone call just prior to the President's speech at the Ellipse, the President said to me, "Mike, you are making the biggest mistake of your life, it will be a fatal mistake." He then hung up. The second reason was I could sense something was terribly wrong with the two Secret Service agents I had with me that day. One was new to me, as he was filling in for an agent that had called in sick, so I did not know him. The other agent was Tim Giebels. Both men seemed very nervous, and they would not look me in the eye. That was very uncharacteristic of Agent Giebel. I just sensed something was very wrong, and that they could not, or would not, say anything to me." Larson asks, "Sir when the President tweeted out at 2:24 P.M. that "Mike Pence didn't have the courage to do what should have been done." What did you think about that incitement of the insurrectionists?" "I just ignored the tweet and got back to work."43 & 44

Larson concluded with," One last question, Mr. Vice President, after hours of many people at the Capitol pleading for help, who was it that finally got the National Guard to assist the Capitol Police" Pence admitted, "I did, that was me." "Was that your call to make?" Larson asked. "Someone had to do it," the former Vice President responded. "Thank you, Mr. Pence. Your Honor, the defense rests"

Dr. Woodman then said to the audience of Truth, "After six long weeks comprising hundreds of witness testimony, the trial of Donald John Trump

THE CROWNING: CULMINATION OF THE NATION

was turned over to the jury to decide Trump's fate. Everyone in the nation knew that what was at stake was not only Donald Trump's freedom but also the nation's ability to hold another election with Trump on the ballot. His ability to lead the nation to wherever he wanted it to go was in jeopardy. His supporters feared he would not survive long behind bars. Throughout the weeks-long deliberation with the jury sequestered in a secret hotel, the protests and riots that had occurred during the trial did not abate but got more violent. When the jury returned to the courtroom the foreperson of the jury, a black woman in her fifties, stood to deliver the verdict. The entire nation was holding a collective breath while the dramatic moment played out. Judge Parker asked the foreperson, "Has the Jury reached a verdict on all the counts?" "Yes, your Honor" she responded in a very matter-of-fact way. "On the charge of conspiracy to defraud the United States, what is your verdict?" The foreperson responded, "We find the defendant, Donald John Trump, guilty." The courtroom immediately erupted into a chaotic mix of cheers and anger. Judge Parker pounds his gavel several times demanding, "Order in the Court!" When the room settled down, Parker continued, "On the charge of obstruction of an official proceeding, how do you find the defendant? "Guilty" the foreperson declared. Again, the courtroom erupted into another chorus of angry shouting, and again Judge Parker admonished the people in the courtroom for interrupting the proceedings. "And on the charge of violating federal statutes pertaining to voter fraud, how do you find the defendant?" "Guilty," the foreperson replied. "And on the charges of seditious conspiracy against the United States of America, how do you find?" asked Judge Parker. "Guilty," the foreperson announced in a louder voice than previously used. The mayhem that ensued before the entire nation was unlike anything ever seen before inside a courtroom. People were screaming at the judge and the jury. Judge Parker, not yet finished with his duties, pounded his gavel twice as hard as before to regain order. "Order! Order in the Court!" He yelled. It took a full ten minutes before the Judge could speak. "Mr. Trump, please rise," he said, looking directly in the former president's direction. Trump sat in his chair indignantly, refusing to get up. His attorney whispered in his ear something and Trump said back, loud enough for everyone to hear, "I am the President. I stand when I am good and ready to stand." Judge Parker ignored Trump's show of disdain and contempt and gave his instructions. "I order that you surrender your passport to the court immediately, I order that the FAA immediately take possession of all planes owned by Mr. Trump or the Trump Organization. The penalty phase of this trial will begin after the holidays in mid-January of next year. I am setting a date for sentencing on January 22nd, 2025. You will be confined to house arrest in your suite in Mar A Lago, Florida until that date. Mr. Trump, you have a full month to get all of your affairs in order beforehand." Then hitting the gavel, once more, Judge Parker said, "We are adjourned". Trump suddenly stood up and with a scrunched red face rage, screamed at the top of his lungs, "I am not going anywhere! I am the chosen one!" He then stood up, straightened his red tie and defiantly marched out of the courtroom.

Chapter 28
Transfer of Power
Tampa, Florida
March 5th, 2025

Tully and Catherine were fixated on the documentary, Truth, which was approaching its last hour. They hung on to every word, hardly breathing and never talking. The camera turned to Chester Colt to complete the project as the host, the same host who began the series. Chester looked into the camera and spoke with a tone of finality. He knows he is taking the reins of leading the discussion of the post-trial events that ultimately changed the entire world. Colt began with his trademark straight and serious face, but that look was demanded by the story he is about to impart to the audience. Until now, most Americans knew the events of the history, albeit without the detail provided by the Truth, but most Americans were not privy to much of what had happened after the trial. The entire audience, just like Tully and Catherine, yearned to hear what had really happened as the news had been devolved, altered, and suppressed from the public for the last two months. Immediately after the verdict, the riots in cities around the nation became even more prevalent and violent, shifting from the courthouses and government facilities to the streets of the cities. Stores of all kinds were looted and burned, reminiscent of the riots of 2019 after the George Floyd murder. The National Guard was ordered to protect the buildings, highways, and infrastructure of every large city in the country. Curfews were instituted and arrests were rampant. The country was in full crisis. The white supremacist groups were fueling the hostilities with their own brand of atrocity and spreading abhorrence for anyone non-white or Jewish. Despite the efforts of the police and Guardsman, the streets were owned by the thugs. Antifa entered the picture with their protest and counter-violence, just exacerbating the situation threefold.

Dr. Woodman explained to the audience of Truth that the election of 2024 was turning out, after the primaries, to be marred by nationwide marches, protests, and continued violent riots. The chasm between the factions, of Republicans vs. Democrats; of the White Supremacists vs. Liberal Anti-fascists; of rural dwellers vs. city dwellers; of those opposing LGBQT+ vs. those supporting, all of them became even wilder as the election approached. "The conviction of Donald Trump on all charges virtually knocked him out of the race for President, propelling Ron DeSantis to the top, and sure to get the nomination." Chester Colt then inquired of Dr. Woodman, "And what about the choice of DeSantis's running mate? How did that factor into the increasing national revolt taking place in every state of the country?" Dr. Woodman replied, "Well Chester, it was like throwing gasoline onto an already raging fire. DeSantis, from Florida, chose the Senator from Missouri, Josh Hawley. That choice was meant to bring back into the fold, all the pro-Trump right-wing faithful. Hawley was perceived as a White Supremacist sympathizer, and DeSantis felt this move would solidify the Republican Party. At the same time, what took place on the Democratic side of the ticket also detonated increasing vehemence. President Joe Biden and Kamala Harris swept the Democratic Nomination, despite the withdrawal from Afghanistan and the economic issues that scarred his first term. The bombshell that occurred was what happened at the Democratic National Convention when President Biden announced he was not accepting the nomination because of his recent serious health issues. At 82 years old, Joe Biden looked weaker than ever before, after a grueling schedule during the primaries. Biden then threw all his weight as the presiding President of the nation and leader of the Democratic Party, all of his political capital and influence into supporting the elevation of Kamala Harris as the new nominee for the Democrats for President. This, of course, propelled the Democratic Convention into a crisis. Inside the Convention Center, the political maneuvering was in high gear, and the question of who would be on the Harris ticket as her running mate was a major controversy. Every Democratic leader was vying and positioning for that opportunity. Pete Buttigieg was initially favored among the delegates. He was white, and to give racial balance to the ticket, he was brilliant and an excellent communicator and yet he was a minority as he had a husband. When the

THE CROWNING: CULMINATION OF THE NATION

debate ended, and the dust had settled on the dilemma, the person who became the nominee for Vice President was named. It would be Stacey Abrams. This of course set up an election of extreme contrasts; on the Republican ticket were two white men, both thought to be far-right extremists within the Republican Party, and on the Democratic ticket, two very liberal black women, running for the highest office in the land. While this is clearly unprecedented in our history. It also set up even greater division throughout the country, and the violent protests only intensified by the infusion of racial tension into what was already incendiary and explosive times. That is exactly what happened in the months leading up to the election of 2024. Rallies and public speeches had to be canceled, and debates were held on T.V., but they were not open to the public. Only the family members of the candidates and their immediate closest staffers could attend."

After over an hour of the final broadcast of the program, Truth, Dr. Woodman asked for a ten-minute break. Chester Colt announced they would take a fifteen-minute break and return for the final segment. The word "Truth" appeared on the screen for fifteen minutes. Taking advantage of the temporary hiatus, Tully and Catherine went downstairs to the kitchen to get some cookies. They talked about what they had just seen and how dramatic the trial was, and how crazy the country, and even internationally, how crazy everyone reacted. Tully opined, "For half the nation, Trump's conviction was a miracle from God, and their fears were now behind them, or so it seemed. For the other half of the nation, Trump's conviction was just one more egregious tragedy that seemed to plague the greatest president the nation had ever known. Their frustration churned into a rage, and someone had to pay; someone had to be sacrificed as retribution for the workings of the deep state." Catherine agreed, adding, "That second group, they knew Trump would not survive long in a prison cell, and many were probably plotting an escape plan." They both thought about Catherine's prediction while chewing on a chocolate chip cookie Tully had made for Catherine with some of the frozen cookie dough they had saved in the freezer. " I doubt he will survive long enough to escape," Tully decided. Catherine looked at the clock on the wall and said, "We better get back, the program is going to start back up." Tully helped Catherine back up the stairs and into her bed.

THOMAS J. FEELY

Chester Colt was back on the screen with Dr. Woodman's head in a virtual box in the upper left corner of the screen. "Thank you for your patience," Colt said to the audience. "And now we will turn it back to Dr. Woodman to complete our nation's history up to the present. Dr. Woodman, we left off with the Republican ticket and the Democratic ticket determined for the showdown, and the two sets of opponents could not be more opposite. For the historical record, tell us what we definitely know has happened, and I am going to ask, or rather insist, that because we are being hunted right now, and we want this story told without premature interruption, to stick to the facts that are necessary to preserve the historical truth. "Again, I will do my utmost to make this brief," Woodman replied, "but it won't be easy."

Dr. Woodman described, in brief, the lead-up to the general election for the nation's top job, as well as the massive violent upwelling that took place wherever any candidate for office took a stage to plead their case for election. "No rally was left without fights taking place both inside the venue and outside. The various news media covering the rallies spent more time recording and reporting on the violence as they did on the candidates and their message, which increased the motivation to attend the rallies to fight the opponents face to face. The democrats decided it was too risky to continue to send their candidates into harm's way so they did all their rallies online and with T.V. coverage from the networks that were happy to air the crowd-less speeches. An indoor auditorium filled with Democrats that had been carefully vetted was substituted for the outdoor rallies. The Republican candidates, DeSantis and Hawley, both favored the continued venue of outdoor rallies, as the energy from the always engaged and sometimes enraged crowds was fuel to their message of anger and retribution for the last stolen election. Law and order was their theme, and fabricated issues creating villains that in real life did not exist was their strategy. Their followers and supporters all echoed those problems so often and so loudly that they seemed on everyone's mind. Elementary teachers were cast to be pedophiles grooming their prey and perpetrators of a race war by teaching to children "critical race theory." School boards were accused of plotting to create a socialistic society. Men and women of science, medical doctors, researchers, and scientists of climatology and immunology were painted to be greedy

THE CROWNING: CULMINATION OF THE NATION

criminals plotting to use their positions to make themselves rich at the expense of the rest of the world while they were fabricating fictional world-ending crises. The Democrats wooed voters with promises of getting the government to pay for their largest expenses and past debts. "Politics as usual", morphed into a new version of mutual self-destruction, and the two sets of candidates only solidified these diametrically opposed world views in this nation. There was no room for middle ground anymore," Dr. Woodman explained.

Chester Colt, eager to steer the historian to a more concise report of the events to follow asked, "Dr. Woodman, what had changed between the election of 2020 and 2024 that would impact the 2024 election? "Well Chester," Dr. Woodman replied, "a lot of things changed, but the most significant change was the election laws in many of the key swing states throughout the country, especially Florida, Texas, Georgia, Arizona, Wisconsin, and Pennsylvania. In these historically red states, the election law revisions were not only designed to repress the minority vote, but just as important, laws were passed adjusting the powers of the state legislatures to supplant the counties election officials, remove them and take over the election counting process, and if necessary declare a winner different from the vote count showed. This resulted in four states, Arizona, Georgia, Wisconsin and Pennsylvania certifying a set of electors in 2024 that differed from the party that had earned the most votes for president in that state."

Chester Colt reminded the audience, "That same plot was attempted in the 2020 election in Arizona, Wisconsin, and Michigan, but it failed, correct?" Dr. Woodman quickly replied, "Yes, the first time it failed because the state laws required them to only send electors from the party that had won that state's election, and when those three states attempted to send a second slate of electors, their efforts were thwarted. This time they had learned their lesson, and changed the laws in their respective states to enable them to control which electors they wanted to send, regardless of the popular vote in that state. Also, federal bills intended to fortify the election process were defeated because of the rules of the Senate requiring at least 60 votes, instead of a simple majority, to pass a law, a process called the filibuster."

Chester Colt, still working to keep Dr. Woodman from pivoting to other topics, steered the discussion back by asking, "So tell the audience, and the world what took place in the time between when the states sent to the National Archives the "Certificate of Electors" and the day The Senate and the House met to certify the certificated electors and count the electoral votes?" Dr. Woodman, ever the college professor, put his teaching hat back on by saying, "The electors record their votes on six Certificates of Vote, which are paired with the six remaining Certificates of Ascertainment. The electors sign, seal, and certify six sets of electoral votes. A set of electoral votes comprises one Certificate of Ascertainment and one Certificate of Vote. On Jan. 8th, 2024 the Senate and the House convened for what is normally a ceremonial event signifying the transfer of power to a new administration. Everyone in the nation knew that after the 2020 debacle, this was no longer a formality, anything could happen, and it did. The outgoing Vice President, Kamala Harris, The President of the Senate, was also expected to be named the new President-elect, having won enough states to get to the mandatory 270 electoral votes, but word had leaked out to the media that the four states, Arizona, Georgia, Wisconsin, and Pennsylvania had changed the slate of electors to shift their state's electors to the set that pledged to vote for DeSantis and Hawley, back in December. Under the 12th Amendment, the House of Representatives decides the Presidential election, if necessary, the House would elect the President by majority vote, choosing from among the three candidates who received the greatest number of electoral votes. The vote would be taken by each state, with each state having one vote. The Senate would elect the Vice President by majority vote, choosing between the two candidates who received the greatest number of electoral votes. Each Senator would have one vote.

When it came time for the Vice President, Kamala Harris, to read the votes of those for the state's electors, Democratic House members, and a paired Senator objected to the reading of the elector's votes for that state, throwing all four into a one-hour debate in each chamber. In the end, Kamala Harris was expected to accept the electors presented to the electoral college. But she did not do so, saying that the slate of electors was "not in accordance with the will of the people of that state." Harris knew that having done so since neither side would retain enough electoral votes to be declared the winner, the election would be thrown into the House of Representatives

THE CROWNING: CULMINATION OF THE NATION

to determine who would be declared the President, and to the Senate to determine who would be declared the Vice President."

Chester, bringing Dr. Woodman back to the point of this historically monumental milestone asked, "So tell us the outcome, Dr. Woodman." Dr. Woodman sensing Chester Colt's frustration with him, replied, "The House of Representatives, who had more Republican-controlled states represented in the House, as expected, decided the Presidential election would go to Ron DeSantis. The Senate, which the Democrats also controlled, but only by one Senator giving it a 51-49 majority, voted for Stacey Abrams to become the new Vice President over Josh Hawley. Hawley was despised in the Senate by many, if not most of the other Senators, regardless of their party affiliation. This historic situation created a new dilemma, Republican Ron DeSantis would become the 47th President, and Democrat Stacey Abrams would become the new Vice President." Before Dr. Woodman could speak, anticipating that path of historical comparisons to other elections, Chester Colt fired off a new question by asking him, "So how did the nation react to this development?" Woodman replied, "No one was happy, everyone felt cheated out of the rightful outcome, and everyone protested, through marches and protests throughout the country and online in social media. The frail fabric holding the democracy together was tearing more loudly each day." "So Dr. Woodman, that brings us to the Inauguration of President-Elect, Ron DeSantis, and Vice-president elect, Stacey Abrams on January 20th, 2025. Please give us a concise description of that peremptory event."

Dr. Woodman took a long breath and exhaled slowly and audibly before saying, "Peremptory, fateful, and transformational are the exact words that come to my mind when talking about that day. The Inauguration is normally a huge event held on the very steps of the Capitol building, but because of the cataclysmic reaction of the nation, the daily violence and bloodshed, the decision was made to hold the Inauguration inside the Capitol, allowing the mainstream networks to air the event to the world, and inviting all members of Congress, family members of the newly elected, past presidents and their family members and distinguished guests, all vetted carefully before receiving the invitation. Only the Secret Service would be allowed inside to protect the proceedings while the Capitol Police, and the National Guard, supported by elite teams from the U.S. Army held guard outside behind a reinforced barricade. Tensions were high, but the planners of the DeSantis Inauguration Committee worked hard to create a professional yet joyous atmosphere. They placed a large screen, some twenty feet tall and 30 feet wide behind the stage where the Presidential Inaugural address would follow the swearing-in ceremony. Before the beginning of this auspicious occasion, the screen projected a picture of Mount Rushmore while soft patriotic music played, creating an atmosphere of tranquility in the nation led by a legacy of great and strong leaders. As the guests of honor, the President and Vice President-elect took their places in seats on the stage, and the invited guests settled into their seats the screen slowly went dark. As it faded back into a foggy view of something indiscernible. Everyone began to murmur, looking at each other with either confusion or amusement at what appeared to be a technical glitch, the blurry figure faded away, and in its place was a man, actually there were two men standing at attention. As the picture came into focus, the two men were easily recognizable. On the right was Xi Jinping, President of the People's Republic of China, and on the left was Vladimir Vladimirovich Putin, President of Russia. A buzz occurred among the attendees of the Inauguration, including George W. Bush who leaned over to Michelle Obama, who was sitting next to him, and Bush whispered, "And I thought the last Inauguration was some crazy sh*t." Michelle Obama smiled back but would not break protocol by returning a comment. The speakers squealed for a second, startling the Inauguration guests, then a deep booming voice announced, "May I have your undivided attention. This is a message of the utmost importance to every citizen on Earth." The people in the Inauguration audience began chuckling, thinking this was a weird joke. "This message is being translated into every official language of every country around the globe. The T.V. networks around the world have been preempted to carry this message on the world's news networks to everyone around the planet." The booming voice continued to speak in English, while the two presidents on the screen also spoke in their own native language, presumably saying the same thing but translated into the language of the listener. "We are here today for an epochal and momentous announcement. This good news will change the course of world history forever and ensure that peace will be guaranteed in every corner of the world throughout all of

THE CROWNING: CULMINATION OF THE NATION

mankind and through all the thousands of years to come. The great nations of China, Russia, and the United States of America have agreed to form a single all-world nation. This new world order will be called Cerberus. Cerberus will be divided into three equal and sovereign nations, The nation of Russia will include all of Europe, the Middle East, the Mediterranean, and all of Africa. Vladimir Putin will remain the President of the new Russia. The nation of China will be named China, and it will include all of Asia, except for that part of Asia that is in Russia, all of the Indonesian islands, all of India, Pakistan, Bangladesh, all of Japan, Vietnam, and Korea; all of the Pacific Islands including all of New Zealand and Australia; all of the Indian Ocean and all lands and island countries. The third part of the new World order will be called America and will include all of North America, Central America, South America, Cuba, Greenland, and Iceland. Finally, the Antarctic Continent will be included in the Cerberus empire but will be jointly shared by the three nations, as will the Arctic Ocean."

Dr. Woodman took a drink of water, then pressed on despite a huge lump in his throat. He said, "I doubt most people would believe what they were hearing and try to rationalize it as some sort of sick prank by hackers, but what happened next would change that perception. Just as the booming voice stopped for a short pause, the Secret Service in the auditorium for the Inauguration began moving toward the stage where DeSantis and Abrams sat. Puzzled by what they were doing, Ron DeSantis asked them, "Are we in danger here? Do we need to evacuate?" "No, Sir," replied the head of the Secret Service detail, assigned to the President-elect and Vice President-elect. "We are not here to take you to a safe place, we are instructed to arrest you." Shocked and speechless, DeSantis stood there with his mouth open, saying nothing. The booming voice of the translator then continued, "Mr. DeSantis, we are sorry to, as you say, 'rain on your parade,' but you and all members of the American Congress are all under arrest for treason." An uproar could be heard from the entire guests attending the Inauguration, so loud the military units outside the Capitol building heard it. Congressman rushed for the exit doors only to find them all locked. The booming voice continued saying, "We have two more important announcements to make, and I know everyone is going to want to hear them so please remain calm. Thank You. The new America will also have a President, one who has earned the honor, and he is here with us now." Walking on the screen, bigger than life, came Donald J. Trump, who wears that fake/serious face he uses when he wants to be feared." "Walking on the screen, bigger than life, came Donald J. Trump, who wears that fake/serious face he uses when he wants to be feared. The booming voice continued, "Our second announcement is for the entire world. You may want to resist this new World Order, if you do, I want to remind you that between Russia, China, and America, we have 98 percent of all the nuclear weapons in the world, and we promise you we will not hesitate to use them. You must capitulate, or every man, woman, and child in your country will be annihilated. In America, President Trump has complete control and the loyalty of the United States Army, and he is declaring Martial Law effective immediately. Also, all media outlets worldwide are shut down except for one, One Cerberus News. That is the only media outlet remaining on the planet. We will have peace, worldwide peace."

The people in the audience were silent, trying to process what they just heard, yet unable to translate that into an emotion. No one said a word, until George W. Bush whispered to Michelle Obama, "shit!" At first, the former First Lady did not respond, she, too was in shock. Then she whispered just loud enough so that former President Bush could hear, saying, "The Culmination." President Bush looked at the former First Lady and said softly, "What?" She responded without looking his way and said, "The culmination of the nation." Still perplexed by what she meant he looked at Michelle and shrugged indicating he was perplexed, so she clarified, looking over at her friend and said, "The end of democracy. This is the end."

THE CROWNING: CULMINATION OF THE NATION

The scene on the giant screen of the three presidents faded into darkness and was replaced with a symbol of the new world order:

Epilogue
American Carnage

Tully and Catherine had never actually heard the description of the Inauguration on January 20th, 2025 before, because for some unexplained reason, every news program, local, national and international, all of them were replaced with just the one, called One Cerberus News, which spoke little of the Inauguration, or what has happened to all the politicians that were in attendance. They seemed to just no longer exist. Every member of Congress, every member of the former administration, except for President Joe Biden, who was too sick to attend the Inauguration, and every member of the entire judicial system throughout the country, vanished. There was no word, no news outlets, no social media, nothing but word of mouth to find out anything. The only way to learn anything besides word of mouth was to attend the protests that were everywhere, in every city, to read the signs and hear the chants. One Cerberus News only spoke of President Trump and the "courageous" or "brilliant" executive orders he issued daily. Apparently, he is a dictator, as he alone has power, and he has the Army backing him up, an army rebranded as the "American Army."

After two weeks, the only communication Tully had was with his children, and all by text message. One afternoon, Tully gets a group text from his youngest son, Michael, who has been not heard from since he was moved to an unknown assignment. Michael's assignments were always kept secret because he was in Intelligence for the Air Force. His specialty was his linguistic skills being fluent in Mandarin Chinese and the Russian language. Beyond his extensive knowledge of these languages, he never divulged his responsibilities or activities. Michael wrote to the family, his brothers- and sisters-in-law, his parents, his aunts and uncles, and all his cousins, including his wife's parents and siblings; one single text, that cryptically read: "Extremely Confidential, write the words, then immediately delete this text. At exactly 8:00 pm tonight I am asking each of you, no matter what you have

THE CROWNING: CULMINATION OF THE NATION

planned, to attend an online meeting with me. I will send a text to provide the link to that meeting exactly one minute prior to the meeting, 7:59 P.M. Click on the link, and as soon as you are connected, delete the text. It will be like Zoom but much more secure. I can't say any more but implore you to attend tonight." Tully shouted to Catherine and read her the text while she wrote the words on a paper notebook. They wondered all day what that clandestine family meeting would be about and why he had to be so secretive about it. They could hardly eat a bite for the rest of the day as their stomachs were sick with worry. No one replied to Michael's text, which told Tully they were doing what Michael asked of them, and that was good.

At 7:59 P.M., Michael sent the link, which Tully quickly clicked on. When the connection was confirmed, he obediently deleted the link, hoping he would not become disconnected before the meeting ended. Virtually everyone logged into the session within seconds of each other. Michael spoke as soon as all invited attendees were accounted for. "Hello, everyone. I have some very troubling news for you. I can't get into how I know this information, so I ask you to trust me and don't ask me that. Ever since President Trump became president again, a lot has happened that the public does not know about, but it affects everyone personally. I don't have time now to tell you everything, but I will tell you the most important information that impacts our lives. First, as you probably figured out, Trump was the benefactor of a coup to take over the nation, engineered by Russia and China. He is the puppet dictator placed in power to control the U.S. and all lands described now as "America." Trump has gained control of the U.S. Army, which is growing exponentially as the armies of all the other countries in North and South America and Central America declare their allegiance to the new American President. He does not control the Navy, the Marines, the Air Force, or the Coast Guard." "What about the Space Force?" James asked. Michael responded, "Trump always had control of the Space Force, which was planned from its inception, so he insisted it be separated and independent from the Air Force. That new branch will be a powerful weapon at his disposal. I can't go into why that is now," Michael replied. "His power depends on acquiring control of all branches of the military, but he is getting great pushback from the top brass of each branch not yet in his fold. We, the non-compliant military branches, hold the key cards to "prevent a run." Tully knew the last comment was a phrase the entire family understood well from their favorite family card game, "hearts." Everyone was taught from early childhood to preserve certain strategic cards in their hand to prevent an aggressive player with a strong hand from "shooting the moon" or "running it." Tony jumped in, asking Michael, "So what is so urgent that impacts all of us so personally."

Michael answered with carefully measured and chosen words to try not to create a panic. "I know Australia is not going along with the demands to accept Cerberus rule, especially under the Chinese umbrella. They are a very proud and independent country that will reject any kind of domination by a foreign country. They will reject China's demands, but unfortunately, China wants to make them an example for the rest of the world. China will turn the entire continent into a radioactive wasteland supporting no life for a thousand years. That will set off other reactions from rogue countries, and before you know it, we will be in a worldwide nuclear war. "What about the U.S.?" Patrick asked. "Will we be involved in the nuclear war?" "Here is where things get weird," Michael replied. "Trump does not have access to the nuclear codes yet. Those codes were not transferred from Biden to DeSantis because DeSantis was not sworn in, and his whereabouts are unknown. Biden still has control of those codes, as well as the military services other than the Army and Space Force. The Space Force has a secret weapon designed to destroy nuclear bombs hidden underground or already launched, so they theoretically could use these weapons against us. We could be involved in a war against ourselves and consequently destroy ourselves. We have run many potential scenarios, and they all end in destroying most of the planet, including America." The last statement was met with a gasp by many people on the call, but no one spoke for at least two minutes. Finally, Michael told everyone, "But I have a plan I want to tell you about tonight." Patrick's wife, Colleen, said, "Michael, what is that plan? Tell us before we have a stroke!" "Michael responded, "Bear with me here. It is radical but also possible. Years ago, early in my training to become what I am today, I was assigned a project to research and document islands worldwide in all the oceans the U.S. Army-Airforce used during World War Two to land and refuel. We gained islands all over the planet uninhabited or inhabited by indigenous people and built airstrips on them and the needed infrastructure

THE CROWNING: CULMINATION OF THE NATION

to keep our planes flying around the globe. It was a team project, and my assignment for the team was to research the islands in the Indian Ocean. There was one I found that was far away from the Maldives or any other country. This island was so unknown that we gave it a number instead of a name. It was the size of Tahiti, and the Army Airforce built two airstrips on it, one on the east end and the other on the island's west end, with necessary buildings to house the troops. After the war, it was abandoned, and virtually no one has stepped foot on the island since. WWII was eighty years ago, so there is no telling what shape the buildings are in, but I learned in my research that it had a large cache of plane fuel in its tanks, which were 95% full when the war ended. That is important because if a plane were to fly there, there would be fuel to get the plane to somewhere else." "Wait! Michael, are you suggesting that we go to this island on the other side of the planet, in a region declared to be newly controlled by China, where the few buildings there are 80 years old, and the only resource is fuel?" asked Tully's oldest brother, Brian. "Well, yes, actually I am because I believe we may all die if we stay here in the U.S." "When?" asked James. "The sooner, the better," Michael replied to his brother. "We estimate the nuclear war is just a month or two away." James retorted, "We can't leave my wife and daughter, Grace, stuck up in Michigan. Suzanne was released from the hospital. The treatment saved her life, so she was moved to her sister's home in the U.P. of Michigan. I could never leave them, nor would my other children leave them."

Michael responded, 'What if we could get her and Grace from Michigan so they could come with you?" James countered, "That could work, but all of this is theoretical, requiring planes none of us own." Tully jumped into the discussion, saying, "James has a good point. We would need to solve the acquisition of planes, or none of this is possible. I will call my good friend Manny and see if he has any ideas." Suddenly Tully's brother, Allen, spoke up. He is nearly 80 years old but still works as a scientist for N.O.A.A., saying, "I will look into borrowing one of our planes we used to hunt hurricanes, planes we used to predict storms. N.O.A.A. owns them, but I don't know which government agency has jurisdiction yet. Perhaps, Paul could fly the plane for us?" Paul was the only Stone family member not on the call because of his duties with the Coast Guard and the only one in the family with the training to fly a plane. "I will check with him," Michael said. "So we all have some work to do, mostly deciding if you want to take part in the immigration to an abandoned island thousands of miles from civilization. We should plan one more meeting to determine who is in and who is not in. If we can get two planes, best-case scenario, it might still take two round trips, depending on the numbers of people taking part, said Tully. Catherine said, "We will never see each other again when we split up. This decision is permanent. Think it through thoroughly." With that final thought, the call ended. All agreed that Michael would text the family in a week to set up the last call. A call that would forever determine who in the Stone family survives and who does not.

Tully and Catherine decided without debating; they knew what they would do, but what about the rest of the family? It was complicated. They had to factor into the decision that going to an unknown, deserted island, as far away from home as one could get, would mean we would not only be cut off from the rest of the world, but our survival on the island would be extremely difficult. None of the modern-day conveniences would be at our disposal. There would not be food, except for whatever food the island naturally provided, which could be almost nothing. We would not have medical care or access to medicines. We probably won't have any access to power other than fuel for planes. Survival on an island in the Indian Ocean could be a slow death vs. death by nuclear bombs or the radioactive fallout.

Tully was in his home kitchen when the text came from Michael for the ultimate group online meeting. He felt sick to his stomach with the anxiety over what everyone will decide and how that will impact our futures. Catherine, also torn up and almost despondent because of the distress this call elicited, was at Tully's side when he clicked the link to bring the couple to the most consequential meeting of their lives. As before, within minutes, the entire family, even Paul, attended the meeting. Michael began speaking, "Welcome everyone. Before we announce our decisions, we should get an update on the progress of acquiring planes to make the trip possible. Dad, what did you find out from your friend?" Tully reported, "My friend Manny, who was a pilot for the Air Force, and he is the one who loaned us his plane to transport Suzanne and Grace to Michigan, has agreed to fly us to the island. It is a little more complicated than I just made it sound. His plane is too small for that kind of trip, so he has offered to sell his Cessna and purchase a Beech 300, capable of flying that far and carrying a maximum of

THE CROWNING: CULMINATION OF THE NATION

12 passengers at a time." Michael interjected, "Dad, why would he do that for us? A Beech 300 is very expensive." Tully replied, "Yes, it is, but he has one condition. He will fly us to the island and then check it over himself, and if he believes it is suitable, he will bring his family there, as well. We must agree to that condition. His family is much smaller than the Stone family. He has two children, their spouses, and three grandkids. So with his wife, it is nine people. I can vouch for him as being a super guy. I have never met his family, however." Michael added, "And he is a former Air Force high-ranking officer. If he returns with his family, we will have a good plane on the island. That would be a game changer."

Tully's older brother, Allen began speaking, "I can get us a plane that will carry 20 passengers plus a lot of cargo room as well from N O A A. if we can get a qualified pilot to fly the plane and return it to one of the Coast Guard bases in the U S." That is when Paul jumped into the discussion with, "I can fly that plane. I have already trained on it during my pilot training for the Coast Guard. NOAA pilots train with the Coast Guard pilots, so everyone gets trained on the same planes. These planes are solid and can endure the worst conditions; they fly right into the eye of hurricanes. I must return to my assignment in Miami, but I can bring the plane back there."

James spoke up, saying, "I think we should do it. He would make all this possible." "Catherine spoke up, saying, "So that would mean, Paul, that you must stay in the States?" "Yes," Paul replied. "I can't just go A.W.O.L. and then be allowed to fly a government plane to the Indian Ocean, then just not return. That can't happen." "I can only do this with the blessing of the Coast Guard."

Michael said, "Well, we may have two planes, one that can carry 12 passengers but not much else, and another that can carry 20 passengers and a lot of cargo. So with that in mind, it is time to declare 'In or out,' I will start with the oldest generation, Dad, in or out?" Tully said, "Catherine and I are firm on this. We want to be wherever most of our family is, regardless of the location. So we must defer our decision until we hear the other's decisions." Michael replied, "Well, Lindsey and I are going. What about you, James, in or out?" James responded, "As long as we can bring Suzanne and Grace with us, we are all going. Hopefully, we can get Grady released from custody so he can also join us." The attorneys James and Grady's father hired were working hard to get his name cleared so he could be freed. Time was running out, and the authorities were in no rush. Tony spoke up next, saying, "We are going too." Next, Patrick declared, "We are all in as well."

Michael asked, "Brian, what about you and your family." Brian cleared his raspy throat and said, "I am 81 years old; I am not leaving my home. My children and grandchildren have decided to stay put. We will gamble that this world nuclear war will not happen. After a moment of silence, Michael inquired, "Allen, how about you folks?" Allen replied with his usual very deliberate way of speaking, "No, we are staying here, but we will move to southern Arizona where we think we will be safer should the nuclear war begin."

Michael said, "Uncle John, as a doctor, we could use your skills on the island. What is your decision?" John spoke with clear conviction saying, "We are going with you to the island. Having that plane there to get us back, or somewhere we may need to go, is our game changer. We are all in." Tully was keeping count of those who declared themselves refugees from a war that may never happen, and he figured it came to 21, plus he and Catherine make 23. He then piped up, saying, "Catherine and I are in, and by my calculations, that makes 23 of us, which we can handle between the two planes on one trip there. Manny's family would add nine more people if they joined us." The family stayed on the call for another hour because they knew that this would most likely be the last time many would see the faces and talk with their loved ones, not making the same choice as they did tonight. There were flowing tears as they said their last farewells. Catherine was so upset she could not even talk. Tully talked, but his voice was shaky, fighting off the tears.

April 1, 2025 (30,000 feet above Madagascar)

Tully was sitting in the co-pilot seat of his friend's new plane as they passed over the land of Madagascar and flew at 30,000 feet above the endless Indian Ocean. The Beech 300 was carrying himself and 11 of Tully's family members while the others flew in the much larger plane about a few miles behind them. They refueled one more time on the island of Mauritius, a small airport just outside of Port Louis, their last stop before their final and very long leg of the journey to the unnamed island, another 800 miles to their east.

While refueling both planes, Tully walked over to the loaner plane being piloted by Paul and his commanding officer serving as the co-pilot. The plane they were permitted to borrow was a Hawker Beechcraft King Air 350ERISR. The ER in its' name stands for extended range, and it is developed for intelligence, surveillance, and reconnaissance. Accommodations include a two-pilot cockpit above a heavily armored floor.

Tully and Manny went into the cockpit to greet his son, Paul. Paul then introduced his co-pilot, Captain Boton, who was too busy checking the plane's instrumentations to even acknowledge Tully's presence. The man wore sunglasses, a Coast Guard hat, and a uniform and did not speak to anyone. Tully was a bit put off by being ignored by the Captain but wrote it off as a man who takes his responsibilities seriously. He thought that Captain Boton must have had a stressful life as he seemed to have aged way beyond his years. Tully had a gut feeling he had seen this man somewhere before. He was vaguely familiar, but Tully could not put his finger on it.

Manny told Paul, "I don't know how you managed to acquire a plane of this caliber, but I can't imagine a more perfect aircraft for this mission." Paul glanced at his co-pilot, winked, and said, "It's all about who you know." That brought a very brief smile to the co-pilot's face.

When back in the sky over the Indian Ocean, Tully watched as the last inhabited island on their charts, named Port Mathurin, drifted silently by and then disappeared beyond the horizon, leaving only the never-ending blue waters of the Indian Ocean. He was confident that would be the last time he would have a glimpse of civilization for the rest of his life, and he felt dread, the dread that comes when a man is sentenced to life behind bars; only these bars were made of salt water. As he looked through the cockpit window into the horizon, all he could see was the blue ocean. He wondered to himself, 'Did we make the right choice? There is no turning back now. I pray we made the right choice, but (remembering his friends and family who remained behind) I hope we are wrong.'

Note: This story continues in the sequel, The Crowning: Exodus from Cerberus due to be published in late 2023.

BIBLIOGRAPHIC REFERENCES

1. Keyssar, Alexander. *Why Do We Still Have the Electoral College?* Harvard University Press. Pages 373–374, 2020
2. Serwer, Adam. *Birtherism of a Nation: The conspiracy theories surrounding Obama's birthplace and religion were much more than mere lies. They were ideology.* The Atlantic. May 13, 2020
3. Leonig, Carol and Rucker, Phillip. *I Alone Can Fix It: Donald J. Trump's Catastrophic Final Year,* Penguin Press 2021
4. Fadel, Leila. *Trump To Proud Boys: 'Stand Back And Stand By'* NPR 2020
5. Rupar, Aaron, *What the new IG report about the gassing of protesters around Lafayette Square actually says,* Wikipedia
6. Klein, Rick. *"Charlottesville News & Videos - ABC News."* ABC News August 12, 2018
7. Burris, Sarah K. *Intelligence expert explains how Trump took over Russia's war against the US with his own* Raw Story October 17, 2021
8. Naylor, Brian. *Read Trump's Jan. 6 Speech, A Key Part Of Impeachment Trial* NPR Feb. 10th 2021
9. Leonig, Carol and Rucker, Phillip. I Alone Can Fix It: Donald J. Trump'sCatastrophic Final Year, Penguin Press 2021
10. Hutzler, Alexandra. *Trump Started Tweeting About Election Fraud in April 2020, Eight Months Before Capitol Riot.* Newsweek Nov 07, 2022
11. Deliso, Meredith, Thorbecke Catherine, and Nathanson, Marc. *Election 2020: A look at Trump campaign election lawsuits and*

where they stand. ABC News December 12, 2020

12 and 13. Deliso, Meredith, Thorbecke Catherine, and Nathanson, Marc. *The campaign has filed numerous suits in several battleground states.* ABC News December 12, 2020

14. Rubin, Olivia and Mosk, Matthew. *Judges want more evidence from Trump campaign as election cases get tossed* ABC News November 7, 2020

15. Karl, Jonathan. *Betrayal THE FINAL ACT OF THE TRUMP SHOW,* Penguin Random House Nov 15, 2022

16. Liptak, Kevin and Brown, Pamela. *Heated Oval Office meeting included talk of special counsel, martial law as Trump advisers clash* CNN December 20, 2020

17. Alemany, Jacqueline, Brown, Emma Hamburger, Tom and Swaine Jon. *Ahead of Jan. 6, Willard hotel in downtown D.C. was a Trump team 'command center' for effort to deny Biden the presidency* The Washington Post Oct 23, 2021

18. Gearan, Anne, Dawsey, Josh, Reinhard, Beth and , Itkowitz, Colby Trump grants clemency to high-profile individuals, including Rod Blagojevich, Michael Milken and Bernard Kerik. Washington Post February 18, 2020

19. All in with Chris Hayes on MSNBC

20. https://en.wikipedia.org/wiki/John_C._Eastman#cite_note-chapman_profile-1

21. https://en.wikipedia.org/wiki/Eastman_memos#First_memorandum

22. https://en.wikipedia.org/wiki/Attempts_to_overturn_the_2020_United_States_presidential_election#False_

23. https://en.wikipedia.org/wiki/2021_United_States_Capitol_attack

24. Woodard, Bob and Costa, Robert. *Peril* Simon & Schuster 2022

25. Raskin, Jamie. *Unthinkable: Trauma, Truth, and Trials of Ameican Democracy* HarperCollins Publishers January 4, 2022

THE CROWNING: CULMINATION OF THE NATION

26. Henderson, Alex. New timeline shows a revealing pattern in Steve Bannon's rhetoric leading up to Jan. 6 Salon October 30, 2021

27. Kuznia, Rob, Devine, Curt and Griffin, Drew. How Trump allies stoked the flames ahead of Capitol riot. CNN January 18, 2021

28. Atlantic Council's Digital Forensic Research Lab. *#Stop The Steal:Timeline of Social media and Extremist Activities Leading to 1/6 Insurrection* February 10, 2021

29. Walker, Hunter Two Jan. 6 Organizers Are Coming Forward and Naming Names: 'We're Turning It All Over' Rolling Stone December 13, 2021

30. Richardson, Heather Cox Dec 30, 2021

31. Raskin, Jamie. Unthinkable: Trauma, Truth, and Trials of Ameican Democracy HarperCollins Publishers January 4, 2022

32. Cillizza, Chris The single most damning email exchange in the new January 6 committee filing CNN March 3, 2022

33. Gavin, Kara of UM Health Lab; *ECMO offers sickest COVID patients a chance to survive, but a slimmer one than previously thought.* Sept. 29,2021

34. Cheny, Kyle. *How Pence used 43 words to shut down Trump allies' election subversion on Jan. 6.* Politico 03/11/2022

35. Wikipedia. *Second impeachment trial of Donald Trump* Feb. 2021

36. https://worldpopulationreview.com/country-rankings/nato-countries

37. Nance, Malcomb. *The Plot to Destroy Democracy: How Putin and His Spies Are Undermining America and Dismantling the West* Hachette Books Jun. 26th, 2018

38. Wikipedia. Konstantin Rykov

39. Anthony Rivas. *Fired DHS cybersecurity head Chris Krebs says Trump should be convicted for inciting insurrection* ABC News January 19, 2021.

40. Plot to Overturn the Election (full documentary) PBS Frontline Mar 29, 2022 https://www.pbs.org/wgbh/frontline/documentary/plot-to-overturn-the-election/

41. Pence, Mike. *So Help Me God* Simon & Schuster 2022. Quoted in Haberman, Maggie: In New Book, Pence Reflects on Trump and Jan. 6. New York Times Nov. 9th, 2022.

42. Haberman, Maggie: In New Book, Pence Reflects on Trump and Jan. 6. New York Times Nov. 9th, 2022.

43. Pence, Mike. *So Help Me God* Simon & Schuster 2022. Quoted in Olander, Olivia. *People are Gonna Think You're Stupid': Trump warned Pence not to 'wimp out' before Jan. 6, Pence writes.* Politico Nov. 9th, 2022

.44. Olander, Olivia. *People are Gonna Think You're Stupid': Trump warned Pence not to 'wimp out' before Jan. 6, Pence writes.* Politico Nov. 9th, 2022

45. Truth and Trump: An Evening with Bob Woodward | TVO Today Live February 2023

46. The Beat with Ari Melber Highlights: April 26, 2023; MSNBC

About the Author

Tom Feely earned a Bachelor Degree from the University of St. Thomas in St. Paul, Mn. in 1974 and a Master's Degree from University of Minnesota/Mankato in 1980. He studied Sports Psychology at the PhD. Level at Florida State University earning an ABD. In 2006 he earned National Board Certification in the field of Counseling. He had a 43 year career as a teacher, counselor and athletic coach before retiring from education in 2016.

Utilizing his educational background and his lifetime love for writing, he launched his 2nd career as an author in 2021 with his first book titled, The Tales of Big Cat. The Crowning, Culmination of the Nation (2022) is the first in a series of dramatically exciting action packed books in the genre of historical fiction. Follow the pulse pounding events of the Stone family while they navigate surviving the nation's 2nd Civil War in the U.S. and World War 3 globally.

Read more at https://Feely.Life.

Printed in the USA
CPSIA information can be obtained
at www.ICGtesting.com
CBHW061058151023
1335CB00002B/4